KATHLEEN EULL

INTERCESSIONS

Black Rose Writing | Texas

ISBN: 978-1-68513-322-1
PUBLISHED BY BLACK ROSE WRITING
www.blackrosewriting.com

Printed in the United States of America
Suggested Retail Price (SRP) $22.95

Intercessions is printed in Minion Pro

*As a planet-friendly publisher, Black Rose Writing does its best to eliminate unnecessary waste to reduce paper usage and energy costs, while never compromising the reading experience. As a result, the final word count vs. page count may not meet common expectations.

For my sisters—
Those I was born to and those I've found.

INTERCESSIONS

Shaking
the packet of seeds
asking, *are you still alive?*

-Kiyoku Tokutomi

CHAPTER ONE

I LIVED IN other rooms when he was gone, returning to the haunted summerhouse of my mind. I had practice. At night I would open the door and drift through the rooms, among ghostly shapes draped with dust covers and my own footsteps, a lonely echo. It became a strange routine and yet each time uncertainty plucked a nervous chord. Would this time be the time I didn't return?

Even as a child, I lived in hidden rooms. A dreamy child, they said, or less kindly, flighty. There were neighborhood friends, but I was equally content to be on my own. In what was then more country than suburb, space was never an issue. Step out of the yard and it wasn't long before feet found woods or fields. I would gather bits of plants, berries, acorns, and smash them with rocks that seemed to heave from the ground overnight. There were potions I was smart enough never to drink and inks that I used to tattoo my young body. I was part of something larger. Something, I soon realized, not everyone could see. Summer days passed in this wisdom, grasses and cattails rustling, slicing up my bare legs, and grasshoppers bouncing against me, springing like popcorn. I could still feel it, hear it, on a hot, muggy day like this one—the tall grass of Midwestern summer. It was the stretch of time that Rilke called "the wise unknowing." Things were safe and if they weren't safe, at least I didn't know any better. I dreamed of monsters. Every child does. But now my monsters had faces, the walls were covered with moving clouds, and babies were left in infant seats in the middle of the road.

This morning when I woke, every window was covered by thick condensation, which in my half-state, I first mistook for fog. I looked and looked again. The world was a picture that had been snatched from the frame. I became disoriented and afraid until the hum of the air conditioner reminded me. I closed my eyes tight and waited. When I opened them again, the watery morning sun had returned. I reached under the mattress and pulled out a leather-bound journal and the short pencil I kept secreted in its folds. As I turned, a book slid to the floor. *The Campaigns of Alexander.* Slowly, I remembered. It had been such a hot night, even by Midwestern standards, that I couldn't sleep. It hadn't rained in weeks, but at last the sky had blackened with the real promise of rain. The air hung thick with it. For me, sleep never came fast or lasted long. It was always the same. Waking with a start at three or four in the morning, feeling like I couldn't breathe. Wandering the apartment, I had run my hand along a stack of books Sean left on the coffee table until I had found this one. I took it back to bed with me and was a good twenty pages in when his bookmark fell out. I knew it was his bookmark because he had the peculiar habit of using ticket stubs. This one was from a concert. In London. I stroked my cheek with the stiff paper edge, remembering when he wrote to me about that concert. I had let myself imagine him there, his dinner out beforehand and the walk to the pub near his hotel after, him naked in his bed and his breath heavy from the drink. How many pages had this ticket traveled in the time since? I tucked the stub back a few pages. I would save it and use it as well. Five pages back in, I was suddenly aware of myself reading. I could watch myself read like I was somewhere above. I saw my fingers turn the pages. Knowing that he had held this book, every word changed for me. I was no longer reading it with my mind but his. It was as if I had accidentally triggered the secret catch on a box and the pages opened to me, the text opened to me, and I read it as I believed his mind would read it. I liked that. It made me feel close to him. I fell asleep with his book and the sound of the rain which finally fell in large merciful drops.

Pushing that memory aside, I returned to the journal, scribbling as fast as I could before the dream fell apart. I stopped, my pen hanging just above the paper as I lifted my head to listen. A conversation in the hall. Two women speaking rapidly. Another language. Slavic by the sound and rhythm. Something was wrong. Their words sounded so urgent I wished I knew what they were saying. I crept from the bedroom, trying to hear. The voices were loud now, stopping right outside the door. I froze and listened. They talked over each other, their voices rising and becoming more insistent, even angry. Then nothing. A pause. Something said lower. Finally, I heard them move away down the hall, their voices and footsteps moving into the distance. It had been so long since I lived with other people, I had forgotten what it was like to have the sounds of other lives around me; the footfalls, deadbolts and chains sliding home, muffled conversations, bits of music, greasy, stale cooking smells. I didn't know their names and didn't care. They were a kind of company, even if we never spoke. The safe kind. I touched the door gently as the voices faded.

There was a man who lived across the courtyard, our balconies hanging like a handshake not yet fully extended. He was the closest thing to a friend here, though we never spoke. He sometimes waved hello to me. I didn't know his name either, but once he caught me standing and staring from the glass door which opened onto the metal balcony. Strains of Bob Dylan were drifting out from his open door. I had been so caught up in the beautiful way the music floated in the space between our two balconies I hadn't noticed he was watching me. Something pulled me back from where I had gone. An unsettled feeling. I looked across and there he was, watching me from his doorway, a slight smile tugging at his mouth. I started to smile back in polite reflex, but I couldn't manage even that. It clawed up from my gut as it always did. That feeling from long ago. My mind started racing. It was a smile he gave me, right? In my mind, it twisted into more of a leer.

I hurried inside and flattened behind the open door, my heart pounding. I stayed that way for at least fifteen minutes. Still, from then on, he opened his door and played Dylan every Saturday morning until the weather grew too cold. Every Saturday, rain or shine.

The women were gone. I moved from the door and crossed through the kitchen to the balcony. It wasn't Saturday yet, but I found I looked for him more and more. It felt better to know where he was. If he were there, he couldn't be…where? On the sidewalk? In the lobby? Just outside the door? There was a light on. I strained my ears to hear past the sounds of cars sluicing through the rain out on the street. Was that music?

It was Sean's idea that I come to stay here for the weeks he would be gone chasing photos. "That house is too empty, Cori," he had said. "Full of dust and ghosts. The summer is almost done. Hell, it is done. You don't want to be there alone this time of year." It was empty, that was true, but it was my inheritance. The thing I had left of my father. My mother too, but she was gone so long I couldn't feel her move there anymore, except sometimes in the garden. I could still see her there, wearing a huge sun hat and walking across the lawn, her daisy head bobbing.

Ghosts came with me wherever I went. I knew that was what bothered Sean. I had mistakenly told him about my walk along the creek and that it felt as if someone were watching me. How there were rocks in the dry bed that had reminded me of the backs of human skulls. That's when he pulled my suitcase from the closet.

"But I'll be alone at your place. What's the difference?"

"I'll be leaving on Sunday for the research trip with Mark. I can't change that. Would that I could. You know that." He kissed me lightly.

"Yes, I know."

"But it will be good for you in the city. You'll have people around. I'll have Kate look in on you. You might even decide to go out." His sideways glance told me he was trying to coax rather than speculate.

"I might."

The more I thought of staying at his place, the more I brightened. Maybe it would be different there. Maybe I did need to be where there were more people. I packed enough things for a stay of several weeks while Sean lay on the bed telling me how the French countryside looked in autumn light and sang fragments of old French songs he remembered from World War II movies he watched with his father. French always sounded impossibly sad. Romantic, yes, but it is really the sorrow that makes anything so. At least that's how I saw it. Then again, not everyone saw the world the way I did. Once upon a time, I didn't see it this way. But I can remember the exact moment it changed. I remembered it every time a car slowed down or pulled over when I was out walking.

It happened along the same fields that had once opened to my adventures. A fall walk to school past the old farmhouse with my friend Rebecca. We had not been friends long. Her family had just moved in. We were what they used to call "fast friends" in the old Nancy Drew mysteries. In fact, we enjoyed thinking of ourselves as a bit like the girl detective and her friends, except we were more outdoorsy. From the first moment I saw her, Rebecca captivated me. She was everything I wasn't. Blonde and stick thin, incredibly coordinated, endlessly happy, and self-assured. She always smelled of roses and Keri body lotion. I was already curvy. Not at all fat, though I confused it with fat back then. I had a more voluptuous (I had looked up the word in my father's thesaurus) backside than other girls my age at a time when thin as a rail was beautiful. The boys at school barely gave me the time of day unless they were trying to look up my skirt or throw worms at me on a rainy day, but they loved Rebecca.

Whether it was because she was the new girl, or thin, or had that silky blonde hair, she was already one of those girls. The "it" girls. Mostly, she was just my friend. My sister. We did the typical eight-year-old stuff. We played at the things we saw the older girls do and things our mothers did. We polished our fingernails, talked about boys that we were going to marry, how many children we were going to have, and what they would look like. We devised games on scraps of paper that were supposed to tell us who was our best match, our own true love. Truthfully, I was never into the kid part. That was all Rebecca. I played along because it made her happy. She wanted a boy and a girl. She knew what she would name them. Justin and Amanda. I struggled to name the children she assigned me. Twin girls. Like bookends. Like us, she said. Fraternal, I said. We could not be more different looking. In the end, I had let Rebecca name them. I don't remember what she chose. Funny that I would remember about Justin and Amanda. Stupid.

Other times we played cards and told each other's fortunes. We held secret meetings in the woods and discussed things we read in magazines, or we made up a game or climbed a tree. We believed in magic. Or at least we believed it was best not to discount magic. There was always the chance that it worked. For us, the line between reality and imagination was still completely permeable. That was when he came.

If automobiles could be stealthy, that one was, or maybe we were so lost in our schoolgirl imaginations we hadn't heard it until he pulled up alongside us, tires crunching in the bits of gravel that cluttered the newly poured gutter. I knew before he spoke that something was wrong. The tiny hairs on my body all rose. That's not something they make up just for stories. It's real. There I was on the sidewalk, the rabbit in knee socks standing frozen, sensing the hungry fox that hunted. He leaned over and rolled down the passenger-side window.

"Girls," he waved us closer. "Can I ask you a question?" His expression was friendly. Without taking my eyes off the man, I pushed Rebecca in the shoulder.

"Keep walking," I whispered hoarsely. It was barely audible. My mouth and throat had suddenly gone dry. He called to us again and the car rolled forward until it was even with us again.

"Girls, this is a new area to me and I'm a little lost. Maybe you could just help me get turned around?" Rebecca stopped. I stopped. Why did she stop? You are never supposed to stop. She looked at me. I shook my head and mouthed the word no. I remained stock still except for my eyes, which darted nervously between Rebecca and the car. She looked back at me with a cheerful but slightly confused expression. And then she did the unthinkable. She walked nearer the car. I hesitated, then stepped forward, standing protectively alongside my friend. He didn't offer us candy. He didn't ask us to help find his lost kitten. But it was wrong. Everything about it felt wrong.

"We can't...," I began. We can't help you. I said the rest in my head but never got the chance to say all the words out loud. When I got nearer the side of the car, I saw his pants were unzipped, his manhood out and in full view.

"Can I see your underwear?" he asked. His voice no longer held a smile.

"Rebecca, run!" I grabbed her arm, but she hadn't yet seen what I had seen. She turned, looking down at my hand on her arm, still puzzled. I looked him in the eye. His face went dark. Angry. There was a sudden movement. I kept my eyes on the car as I tried to pull Rebecca away. That's when he grabbed her other arm through the open window, her confusion turning to surprise and I guessed later, terror. I tried to hang on, but he swung the long door open and pulled Rebecca sharply around the other side. She jerked out of my eight-year-old hand and into the car with him. *The man. The man in the car.* It would become a call and response as the policemen asked me questions over and over.

"Who opened the door, Corianne?"

"The man."

"The man in the car?"

"Yes, the man in the car." He was the only man there. I had said it quite clearly. I didn't understand why I had to keep saying it. It was just me and Rebecca and the man in the car.

"And what did you do, Corianne?" I couldn't cry. I remember it being like the tear duct equivalent of dry heaves. All the muscles in my face and throat contracted as if I was crying, but no tears came. "Cori, what did you do when the man pulled Rebecca into his car?"

"I couldn't hold on. I tried but I couldn't hold on."

"To the car?"

"To Rebecca. I was holding her arm, but he pulled her. And the car started moving."

"And then what did you do?"

"I ran."

I ran. And in that moment, the entire world opened out. The day was no longer about two friends walking to school, counting how many steps it took to get across one square of cement, hopping over the cracks and things that crawled, or the mice rustling through the grass. It was about monsters driving brown sedans in broad daylight, serious policemen, and terrified parents peering into my face, crying the tears I could not.

I ran and as I ran, the birds in the grasses flew up, circled, and then descended again to the cattails. The world that had cracked open so suddenly collapsed back in on me with a crushing weight. My breath felt thin. It hissed in my throat. I ran.

CHAPTER TWO

WE MAKE OUR lives out of what we are offered, not what we would choose. I got the dark images of that day, the wreckage of Rebecca's abduction and death, as the stuff from which to begin making my life. From that day on, I was two people. The girl I would have been—feminine, open, and curious, the girl who had just started the process of becoming—and the one he made me, a girl who was tentative, lonely, and untrusting.

Overnight, I was older than my classmates were. The world was a darker place. From then on, when I saw the nightly news stories, I never doubted that such evil could exist in the world. I knew it did. I had stared it in the face and, well, lower.

When we first lived there, it was a new housing development with new subdivisions, but there was still a great deal of farmland around us. The search for Rebecca was an agonizing three days. A farmer found her, dumped in the creek that ran through his property. The farm was near to where we had been walking on the brand-new sidewalk that lay between the new road and the old prairie. In fact, the roof of the old white farmhouse was visible from where we had been standing. I hadn't thought to run to the farm for help. I ran all the way home instead. Probably, I thought to myself later, because Mr. Emory was more inclined to chase unwanted children off his property with a gun than offer any assistance. Rebecca and I used to sneak up to the old sagging barn to look for the owl we had heard lived there. He spotted us one time (the farmer, not the owl) and the way he yelled at us as he rumbled down to the barn made my legs shake. Well, that and the gun. I told myself it was only a BB gun, but I suppose it could have been a shotgun. We never let him get close enough to find out. I still think of poor Mr. Emory. He thought it was bad when teenagers would sneak in, smoke weed in the barn and toss their empty beer bottles in his field. I imagined nothing could have prepared him for finding a dead girl, and a farmer sees a lot of life and death.

Mercifully, in those days, people's appetites for gruesome details went unfed. At least when there were children involved. There were no pictures of her body, just footage of policemen in uniforms and detectives in suits, like those who had come to the house to talk to me, milling around in the tall brown grass and water, yellow tape placed around that plot of land in a ridiculous effort to separate it. I didn't need photos. Though the last time I saw Rebecca she was standing there, surprised in her purple and gray flowered dress, I knew enough now to picture what it might have looked like to come upon her, cold, wet, and smudged with dirt, thrown out among grasses and trees where we once played. I didn't know more. I didn't want to know. I couldn't sleep with the images that were mine and the ones I imagined.

I had run. I had run, sure that car would follow me. I ran, without looking back, until my lungs burned. Until I was home.

In the three days that followed her abduction, everyone in our town lived in a state that was equal parts fear and numbness. If our kitchen hadn't already been painted yellow, it would have turned that color from all the nicotine. The memory smells of coffee and cigarettes. For three days, I wasn't allowed to walk out of the house alone. Not even to ride my bike on the gravel driveway. When the phone rang with its old jangling bell, it shook every nerve in the house. Each time it rang, we held our breath. Each time, my mother smiled at me and tried to be reassuring, but each time she stood there for a moment and took a deep breath before lifting the handset with trembling fingers.

The call finally came, the one where they told my mother that they had found Rebecca. I may have been the only one besides the police officers who wasn't surprised she was dead. I knew. I had felt her go.

It was an endless source of conversation and speculation for years. At first, there was disbelief. How could this happen in such a quiet community? These things happen in the city. Why here? Why now? "Oh, that poor Rebecca Ashworth, such a *tragedy* what happened to that girl. And her *parents*. I can't imagine." No one could imagine. But they tried to explain. Teachers ill-equipped for the subject matter made time away from the regular lessons to talk about the dangers of walking alone, going with people you don't know, and the dangers of hitchhiking. Hitchhiking, for god's sake. Rebecca and I were not hitchhiking. She wasn't walking alone. I was right beside her. She did not get into that car voluntarily.

Meanwhile, the police came and talked to parents in the school gymnasium, bringing along an expert on child abduction cases. It had been easy for people to label the man in the car a pervert, which I took to mean anyone who didn't fit in. As they looked for the man under every rock, the people of our town turned a suspicious eye on anyone who didn't seem to knuckle under. The male schoolteacher, single well into his thirties, was a suspect in people's minds even though the police weren't looking at him. Any whiff of homosexuality cast enough aspersions when really it was just an excuse to persecute someone. The policy clarified that "the witness" said he was someone she didn't know. Everyone knew the witness was Corianne Dempsey. Everyone knew it was me. Everyone.

He was, the expert explained, a preferential predator. That meant he had a certain sex and a certain age he hunted. Hunted. People's faces must have blanched at that word. What did not seem to fit was his displaying himself. If the man were just a pervert (that word again), the man would have only tried to lure us to the car, touch us or get us to touch him. I quietly vomited behind the velvet armchair in the living room where I crouched safe and small. Once he achieved his "result," I heard the detective euphemistically tell my parents, he would have left, moved on to another neighborhood, some other kids. Killing Rebecca could have been a panic reaction, but the taking and the killing seemed to point to a different sort of offender and the police had a theory that there was a pair of men working together–one who did the taking and the other who did the killing. I didn't feel better knowing there might be two men instead of just one. I didn't feel better knowing these new words.

They kept me home from school and out of sight for what felt like a very long time. It was likely only a few weeks. I couldn't quite remember. It was long enough that the last of summer gave way. Walking to school, I could smell freshly laundered clothes on the warm, steaming breath of clothes driers billowing out into the cool fall air. I liked that smell now more than ever. Maybe because it was clean, and I hadn't felt clean since that day. I had asked for a ride to school and while my father was inclined, my mother believed I needed to get comfortable getting to and from school on my own again. "Just that much for now," she said. She arranged for a neighbor to walk with me for a while, her only acknowledgement of the fear he would return. Ever practical, my mother shared with me various small updates as the investigation proceeded. I think she was trying to make me feel better. She thought I would feel safer knowing. It was better than the whispers. Still, I pretended a lot. The truth was I never really felt safe again.

Every street has its own smell. I remember Lancaster Drive, for example, always smelled like cooking pancakes. Rolling Hills smelled thick and sticky sweet, like honey. It was a particular tree growing there whose blooms gave off the scent. I could always tell where I was even with my eyes closed. It had become a game Rebecca and I played. Now my eyes were wide open, but the familiar smells were comforting. The sounds were another matter. Squirrels skittering somewhere in the leaf litter made me sure someone was watching me. I often thought I heard footsteps somewhere behind me only to find it was only the sound of my own tennis shoes in the gravel. Every slowing car made me walk faster. Sometimes I broke into a run and didn't stop until I reached school or home or caught up to another group of kids. It got a little better as I got older. Eventually, there were moments when I forgot and found myself caught up in conversation with a classmate or enjoying the crisp autumn air. But I never again liked the colors or light of late September.

CHAPTER THREE

PEOPLE FORGET. IT is in human nature to distance ourselves from unpleasant memories. It works as a kind of protection. Who would live if their only thoughts were about those who died? The kids in my school gradually moved on. They grew tired of the sadness of adults. They forgot about me as the girl who had been with Rebecca. Gradually, they even forgot about Rebecca. I'm sure Rebecca's parents never forgot. They say the death of a child is the very worst. It goes against the natural order. If that was true, I thought, their sadness was bottomless.

People put a lid on their memories and forget, save that one day of the year. That one day when they open the box, take out the horror and grief, and string it like a garland. They look at it from the sidewalk with their candlelit faces and maybe a local television station remembers to send a camera crew. Then again, maybe not. There is too much loss to remember it all. Too many women, too many men, too many boys, too many girls. If anyone remembers, they remember the young. The twenty-third of September was that day, that long night, in Oliver.

I worked hard to be gone on that day, or at least, I tried hard not to go out. It became an old rhythm. It had always been from that

September forward. Afraid of reporters who nosed around the house and turned up at my school trying to talk to me around the anniversary of Rebecca's death, my parents used to take me (and later send me for the summer) to the farm of an old family friend, Evelyn Butchart. My mother was always careful to tell me it was not a punishment, but a way of protecting me. It meant pulling me out of school for a few days, even a week at a time, but there never seemed to be any problem with the school authorities. I simply packed up my schoolbooks and left, returning a week or so later to curious stares from my classmates, but never even a comment from a teacher, save a sad knowing smile. In time, people even forgot why I was gone each year. Just an annual family vacation, as far as everyone was concerned. Everyone except for the reporters, my parents, and the Ashworths. In the beginning it was. My parents loaded up the car and all three of us spent the week at the farm. By the sixth grade, my mother drove me out, visited for the day with Evelyn, and left after breakfast the next morning.

Evelyn and her husband Bill put me to work on various tasks indoors and out, but my favorite was when I worked in the house garden, as Evelyn called it, picking the last rough beans or ripe peppers and tilling under the already harvested rows. I savored the time alone in the autumn sun, the smell of the dirt, the grit of it in my teeth and the bushel basket full red, orange, yellow or green. I worked until the smell of my sweat was indistinguishable from the smell of the dirt and my hair was stringy and wet. When I went in to wash up or rinsed off at the hose, my skin changed colors as the water cut paths along my arms and hands, both still pale underneath, but now with a fresh crop of freckles.

Everywhere I kneeled there seemed to be stones. Some were large enough to call rocks, I guess. It never mattered how many stones I moved or rocks I had dug, the next day, the next row, there were always more. In the beginning, I tossed them in a pile near the wire-mesh fence meant to keep out the rabbits. As I became more interested in the stones I removed, I put the most interesting ones in my pockets and carried them away to a spot under the trees that formed the windbreak between the garden and the larger fields of corn and other crops. Before I delivered the vegetables to Evelyn in the kitchen, I would stop by the windbreak and empty my pockets under a particular oak tree, its bark deeply furrowed. There was a time in the late afternoon when the work of the house and garden stopped, a time when the meat was already in the oven, the accompanying vegetables and potatoes were in the pot, and Evelyn would rest with a magazine and a cold drink. Bill would still be out in the fields taking advantage of the last long light. That was the time I would sneak back to the windbreak and inspect the day's finds. At first, I just lined them up. Then I began to stack them carefully with consideration to size, shape, and function. I liked the way they bleached in the sun. I liked the way they went from being buried things to bleached and watered clean by any rain. My small dolmens of limestone and granite. The prize piece of quartz I kept. I still kept.

The first time I crept off to my spot under the tree I didn't tell anyone—nor did I keep track of how long I was gone. After calling and calling after me and looking in every likely spot, Evelyn was frantic. When she ran out to the field to find Bill, to tell him I was missing, she found me sitting cross-legged in front of a small pile of stones.

"Cori, what on earth? Didn't you hear me calling? You nearly scared me to death." Her tone was stern. I scrambled to my feet.

"I'm sorry. I didn't hear you," I answered lamely, standing in front of her and squeezing the small lump of quartz until its sharp bits dug into my fingers. It was a lie. I had heard her as she made her way from the house calling my name, but I couldn't, or wouldn't, raise a sound from my throat in response or acknowledgement. I sat with eyes fixed on those stones.

"Well, no harm done I guess, but do remember to mind the time." Evelyn tried to look angry with me, but the relief was too plain on her face. She took me by the arms and looked at me with a deep sadness that I sensed had nothing to do with me. Then she hugged me to her. The soft cotton of her well-worn floral blouse felt good on my face. I hugged her back, dropping the quartz stone into my pocket, hoping my thin arms wrapping around her did something to ease her sadness. I understood sadness.

After that, I tried to be more aware of how long I was gone. I can't say I kept an eye on the time. I never wore a watch. I tuned more to the time of day and the rhythms of work. I learned for instance that if I helped Evelyn prepare the side dishes for dinner before she took her rest, I could go to the windbreak and stay until Bill started back in. I had enough time to run back to the house and help get the rest of dinner ready while Bill finished in the barn and washed up. I listened for the tractor. I noticed the position and angle of the sun, even how the temperature began to drop slightly as the sun slid toward the horizon. Bill must have promised Evelyn to keep an eye out for me. As he motored or walked back toward the barn, he always seemed to come by my special spot. Soon it became a kind of game between the two of us. He would raise a hand and holler to me, "Hey girl, you're gonna be late." At which point I would scramble to my feet and run back to the house, racing the tractor or vice versa. I arrived at the house breathless and laughing. It felt good running again, through the tall grass or cornfields, silk tassels grabbing at my hair, knowing that Bill was alongside me somewhere, watching to make sure I was safe.

At dinner, Evelyn would ask about my schoolwork or talk about the neighbors, but it was Bill I watched over my fork. His strawberry blond hair fell in a wave across his forehead, painted with silvery gray except for his sideburns, which had grayed outright. His skin weathered from the years of sun and outdoor work. It made him look older than his almost forty years. When he spoke, I noticed his teeth didn't sit in a straight line in his mouth. Some of them turned a bit and those seemed set further back, but when he smiled there was a delightful and warm crinkling at the corner of his deep blue eyes that I thought must be how happiness looked if you could see inside. I worked hard to say things that earned one of those smiles.

One of the times with Bill that I remember best wasn't around the dinner table. It was out along my pathway between the house and the fields. I had just finished up at the house with Evelyn. We had made coleslaw to go with dinner and now that it was in the refrigerator chilling and the kitchen was tidy, I was released to go off on my own. I had a pocket full of new stones to add to my pile under the tree. Now I was picking them up anywhere I came across an interesting one. Bill started bringing me stones he found walking the fields that he thought might be good additions. Some were, some weren't. It was truly the thought, as they say. As I galloped along like a much younger little girl, arms spread out to ride the wind, something in the taller grass to the side of the path I had worn caught my attention. I stopped. Recognizing that it was an animal, one of fairly good size, I moved slowly toward it so I wouldn't startle it. No need. It was dead. A dead rabbit. Something had torn the body open and bits of brown and silver colored fluff blew in the wind. Its eyes were open and staring. I felt it. It was dead, but I felt it. Felt the death of it just as surely as I had felt Rebecca go.

If I looked at where it was torn open, looked at the red mess of it, my stomach lurched. Instead, I kept looking into its dark round eyes. Flies were crawling around the gaping hole. One of them flew up, landed on the rabbit's face, and started crawling on its round glassy open eye. I shooed it away and all the flies rose up and then settled back down, but they left the face alone after that.

Bill must have seen me standing there and staring down. He walked across from the field and came through the rough to stand opposite me on the other side of the deceased. I didn't look up. I was still fixated on those chocolate brown eyes. I felt I knew what they had seen. That somehow that half-eaten rabbit and I shared a knowing.

"That's a damn shame," Bill said quietly. "Looks like a hawk, maybe. Or a coyote." As a farmer, Bill should have been glad that rabbit was dead. One less garden marauder after all. If he was glad, he made sure not to show it. After what seemed like a long while, I found my voice.

"We can't just leave it here."

"Something will come for her. Maybe the hawk that killed her. Something." Bill said, still speaking softly.

"We can't," I insisted.

"Okay, okay. Let me get a shovel." Bill walked back to the barn to get the shovel and I stayed there, standing guard over the body.

"Should we bury her or just move her someplace," he asked, looking for a likely spot as he walked back to us, a spade in one hand and a small bag of something in the other.

"Bury her," I said. "Over there." I pointed to the windbreak.

"Yeah, that's a good spot, Coriander. Really pretty. Yes, that's a nice spot." Bill lifted the body gently with the shovel and as I walked alongside, he carried it slowly to the island. He tested the ground with the shovel in a few places until he found a section where the shovel seemed to sink more easily. He dug a deep oval and sprinkled a handful of white powder from the bag into the hole.

"It's lime. So she won't get dug up."

"How does that help? Does it cover the smell?"

"No, I don't think so, but she'll break down into the plants faster."

He took the shovel, lifted the rabbit again and put her in the hole. The body hadn't really stiffened yet. The weight of the hind quarters make it slide headfirst and settle solidly into the dirt and lime. Shovel by shovel, the brown and gray fur disappeared. Bill was careful to cover the face first. When the rabbit was completely covered, he knelt, smoothed the dirt with his hands, and packed it slightly. He still wore his baseball cap, but as he bowed his head, I saw the back of his neck grow taut, the slightly wrinkled skin pulling up, revealing white rivers of skin the sun hadn't reached. Suddenly, I wanted nothing more than to reach out and touch those white lines with my fingers. To touch the skin that remained hidden from the sun.

"That should do it." He half grunted as he got back up on his feet. "Are we good now, Cori? Should we say something?"

"No," I said. We stood there together a moment longer. Finally, I pulled a stone from my pocket and placed it on top of the fresh mound of dirt.

"That's nice, girl. That's nice." Bill put his hand on my shoulder. I looked up at him for the first time since he found me and knew in that moment, I loved him.

"Why did you call me Coriander?" I looked at him squinty and sideways.

"Because you are older than you know…and you grow wild."

I was sixteen the last time I went out to the farm. It was cold and gray, I remember. More like October than late September. Just a few weeks earlier there had been record-setting heat and the lawns were brown and dry like this year, but it changed suddenly with one storm front. That's how it happens. Even in the heat of August, autumn is there waiting. You can smell it long before it arrives. My mom seemed distracted by something as we made our way to the farm. Even so, she would look over and smile reassuringly at me there in the passenger's seat, legs tucked up and held tight.

"You know it's supposed to be cold all week. I hope you packed warmer things than that." She was referring to my defiantly wearing cut-off jean shorts even though the temperatures had dipped low into the fifties.

"I'm fine." I shrugged, pulling my hands into the sleeves of my powder blue sweatshirt "Besides, I'll be working so I'll just get all hot anyway."

"Corianne." The tone of her voice warned me.

"Fine. I packed jeans. You worry too much." I resumed looking out the window and she resumed her thoughts. We were quiet the rest of the way. When we arrived, Mom and Evelyn seemed happy to see each other. They chatted away almost as if Bill and I weren't there at all. After dinner they put on their jackets, each grabbed a blanket off the chairs in the living room and went out on the porch to talk some more while Bill and I cleaned up the kitchen.

"What do you think they talk about?" I asked him, a glass in one hand and white dish towel in the other.

"Oh, I'm not sure. A little bit of everything, I guess."

"You know everyone thinks I don't remember why I'm here." I threw the towel over my shoulder and gathered up the dry glasses, lining them up one by one on the long pantry shelf where the others sat waiting. "No one thinks I remember anymore."

"I don't think anyone thinks anything of the sort," he said after a long pause. "But I think they hope for you."

"It was starting already last week. Every year they start talking about her. About what happened. Every year it's the same. I don't know that anyone even remembers why they're telling it anymore."

"That's why you're here Cori. Or that's why you started coming here. No one wanted you to have to relive that stuff."

"I don't. Not all at once. Not all at one time."

Bill dried his hands and looked at me. He looked me right in the eye. No one else did that. Everyone else looked somewhere near me, but never right in the eye. Bill always looked me straight in the eye. He turned and walked over the few steps to the refrigerator, took out a longneck bottle of beer, popped the cap off against the counter, and took a long pull. Looking back at me again, Bill said nothing. He just turned back to the refrigerator and pulled out a second bottle of beer. He held it up and motioned toward me, lifting his eyebrows.

"You want one?"

"What? Yeah, but can I? I mean mom will freak out. I'm only sixteen." Bill stopped, turned his head, and listened. We could hear the rise and fall of conversation on the porch.

"They'll be at it for another hour at least," he said popping the cap off the other bottle. "Here. You've seen enough. Sure as hell a beer isn't gonna kill you."

I took a slow sip, followed by a longer one, aware that Bill watched me for some sort of reaction. This wasn't my first beer. I'd had it before and not just stolen sips at family picnics. My eyes closed as the slightly bitter wash hit my throat. It tasted good and there was no use pretending it didn't.

"That's what I thought." Bill pulled out a chair out from the kitchen table and motioned for me to sit down too. "Set it down between us in a hurry if you hear the front door. I'll just look thirsty."

I nodded and sat down. He drank. I drank. My eyes stayed on the chipped fake marble Formica tabletop. I opened my mouth to say something and then stopped.

"What's on your mind, Cori?"

"Nothing." I picked at the label of the beer bottle, peeling up the edges. "We're reading Shakespeare at school. *Hamlet*. Have you read it?"

"I don't think so. I remember we had to read something by Shakespeare. *Romeo and Juliet* maybe. Do you like it? *Hamlet*?"

"Yeah, it's alright. Everyone in my English class is complaining. Why do we have to read this? It's so hard." I drew out the last word in imitation of the girls in my class who had complained the loudest about the assignment. "It's weird, you know. Because the words are the same ones we use, but it doesn't mean the same thing. It's like another language. But it starts to make sense. Or I think it is." I took another healthy sip of beer. "There's this girl, Ophelia. She's supposed to marry Hamlet, but he's not really that into her and then her father dies, and she totally loses it. Drowns in the river. There's a lot more to it than that. Still, that's pretty much what happens. I think she kills herself. I mean, he's kind of vague. No one really sees her, and her mother says she fell in, but I think maybe she did. I like Ophelia."

"You're not thinking of killing yourself, are you?"

"No. Not today," I said matter-of-factly.

Bill froze with the beer bottle halfway up to his lips.

"I'm kidding. Jeez." We sat again just drinking and listening. I picked some more at the label and now, wet with condensation, it gave way completely. I pulled it off and laid it on the table. "They were having a candlelight vigil. For Rebecca. They were having a candlelight vigil again."

"I suppose they would."

"You know I've never been at a single one. Not one. I'm always here. Oh, I'm not complaining. God that sounded bad. I love it here. I just meant—"

"I know what you meant. It's tomorrow, isn't it?"

"Yeah."

"Tomorrow then." Seeing my confused expression, Bill added, "Tomorrow we'll light a candle if you like. Evelyn must have something around here in one of these drawers." He drained the last of his beer.

"I'd like that." I felt like I might start crying, but I swallowed hard on the lump that rose in my throat and washed it down with the last of the warm beer. Bill took the empty from my hand.

"You better get a head start up to bed."

"You're probably right. Goodnight Bill. Thanks."

"Goodnight."

I heard the empties clink into the garbage can and was halfway out the door and turning to the stairs when he called after me.

"Was she the one who killed herself by filling her pockets with rocks? Ophelia, I mean."

"No, that was Virginia Woolf. She was a writer."

"That's right."

CHAPTER FOUR

WHEN I OPENED my eyes the warm morning sun was already streaming through the thin cotton curtains that covered the dormer windows in the bedroom where I slept. It only made the scuffed mint green walls look more tired than they normally did and the white painted dresser opposite the bed more yellow. With my eyes, I traced the lines of the ornate wooden mirror frame rising above the dresser top in a graceful arch until my gaze fell into the mirror itself and onto my figure in the bed.

Lying on my back, auburn hair spilling in waves across the stark white of the pillowcase, for an instant it appeared I was only hair and the blackness of my eyes. The longer I looked the more I could see my own shape underneath the covers, smaller than I pictured myself. Eyes still fixed on the image in the mirror, I guided my hands along the outline of my body beginning where the sheet was folded in a thick border over the old wool blanket. Feeling under my arms with the backs of my cupped fingers, I could detect the top of my ribcage and then the rounded spill of breasts. Creeping upward I cupped each breast, enjoying the swell of them beneath my hand, the weight of them as my chest rose and fell. I had a woman's figure now. My eyes fell closed again. I slid both hands along the line of my torso, the curve of my hip, and up across my stomach. My breath was coming faster as I let my hands drift down. Slowly. Gently. At the sound of an engine revving outside, my eyes snapped back open.

I sat bolt upright with the covers clutched in my fists. The engine revved again out on the driveway. I turned toward the window, then to the door, listening with a pounding heart. But no one tried to enter. The car engine continued to idle below. I allowed myself one glance back in the mirror, but I could not hold my own gaze and quickly looked away as I climbed out of bed to dress facing the closet door.

The heavy, slightly nauseating odor of frying bacon and eggs combined with diesel fuel wafted up the stairs as I headed down to the kitchen. Evelyn hovered around the stove while my mother sat at the kitchen table drinking a cup of coffee and looking very much like she was holding court.

"Oh good, Cori, you're up. I thought I was going to miss you." She put her hand out to me. When I ignored her gesture and moved toward the open seat at the table, she reached out and took my hand anyway. "How did you sleep?

"Fine. Can I have some coffee?"

"Really, Cori? I didn't start drinking coffee until I was in college."

"Mom, it's not like it's going to stunt my growth. Evelyn, tell her."

"That's between the two of you, but you know where the cups are. Help yourself."

I smiled sweetly at my mother as I sashayed past and pulled a short, thick coffee mug off the shelf. She made an exasperated face and then just laughed.

"I know when I'm outnumbered."

"Say, what's with all the racket out front?" I lifted the ancient silver percolator, poured a full cup of the strong black brew, and helped myself to a piece of hot bacon. "It sounded like an auto shop underneath my window," I said between bites of bacon.

"That is entirely my fault, I'm afraid. I got it into my head that I wanted to get an early start. Unfortunately, my car had other ideas.

Wouldn't start. Bill thinks it's the battery, so he's out there trying to jump start it."

"I thought car batteries went bad in the winter?" I took a sip of Evelyn's coffee and grimaced as I sat down at the table opposite my mother. "Pass the milk?"

"Well, it seems they get old, like the rest of us," she said handing me the glass milk carafe. Evelyn let out a clear high laugh. "Alan keeps track of these things better than I," my mother added.

"Apparently, he could do a better job of it too." Evelyn laughed again and this time my mother joined her as they shared their little joke.

"Is Dad coming out at all?" I poured the cold fresh milk into my cup, turning the strong dark liquid into a pleasing caramel color.

"No, he's working this week. I told you. But he'll be out to pick you up on the weekend."

"That'll be nice. We haven't seen Alan in a long time. Too long. What is it that keeps him so busy he stays away from the farm?" My mother and I shrugged simultaneously. "Cori, put this plate of toast on the table and then go tell Bill it's time to eat, will you?"

"Sure." I took the plate and snagged a hot piece of toast while the butter was just starting to puddle, then put the rest on the table. I slipped out the back door in the kitchen and walked around to the driveway, sinking my teeth into the toast as I went. On the driveway, Bill was just disconnecting the jumper cables from our blue sedan and slammed the hood.

"Is it fixed?"

"She's got enough juice to start up and get home, I hope. Think I'll leave the cables here just to be sure. You got any more of that toast?"

"Not with me, but there's a ton in the kitchen. Sorry, this one's got a bite out of it."

"I don't mind if you don't."

I took one look at his greasy hands and held out the piece of toast, one corner gone. Bill took a generous bite, leaving me holding a chunk of crust. I tossed it into the lawn where dozens of starlings were patrolling the short grass for insects, their purplish black heads shining as they bobbed up and down. The birds hopped out of the way as the crust came bouncing in. When it failed to menace them, they returned to investigate, one of them greedily snapping it up sharply in its yellow beak.

"I'm supposed to tell you it's time for breakfast."

"Well, we better not keep the ladies waiting," Bill said, wiping his hands on the red rag he pulled out of his pocket. "After you." He gave a playful bow.

My mother left just after breakfast, promising Bill she would drive straight through to Oliver and get the car battery replaced that same day. I had some work to do for Evelyn in the garden and I was happy to get at it. It felt good to be outside. Good to be on my own. The first bright sun of the morning cooled to a warm glow lying on the horizon, pinned by a dome of darkening clouds. As I kneeled among the shrubby rows of pepper plants, I paused to take in a deep breath. Above the loam and spice, the air had thickened with the damp scent of rain yet to come, a scent that seemed as heavy as my restlessness. I got to work pulling weeds, picking the last ripe peppers, and trying to shore up the chicken wire fence where something had trampled it down to the ground.

I didn't hurry through my work. Still, I was eager get out to the windbreak to see what, if anything, was left of the stone dolmens. What had survived the summer rains, I wondered, and even more, what had withstood the relentless winter winds, snow, and ice. I had wanted to go there right away when we arrived, but there was too much of everyone wanting to catch up and hear what was new for me to slip away unnoticed. Now at last, having unloaded the peppers back in the kitchen and stowed my gloves and bushel basket, I walked that familiar path past the barn and along the cornfield, looking ahead toward the slight rise where the windbreak sat. From so many summers of walking it, often at dusk, I remembered there was an old furrow covered by matted grass and weeds. I remembered a second too late and cursed as my ankle turned. Wincing for a few steps, I pushed ahead, hoping to walk off the soreness. Rounding the last curve, I emerged from a tunnel of grass and corn stalks at the place. Punctuating the rise, another massive and ancient bur oak stood as broad and burly guardian. The wide lobed leaves turned their silver sides into the wind, sensing the approaching storm.

The dolmens were on the far end like small white beehives, partially tumbled down but otherwise in remarkably good shape—a line of miniature ruins at the edge of the break facing the cornfield to the south. I knelt and began restacking thoughts year by year. Finally satisfied, I went to find the grave under the big tree.

Grass and weeds had reclaimed the ground in the intervening years, though it was even scrubbier looking than the rest of the break. It had sunk in a little, but I could find the grave's outline. I imagined the rabbit's body becoming less and less or more and more a part of the ground itself. I thought of Rebecca's small, thin body in the flowered dress, covered with dirt. I remembered the round staring brown eyes of the rabbit. I had often wondered darkly if Rebecca's eyes were opened or closed. Most times I tried to shake off the thought. Open, I thought now, freeing the small white stone from the tangle of grass and weeds and replacing it gently on the grave. What had they seen? I hugged my sweatshirt close, laid down in the grass next to the grave, and looked up into the sky as the first slow cold drops of rain began to fall.

CHAPTER FIVE

BY THE TIME I got back to the house it was pouring. I had run most of the way, slipping in the wet grass and splotching through ruts and low areas that were quickly becoming watering holes. In the end, no amount of careful running helped. The cold water soaked through my canvas sneakers until my short little white socks were sodden and squishy. Hopscotching the last of the mud puddles near the back of the house, I threw open the screen door so hard it clunked on its hinges as I exploded into the kitchen.

"For goodness sake, Cori! I'll thank you to leave the door attached, please." Evelyn was at the table, her head bent over some papers. She looked at me over the top of her reading glasses, looked back to her papers and then looked at me again. Taking off her glasses and folding them slowly, Evelyn's eyes now swept me up and down, taking full stock of my waterlogged state as rain dripped from my hair and the hem of my sweatshirt. Like her mother, Evelyn wasn't a tall woman, but she could make herself look imposing, even sitting. Sheepishly, I took a step forward to grab the white flour sack towel from where it hung on the back of one of the kitchen chairs, feeling very much like a bedraggled cat. The wet rubber sole of my shoe squeaked on the vinyl floor. I smiled nervously and wiped my face and my legs.

"Something tells me that's not going to do it. Hold on." She got up from the table and pulled a thicker dishtowel from one of the drawers. "Here. Mop yourself up a little. And then I think you better go get out of those wet things, don't you?"

I nodded. I was getting cold now and a hot shower sounded good.

"I had just been wondering where you had got to. Just about time to get dinner out. Bill said he didn't see you when he headed back in. He thought you might want a ride back with him given the rain and all."

"I fell asleep."

"Fell asleep? Where?"

"Out in the barn," I lied. It just popped out of my mouth. There was no reason to lie. It shouldn't have mattered where I was, but Evelyn and I hadn't talked about my spot on the windbreak, not even the day she had found me among my stones. It was her farm, of course. Surely, she must have gotten about other places than the house, but I had never seen her walk that direction. Usually if she went walking, it was out to the road, as she had done with my mother. Suddenly I didn't want her to know about the ruins or the grave. Bill had probably told her already. Married people tell each other everything, right? On the chance he did not, I didn't want her to go looking. I didn't want to have to explain.

"Well, I can keep the pot roast warm a while. You go get warmed up and into something dry."

"Thanks Evelyn. I'm sorry about not being here to help."

"You can do the dishes, how's that?"

"Deal." That reminded me I still had the two dishtowels in my hand. I hung them on the chair and then thought again. Better to hang them up with the rest of my wet things, I decided, balling them up in my hands. As I headed up the stairs, I paused to look down at the empty space on the living room floor where my mother's bags had been before Bill took them out to the car that morning.

Back when we were all at the farm together, my parents slept downstairs in the living room on the sofa sleeper, behind an oriental-looking screen. My mother stayed there even after my father stopped coming along. The space was originally set up for Evelyn's mother when she came to live with them, but she had died years before. I remembered her a little, Evelyn's mother, from when I first started coming to stay at the farm. She was a tiny woman with unruly thick and wiry gray hair that she was always smoothing with her wrinkled hands. She never seemed sickly though. Mrs. Butchart walked every morning before Evelyn even had a chance to go down and make the coffee. She always had a handful of something that she had picked along the roadside, the last blooms of daisies or Queen Anne's Lace with its scent of freshly pulled carrots. She would fill an old mason jar with water and holding the handful, trim the ends with some scissors before tucking them in the jar which she would then put up along the kitchen windowsill. I had called her grandma.

I slept upstairs in the small bedroom at the end of the narrow hallway that was more of a big landing. Evelyn and Bill's room was on the opposite end. The bathroom was at the top of the stairs. Rummaging through my suitcase, I grabbed dry underwear, the pair of jeans my mother and I had argued about in the car, and an old gray t-shirt before heading back down the hall. I clicked on the bathroom light and threw the towels down in a heap on the tile floor. Balancing on one foot, I untied my sneaker and pulled off my soggy sock. It was plastered with bits of grass and the bottom was streaked with dirt that had seeped into my shoe as I ran back to the house. It was stupid of me not to have taken them off at the back door or out on the porch. I hung my sock on the edge of the porcelain sink, trying not to get grass everywhere, and went to work getting the other one off. Pushing back the vinyl shower curtain, I sat down on the edge of the tub and turned the two x-shaped silver knobs until water splashed loudly from the faucet.

It took the hot water forever to come up through the old pipes and then when it did, it was rocket hot. I let it run, tested the water, adjusted, tested, adjusted, trying not to scald myself. When it finally felt right, I pulled the metal bar up and water sprayed from the old showerhead. I almost had my sweatshirt off when I realized there were no towels other than the two soggy dishtowels balled up in the corner. My hot shower was going to have to wait a minute more. Pulling the sweatshirt back on, I stepped quietly out to the linen closet between the bathroom and Evelyn's room and grabbed a thick, neatly folded blue towel from the middle shelf where Evelyn always had all the towels lined up, folds out. Movement in the room next door caught my eye.

At first glance, it appeared the bedroom door was closed, but the wood had swollen from the rain and stopped it just short. Through the small opening, I saw light. When I heard Bill cough, I startled and ducked behind the closet door, half clad, waiting silently. There was more movement. A dresser drawer sliding out and back in. Quietly, I closed the closet door. Then I did something unforgivable. I stopped and peeked through the opening in the door. There was Bill, completely naked and with his back to the door. He was reaching into the chest of drawers for something. The muscles in his back stretched and flexed. My breath caught in my throat. I should have looked away, but even as the guilt began to color my face, I let my eyes travel his body. They lingered where his back met his buttocks, skimmed the long stretch of his legs. Then he turned around and I saw all of Bill. Much more than I wanted and somewhere inside me, exactly what I had hoped.

In one sharp intake, my breath returned. I clapped one hand over my mouth. Heart pounding, I turned and ran as softly as I could back to the bathroom, closed the door, and threw up in the toilet. Riddled with guilt and something I couldn't name, I flushed the toilet and went to the sink. Putting my head under the faucet, I rinsed my mouth over and over. What was wrong with me? Why didn't I look away? With shaking hands, I pulled off my clothes and stepped into the hiss and steam of the shower. But I couldn't get warm. Couldn't get clean. Couldn't wash away the feeling. I had been cold like that once before.

CHAPTER SIX

THE DAY REBECCA was taken, I ran, and I didn't stop running until I was home. Mrs. Arnesen's house was the closest house, but I thought the man in the car was following me. I didn't know for sure he was. I never looked back. I just ran as far as I could—until I didn't feel him behind me. I ran right past Mrs. Arnesen's sunny little yellow house.

At home, I flew through the door looking for my mother. Calling her as I ran in and out of rooms. But she wasn't in the house. When I found her out in the backyard, I blurted out breathlessly, "He took Rebecca. He took Rebecca."

"Corianne, my goodness." My mother dropped a handful of weeds and hugged me close. I breathed in the morning and the warm scent of her shampoo. Like apples. "Corianne, what happened?" She held me out from her a little way and looked at my stricken face.

"Mom, he took Rebecca!"

"Who took Rebecca? Mr. Ashworth?"

"No, no. I don't know who he was."

"Where did he take her, Cori?"

"I don't know. In his car."

I saw my mother's face change from reassuring to afraid.

"Oh my…I'm calling the police, Cori. You sit right here." She motioned for me to sit in one of the garden chairs.

"No!" I called out.

"You're right. Of course, you're right. Come in the house."

I sat stock still there at the kitchen table where she put me, still except for my hands. I remember I kept grabbing at my skirt. I kept it fisted in my shaking hands. My eyes didn't leave my mother's face as she dialed. Her features remained calm. Her voice wavered. "Yes, this is Mrs. Dempsey on Rossmore Drive. I think my daughter's friend was just abducted." She repeated what she knew. Rebecca's name. That we were walking to school. That there was a man in a car. "Yes, Dempsey. Rossmore. R-o-s-s-m-o-r-e. 2317. Yes, I understand."

I remember the sirens coming closer, growing louder and then stopping. My mother getting up to let the first policeman inside. His dark blue uniform. He was talking to my mom. Then he came into the kitchen to talk to me. He knelt in front of me. He had a notepad and started to ask me questions. I couldn't take my eyes off his gun. I had never seen a gun before in real life. He must have realized and turned so that the hip with the gun faced away from me. I stared at his badge as he talked. 403. Then the man in the suit came. I heard Mrs. Arnesen's voice, loud and harsh. It sounded as loud as the sirens.

"I saw Cori running and now the police car. Is everything alright Nola? The new man motioned to the man in the uniform. He left the kitchen, but the man in the suit stayed with me.

"This is my neighbor, Helen Arnesen. She saw Cori and heard the sirens and well, here she is."

The policeman in the uniform started talking. I could not hear what he said. Mrs. Arnesen, on the other hand, was easily overheard. My mother came back into the kitchen, but the man in the suit spoke only to me.

"Corianne? That's your name?"

I nodded.

"Corianne, I'm Detective Hanley. I'm a policeman too," he showed me his badge and then showed my mother. "But I don't have to wear a uniform." He pulled up a chair across from me. I stared back at him. "I'm going to ask you some questions about what happened, alright? You're not in trouble. We want to find your friend Rebecca and you can help us, okay?"

I nodded again.

"Okay, good. Corianne, where were you?"

I told him where we were. Walking to school. I started to tell him about the man.

"The man in the car?"

"Yes, the man in the car."

"Do you know what kind of car?" I shook my head. "That's okay. What did the car look like?"

"It was brown."

"Was it big or small?"

"Big."

"Do you remember how many doors it had?"

"Two."

"Do you remember if there was any writing on the car, or a picture. Like a logo?"

I shook my head again. "But it was really long in the front. And the top was a different color."

"That's great, Corianne. That's a big help. Now, did he say anything to you?"

I looked at my mother. She came and sat on the other side of me.

"What did the man look like?" Detective Hanley tried again.

I said nothing.

"It's okay, Cori," my mother said reassuringly, putting her hand on my shoulder.

"Yes, it's okay, Cori," Detective Hanley echoed. "Cori, that's a great nickname." He paused. "Cori, did the man say anything to you and Rebecca?"

I stared down at my shoes, intent on the white laces where they ran through the silver grommets.

"He said he was lost and asked if we could help," I finally said.

"Did he say anything else?"

My grip on my dress tightened. My mother laid her hand over my balled-up fist.

"Cori, he said something else?"

"He asked—" my voice was hoarse. Fingers twisting on the blue plaid dress.

"He asked you something. What did he ask?"

I looked at my mother. She smiled encouragingly.

"He asked...to see our underwear."

It got very quiet. For a moment, in that room, it was silent. No one in the kitchen said a word or rustled a paper. I could hear Mrs. Arnesen still talking to the first policeman. She had plenty of words.

"Cori, what else did he say?"

"He didn't say anything else."

Bit by bit, coaxed by Detective Hanley and by my mother, I described how Rebecca had walked up to the car. How I tried to stop her.

"Who opened the door, Corianne?"

"The man."

"The man in the car?"

"Yes, the man in the car." We went through the whole thing and then started over again. Any detail I could remember. How he and I had had Rebecca like a wishbone. How he was stronger. How I ran.

"Is there anything else, Cori. Anything else you can tell me?"

I started to shake.

"I'm cold."

"Cori, what else happened?" Detective Hanley said gently.

"He...his pants." I couldn't even look at my mother as I tried to tell them what I had seen. I just focused on a small brown scorch mark on the kitchen floor. "His pants were unzipped. His...I saw his—" I couldn't finish.

"Oh my god," my mother said softly. Her face was very pale, but my cheeks felt like they were on fire, even as cold as I was. I couldn't stop shaking. No one said anything for a long moment.

"Mom, I'm cold." My mother put one of her arms around me and pulled me close.

"Mrs. Dempsey, I think maybe Cori should see the doctor today."

CHAPTER SEVEN

THERE WERE POINTS at which I sat almost forgotten in the constant activity of that day. Once the detective finished talking with me, asking me all those questions, he and my mother stepped aside and talked for a while. Then she was calling Dr. Mullen's office. Then talking to the policeman at the door. It wasn't until then that she had thought to call my father at work. He was to meet us there, at Dr. Mullen's office.

I was still so cold, but no grown up seemed to be listening. I got up from the kitchen chair where I had been sitting since I first came inside and started upstairs to my bedroom. I had made it about three steps when the policeman in the hallway motioned to me to wait.

"Where are you going, Corianne?" It was Officer 403. I don't think he ever told me his name.

"To my room."

"Does your mother know where you're going?"

"I...I don't know. I don't usually have to ask to go to my room. I just go."

"Well, why don't we ask today, okay?" He motioned toward the living room while trying to take my hand, but I snatched it away. Reluctantly, I came back down the steps and followed him into the living room. There were plenty of people there, but not my mother. We filed back into the kitchen. My mother was there talking to the detective again.

"Mrs. Dempsey," he was saying. "I just don't think it's a good idea right now. I'm heading to the Ashworth's. My partner is already there. I'll update them on what we've learned from Cori, and we'll go from there. I will tell them you wanted to come but that you had to get Cori to the doctor. They'll understand."

"Okay. All right. Yes, we should go. I phoned Dr. Mullen's office. They are expecting us." I stood waiting behind Officer 403.

"Corianne, how are you doing?" Detective Hanley asked, noticing me.

"I'm not sick," I said. "I'm just cold. I wanted to go up to my room. To get a sweater. He said I had to wait."

"We don't have time for that Cori. We need to go now. I just need to find my purse." My mother looked from chair to chair, as if that were where she always kept it.

"It's right here, ma'am." The officer spotted my mother's purse next to the telephone and handed it to her.

"Yes, that's right. I left it there…yes, thank you."

"I had a sweater this morning." I looked up at Detective Hanley. "I think I dropped it." He got an extremely interested look.

"You did? Well now, Cori, what color was that sweater? So that if I find it I can bring it back to you."

"It was white."

"I'll keep my eye out," he tried to reassure me. "But if I find it, I might not be able to bring it to you right away. I might need to keep it for a little bit. Would that be okay?"

I nodded.

"Come on, Cori. We need to go." My mother was steering me back through the kitchen to the front door. As she propelled me along, I turned to look back at Detective Hanley. He smiled a little.

"Can I go get my sweater now?"

"We don't have time, Cori. Here." she reached into the hall closet. "Put this on." She handed me my father's brown corduroy jacket, the one with the big square pockets. The one he wore for raking leaves in the yard. I slipped it on. Obviously, it was much too big, down to my knees, and the sleeves covered my hands. But I didn't mind. It was warm and the red flannel around the collar was soft. It smelled faintly of sweat and fresh air. I pushed the sleeves up over my elbows. They fell back down.

Outside, my mother hurried me to a waiting police car, I supposed because my dad had our car. Another officer opened the door to the backseat. I didn't know him. I crawled in and slid across the black vinyl seat to make room for my mother to get in behind me. After she was in, the officer closed the door behind us. A wire screen like the kind they used in dog kennels separated us from the front seat. A sudden blast of static from the radio made me jump. Then there was a woman's voice, more static and then a muffled sounding voice. I couldn't understand all of it, but I thought I heard Rebecca's name—and something about Rossmore Drive.

"It's okay, Cori," Mom said taking my hand. "It's going to be okay." There were tears in her eyes.

The chairs in the doctor's waiting room were in three groups. A couple sat together on the far wall next to the fish tank. They didn't speak to each other. A baby slept in an infant carrier by the woman's feet. An older boy wearing frayed jeans and dirty white tennis shoes sat close to the desk. He had flipped through the pages of a magazine without reading anything, his leg bouncing up and down like a jackhammer. In the center was a low table with tiny chairs, toys, and kids books. A little blonde girl with a high ponytail was carrying a doll and a book, which she held open by its cover. Under her nose was shiny with snot and when she coughed, I could hear that whatever wasn't running out of her nose must have been running down her throat. Her mother glanced up and then went back to her magazine.

"Wait here, Cori. I'm just going to talk with Dr. Mullen first." My mother walked through a small swinging door and disappeared behind the desk.

I inched toward the fish tank.

"Corianne?" A woman was calling to me. It was the nurse, all in white except for her short-cropped red hair. Even her legs were white, covered in tights that made them the same color as her shoes and uniform. All that white made me think again of my lost sweater. I took small steps, making my way toward the nurse as she stood at the little swinging door that rose only as high as the counter, past the boy in the jeans. His leg still hopped up and down.

I followed the nurse down a short narrow hallway and past a bathroom. She could be a ghost, I thought. Except ghosts floated. She didn't float. Her steps were heavy, and her dress made a stiff rustling noise where it brushed against her tights. We turned down an even longer hall. This hall had at least six doors, some closed, and others opened into empty rooms. There was a thick wood railing attached to the wall on one side. Who would need a railing, I wondered? There were no steps. But I reached out, my hand covered again by the too long sleeves of the borrowed jacket, and slid my hand and all along the railing, lifting it a little when the rail stopped at a doorway and then letting it drop again when the wood started again. A baby was crying behind one of the closed doors. Other rooms were quiet. Finally, we stopped at the end of the hall. A low murmur of voices came from the room in front of us. The nurse blocked my view, but I could hear that there were two distinct voices. Both were women's voices. One was lower than the other. It rose and fell in response, but it was always calm. The second voice was higher pitched and nervous. That voice I knew.

The nurse looked down at the folder in her hands. There was a plastic holder about the right size for the folder hanging on the wall to one side of the door. I thought she might put the folder there, but she knocked on the door instead.

"Yes," the calm voice replied.

The nurse swung the thick door open and there was my mother, sitting in a chair. Facing her on a stool was Dr. Mullen. I had already known my mother was here. Hers was the voice that I had recognized through the door. She smiled, but it stayed on the lower part of her face. It was like the smile all the old people had given me at my grandmother's funeral. It came right before they clutched my hand or my arm with their cool, bony hands and see-through skin, telling me with watery eyes how much my grandmother had loved me. I knew she loved me. I didn't need them to tell me. This time, my mother reached for my hand. I wriggled it out from under the jacket. Her hands were nice—warm and smooth.

"Cori, you know Dr. Mullen," she prompted. I nodded to show I did. Dr. Mullen was the one I saw if I had a sore throat or something.

"Hi," I said shyly.

"Hello, Corianne," Dr. Mullen replied more formally. "Your mother was just telling me you've had quite a scare today." There was something softly musical in her words, as if she were really from somewhere far away from here. I used to pretend she was a princess, sent away by her family to keep her safe. Now as I looked up at her from inside the corduroy jacket, she no longer seemed princess-like standing there in a white coat with her stethoscope around her neck. Still, she was very tall and pretty in a strong way. Princesses were tall.

"Why don't you give your mom that jacket." It wasn't a question. "She's going to go hang it up and while she's gone, we'll talk a bit."

"She's been cold. She hasn't wanted to take it off."

"Yes, well, I think she'll be fine in here. Don't you, Corianne?" Again, it didn't seem like a question. Obediently, I slipped the jacket off and handed it to my mother. "Okay, Mrs. Dempsey, we'll see you shortly." The doctor opened the door.

I glanced nervously up at my mother.

"I'll be just outside, Cori. Okay?"

"Okay." I sat down in one of the brown plastic chairs. The plastic was cold and hard on the back of my legs, bare where my dress had caught underneath me.

"Rebecca. He took Rebecca."

"Yes," she murmured. Her expression became very stern, as if I said something that angered her. "Yes, your mother told me about that. Many people are out looking for Rebecca. I'm more interested in how you're doing, Corianne. How are you feeling?"

"I'm cold."

"Yes, you're cold. That's because you were so scared. It's perfectly natural." She paused and then asked more gently, "Does anything hurt? Your arm or maybe your leg." She scribbled something on the papers in the file the nurse brought in. Dr. Mullen wore no earrings or necklaces, not even a chain, just a thin silver band on one of her fingers. Against the white of her coat, her straight dark hair looked even darker. No, not a princess. Maybe she was an animal turned into a person to protect her. Like a mermaid or a swan. But no, those stories usually went the other way.

"Corianne?"

"No."

"No?" The word sounded longer and more drawn out than it did when other people said it. "Okay then. Now, Corianne. I'm going to have someone else come join us." Without picking up the handset, she touched a button on the telephone. Shortly after, there was a soft knock at the door. I expected it to be my mother come back, but it was the nurse. "Even though you say you feel fine, I'm going to look you over and Mary is here to help me. After all, you've been so cold. We want to make sure everything is okay. I'll need you to get up on the table for me."

I stood up and crossed the short space to the table as Dr. Mullen washed her hands in the little metal sink. Ghost Nurse Mary pulled a small step stool from under the table. It wasn't quite tall enough, but I was strong. I turned around and boosted myself up the rest of the way. The white paper on the table rumpled under me. I tried to straighten it, but that only made it worse. It made a horrible crinkling noise. I stopped and clenched my hands, holding my embarrassment in fists that lay in my lap.

Nurse Mary and I waited as Dr. Mullen dried her hands with a thick wad of brown paper towels from the dispenser on the wall. She did the normal doctor things. She took my pulse and listened to my heart with her stethoscope. Then she nodded to Mary who continued to make notes. Dr. Mullen's hands smelled a little like the antiseptic stuff you put on after you skin your knee.

"Corianne, the man who took Rebecca, he talked to you?"

"Yes," I answered, and when she looked at me expectantly, I added, "he said he was lost." My voice sounded small, swallowed up even in this little room.

"Did he do...anything else?"

I began to shake again. I didn't want to think about it anymore. Wished people would stop asking me.

"Did he...touch you anywhere?"

I shook my head no.

"He stayed in the car."

"But he touched Rebecca, didn't he?" Again, it wasn't really a question.

"He grabbed her arm."

Dr. Mullen lifted the top of my dress away from my neck and peered down toward my stomach. Then she asked me to slip my arms out of the shirt part. She looked at my arms and my back. Her hands were cold. Much colder than the stethoscope had been. My belly sucked in. Frowning, she said some things I didn't understand. Mary wrote these things down.

"You're doing fine."

She asked me to lie down and looked at my legs. Then she asked if it was okay to lift my skirt. I didn't really know why. I mean, I knew it had to do with the man in the car, but he didn't touch me. He grabbed Rebecca not me. No one seemed to listen. Could something bad happen to me because of what I had seen? I nodded, biting my lip. Dr.

Mullen lifted my skirt. Then she asked to look down there, under my underpants. She asked if I would bend my legs. I wanted to ask why, but I couldn't. I looked up at the fluorescent light and when that got too bright, I looked at the desk next to the sink. There was a photograph of two young girls with long dark hair, just the same color as Dr. Mullen's. Her kids, I supposed. That made it even worse. Like strangers were there. I looked at the wall next to the exam table. There was a painting of a plant framed in gold. A fern, like the ones that grew in our garden. The painting was slightly blurred. I liked that better than the faces. I kept my eyes fixed on the fern, following the swirling fronds. I went away. To the garden.

"That's fine. You can sit up now Corianne."

She wouldn't really look at me and I no longer wanted to look at her. I pulled my shirt back up and slipped my arms in its sleeves. I was cold again.

"Mary, can you go get Mrs. Dempsey?" the doctor said as she washed her hands again. There was more paper towel and more crinkling as I slid down off the edge of the table, my foot fishing for the stepstool.

My mother came in and behind her, my dad followed carrying the corduroy jacket. I ran to him. He scooped me up like he had when I was much younger. Like I weighed nothing. I buried my face in his shoulder.

"Oh, my sweet Cori. You're as cold as ice." He draped the coat over me like a blanket. "Are you okay?"

"Better now," I whispered just to him. It felt better being back in the big coat and with my father. Now that I was eye to eye with Dr. Mullen and in the safety of my father's arms, I could look at her again. I could see she looked tired. There were dark circles under her eyes. Not that she looked at me. From my new vantage point, I saw how tall and slim she was. I thought again that she looked like something else. Like I could see the something else inside her. A horse. A horse now human. But the horses in the fairy tales I read were always men.

"So?" my mother asked.

"Everything looks fine. I don't have any reason to suspect there's anything more to it."

"What about how cold she is? And the shaking?" My mother touched me on the shoulder.

"She is in mild shock. It's really nothing to be concerned about. If it continues to trouble her, you might give her some cough medicine, so she can rest. My guess is she'll feel herself in the morning." Her voice went up at the end of the word morning.

"I don't know. Really? Is that a good idea? I mean, she's not actually sick. You said she's fine. Right?"

My father looked back and forth from Dr. Mullen to my mother and back again.

"It really is harmless. She'll just sleep. Any other questions?" Dr. Mullen already had one hand on the doorknob, as if she couldn't wait to leave.

"No, no… I guess not."

"Time has a way of taking care of these things," the doctor replied. Then as she walked through the door added under her breath, "God willing."

CHAPTER EIGHT

I STAYED IN the shower as long as I could, trying to get warm. Trying to stop shaking. Rinsing, rinsing, rinsing. I knew Evelyn was waiting to serve dinner. Eventually, I could not justify being in the shower any longer. Drawing in a deep breath, I turned off the water and toweled off quickly, pulling my clothes on over my still damp body. I did my best to do something with my wet hair, then scooped up the sodden towels and clothes from where I had thrown them off and turned to head to dinner.

Bill and Evelyn's voices rose to the top of stairs along with the clatter of plates and silverware. I hung there, looking back at their room. There was nothing to see now but the room itself with its few pieces of antique furniture and the bed, shrouded in the same kind of white cotton bedspread that covered my bed in the guest room. A pair of men's shoes sat in front of an old ladder-back chair, the kind with a wicker seat. The room looked lifeless now save for the breeze that fluttered the lace curtains. I shivered and started down the stairs. The wooden steps announced my descent as soon as I leaned onto the first tread.

"Hey, there's our girl," Bill said with a smile as I came into the kitchen, the carving fork and knife in his hand. Evelyn set the pot roast down in front of him. At the warmth of his voice a heat rose from my core to color my cheeks.

"Did the shower do the trick?" Evelyn asked. "It must have been good and hot. You're all flushed. That old water heater. Bill, we need to get that fixed before one of us cooks like a lobster."

"Yeah it felt good. Didn't realize how long I was in there. I'm sorry Evelyn. I hope I didn't hold up dinner."

"Oh, that's okay. Sure, you had quite a chill. With that wet hair you're going to be back where you started, I'm afraid. But if you had been much longer, we were going to have to start without you."

"Um—" I held up my armful of wet things.

"In the washer for now." Evelyn pointed to the utility room. "Don't bother about separating anything. I think we can just run it all through after dinner, don't you?"

Both to and from the laundry room, I tried to breathe as slowly and deeply as I could. As I did, the flush subsided. During dinner, I kept my eyes on my plate and just listened to Bill and Evelyn talk about the day, about what needed to be picked up from the big garden center and how the rain was slowing the work of getting the fields ready for winter. Eventually there was a long pause. I stole a glance just in time to see Bill and Evelyn exchange meaningful looks.

"You know, Cori," Bill said setting down his fork, "there were a bunch of chickadees raising holy hell yesterday afternoon out by that windbreak. I think they found an owl in one of your old trees and were raising the alarm."

"I thought owls were only out at night." My words were partially muffled by a mouthful of mashed potatoes and gravy.

"That's when they hunt, but they're around during the day. Well screech owls for sure. They like to nap in their doorways, knots in the old trees, and sun themselves. Like us napping on the front porch. They're hard to see for all that. Their feathers are damn near the same color as the bark. Other birds are tougher to fool, I guess. They know they could be dinner."

"So they eat other birds?" I was thinking of the rabbit in the sunken grave. The owls were probably in the same tree as the one nearest the rabbit's body.

"Not just birds. Rodents. Mice, voles—" Bill stopped himself. He must have known where my thoughts had gone, and now I knew his did too.

That was it. I had been having trouble eating anyway but remembering the rabbit with its side torn open I couldn't take another bite of the roast. I set my fork down and let my hands come to rest on either side of my plate.

"Cori, I can't blame you for losing your appetite. Honestly, Bill. That's just great dinner conversation." Evelyn's scolding effectively closed the topic. No one said anything for a bit. Finally, Evelyn turned back toward me and put her hand on mine. "Bill told me you wanted to light a candle tonight. For the anniversary. I put one out on the counter for you. It's small, so it's not the kind you can hold, but I put it in a little jar. I think it will work." She smiled warmly and patted my hand again.

"Thanks. I think I'd like to light it out by that old oak tree, if the rain has stopped."

"Way out on there?" Evelyn's reaction was as I feared. Then her voice softened again. "It's not raining right now. You go get that laundry started. Bill can help me clean up and then," she spoke to Bill now, "get a flashlight and walk her out there."

"You're not coming?" I did not want to exclude her. Thinking of how she patted my hand, part of me felt it would be nice to have here there too.

"No, I think this is a private thing. Something you need to do on your own, in your own way."

Bill got to his feet.

"Let's do it," he said carrying his plate to the sink.

I was still in the laundry room when Bill came to find me, flashlight in hand. It had been easier to be in there and be alone. Easier to keep my thoughts focused on tonight, on the anniversary. On Rebecca.

"Are you still sorting that same load of wash?"

"No, it's in. I was just thinking."

"Well, we better get going before it starts raining again. Here, I brought you a pair of Evie's work boots. They're probably not up to your fashion standards, but they'll keep your feet dry." I took the boots from Bill.

"Thanks." I slid a foot down into one of the boots.

"Well?"

"A little snug, but it works. I guess I never realized Evelyn has such small feet, but she's tiny, so. You know, my sweatshirt got soaked. It's in there." I raised the other boot and pointed at the washer, which shook and sloshed. "I have to look for my jacket. I think it might be in your truck from when I rode along with Evelyn to get groceries yesterday."

"It's pretty warm out. Why don't you borrow this old flannel?" Bill plucked a black and white flannel shirt from where it hung on the doorknob. "It's clean. I promise." He laughed. "Here." He tossed it at me. I pretended to smell it to verify his claim.

"Okay." I slid on the other boot and pulled on the flannel shirt over my t-shirt. It was old and soft and had the same fresh smell as all the laundry at the farm. I ran my hand along the sleeve and then pulling the collar up against my face, remembered another soft flannel collar from long ago.

"Ready to do this?"

"Yeah," I said grabbing the candle from where I had set it on utility table that held laundry detergent and some old wooden clothespins. "We just need a lighter or some matches or something."

Bill patted his shirt pocket. "I've got you covered there too. Do you mind just stopping off at the barn quick? Evie said one of the horses seemed a little off today. I just want to check in on him."

"That's fine," I answered as we headed into the kitchen.

I looked for Evelyn in the kitchen in case she had changed her mind. Maybe she would want to come after all. She was on the telephone. Something about the way she paused when I came into the room made me think it was probably my mother on the other end. I held up my hands in the unspoken question, but Evelyn shook her head "no" and gave a small wave. I gave a shrug in return and turned to follow Bill out to the barn.

Evelyn's boots were smaller than I had first realized. I curled my toes to keep them from rubbing against the leather, with little success. Bill's feet and mine made scuffling noises as we trudged along the gravel path to the barn. There was no need for the flashlight here. Bill knew this walk by heart just as I did and the light shining out from the house allowed us to see a good way ahead. Just as we were losing the last golden rim of light, the old barn came into view.

Bill and Evelyn had two just two horses, Knight and Lucy. Knight was a black Friesian cross. Truthfully, I didn't know what that meant except that it was supposed to be very good. I remember Bill telling me he had named him Knight because in medieval times knights rode Friesians into battle. Lucy was Evelyn's horse and had a less storied past. At least no one talked about her breeding. Lucy was deep brown—almost black really, with a black mane and a white patch on the broad space between her eyes. Her legs looked like she had stepped in white paint. Evelyn spent every morning brushing both horses until they gleamed.

"Which horse is sick? Knight or Lucy?" I had to jog every few steps to keep up with Bill's long legs.

"Lucy. Evie says she's been coughing." He slid open the big barn door.

"I didn't know horses coughed. Well, I suppose why wouldn't they? I guess I just never thought about it." Both horses shifted and looked at us with great interest as we came in.

"Hey, Lucy," Bill called to the ailing horse as he opened her enclosure. She bumped his hand with her nose and seemed pleased when he reached up and put his hand on her side. "Well, that's a very good sign."

"What is?"

"She's looking around, responds when we talk to her, and Evie says she's been eating. Plus, I don't see a runny nose or anything." On cue, Lucy lowered her head to the ground and coughed. "Could be dust. It's been awfully dry up till this rain. She looks good otherwise." Bill sounded almost as if he were consulting me. I liked that and nodded seriously. "I'll call the vet in the morning, but I think she's good for tonight. I'll check back on her one more time before I close everything up. Okay, thanks for making the stop. Let's go do your thing."

"Knight and Lucy, they don't work." We headed out of the barn and turned for the windbreak. "So, they're just here for riding, right?"

"Yep."

"I know you ride," I paused. "And I remember someone's kids coming out once when I was here. Does Evelyn still ride? My mom said she used to. She's out here with the horses, but I never see her ride."

"Not since the fall."

"But that was a long time ago, wasn't it?"

"Yeah, it was a very long time ago."

Bill got very quiet after that. I felt bad for bringing it up. Not that I was entirely sure what I had said. I knew Evelyn had fallen off Lucy a long time ago and was badly hurt, but no one ever said anything more about it. We walked the rest of the way out to windbreak without speaking, which was probably a good thing. Now that we were out past the lights of the house and the barn, walking needed more attention.

It was quiet except for the distant sounds of cars out on the main road, the rustle of some dried-up cornstalks, and our footfalls. It was too late for the daytime animals and still a little too early for any of those that prowled around at night. Bill kept the big flashlight trained on the ground. Sometimes there would be a gap in the clouds just long enough for the moon to pop out and for a little while the yellow beam of the flashlight would be swallowed by the cool white light of the moon. As our eyes adjusted to the dark, I could make out the line of the break. I slowed to a stop. Bill stopped alongside me.

"Rebecca would be in high school with me now. I think about that sometimes. Wonder if we would still be friends. I remember that day. Remember her from before. When we would go play in the woods. Sometimes I think about how... I think I know how she must've—" I stopped myself. "Sometimes, I wonder what she would look like now. I wonder what I'd look like if it never happened. It shows you know. It follows me around. People don't always know what it is when they look at me but it's there. She's there. She's here. She's always here. It's like her shadow is around me, like a dark outline around my body. She can't live any other way. She wants to still live. I know whenever they look at me, they can see it. I look in the mirror and there she is. Not just me. Me and Rebecca. It's like those old religious paintings. You know? The ones where there is the holy light that shines around the saints or Mary. Except mine isn't light. Or holy. But it's there all the same. I think it will always be there."

I pulled the candle out of the jar and held it out to Bill to light. Setting down the flashlight, he reached into the breast pocket of his jacket pulled out a small disposable lighter. After three empty tries, the small flinty wheel sparked a flame. Bill held it to the wick of the candle. It took a while for the waxy coating on the long new wick to melt enough to catch, but it did. I had the glass jar ready.

"Don't burn yourself," I cautioned as Bill worked to lower the small votive candle into the jar without tipping it and snuffing out the candle. "I can do it if you want. My fingers are skinnier."

"I got it, I got it." He handed the candle jar back to me cupping his hands around mine until he was sure I had it. I could feel the muscled strength of his hands and yet his touch was tender. My hands felt small inside his. Safe.

Carefully holding the jar toward the bottom where it was still cool, I carried it to the small grave and knelt. Patting the ground, I felt for the flattest spot near what I remembered being the head. There near the small white stone. I set the candle down and rocked back up on my heels. Bill looked at me expectantly.

"Do we need to say anything?"

"No. It's about the quiet. Remembering." We watched the candle flickering, highlighting the texture of the nubby weeds and grass, lighting up the stone. "Hold on," I said after the first few minutes went by.

I walked back over to the big tree. Bill stayed in front of the grave but turned to watch me. There was a flat bit of fieldstone near the base of the tree. Kneeling, I pried the fieldstone from its bed and from the hole underneath produced a metal tin. I pulled out a pack of cigarettes, took two out of the pack, and replaced both the pack and the tin under the rock. An old aluminum can lay nearby, half-covered by weeds. I pulled it free and walking back to Bill, I held up the two cigarettes.

"You don't mind, do you?".

"You are just full of surprises, aren't you?"

"Want one?"

"Yeah, alright," he said.

I put a cigarette to my mouth and handed him the other. Bill took the lighter back out his pocket and lit mine first and then his. He exhaled a long train of white smoke. "So how long has this been going on? The smoking?"

"I don't know. A while, I guess. It's not like I smoke all the time."

"Your folks know?"

"No. Don't need the lecture. No, I go for a walk or something. Wait till they're out."

"I'm surprised they don't smell it on you when you get back." He thought about it a while longer. "They must." Bill flicked the long ash-end into the can. The cigarette looked much smaller in his hand than in mine.

"Well maybe they do smell it, but they never say anything. They don't like to know things, you know?"

"You smoking anything else?"

I frowned and shot Bill an angry look.

"I'll take that as a yes."

"It's just sometimes. To relax. You know. Sometimes the dreams get bad."

"You ever talk to anyone about that?"

"I'm talking to you." I snubbed out my cigarette on the top of the can and tossed in the butt.

"Okay. You're talking to me. Do you want to tell me what they're about?"

"They don't always make sense. Sometimes I'm running. Sometimes, I see ... sometimes it's just a jumble of things. But it's always cold. Cold in my dreams. Cold when I wake up."

We let the silence fall again and just stood there, close to each other.

"It's been rough, you know. On Evie. Since the fall."

I nodded even though I didn't really know what he meant.

"She was hurt badly. Concussion, broken pelvis, she couldn't even get up out of bed for six weeks. She could have died. If I hadn't found her when I did. And it's not like the ambulance is down the block here. She had to have a couple surgeries. They put in two rods and a bunch of screws."

"I didn't know. My mom never told me that part. She just said Evelyn had a bad fall once. But she's okay now. I mean, she can walk and everything. Everything healed, right?"

"Yeah, pretty much. But she won't ride ever again. She's too afraid."

"I know how that feels."

Bill snubbed out his own cigarette and set the can down carefully on bare spot of dirt. I could feel him looking at me, but I stared ahead, at the ground—at the grave. Anywhere but at him.

"Cori," he said quietly. "It's been rough for you, I know. But there are lots of people who care about you."

I could feel the lump starting in my throat. The one that always came before the tears. They welled up, but I would not let them fall.

My eyes stayed fixed on the candle now. The wind was picking up again. The flame bowed down as a gust went over the top of the jar, and then stood back up, burning even stronger.

"I care about you. Evelyn cares about you. Your mom and dad. Your friends."

"I don't have a lot of those." I bent down and picked up the jar, then curling my palm around the rim, carefully blew out the flame. The little patch of light on the grave disappeared. My eyes struggled to adjust to the darkness as a bit of moon slipped in and out through the veil of clouds.

"We should get back," I said as I began carefully picking my steps. Bill touched my arm gently. I stopped.

"It's not fair, Cori. It's not fair you had to go through all that." He kept his hand on my arm until I turned around. When I looked at his hand, he pulled it away. "I'm sorry. Does that bother you?"

"It's okay. Don't worry about it." I shrugged, wedging my free hand into the pocket of my jeans.

He reached out and with two fingers, lifted some hair from where it had blown across my face and tucked it behind my ear. I could feel the warmth coming off his skin as his hand came close to my cheek. The pungent aroma of raw tobacco and fresh smoke lingered on his fingers.

"It's okay," I repeated.

With his thumb, he traced the line of my cheekbone. My breath was coming faster. I relished being this close to Bill. I let him touch my cheek. I didn't stop him when he reached through the angle of my arm to touch my waist. I just stood perfectly still, my eyes never leaving his face. I was sure he must be able to see my pulse pounding in my throat, even in the dark. Tightening his arm around my waist, he pulled me against him. The place where he was hard pressed into the ridge of me. I hadn't expected that. I flushed again. My whole body was charged and alert. It felt good. I stiffened in his arms. With one hand on the small of my back and the other wound in my hair, he kissed me, softly at first. Opening my mouth, I kissed him back. His kiss deepened, became harder. More urgent. Then he just stopped.

The electricity that filled me drained away and the hollow space filled back up with fear. He pulled away.

"Jesus, Cori. That was... I don't know what that was ... I'm so sorry." He drew his hand through the thick waves of his hair. With his eyes closed, his jaw set, he just kept shaking his head. "Oh God, this was a mistake. What was—?"

The sick feeling returned.

"It's my fault," I said.

"No. No. That shouldn't have happened. It's my fault. I'm ... this past week... I felt ..." he tried to touch my cheek again. I pulled way. "It shouldn't be me, Cor. It can't be me. Understand?"

Without a word, I handed the jar candle to Bill. My hand shook so much that the candle rattled against the glass. He just looked at it. Looked at my shaking hand. I gestured again. *Take the damn candle.*

"Coriander."

I threw the candle as hard as I could at the tree. It wasn't a great throw, but it was enough. The first hollow sound of the jar hitting the tree was amplified by the smaller, sharper noises of fragments flying, breaking open the night. I flew too, running blindly.

The moon was gone, blanketed by heavy clouds. I had no flashlight, but my eyes were used to the dark now. Muscle memory guided my steps. I caught my foot anyway. Feeling myself going down, I put my hands out. I landed hard on my hands and knees but avoided hitting my head. I felt the impact first in my wrists, then the jolt as it shot up my arms and into my shoulders. The evening's rain and mist seeped from the grass into the fabric of my jeans. Bill was calling my name now. Over my shoulder, I could see the halo of the flashlight beam bobbing in the fog that was settling over the fields and low spots. Ignoring the pain in my knees and arms, I got to my feet and kept running.

I had not known where I was going to go until I saw the light outside the barn. Then it was a sprint to get there before Bill caught up with me. At the barn, I glanced over my shoulder. I saw no hint of him or the light of the flashlight. In the fog, he had no way of knowing which way I had gone. I lifted the latch and ran inside. Knight and Lucy shifted and whinnied.

"Shh," I whispered at them, holding my finger to my lips. "You have to be quiet." I moved around to the wall opposite their stalls and slid down in the hay. I ached from the fall. My hands were muddy. Wincing, I rolled up the legs of my jeans. Both knees were red and scraped. Dark bruises were starting underneath the red patches, but at least I wasn't bleeding. I rolled my jeans back down and instinctively hugged my knees into my body. I winced again as the fabric pulled taut, pressing against the tender spots. Bad idea.

Hissing through my teeth, I straightened my legs back out. The stinging lingered, pulsing as the skin had to flex again and the fabric came away, but the stinging of my knees was nothing compared to what I felt when Bill pulled away. I liked the feeling of him against me. His warm tongue in my mouth. I had wanted to him touch me. I wanted more and I wanted none of it. It was wrong. I was wrong. My lips felt swollen, and I could feel where his whiskers had rasped against my cheek. The dampness between my legs. My body had betrayed me. I had wanted so much to touch him. To know what he felt like. Closing my eyes, I saw Bill. I remembered the heat of him searing through my clothes. Then it wasn't Bill, it was *him*. He was there again, in my head. The man in the car. Bill's face became his face.

"He's gone. He's gone," I repeated, rocking myself. Closing my eyes, I tried to shut it all out. It was no good. It was all rushing in again. The man. Rebecca in her flowered dress. Her look of surprise. My stomach lurched. I ground the heels of my hands against my forehead as if I could force it all from my head. Trying to force him out of my head.

"Get out. Get out!"

Knight looked at me with those dark, dark eyes as if he knew what I had done. As if he knew my thoughts. My sins. That animal's eyes condemned me as another dark pair of dark eyes had eight years ago. I turned my face away.

CHAPTER NINE

I WEDGED ANOTHER pillow between the low track arm of Sean's gray sofa and my neck, trying to get comfortable. It had been raining for days and the damp and gloom permeated everything, including my body. There was nothing else to do but make the best of it. I never minded rainy days before, but in the city the gloom seemed solid and inescapable. There was so little sky. It was one of the reasons I was grateful that Sean lived on the sprawling top floor. There were fewer units on the top floor than those below, so snagging a corner apartment meant an abundance of windows, especially in the living room. From this vantage I could see more of the sky, watch it move and change from ocean gray to ink and back again. I read once that the Japanese had at least fifty words for rain including times of day for rain and types. I knew they must have a word for the cold drops that dashed against the panes of the large atelier windows as if the drops themselves were made of glass.

The city seizes some people. Sean was one of them. My father was another. Both could describe every street, every brick, tottering bits of litter, in rhapsodic detail. People like that loved the greasy smell of it. Loved the press of bodies surging, moving, breaking wave upon wave in the crosswalks. The iconic yellow taxicabs with their stale back seats—a noxious mixture of body odor, vinyl, stale smoke, and car exhaust. I never much liked riding in taxis. It was too much like riding in the backseat of a police car.

In that way, in that love of things urban, my father and Sean were the same. Not for all the same reasons. Buildings fascinated my father. People did not. Maybe it was the reason he was at the office such long hours or bent over his drafting table at home. Buildings spoke to him. He would talk to me about buildings sometimes. The theory and the art of them. Looking over his arm, I was more interested in the rooms within, tiny containers separate in their lives and purposes. He heard the conversation between them. To him, buildings were a miraculous expression of the human spirit.

He had grown up here. The Dempseys had always been city folk or at least they had been since my great grandfather made his way from Ireland. I remember my mother telling me how proud his parents were—their son, Alan Dempsey, the architect with his fine family and a house in the country. Funny, they had always endeavored to leave the city and my father tried desperately to get back.

Dad told me we lived outside the city for my mother. My mother said we lived there for me, so I would be safe. She distrusted the city. As it turns out, there are no safe places left. Not the open fields. Sometimes not even your own body.

Three years after I left high school I had almost started to believe again. Not that the best years of my life were ahead. Those ended the day the car pulled up to Rebecca and me. Yet gradually I started to let myself believe that just maybe the worst days were behind me. Of course, everything is relative. Some things that made me odd in high school, like burying myself in books, were encouraged on a college campus. And being away, meeting people who did not know what had happened in Oliver, or better yet, had never heard of Oliver, that was the closest I had been to normal since Rebecca's murder.

Distance is relative. I did not need to go far to find a place that had no memory. Never even crossed state lines. Whether that was a lack of courage or common sense depends on your perspective. My parents thought it was best that I stay within a couple hour's drive, and I guess I wasn't inclined to go too much further. I rejected their idea of going to a small private all-girls college just across the border in favor of the small liberal arts college three hours away. That I lived in a world also occupied by men was not something I could suddenly deny, an insight supported enthusiastically by my shrink, Dr. Lawrence. Anyway, I liked to think he was more concerned with my insights than the fact that he would still be able to bill my parents monthly.

Dr. Lawrence and I talked quite a lot about my dreams. In fact, he was the one that encouraged me to start writing them down. It felt wrong to pour it all into an ordinary spiral notebook, so I went to the bookstore at the mall and bought a handsewn leatherbound journal about the size of my hand. I toyed with labeling the title page *The Consciously Unconscious Mind of Corianne Hayden Dempsey* but resisted in case my parents ever went snooping through my room. The cigarettes I kept hidden would be a lot less shocking to them than the images that filled my head at night.

It became a ritual, kneeling next to the bed and taking the journal from where I kept it hidden between the mattress and the box spring—not right at the edge where you might find it changing the sheets, but further in so that you had to reach in and dig for it. When I first started, I would try to wait until the morning to write everything down, but the details would be hazy by morning time, so I began writing them down just then—as I woke in the night—when my skin was still damp, and those worlds were real. The rich warm scent of the brown leather was comforting and the way it took on soft creases from all the opening and closing made it looked lived in rather than worn out. Men's faces were like that. Warmer and more lived in for the years. Bill's face had been like that.

At least in my dorm room I didn't need to hide my cigarettes. I did continue to hide my journal. My roommate for the first two years of school was a girl named Lisa. She came from a small northern town ironically named Freedom. If I thought Oliver was small and oppressive, her stories about Freedom made me feel positively cosmopolitan in comparison. Apparently, in Freedom you went to the Catholic school or the public school. Your parents either farmed, owned a business related to farming, or worked in one of the industrial parks in the next county. It being a conservative and religious community, as a teenager your extracurricular choices were sports, volunteering at church functions while your parents were watching, and copious amounts of drinking, smoking weed and sex when they weren't.

Lisa embraced her college emancipation, but she was easy prey for slick college guys who were interested in how fast they could charm her into bed. There was something quite young about her. She was cute. Not pretty, but cute. She never lacked for attention. Her face was open, so when she laughed, you laughed, and when she was upset, you knew it. Everything was right there on her face. I liked that about Lisa. Even underneath all her black eyeliner, there was real honesty. Deep down she was just a nice girl afraid she would never get out of Freedom and just as afraid that she would never amount to anything outside of Freedom.

Next door lived Nicky and Cassandra. It was a totally different story there. There wasn't an honest thing between them. If I had worked through high school not to be *too* anything, these two were the kind of girls who worked hard to be everything. They relished the trail of young men drunk on the smell of them and the sight of their breasts spilling over their low-cut tees and their tanned summer legs stretched out long beneath shorts that showed the curve where those legs met their assets. They liked the power of it.

No, I much preferred Lisa to those two, though I tired of the parade of men and having to go study in the Student Union. It wasn't the studying somewhere else that I minded. The bustle was okay, and it was preferable to the panting and moaning going on in my room, but I never liked the walk back in the dark.

"And how do you feel about your roommate having sex in your room?" Dr. Lawrence asked me at our session over Christmas break.

"Whatever. It's her life. I just don't want to listen to it, you know?"

"I think that's a reasonable request. Have you tried talking with her about it?"

"About what?"

"Telling your roommate that it makes you uncomfortable that she is having sex in the room you share?"

"I didn't say that."

"Okay, but now I'll ask. How does it make you feel?"

I curled and uncurled my toes in my shoes.

"I don't know." I shifted uneasily in the chair. "I worry about her I guess."

"What specifically worries you?" Dr. Lawrence asked with that infuriatingly placid expression he always maintained. Not even the skin on the top of his bald head ever moved. Occasionally his eyebrows would lift ever so slightly if he thought I'd said something new or interesting. Next, he would put on his reading glasses, which he had been holding by the stem, uncross and cross his gray-trousered legs, and make some notes. I presumed so we could come back to whatever it was I had said.

It was so quiet I could hear sound of myself swallowing thickly.

"It doesn't seem very safe," I finally managed.

"Safe?"

"You know, a lot of guys. Getting pregnant. Diseases."

"What about her physical safety? Do you ever worry one of these guys will hurt her?"

"I don't know."

"Do you ever worry for your safety?"

"You know, I've got something I want to talk about today. That's okay, right? You always tell me this is where I can bring things to work on them."

"Of course." He put the emphasis on the second word.

"My mom told me she has cancer."

Dr. Lawrence's calm, unflappable expression did not dissolve at my announcement, but it did waver. His eyebrows went up slightly.

His mouth flattened into a harder line. He set down his pen on the notebook and then slowly removed his glasses.

"I'm terribly sorry to hear that, Cori."

In retrospect, I told him, I should have known something was up. My parents weren't exactly joined at the hip. My father had his work, which meant long hours in the city and drafting late into the night. My mother had not worked full time as a landscape designer since I was born. She still had her gardens and took the odd side jobs designing gardens for other people. She rose early and was curled up reading or sound asleep by nine or ten o'clock at night. She had her things and her friends. He had his work. Yet they both came to pick me up at the bus when I came home after my final exams at the Christmas break, my father dashing over to help me with my small suitcase and my mom waiting by the car. She looked tired. Her eyes. There was something about her eyes. She had not looked at me like that since I was a little girl. Love and sadness mingling unmistakably in an unwelcome new knowledge.

They wanted to tell me right away that night. They wanted to unload the awful secret that they carried between them, but then neither one of them could do it. Not that I could blame them. How could I blame my mother? It's Christmas and you've got cancer. Who wants to tell anyone that? Then again, how long can you really keep that secret before it becomes unfair. She told me at breakfast the next morning. It wasn't exactly, "please pass the jelly and by the way, I have cancer," but she didn't spend time with a long lead in to soften the blow. It was better that way, I think. Just to say it.

As she said the words, just as she started to tell me, I felt my limbs grow tingly as the adrenaline flooded my body. My heart pounded. My mind raced. I wished I could say I was thinking ahead to her treatment, to her prognosis, but I wasn't. I wanted to get away. Part of me continued to listen, nodded as my mother talked about those things. I heard the words—stage three, surgery, chemotherapy–and in between was white buzzy static. My father sat next to her, his hands covering hers.

I was rambling. It was the sort of rambling shrinks normally loved. No telling what treasures I might accidentally reveal.

"What kind of cancer?" Dr. Lawrence interrupted me.

"Lymphoma." My voice sounded flat in my own ears. "Really common, I guess," I added after a long pause, as if that made it better somehow. Less destructive.

"Has she started treatment?"

"No, not yet. She refused to do it until after the holidays. She looks okay, you know? Tired, but okay."

"Have they talked about a prognosis?"

"Umm, yeah, yeah. She said the fact that she is younger and can still do her everyday things is good. I mean, it's still stage three. She's trying to be really positive."

"And you said your father was being very supportive."

"Yes, he's right there."

"So, let's talk about your reaction, Cori. You said you felt like you wanted to get away. Tell me about that."

Every muscle began to tighten in resistance. I stared at the same red and brown swirl in the Oriental rug until it began to dance and shift.

"Cori?"

"I was wrong. I can't do this."

"Can't do what?"

"This. I can't do this. Not today." I plucked my handbag up from the floor as I stood and grabbed my jacket off the coat rack. "I'm sorry." I closed the door without even looking at Dr. Lawrence.

———————————————

By the time I came home for the summer, my mother had finished her chemo. It's weird how quickly you get used to saying "chemo" and talking about ports and scans. That spring semester, I came home when I could despite her insistence that I stay focused on my studies. I did my best to help my dad when I was there. Each time I came home she was a little less my mother. Her appetite went. Then her energy. Then her color. Finally, her hair. I think she minded that more than the rest. Until then, she had glossy and thick dark hair. I had always envied her that beautiful hair. My own was only a vague echo of hers, thick and auburn, but without the sleek sophistication given the waves. She tried on wigs that her hairdresser brought over for her and in the end decided just to shave her head completely. The hats and scarves she wore were more a concession to the cold Midwestern spring than modesty. She bore that as she did everything else, with a steadfast determination.

My mother was never overweight a day in her life, but after a few cycles of chemo she grew so thin I could hardly look at her. Her oncologist wanted us to get her to eat more. I tried making her favorite soups. She would muster a smile and tell me it smelled delicious. I knew most of the time it was probably a polite lie. We were pretending. If she was hungry for something, anything, and we didn't have it in the house, I would dash out to get it. By the time I got home, she could manage only a few small bites. I even tried to ply her with chocolate shakes, a treat she almost never let herself have. She said the chemo made everything taste bad. Like metal.

Throughout the summer, she improved, albeit gradually. Her hair was growing back, but its texture had totally changed. It grew back in much coarser and without its gloss. From then on, she chose to wear it cropped close to her head. She said it was because she had discovered how much easier it was, but I knew. Her doctors would never say she was cured, just that her scans showed nothing abnormal. Remission. From the Latin *remissio* or the Old French *remittere*, to send back or restore. I had looked it up. Except you never really could send something like that back. The cancer could still be hiding in her body, somewhere their scans and blood tests could not see, waiting. It almost certainly was.

As she became stronger, my dad was back at the office more and more. I split my time between looking for a job and looking after my mother. She said she needed no looking after, but I noticed she was often short of breath and her weight hadn't really come back up. Not enough. When she was sick the first time, she didn't really want anyone around. I had tried to sit with her, tried to talk with her, but she was too tired or too angry. Eventually the anger subsided, but she still preferred to be alone most of the time. Dad, even more than I, had to make excuses to many of the neighbors and friends who wanted to come by. It was a bad day. She's tired. Maybe in a little while when she's feeling stronger. By avoiding the most obvious topic, the house grew quiet.

I closed my eyes and listened to the taxi horns on the street. Theirs was a new language I learned. A short sharp honk alerted the fare waiting in a doorway. A series of broken honks greeted another cabby. The long lean on the horn was for a driver who had cut them off in traffic. Tonight, I found the whoosh of bright yellow cabs on dark rain-soaked streets late into the night a reassurance.

It's not that I didn't think of my mother. I did. I missed her. Missed both my mother and my father. But I hadn't thought about her that way, thin, pale, and breathless, not for a long time. I remembered her in the garden, among her plants upon which she lavished her tender affections, trimming, watering, and pruning. She spoke to them as if they could hear her, even as if they answered. Just as I had all those years ago out in the house garden at the farm. After all, I learned it from her. I could still see that faraway look in her deep blue eyes—peaceful, as if she never came all the way back from wherever it was she went in the worst of those months.

I roused myself from the sofa and the memories of my mother.

"Come on, Maud. It's time for bed." The cat looked down at me lazily from where she already dozed along the back of the sofa. "Okay, fine. You stay here. I'm going to bed."

I picked my book up from the table and clicked off the lamp. The room fell into gray and black shadows, the streetlights, and the lights of the building across the courtyard providing a false moonlight. From the dark of the living room, I could see into the apartment across the way. The music man was home. His lights were on. A shadow figure moved deeper in the apartment. I guessed he was listening to jazz. No, blues. Yes, blues with this kind of cold rain. Howlin' Wolf, maybe. I tried to hear it in my mind. It had become a pleasant distraction trying to imagine what he would favor. More movement from the apartment pulled me from my game. The shadow moved closer to the balcony door and then became the slim silhouette of the man. He swung open the door, leaned against the frame and peered out into the rain. Instinctively, I froze. Could he see me? No, that was impossible. The only light on was down the hall and that didn't cast enough light here. I watched. He watched.

With only a soft thud letting me know she had moved from her perch, Maud jumped off the back of the sofa and came to sit at my feet. She looked up at me and then at the doorway, her tail held still and slightly aloft. She watched the man too. After what felt like minutes, he stepped inside and closed the door. Maud looked at me and meowed once to let me know she was bored with our game.

"Yes, yes, I'm coming."

The cat trotted ahead, silent on her delicate paws, her ash-gray fur blending with the darkness as she moved in and out of it. She had taken to sleeping on the bed with Sean gone, something I never let her do when we were at home. I had no illusions that she slept there out of loyalty to me. On Saturday mornings, as soon as I got up to make tea and get the paper, she jumped up to curl up happily with him, nuzzling under his chin and grizzled whiskers. No doubt she was already settling into his spot.

Standing barefoot on the cold tile floor of the bathroom, putting the toothpaste on my toothbrush, the sense of something familiar haunted me. Hanging at the edge of my mind and just out of reach. I had stayed here dozens of times. Surely that was it. The Déjà vu experience as the memory of having stood here like this before leaped off the edge of a synapse and plummeted before making it all the way across. Inexplicably, my hands shook as I tried to screw the cap back on. It bounced into the sink.

"Dammit," I muttered, chasing the small white cap as it rolled around the slick porcelain. Then it happened. *Now* crashing into real memory. I was back standing on the blue and white tile floor in the bathroom at the farm. The feel of it slick and cold under my feet. A body memory, I suppose. My arms and legs felt numb and heavy. Grabbing the edge of the sink, I looked in the mirror. I wasn't sure I knew who looked back. I wasn't sure I wanted to know. I cast my eyes back to the sink and finished brushing without looking up.

I padded back down the hall just as I had that night, heading to the bedroom as fast as I could and pushing the door closed. Maud's amber eyes glowed from the bed as she opened them to acknowledge me. I undressed hurriedly and climbed under the covers, pulling them up tight. But this bed smelled of Sean's soap and cologne, not cedar and fresh air. The duvet was fine and smooth, not the nubby texture of the patterned hearts on the old white cotton bedspreads Evelyn favored. Yet, I could swear I heard a screen door open and close downstairs. I held my breath. There was Evelyn's voice, then the low murmur of Bill's. I couldn't make out what was being said. I strained my ears again the dark and distance, listened for a raised voice or the footfalls of someone running up the stairs, but the talk was quiet and warm, like my parent's night talk. I breathed out a long, ragged breath. He wouldn't tell her. Evelyn came up stairs first. I heard her humming softly as she washed her face. I fell asleep still listening for Bill's footfalls on the stairs. When I woke, I knew I'd have to go back. Back to Sheerfolly Chapel. Back to the farm.

CHAPTER TEN

SHEERFOLLY CHAPEL. POPULATION 2,261. I always wondered who the one was. Unlike some towns that were rediscovered, or re-made, Sheerfolly was not on its second or third life. It had only the one long rusted existence. It was a small rural town on the road to somewhere else, no doubt named by settlers who had pulled their own share of rocks from the soil as they attempted to farm here and instead moved on, leaving behind the small white clapboard roadside church with its steeple rising as consolation to the tenacious folks who stayed and found life in the rich, albeit rocky soil.

Situated within an unremarkable landscape save the river which carved its way just past the center of town, Sheerfolly Chapel was pretty in an uncomplicated way. Along the river, it was a different story. There were gently rolling hills covered with trees that made rich greens in at least a half dozen different shades if you looked closely. Everywhere else it was neatly rowed crops, scrubby trees, and dusty roads, but at the river there was a beautiful tumbling chaos. In town itself, an old stone bridge arched across the river, built from the same rock that heaved itself from every field in the spring and lay smooth and cold underneath the burbling water. Constructed when horse and cart ruled the road, it was only wide enough for one car to pass. It had been closed to cars for the last sixty years. Evelyn had told me. Engineers had deemed modern cars were too heavy and would damage it. The old stone bridge was just a footbridge now. A bigger, wider, and purportedly better concrete bridge had been built outside town at the widest part of the river. One that could handle the trucks coming to and from the dairy farms from the highway bypass.

When there were morning errands to be done in town, I would ask to ride along. Usually, it was with Evelyn. While she went to the market or to the doctor or got her haircut, I was free to roam the mile or so that made up Sheerfolly proper. My only assignment was to walk up to the Post Office and pick up the mail. From her pocket, Evelyn would produce the box key, tied to a red and black braided cord. She didn't carry a purse, which she still called a pocketbook, unless she went to church. There was just no use for them here, she said.

Next to the county courthouse in Pigeon Falls, the Sheerfolly Post Office was the most ornate building in at least 250 miles. With no home delivery, everyone had to go to town to retrieve their mail from the slender gold boxes that recessed into the marble walls of the Post Office. At first, I'm sure it was just something she did to keep me busy and make me feel important, but I didn't mind. On a hot summer day, I welcomed the coolness inside and the old smell of it. It reminded me of the time we had gone to the natural history museum on a class trip. What I liked best about it were the secrets of that locked box. Opening it with the key. Waiting to see if there would be the angled stack of envelopes, or a claim slip for a package, or just the gold sheen of the empty box and the light of the hidden room on the other side.

The creek in Oliver, the windbreak, and the stone footbridge here; these were my cherished spots. I gravitated to the bridge because it reminded me of the creek. I felt closer to life in those places. And I suppose, closer to death. I spent hours on that bridge and under its shade, feet slipping on wet rocks, hands pressed to the cool low underside of the stone where it climbed into the arch. I contemplated the algae-colored crayfish who took respite there with the same interest if not the same intensity with which I considered the fate of Ophelia.

When he wasn't in the city, my father liked places the new bypass didn't reach. Towns like Edgewater with its fine cottages and resorts. In between were run down old motor inns or cabins with names like Arrowside or Breezy Point. Edgewater had caught the eye of an artist who bought one of the old, dilapidated resorts and rented out studios to other writers and artists looking for cheap space and privacy. They saw charm in the peeling old signs and the defunct supper clubs. A developer named John Everett saw dollar signs. He started buying up the boarded up old places and renovating them into posh resorts. The kind with spas. Suddenly, there were restaurants, galleries, and boutiques. My father had known the old town well. He took us once for a weekend after the redevelopment and promptly declared Edgewater ruined. As an architect who spent every day going to an office, he had preferred being away, being with artists who chose to live in a smaller way. Someday, he told me, he would go back to living that way. Closer to the bone. The way it had been.

Despite his objections, my father still preferred any town to the Butchart farm, so while my mother and I were in Sheerfolly, sometimes even when we were at home, he would be in Edgewater or some other place. His version of close to the bone did not involve the earth in the same way it did for my mother. Some people have that in them, I guess. Some people prefer buildings. Though he spoke of John Everett with disdain for the way he had commercialized Edgewater, I always thought I detected a note of jealousy. Not vitriol. Envy.

I thought about telling Sean about my plan, about my need to return to Sheerfolly Chapel, but that would open too many things we hadn't talked about yet. I laughed to myself. It had been more than six years. What was I waiting for? But then some secrets are hard to tell. He didn't know about Bill. I had not told him. I told no one except Dr. Lawrence. I worried Sean would be angry with me, disgusted even. Or jealous. Then I was afraid he wouldn't be. And the truth was, I still loved Bill. No, not yet. The time wasn't right, and Sean wasn't in one place long enough for those kinds of conversations. Besides, I had plenty of work to do here before I retrieved my car from the long-term lot and drove to Sheerfolly.

CHAPTER ELEVEN

FOR THE TEN months between my mother's cancer and the recurrence, she was quiet. The year she died she was big into talking. Truth telling. It happens when people are dying. They know. They prepare even when they are not aware they are preparing. Suddenly, there are all the unsaid things coming into words. It is the soul pinning its laundry up in the sun and eternal wind. All you can do is stay near and keep handing the clothespins. My mother knew.

As we went along with this process, it wasn't really shocking that some of my mother's existential laundry had to do with me. I was her daughter after all. Part of me enjoyed this time with her though I tried not to spend time thinking about why it came. She was suddenly more open about her own life, her own choices. What did surprise me was that there seemed to be no limit to what she would say to me now.

My father continued working long hours as usual. Sometimes after dark, I would slip outside for a cigarette and see the glow of the light on his drafting table. I would watch him through the window, watch him draw and pause to take sips from the glass of whiskey he kept on his table. There were nights he slept in his studio. That had started during the chemo when the slightest movements around my mother disturbed her sleep. Later, it would be the small movements that brought her pain.

She and I were alone in the garden, enjoying a July evening, when she took my hand and smiling said, "You know, I hadn't expected you, Cori. You were a wonderful and terrifying surprise."

I blinked, not quite sure what she meant or how to react.

"I wasn't supposed to be able to have children at all."

"Why?"

"A botched appendectomy when I was in my twenties. It was terrible. I was in the hospital for weeks. They thought I wouldn't be able to get pregnant after that. No one was more surprised than I was when I realized you were on the way. Except maybe your father." She paused and then a small smile came back to her face. "But he was thrilled, of course."

Yes, of course. But the way she said it made me wonder if after everything he was. Why would she tell me this? To make me feel special? There was something odd about the whole conversation.

"We just thought we would never have children is all. It was quite a shock. Adjustments needed to be made. You remind me so much of him."

"Of Dad?" My disbelief was plain in my voice. I often thought we couldn't be more different.

"No, not Dad, though I guess in ways you are like him too."

The old familiar sense of foreboding seeped in. What was she saying? I leaned forward, pressing her.

"Who? Who am I like?"

"Martin. Martin Hayden."

"Hayden?" Hayden was my middle name. My pulse quickened. "Mom?" Martin Hayden was a name I had never heard uttered. Not in any story my parents ever told. Now I found out he was important enough that I was named for him. There was something else. A look I had rarely seen before. A deep grief.

"Mom," I said slowly, "what are you saying? That I'm not Dad's kid, but some guy named Martin's?"

"No, Cori. No. Your father is still your father. I'm sorry. I didn't mean to imply… I just think I made you like him."

My heart was still thumping, but the sound of blood in my ears had receded again. I relaxed back into the silvered Adirondack chair, my spine crunching vertebra by vertebra against the high back. So, there was someone before my father. It wasn't a fact I had ever stopped to consider, but of course. My parents hadn't met until they were well into their twenties. There would have been other people. That I was in fact the biological child of my mother and father was no longer in question. I drew air a little deeper into my diaphragm, practicing the breathing exercise Dr. Lawrence had first taught me when the anxiety attacks began. I was lightheaded. My vision grew dark for a moment, then returned in prickles and waves of light. I inhaled again, drawing the air down even deeper. I could feel my pulse slow down to a more evenly spaced thud, thud, thud, but the nauseous feeling remained.

"Mom, forgive me, but what the hell are you talking about?"

"You're the child of my heart, Corianne. Yes, you have your father's eyes and you're alone, solitary like he is, but the rest … if we had been able to…I can't expect you to understand right now. Someday you will."

I did. I understood. The rest of me was born of the love for him, this other man, love that she had poured into me. I had been named for him.

"What happened," I whispered.

"A car accident. On the old highway heading into Sheerfolly. I was at the farm. Bill…Bill found me. He told me what had happened."

"Does Dad know?"

"Maybe. Yes." She looked down at her hands. "Corianne, I'm telling you this because you feel it. I see that you do. There is more distance between your father and I than this damn cancer. And I want it to make sense. I almost told you that last trip out to the farm. Evie and I have talked this over a hundred times. She said it was wrong to tell you. That you'd already been through so much. She was right then. But you're older now. And I'm not going to be around much longer. I don't want it to be for you like it was for me. It hasn't been a bad life, but secrets are a bad thing. You should know this wasn't always my life."

I had no words. I sat like a stone as my mind limped from thought to thought.

"Don't talk about dying, Mom." I finally said.

"It's going to happen to all of us one day," she said matter-of-factly. "It's just going to happen to me sooner." Her eyes said there was still something struggling, something that hadn't quite let go.

"Here." She reached down and produced a small leather box from underneath her chair.

"What've you got there?" My father's voice burst in cheerfully.

She never got the chance to finish. My mother's voice had trailed off and I followed her eyes. Dad, Alan, strolled across the lawn. My eyes darted from my father to her. We weren't done. How could I just go on as if nothing has happened? But I saw the look in my mother's eyes, part warning and two parts unmistakable sadness. This conversation was over.

"Take it." She handed me a leather-covered box about the size of a cigar box. The sort of box a young girl uses to keep special things in. Found things and things not yet found— stones picked up along the beach, tiny rings that no longer fit, the odd lucky penny. All these things were talismans meant to keep away the bad things and attract good fortune. Bring love.

I held out my hands numbly to take the box. Lifting the lid, I saw envelopes addressed to my mother. Love letters? I quickly snapped the lid down. Dusk had fallen while we talked. I looked at my mother's face and noted how it seemed all light suddenly left her as well. Her face, alive a moment ago with sorrow and tenderness, now just looked tired.

"Read them. It will explain things." She got up and kissed me on the top of the head. "I'm going to bed."

She was right. I knew. Had known. The love that was in my mother's face when she looked at me, that was so apparent when she spoke of Martin Hayden was never there when she looked at my father. There was kindness and a different kind of love, but no light. I bore the last name of Alan Dempsey who I adored, and I even resembled him, but to my mother the rest of me was like Martin, the man I never knew. She saw his mannerisms in mine and traits that seemed by some power of spirit to manifest in me the man she deeply loved and lost. It seemed I was always going to be two women—my father's child and the child of my mother's devotion to another man— just as I had become the girl before the murder, and the one after.

Lost love letters indeed. How does a girl fold herself into a small leather box?

CHAPTER TWELVE

MY MOTHER DIED in October as the first golden leaves fell and the spent grasses and wildflowers of summer tottered on their dry stems. We were with her, my father and me, sometimes together, sometimes taking shifts, for four labored days and nights.

She had not been strong enough to climb the stairs for weeks and before that, she was too unsteady from the pain meds they gave her. My father had seen this before with his own mother's brutal battle with cancer. He was fourteen. Not old enough to do anything and just old enough to feel the full weight of helplessness, uncertainty, and loss. He didn't say it out loud, but he wanted things to be different this time. He wanted to do things for my mother, help make her comfortable in ways he could never do for his mother. The stairs had become a problem and my father was determined to find a solution that made her happy. He proposed converting the large screen porch into her bedroom. My father spoke with her as a potential client, consulting and making notes. I never saw them collaborate on anything like they did that room. The plans were drawn. Her requirement? That it be a place that let her spend that last summer of her life still tending her garden, albeit this time from the big wicker rocker that had been brought in from the garden and adorned with plump new cushions covered in a pink and red Victorian floral–or a hospital bed when the time came. The project was his solace that last spring, and his last gift to my mother.

As exhausted and sick as she was, my mother was extraordinarily patient with my father as he rushed around with plans in his fists and drafting pencils behind his ears. Workmen trooped in and out for weeks, drilling, hammering, and sawing as modifications were made. Normally, the porch was rustic and simple, not unlike one of those giant canvas tents erected over wooden floors at old summer camps.

"It's unpretentious," my father said, taking stock as he and I sat on the porch one last time before the remodeling was to begin. "Like Teddy Roosevelt on one of his expeditions."

"Dad, Teddy Roosevelt would have done it with a dirt floor and a hell of a lot more whiskey."

He laughed and his eyes laughed, crinkling at the corners in lines that remembered a joy that had long been absent. I was suddenly glad I had made him smile. To hear him laugh like when I was a little girl, before the shadows moved in with us and before my mother's cancer, it made me smile too.

"You're probably right, Cori. You're probably right." He raised his glass of whiskey in a toast and from that point forward, he took to calling the construction project "The Great Migration."

Things had to change considerably to make a rustic retreat comfortable for a dying woman, this dying woman. It needed to be open to the garden and yet insulated, heated when necessary. She got cold so easily, all her bodily stores long since spent. She was as thin as a rail and wore at least a light cardigan even on the warmest days. It had to have more outlets. More places for medical equipment to be plugged in. She didn't want any extraordinary means. My mother was clear on that. She wanted to die at home and not hooked up to a bunch of machines. But her doctors had prepared us. She would need a hospital bed eventually and an alternating pressure mattress underneath her that would circulate air in regular intervals in changing patterns to relieve pressure points, keeping her comfortable and preventing bed sores. For now, she was on pain pills, but when it got bad enough, when she couldn't swallow anymore, the hospice nurses could give drugs through the port just below her collarbone, as they had done with her chemo drugs. Dying at home was a more complicated business than any of us could have imagined. I remember hoping that when my time came, I could just lie down somewhere green.

Despite all the medical realities, or perhaps because of them, my father saw to it that every detail of the refitting was perfection. Screens on two sides of the porch were fitted with removable glass storm panels to help insulate the room without robbing the view. Because my mother would not tolerate them being shuttered, the eight-foot screens in the front were rigged with large, hinged panes that could be closed against a storm or cold, or opened fully and hooked to the walls. Electric baseboard heat was installed. The rough-hewn wood replaced with a smooth, warm maple veneer. It was all beautiful, but the beadboard ceiling? That was exquisite. Dad had carefully measured to calculate how many boards it would take and then he searched out reclaimed wood. Wood from an old barn in Sheerfolly Chapel. It was probably the most time he ever spent there. For weeks, the carpenters my father hired worked cutting the boards to the right widths, sanding them until the surface of each was as smooth as felt. Then they were stained to match the maple. Sawhorses straddled the lawn, and the sound of miter saws and pneumatic nail guns pierced the dewy mornings of early summer. On one of the first days, I went out to talk to Chuck Marshall, the lead carpenter on the project.

"Chuck," I said putting one hand on my hip and gesturing with the other. I had become emboldened by being my mother's protector. "I know this is all for my mother, and I love it, I do, but I want you to know that she rests every afternoon at two o'clock. She *needs* to rest, and I'll not see those two hours of quiet interrupted." He nodded solemnly and as I walked away, I saw him give one of the other guys a look and shake his head, but never did he pound a single nail after 1:55 PM.

Chuck grew fond of my mother. At the beginning of the summer, she would still go out accompanied most days to survey her garden. She could no longer do the work save pull a weed or two, but she was good at telling me what work needed to be done. I worked under her direction as I had once worked for Evelyn at the farm, and as I worked, she would talk with Chuck. She had a way about her, a way of disarming people, asking them questions so directly that there was no room to be evasive. They began talking about their lives. I kept quiet and listened when I could.

Chuck was about forty, I guessed. He came every day in his tattered khaki cargo shorts and a t-shirt. From being outside so much his dark hair had bleached the color of a sand dune, the silver in it like driftwood. He always stopped at the house first, and often he would walk her out to her chair in the garden. It became common to see the two of them strolling across the lawn, arm in arm, like something out of a nineteenth-century novel. As Chuck prepared the wood to accept the stain, his story unfolded on to the lawn. My mother gathered it up in her lap, nodding patiently and offering her matter-of-fact advice. I was not always privy to their talks. I just know that as Chuck talked to her, this gruff and quiet man became softer.

Sometimes I sat with my mother and watched Chuck work while pretending to read. I became entranced by the strength of his forearms, his hands, tanned and scarred, and how as he sanded, he would blow or brush away the sawdust, and then run his hand slowly along the board, his palms feeling for any roughness, any blemish. I fantasized about being under those hands, feeling them run the length of me. I thought about touching those arms, lifting his t-shirt, and running my hand along his stomach, feeling the trail of hair and the heat. Once I even came softly and quietly there in the chair, watching Chuck work, imagining what those hands could do.

It was also during that summer that I met Sean. I would like to say it was like a lightning strike, but our first meeting was nothing so glamorous. I had taken my mother into the hospital to have her latest set of scans and meet with her oncologist. My father rarely came to these appointments anymore. He said it was because he was supervising the project, but the truth was he didn't like hospitals. It became my job to drive her and sit and wait. She hated me sitting around in waiting rooms while she had her procedures. I never complained, but she knew. She remembered. She sent me off to the hospital café to get some breakfast.

"Go," she said. "I'll be fine. You can meet me back up here in an hour." When I looked skeptical, she added, "I promise I won't talk to the doc without you. Cori, go. Go!"

"Well, since you put it that way. But I'm going to wait with you until they take you back." I insisted.

Truthfully, I hated being at the hospital as much as my father did. I hated the waiting rooms that pretended to be living rooms, as if soft colors, a battered copy of *Ladies' Home Journal* and a tank full of fish would make people forget they had cancer. The music was the worst. I hated the exam rooms with their closeness, the vinyl chairs, metal sinks and red sharps bins. The hallways were no better. Shiny tile floors, coded pages, and the warning signs around the radiology department reminding everyone who was paying attention that fighting cancer was like trench warfare, replete with machines and deadly biologic agents. I hated it, but I could never leave her alone there either. We were a team.

Hungry did finally get the better of me. I went down two floors to the café, ordered a large, iced coffee and looked over the bakery. My eyes settled on the last blueberry scone even though I could predict that waiting for the latest results, it would just stick in my throat. Just as I reached for it, the man next to me plucked it out of the case. I didn't even look at him. I just sighed.

"Oh, wow. I'm sorry. You had your eye on that, didn't you? Here," he extended the plate with the scone to me, "you take it. Truth is, I don't even really like scones. I'm more of a stale Danish guy." He grinned at me, revealing perfect white teeth. It was crap about the Danish and we both knew it, but it was a nice gesture and there was a kindness in his smile, in the offering, that I hadn't felt from anyone in a long time.

"Why don't we share it. I'm not very hungry anyway."

He smiled again.

"It's a deal." Before I knew quite what was happening, he had paid for both orders and guided me to a table. "By the way, I'm Sean."

"Corianne," I replied extending my hand. He enveloped my hand with his perfectly sculpted one and held it just a moment too long.

"Corianne, it's an absolute pleasure."

For the next hour, he guided me through conversation as easily as he had steered me to the table. I talked about my mother, the reason for our being at the hospital, and her prognosis. He asked questions. Knowledgeable questions. I realized at the end of an hour, I had spilled my guts to a total stranger. So much for always being guarded and vigilant. I looked at my watch.

"Look, I've gotta go." I pushed my chair back and rose to my feet. "My mom, she's going to be out of her scan, and I'm supposed to … well, I've gotta go." Damn him. I'd almost done it again. He had that way of making me volunteer more than I wanted.

"This was nice, Corianne. Corianne what?"

I hesitated.

"Dempsey. Corianne Dempsey."

"Maybe we could do this again sometime Corianne Dempsey. Somewhere else."

"Maybe." I grabbed my lidded coffee cup off the table and started walking away. I stopped and turned back. "Hey, Sean, you never said why it is you're here."

"You wouldn't believe me if I told you."

"Well at least tell me what you do for a living."

"I teach biology."

I laughed. "I bet you do."

CHAPTER THIRTEEN

AS IT HAPPENED, Sean Michael Parsons hadn't taught biology in five years. He had been a celebrated secondary school biology teacher, but only to pay the bills until his career as a nature photographer took off. Landscape photographer he would specify. He didn't like people at parties thinking he was some amateur taking photos of birds he lured to a backyard feeder. He had told me the bit about teaching biology because he said it sounded less like a come on. Now he had the career he wanted, which involved being a sought-after photographer, asked to travel around the world for just the right photos to accompany stories about endangered landscapes and species or documenting the few that weren't yet. Currently, that was in France's Dordogne Valley. For someone with those skills, tracking me down had been no problem at all. I had to give him credit, he didn't just call when he found me. The first thing he did was send me a box of scones from Babineaux's, the finest bakery in the city. No note. Just the scones.

When I put out the plate of scones with coffee the next morning, my mother, always alert for a mention of a man in my life, smelled testosterone in the air and perked up. The questions began as she considered a pecan scone, holding it aloft over the steaming jasmine green tea she favored since the chemo had first turned her stomach.

"Your father tells me these were delivered to you yesterday. Kind of extravagant, don't you think, ordering one box of scones from Babineaux's and having it delivered out here? Not that I don't appreciate the thought, but you know I don't have much of an appetite." She looked over the top of her glasses at me as she finished, the hint of a smile pulling at the corners of her mouth. She knew full well I didn't order them, but she'd offered me a plausible, albeit teasing alternative, and then waited to see if I'd take it.

"I wish I'd been that thoughtful, Mom," I confessed. "A friend sent these over."

"A friend?"

"A guy. A man. Sean. Someone I talked to at the hospital the day you were having your scan."

"Is he a friend or a guy?"

"He's just some guy."

"Some guy doesn't send you a box of bakery." My mother's tone was still interested, but I noted it also carried a note of concern.

"It's just a stupid little joke. We both wanted the last blueberry scone. It was stupid." I gritted my teeth and poked angrily at a blueberry that had fallen out of the scone on my plate. Truthfully, the attention was flattering, although it had made me uncomfortable that he had found me so easily.

My mother laughed. Her voice was thinner than it used to be, but not brittle. Her laugh still had its music.

"Watch out for that one, Cori. You'll lose your heart before you're even in his bed."

"Oh god, Mom."

"Hey, I'm not dead yet." She lifted the tall brown coffee mug to her lips and then lowered it again. "I'm just saying be careful. Have fun. But be careful. Well, there's no denying he's got good taste."

"God, I'm not sleeping with him. He sent me a box of bakery." And with that I got up, picked up the box of scones and took them outside. Chuck and his assistants Phil, who they called Puck, and John were already at work staining wood. They looked up as I walked across the lawn.

"Breakfast, boys." I dumped the box unceremoniously onto one of the empty sawhorses, and turned on my heels.

"Hey, thanks Cori!" the always easygoing Puck called out.

I could feel Chuck's eyes follow me across the lawn. Feel them slide down my spine like the exhilarating torment of an ice cube, following the line of my hips as if I had left my white denim shorts and sleeveless blouse lying forgotten on the bed in my room that morning. I shivered involuntarily despite the heat.

A week later, Sean called to ask me out for coffee. I put him off with an excuse about needing to stay with my mother. Another week went by and then he called to ask me to the jazz concert in the park that Friday night. Again, I declined, citing my mother's poor health. On Friday, he showed up at our front door.

"I took a chance that you might be home," he said grinning as I opened the door.

"You're cocksure of yourself, aren't you?"

"And you've got quite a mouth."

I felt myself blush, but quickly pivoted from embarrassment to apparent bored exasperation. "Why are you here, Sean?"

"I thought you could use a break, so I brought the park to you." From behind his back, he produced a small basket holding a bottle of wine, crackers, and some brie. I eyed it over carefully.

"I don't see any glasses. I suppose you thought we'd just pass the bottle back and forth?"

"I took a chance that you'd have some."

"And the music? Were you planning to hum?"

He produced his phone from his pocket.

"Kind of small, don't you think?"

"You are the saucy one." I looked over my shoulder. My mother was at the kitchen table answering one of the letters that came for her every few weeks. My father was out on the porch evaluating the day's progress. The remodeling was almost complete. Another week, maybe two, and the migration could begin.

"Okay, but go around back to the garden."

I ducked through the dining room and snatched up the two wine glasses sitting next to a decanter on the old Spanish sabino door my father had converted into a library table, then slid out the French doors unnoticed. Sean had opened the bottle of wine and set out the spread of crackers and cheese on the table between the two chairs where my mother and I always sat. Strains of Miles Davis "Kind of Blue" wafted out of the phone's small speaker.

"Not bad," I said, handing him the glasses.

There was something very compelling about this Sean with his starched white shirt and almost boyish grin. Something safe. I relaxed into the wine and the sound of his voice as he talked about his work, about where in the world it had taken him and where he would go next. I sunk into the soft light of evening, the wobbling flight and squeaky song of the goldfinches who, undaunted by our presence, came to the nearby bird feeder for a late snack of thistle seeds. I indulged myself, thinking the sound of Davis's horn called to something deep in them as well.

My father spotted me with my visitor. He never came out, but I noticed him walking past the dining room doors from time to time. His way of letting me know he was nearby, should I need him. After two hours had passed, I sat forward in my chair and announced the evening was over.

"I admit this was nice. But I've had a long day, so we need to call it a night."

"It was nice. Maybe next time you'll let me take you out to dinner."

"Maybe," I said getting to my feet.

"So, there *is* a next time."

"I didn't say that."

"Yes, you did."

I frowned, feeling backed into an answer I had not intended to give. He picked up the wine glasses.

"Just leave them." I suddenly wanted him gone as quickly as possible.

Following Sean as he made his way toward the front of the house, sandals in hand, I glanced over my shoulder again at the dining room. My father was nowhere to be seen. As we rounded the corner to the driveway thickly bordered by a hedge of boxwoods, Sean, hands in the pockets of his charcoal linen pants, turned to me. Trapped between the hedgerow and his body, I felt every inch of his six-foot frame. I smelled his freshly laundered shirt mixed with the subtle spice of his cologne. He leaned in to kiss me, but I turned my head. His lips brushed my cheek.

"You don't trust anyone, do you Corianne?"

"No," I said matter-of-factly.

"Goodnight, Corianne," he whispered into my hair.

CHAPTER FOURTEEN

THE FULL HEAT of summer arrived the last week of July that year. Tennessee Williams hot. The air was stagnant, oppressive, and pungent with the smell of rotting things. Sweat sat up on my skin, making my cotton halter dress feel limp and stick to me as I carried a box of my mother's books from her bedroom upstairs to her new room downstairs. I half expected to look down and see the antique pink roses on the fabric drooping limply as well.

"I think that's about it, Mom. Except your clothes and stuff from your bathroom."

She sighed heavily. "I'll have to go through that all myself. There's no sense in bringing it all down here."

"You shouldn't be going up and down the stairs, Mom."

"I have no intention of going up and down the stairs. I plan to go up, do some sorting and then take my nap. Besides, Chuck is going to be here to put the finishing touches on that bookcase your father commissioned. I really would have been fine with something out of a box, but he insisted." She shook her head. "You know, Cori, you should have it. You are not going to live here forever. You'll need some things. Or is that too ghoulish to have your dead mother's bookcase in your apartment?"

"No, Mom. Of course not. But it is ghoulish to keep talking about yourself in the past tense."

"It is what it is. Everyone dies, Cori."

I opened my mouth to say something, but Chuck knocked on the door.

"Hey, Mrs. Dempsey," he said warmly. "How are you feeling today?" At the sight of Chuck, my mother brightened.

"Chuck, come in. I was just telling Cori that it doesn't do any good to wish things away." I noticed my mother had not answered the question.

"That's a fact, Mrs. Dempsey." He nodded in solemn agreement and after a polite pause added, "I'm here to bang that bookcase together and cut the last couple trim pieces for the ceiling. Is that going to bother you too much? It's almost one o'clock," Chuck glanced over at me, "and I know you'll be going to lie down soon. I've got another job tomorrow afternoon, but I could come by in the morning if you'd rather."

"No, no, no. Do it today. It's fine. I'm going upstairs soon anyway, but I do have some work to do here first. Start with the ceiling if you don't mind. And then by the time I'm done, you'll be on the bookcase. I can just close my door."

I marveled at the way, even as ill as she was, my mother continued to orchestrate the life of the house.

"You sure? Like I said, I'm going to be making some noise."

"I'm sure." My mother had spoken, the matter settled.

"Okay, I'll go grab my stuff out of the truck and get those pieces in from the garage." Chuck headed back out, his brown work boots making a soft thudding noise on the slate floor. He always had curiously perfect posture, held his back perfectly straight. His oatmeal-colored t-shirt pulled taut across his broad and well-muscled back.

"Mom, can I fix you some lunch before you go up?" I asked, finally bringing my eyes back to her.

"I'm not really hungry."

"Alright, Dad or I can always bring you up a snack later. Hey, where is Dad?"

"He went into the office today. He had some meetings scheduled. A potential new contract and something else. I forget." She waved her hand dismissively.

"Well why don't you head up? I'll bring you some water. It's awfully hot today."

"I like the heat." She was feeling contrary today and I was not going to get it right. "Chuck can walk me up when I'm done."

My mother never liked air conditioning anyway, and now that she was always cold, she liked it even less. As a concession, my father and I endured the heat, keeping the central air-conditioning system switched off, although he had bought me a window unit for my bedroom. He installed it after making me swear I would keep my door closed so she wouldn't know.

I decided to fix a snack for my mother anyway and take it up to her. Hopefully, she would feel more like eating once it was in front of her. I heard the pneumatic nail gun fire up and knew Chuck was back out on the porch working. He was so good with my mother, tender really, and then with me—well, I felt something different altogether. Knowing this was probably his last week at the house, I felt an odd regret setting in. And an urgency.

The ringing phone pulled me away from thoughts that were growing in intensity. I hurried for the handset before the ringing could disturb my mother. Well-intentioned friends and nosey neighbors were always calling and if she got caught on the phone, she was too polite to say she did not feel like talking. Even now, there was always a moment of anxiety and fear as I lifted the handset to my ear.

After Rebecca's murder, after the police went away, the phone calls had started. I would say hello and there would only be a thick, dark silence in reply. That went on for a while, sporadically. There was just enough time in between that I would forget the last one. If my mother or father answered the phone, whoever it was would quickly hang up. My mother shrugged them off as wrong numbers or some neighborhood kids pulling pranks. Then the calls changed.

Instead of silence, my hello was greeted with the sounds of breathing. Heavy breathing. The worst calls were the ones where he spoke. His voice, somewhat high pitched and smooth, asking me if I knew what he wanted to do to me. Sometimes he would describe it. The first time he spoke, the first word, the sound of his voice convinced me of what I dreaded most. I was convinced it was him. In my terror, I had frozen for a second or two. Then I'd hung up, slamming the receiver down just as soon as I came back to myself. I got faster at sensing the man before he spoke, faster at hanging up. But it was too late. I couldn't unhear those words. Coarse words, disgusting words, the exact meaning of some I couldn't even know yet. Words that as a young girl, I should not have known yet. But in their sounds and the way he formed them, something rotten and dark rose, reaching out for me and into me with such a coldness and evil, I knew what he meant to do. I would shake for hours.

I never told my parents about the calls. He had never warned me not to tell, and yet I said nothing. Dr. Lawrence said once that he counted on my being too traumatized to say anything. That was his power. He got off on being able to get to me. And he got to me. Over and over and over. Then one day the calls just stopped. Maybe he got locked up. Maybe he was dead. I remember hoping he was dead. I thought of it all in that split second between answering and waiting.

"Hello?"

"Nola?"

Relief flooded my body. It was just a friend of my parents looking for an update.

"No, I'm sorry, she's not available. Can I—?"

"Corianne?"

"Yes, who is this?" It was a little too late for caution. I swore at myself silently and I could feel the little tremor in my hand begin.

"My god, of course it is. Cori, it's Bill."

"Bill." The name rushed out of me like air out of a sealed tomb.

"I was calling to check on your mom," Bill said, trying to recover from his own surprise at hearing my voice. "She hasn't called in a while and well, with things the way they are, Evie was getting worried."

"She's okay. Well considering, you know. She's stopped treatments."

"Yeah, I did hear that."

"She's still up and around. But we had to move her bedroom downstairs. We are moving her today actually. Going up and down the stairs is getting harder for her, and the pain meds make her woozy. Dad and I are afraid she might fall. We can't leave her alone for too long. Shit, I'm babbling."

Bill laughed. It was the warmest sound I had ever heard.

"It's fine, Cori. I asked, remember?"

"How are you?"

"I'm fine. Evie, she's having a tough time. Not like your mother. Evie's had some trouble with scar tissue from one of the old surgeries. She's in a lot of pain. They're going to need to go in there again."

"I'm sorry to hear that. I know she's been through a lot already."

"Yeah, and you know Evelyn. She won't complain. She just keeps trying to do everything."

"That sounds familiar," I said, thinking of how my mother was earlier and remembering Evelyn's efficient way of doing things. "No wonder they're such good friends." There was a long pause, a silence large enough to hold the things we weren't saying. Finally, Bill spoke again.

"There's not a day goes by that I don't think of you, Corianne. You know that."

I closed my eyes, feeling tears welling up from somewhere I had not dared to go for years. I nodded my head.

"Corianne."

"Yeah, I know." The words were ragged as I fought to hold on to them and let the cry sink back to the place from which it had risen. I heard a train in the background, the long loud low whistle of the train that ran past Sheerfolly Chapel near the farm, its tracks laid like a zipper between the farms and the town that rose beyond them. It was always loudest and clearest at one spot on the farm. A place where the land swelled up into a little rise. I had lain on it may times and listened to the trains.

"Bill, where are you?"

"I've gotta go, Cori. You'll tell your mom I called to ask after her, okay? But don't tell her about Evie. She'll worry and she doesn't need more of that. If she's feeling up to it sometime, I know Evie would love to talk to her. She's just doesn't want to intrude."

"I'll tell her."

"Bye, Coriander."

"Bye," I whispered.

Years of unspent emotion and unsaid things rattled the door of the closet where I had stuffed them all like Bill's flannel shirt after that night on the windbreak. I felt young and undone as they came back to me. Sights, sounds, signs, touches. I still held the phone tightly in my hand, in both hands, as if by squeezing the phone I could shut out the noise that rumbled up.

"No, I'm not doing this right now." I set the phone down and busied myself making a tray to take up to my mother. As I put the water glass under the faucet, my hand shook. "Not now. Not now." I repeated the words over and over, like a mantra. Or like a chair, shoved up against the door.

CHAPTER FIFTEEN

I STAYED UPSTAIRS with my mother, sitting next to her on the bed, talking, trying to distract her so that she would forget that food didn't taste like much and absentmindedly eat a few bites. It felt good to be there with her, in the room that had always felt like a refuge after Rebecca's murder. Bright even on a cloudy day, it had windows that overlooked the garden, and it was warmed by the scent of lavender perfume and my father's shaving soap.

I casually mentioned Bill's phone call but lied and told my mother Evie had been the one who phoned. I'm not sure why I lied. I hadn't planned to lie. I thought it would cheer her up more to hear from Evelyn, or maybe I was afraid that even saying his name, there would be too much on my face.

"I'd like to go out to the farm again sometime," my mother said as she settled back sleepily on her pillows. Her pain meds were beginning to work. "Wouldn't it be fun? To drive out there together like we used to?"

"You're falling asleep. We'll talk about it later." I kissed her on the forehead. Her skin was buttery soft and warm. Her eyes were already closing. Though the heat in the room seemed oppressive to me, I knew the ceiling fan would make her feel chilled. Rather than turn it off, I picked up the pale blue cotton throw blanket from the chair by the window and covered her arms. Her breathing was deep and steady. She was asleep before I closed the door.

Downstairs was less peaceful. The entire lower level was reverberating with the thudding of wood on wood and the pounding echo of hammering as Chuck worked on assembling the bookcase. I had forgotten he was here. Hearing Bill's voice had temporarily erased everything else from my mind—the room, the cancer, the heat. I turned back up the stairs and went into my bedroom. Now, unlike my mother, I was feeling the heat of the day. Grabbing an elastic hair band from the small ceramic dish on my dresser, I gathered my waves into a thick ponytail. As I finished winding the band around, I looked in the mirror at my raised arms and the lines they formed, the lines of my torso accentuated by my dress as it skimmed my ribs, snugged at my hips, and then dropped into the full skirt that stopped just above my knees. I lowered my arms slowly. The last time Bill had seen me I was in a shapeless flannel shirt. I ran my hands along the length of my neck and let a finger trail into the deep "v" neckline, wiping away the drop of sweat that threatened to roll between my breasts.

The knock and the voice came altogether. I jumped guiltily away from the mirror.

"Sorry to interrupt," Chuck's tone was one of amusement, but he looked at me with the same hunger I had felt whenever he watched me.

"Jesus! Haven't you heard of knocking, Chuck?"

"I did knock."

"Well, what the hell are you doing up here anyway?" I pretended to make a last-minute adjustment to my hair. "You know she's sleeping."

"I was looking for your father. I had a question for him on the bookcase. Seems I found something altogether more interesting." His eyes swept my body again.

"He sure as hell isn't in here." I tried to keep my voice low so as not to wake my mother. I moved to the doorway, but Chuck's body blocked my exit. "Excuse me." I said with a bravado I wasn't feeling. Chuck turned his body but didn't move out of the doorway. "Fine." I started through, dragging my spine along the wood frame so that I could clear the doorway without touching him.

When I was halfway through, he stepped forward until his chest just brushed mine. He ran his hands, the hands I had watched lovingly skim the wooden boards that became the dying room, along my shoulders and down my bare arm.

"Now, Corianne. You can't tell me you haven't felt it. I see the way you look at me, just like you know I'm watching how you twitch your way across the yard." As if to emphasize his point, his hands settled on my hips. He leaned forward and kissed me, gently at first. His lips were soft and full, his mouth tasted like an odd combination of cigarettes and lemonade.

"Not here," I pulled away. Taking his hand, I led him back downstairs. After I looked in my father's study and the garage to make sure he wasn't back, I led Chuck into the laundry room. He backed me up until I was against the wall and pushed the door closed with his foot. With his thumb, he traced my breasts where they thrust against the fabric of my dress. I felt the rush of desire. Trembling, I reached up under his t-shirt and ran my hands across his chest and up his back. I could feel the muscles moving as he shifted, nudging my legs apart with his knees, his hand sliding up my leg, underneath my dress. I felt the heat from his hand as he slid it over my sheer black lace panties, the heat and the pressure of it and the way it enveloped me. He lifted his face from where he had buried it in my neck. His expression was one of hunger and delight.

"How long did you say your father was out?"

"Shut up, Chuck."

When he probed inside me with his fingers, I moaned. He clapped his hand over my mouth. I should have pushed him away, but the whore-child clung to him, writhed, and came wobbly legged. His breath was hot and moist on my skin and though my eyes had closed, I knew he was watching my face.

"That's a good girl."

CHAPTER SIXTEEN

THAT WHOLE SURREAL summer, Sean called at least once a week, wanting to see me when he was in town. I put him off. The memory of what I had done with Chuck made my cheeks burn. And with my mother dying upstairs no less. I was certain Sean need only look at me and he would know. Not that I owed him anything. Still, it wasn't his fault. I was not who he thought I was. There was something dark inside me. There was nothing.

I didn't want to go out. When I had to be out, I didn't like how it felt. At the house, things were close and quiet. Something was slowly opening inside the house and in the garden that I could not reconcile with the noise and activity outside. Everything out there seemed empty and unimportant, all pointless rush and meaningless conversation. My senses felt heightened. It felt like too much.

Sean came back to the garden as the trees turned their finery to autumn, the first crimson leaves standing out in the August green. The garden was the only place I would agree to meet him. I did not want him in the house. It was not for outsiders, not now. Not ever. I needed to be with my mother, I told him. He accepted my explanation without question and brought wine and delicacies to the garden. We talked surrounded by the thick and lush green where only the snap-dragons and hollyhocks could turn their heads to listen.

In those weeks, my mother was growing noticeably weaker. Her coloring began to change. To say she grew paler would be an under-statement. It was as if a cold had touched her. The kind from the fairy tales. The skin on her face grew white with a milky blue underneath, like frost had settled around her bed, and the normal pink flush I had known on that face my whole life grew smaller until it was just faint streaks along her cheekbones and forehead. The plumpness of her face, the little that had remained, sunk away. When I held her hand, it felt soft and fragile in mine.

There were no last words when she died. Not hers anyway. She had been in a coma for days. At first, the hospice nurses came three times a day to monitor her pain, give her morphine and clean the port that still lay buried in her chest just below her collarbone. There was little else to do. Her body was shutting down. My mother had always been slender, and then painfully thin as the cancer fed on her body, but as the end came closer her abdomen bloated so there was a little swell underneath the blankets keeping her warm. It was that—the out-ward sign of the decay within that bothered me more than anything else I saw in the dying room.

My father and I took to sleeping in her room, or tried to sleep, him taking the chair and me stretched out on top of an old sleeping bag I spread out on the floor over a couple of old blankets I used as padding. I laid face up staring at the ceiling, or with closed eyes, fixated on my mother's breath, soft and regular at first and then more ragged, rat-tling in her chest. I would try to match my breathing to hers. Sometimes it would just stop. My eyes would fly open, and I would sit bolt upright. Frozen. Listening. I would call out softly, "Mom?" Then with a small groaning in it would begin again and I would lie back down, my heart beating faster, each knob of my spine crunching against the hardwood floor, despite my bedroll. *Had I called her back?* I supposed that wasn't fair.

Eventually there was only the one nurse, a woman in her fifties, and she stayed with us at the house. She padded in on her rubber-soled shoes, the fabric of her soft pink scrubs rustling like the bed sheets at the farm as she felt for my mother's pulse, in her wrist and then, folding back the covers at the end of the bed, in her feet. Deidre, I remembered. The nurse's name was Deirdre. Deirdre of the Pink Scrubs. She wore her silver watch turned around on her wrist, so the round blue face was toward her. She watched my mother for any signs of discomfort, speaking to her softly as she tended, smoothed, and soothed, adjusting the covers so that they did not put too much pressure on her toes. I opted to step out when it was time to for the next dose of morphine. My father stayed. When Deidre came back out of my mother's room, she would bend her head toward me and say reassuringly, "She's very comfortable." I wondered how she could know, but then as a hospice nurse, she knew a lot about the dying. I only knew about death.

Watching my mother's face became a strange fascination. It was peaceful enough. The morphine had smoothed the furrow that had deepened between her brows over the years, but I could still see the trace of it. If I watched closely enough, now and then I could see her forehead ripple ever so slightly and her lips part as something unseen moved through her, or toward her.

The morning she died it was cool and stormy. I had gone to the kitchen to make some tea, one of the brief moments I left. Coming back, I stopped just outside the door. I could hear my father speaking to her, choking back a sob. "My brave Nola. My sunflower." I knew without being told. When I stepped in, the room had changed again. Something was, if not gone, no longer as it was. Whatever had opened now closed again. My father sat there at her bedside, holding her hand. He looked up at me and nodded, his face wet with tears. I stood there for what felt like ages, dumbly holding my cup of tea, watching the steam rise. Outside it was gray and windy and the large maple trees swayed in their skirts of leaves, but in that room and for that long moment, only the steam from my hot tea stirred.

The nurse materialized from wherever she had been, I don't quite remember, and took the cup from me saying, "Spend as much time with her as you need." I hugged her. Deirdre of the Pink Scrubs, who I did not know. Deidre who cared for my mother in ways I could not. She had a jasmine bloom in her hand from the garden. One of my mother's favorites. She gave it to me.

I walked over to the bed slowly and looked down at my mother. I did not cry. Not at first. I pulled up the other chair and sat next to the bed, opposite my father, holding her other hand, setting in it the jasmine flower. We sat that way together for a long time, not speaking. Finally, Deirdre came back and stood quietly just inside the doorway. After several minutes, my father stood up, kissed my mother's forehead, and stepped out to speak with Deidre. I heard the words *prepare*, *funeral home* and *priest*.

I stayed there, holding my mother's hand until the warmth left it.

CHAPTER SEVENTEEN

THE SIGHT OF the hearse parked in the driveway drew the neighbors like flies. They gathered on their lawns and on their porches, and finally on our lawn and on our porch. There was something unholy about the way they collected, whispering and probing, after the sanctity of what had happened in that room.

Looking out the window, I saw Sarah Arneson, her arms outstretched, turning people back. Her mother Helen, the neighbor who had come to my rescue all those years before, had died just ahead of my mother, a weak heart finally doing her in as she sat on her front porch watching the neighborhood kids climb off school buses and run home. Sarah, long divorced, had moved into the house with her two kids. Now Sarah, like her mother before her, ran interference with the people who came to offer their condolences and their gossip. She turned and I stepped back quickly, shrinking into the shadows, hoping she had not seen me. I was not quick enough. Sarah had seen me. She stared at the empty window as if she could still see me and nodded sadly.

The morning of my mother's funeral, a thick mist settled on the lawn and hid the garden. Descending the stairs in my knee-length black dress, black hose, and heels, I saw my father standing in my mother's room, what had been her room, in the big space that had been occupied by the hospital bed. Around him were the things we had brought in to make her comfortable—a bedside table, the chair, and the bookcase. He looked small standing there in the center of the hardwood floor surrounded by those things. Tears burned behind my eyes, but I blinked them back. I would have to be the strong one today.

"It's almost time to go," I said from the last step as a way of announcing myself before the sharp sound of my heel rapping the floor could startle him.

"Yeah. I just was walking past."

"I know." I put my arms around him. The lining of his suit jacket rustled as he raised his arms, hugging me back.

"I'm not sure what to do."

"You don't have to do anything, Dad. We picked everything. Let Father John worry about it." I said it firmly, with authority, but I knew he was not talking about the funeral.

Knopf, Page and Niedel Funeral Home and Cremation Services squatted on Jackson Boulevard, looking imposing and ominous in the fog on a quiet Saturday morning. There was a soft gray smoke rising from the chimney as my dad turned into the parking lot. I tried not to think about what, or who, that smoke might be. Chimes sounded as we pulled on the brass door handle. Inside, it was just as quiet except for soft, very generic orchestral music. The big double doors to each of the main visitation rooms were all closed, their curtains drawn. There was no one in sight. It was so cold I was surprised I didn't see our breath as my father and I whispered to each other.

"Do you think we're supposed to tell someone we are here?" he asked.

"Let's wait a minute. They know we're coming." The smell of the place was making my stomach turn over. It was everywhere, even in the little conference room we had sat in with the funeral director while we chose everything. A sickly odor mixed with flowers and something that smelled like an old drawer sachet. It made me want to vomit. As

I tried to think my way out of being ill, Kevin Page, the ever-serene funeral director emerged from a long hallway.

As he reached out and took my father's hand, he smiled in a way I'm sure he thought was reassuring, but I found creepy. It made me as nauseous as the smell that was everywhere. I did not want to touch him when he reached for my hand and did not extend mine. He placed his hand on my arm instead. I glowered at him.

"Nola is here," he said, motioning with a thin pale hand toward the second of the large rooms as if he were some sort of butler and we had just called to see the lady of the house. "We'll give you some time with her." He said "we" even though no one else was visible. I wondered if Niedel and Knopf were lurking in the back room. "She looks lovely, but if you see anything that you feel is out of place... of course we want to be sure everything is how you'd like before we leave for the church. Are we ready?"

My father and I held hands and nodded mutely. Kevin opened the doors and a wave of even colder air washed over us. We walked slowly to the front, Kevin accompanying us down the center aisle between rows of folding chairs to where the open casket rested on a skirted platform. My right hand still held my father's while my left hand fidgeted at the seam of my dress. As we reached the front, my father's hand tightened on mine and then let go. Standing in front of the casket, his shoulders hunching, he began to weep silently. I waited a moment and then stepped forward. There lay my mother upon her pillow of eggshell-colored satin, her hair done up as if she were going out for the evening, and her thin face painted within a facsimile of life. The dark sweater we had picked out for her came up high at the neck and down to the tops of her hands, which were also painted and folded around a crucifix. They had tied the red silk scarf, the one with the Asian floral print, at her neck as I had requested.

"She looks good, don't you think?" my father asked me with an imploring look.

"Yes, she looks very nice."

"She'd be happy about the scarf, Cori."

I forced a smile I didn't feel on the inside. "Yes, she wouldn't have wanted to be all in black, that's for sure." Not like me, I added in my head.

Kevin stepped forward again. I clenched my teeth.

"Alan, I need to ask if there is anything you would like before we close the casket at the church. Her scarf, the crucifix, her wedding ring?"

My father shook his head and looked at me. "Cori? What do you think?"

If I had not already felt like vomiting, the thought of ever wearing the scarf currently wrapped around her neck pushed me over the edge. I swallowed down on the bile that rose, burning my throat and shook my head.

"Okay then. We like to ask because sometimes people regret not keeping things like jewelry."

"Her ring," I said to the floor.

"What's that?" Kevin asked leaning close. His breath smelled of onions.

"Her ring." I thought of the box of letters she had given me in the garden. Of how much she loved Martin. How much she missed him. "Don't bury her with her ring."

My father looked puzzled for a moment.

"Oh, Cori. I never thought to ask if you wanted it. Yes. Her ring," he spoke over my head to the funeral director. "We'll keep Nola's ring."

I nodded.

After the private viewing, we waited outside while two young men in gray suits, funeral assistants, emerged from the building and pulled the hearse around to the front. They climbed out of the car as their boss stepped out onto the all-weather carpet at the doorway and motioned, first to them and then to my father. As my father walked over, Kevin leaned over and whispered something to the young men, who stood with their hands folded in front of them as they listened, nodding. A moment later, the silence that had hung over Knopf, Page and

Niedel was broken by the sound of two bolts sliding home as the assistants slid the brass pins at the top of each door into their wells. They turned and went inside. My father followed with Kevin behind him. The damp quiet settled again.

I knew what was coming. Moving toward the backside of the parking lot and keeping an eye on the door, I slid a cigarette out of the half-empty pack in my handbag and lit up. The paper and dry tobacco crackled for a moment as they caught and then the first wisp of smoke drifted up. The heat licked at my fingers. The smoke stung my eyes. It felt good, felt like something real in a series of days that had felt suspended in time or like I was watching them happen to someone else. In my head, thoughts remained muted and slow. All week, everything else in the world had continued to move as if nothing had changed. This morning was different though. Hushed. As if everything that lived acknowledged another life had left.

The two young men emerged first and opened the back door of the hearse. Its empty maw gaped, waiting to swallow and hold. Next came the casket with its warm mahogany lid now closed, rolling on a folding metal stand, led by the two assistants with their serious looks. As my father and Kevin came out, trailing behind the casket, I threw my cigarette down to the asphalt and ground it out with the toe of my black suede pump. The casket was lifted and slid into place in the back of the hearse, which swallowed it like a python eating a large rodent. With absolute efficiency, and a minimum of noise, they collapsed the metal stand and then loaded into the hearse as well. The curtained lift gate closed with a solid thump.

"Corianne," Kevin opened the back door of the car and motioned while I tried to imagine what it was like growing up in the funeral home business, "you and your father will ride to the church with your mother." He used the artificially soothing tone again. It might have worked on other people. It just made me want to get away from him.

"Dan and I will drive you and Ben will follow with your father's car, okay?" He placed his hand on my forearm again. Again, I pulled it away.

"Fine," I said and bent down to slide into the back seat of the hearse.

"She's not herself," my father murmured as he climbed in next to me.

"Nobody is at a time like this, Alan," Kevin nodded sagely. "Nobody is." With that Kevin closed the door behind us.

CHAPTER EIGHTEEN

I REMEMBER LITTLE of what was said at the funeral. Mostly I remember how it smelled. Incense and chrism mixed with the smell of fresh flowers and the overwhelming powdery, heavy perfume of old women. Before the mass began, I had walked around reading the cards and sashes that announced each arrangement. Beloved wife. Dear Niece. Dearest Mother. I could feel the chill coming off the flowers that had just been unloaded from refrigerated delivery vans. I pulled a white rose from one of the arrangements and walked to the statue of Mary. Looking up at the blank marble of her eyes and her outstretched hands, her blue mantle gently draping, she felt like the only one in the room who could understand the magnitude of my grief. I placed the rose gently at her bare feet.

People spoke to me, gripped my hands, hugged me, and cried. They told me how terrible it was that my mother was dead. How devastated they were. How awful it was for my father who was now alone. How sad it was for me, losing my mother while I was so young, "and after everything." They never said what "everything" was. They didn't have to. I was Corianne Dempsey, the girl prematurely and persistently shadowed by death. Ushers took us to our seats. I took my place, sitting next to my father, without speaking, barely moving. Trying not to look at my mother's body laying before us in the casket, I studied the stained glass behind the altar. Each panel depicted a scene from the gospels. To our left, Mary stood serenely in her nave. I focused on Mary. I sat quietly with her as my witness.

Just before the mass finished, my father and I were invited to the front and given a last moment with my mother before the casket was closed for good. We stood together, unsure what to do, each of us thinking our own private thoughts. I heard my father snuffle and sigh.

"Goodbye Nola."

There were no words in my mind or on my tongue, even if I could get them past my throat, now dry and raspy from all the incense. There was nothing to say. There was only the lonely finality. I reached into the casket and put my hand on my mother's arm. The cold rose from her as it had from the flowers. Her arm, which had so often been a source of warmth and comfort, was stiff and hard as a dress manne-quin. I pulled my hand back quickly, unable to suppress a shiver. I never would forget that feeling or that cold.

Back at the house, there was an endless parade of people and even more food. I wondered who it was who had started the tradition. Who decided to descend on the grieving with huge quantities of food they did not feel like eating, bringing company they wished would go home? Still, I had to admit the attention was nice for my father. All the ladies from the neighborhood fussed over him, taking care of the dishes, and answering the door. Everywhere I went, every room I en-tered, there were more people and there was more food. It was easy for me to slip out unnoticed through the garden door.

Hurrying out across the lawn, I moved stealthily, as if the heels of my shoes could give me away instead of sinking into the grass and soft earth like spikes. I stopped long enough to slip them off and peel off my black hose before continuing the rest of the way through the back-yard barefoot, feeling the long autumn grass soft and cool under my feet. Slipping between two panels of white fencing, I stepped out into the neighborhood and disappeared. I must have walked more than a mile through the lawns and terraces belonging to people I didn't know. I walked until the neighborhood and sidewalks I knew fell away and long wooded roads forced me to walk in the street or on the easements, mown back like surgical scars in front of the driveways.

Fallen branches and gravel dug into the soles of my feet. The hills rose and fell as the road continued to twist and wind its way under the canopy of trees and then yawned wide again. Large homes were set well back from the road, partially hidden among the trees and blazing sumac while small little ranches, with their sparse landscaping and precision lawns cut high and tight, sat closer to the roadside. I turned my mind loose to run along the road, but it kept coming back to the heavy and inescapable reality of the day.

The road turned once again, and lawns gave way to a line of weeds and scrub trees rising about five feet from the road. In front of the trees, among the tangle of weeds, was a pile of bare dirt and rock. A few old broken timbers lay crossed, forming an inverted V. It was a no-man's-land misplaced among the sprawl of houses. Bits of a purple wildflower still bloomed, scattered here and there on emaciated stems. From deep inside me, something began to surface. Not sadness. Not even grief about losing my mother. It was something even older. I lifted my head, closing my eyes and exposing my throat to the cold, to the coming night, to everything. Yet nothing came to take what I offered. I ran my hand along my throat and felt its velvety softness and the warmth coming from my own skin. My hand could reach from one side to the other just under my chin. I wrapped my cold hand around my neck, feeling my throbbing pulse beneath my fingers. When I lifted it away, I could still feel the cold as if an invisible hand tried to hold me there. I wrapped my arms around myself tightly and wandered on down the hill.

Another road came in on the left, but I stayed to the right, following the first road where it bent again under a canopy of great oaks. It was quiet. Not even the sound of the cars on the main road penetrated here. Walking to the middle of the road, there on the curve, I spread my arms out, reaching as if I could touch the giant trees on either side and be part of their silent family. Asking them to take me. But I was just a silly girl in a black dress. Tipping my head back, I looked up into the branches spread against the deepening twilight, playing the child's game of looking at the world upside down, turning it over like an hourglass. Almost bare, the oak's gnarled network of branches could just as easily have been roots. My hair hung down my back, sometimes blowing and brushing against my arms where the cap sleeves of my dress stopped. The thin fabric did little to keep out the damp and cold that were beginning to settle as deep into me as into the grass and fallen leaves. Heat trapped in the asphalt radiated up, keeping the soles of my feet warm, sometimes wavering to lick at my legs before a bit of soft wind scattered it. The trees sighed. My face still turned upward, I closed my eyes, wobbling a little as I imagined my hair spread out like the roots of the trees above me. I thought about how peaceful this place was and how much I wanted to be part of it. Part of the vigil of the trees. Just for a few minutes to be rooted.

I cannot say how long I stood there. It seemed like a long time. The darkness had fallen so softly and slowly I was not aware of the minutes passing. I was simply there, present to the trees and the wind that rustled the dying leaves that had yet to fall. The smell of a wood fire drifted on the crisp air. I wondered if the trees knew it was one of their own split open and lying on someone's fireplace grate. *He was very old*, I imagined them saying to each other wisely. My thoughts were interrupted by the screech of brakes and the slam of a car door, but I was so enraptured, I could not react.

"Corianne? Jesus Christ. Corianne." It was Sean's voice. As I opened my eyes and turned, he came rushing toward me. "Are you okay? His sharp photographer's eyes were scanning my body for signs of injury or trauma. There were none. I tried to form words, but again my voice would not come. It was locked away. I was glad he was there. I tried to tell him but there was no sound. I put my hand to his cheek.

"You're as cold as ice." He pulled off his suit jacket and wrapped it around me. "Are you hurt anywhere?"

"No," I mouthed.

"What the hell, Corianne? I mean, what the hell?" he repeated, pronouncing each word clearly and distinctly. "Standing in the middle of the road. No shoes, no coat. That's a great way to get yourself killed or freeze to death if a car doesn't get you first. How long have you been out here?" I didn't have an answer. He peered into my face for a long moment and then gathered me up in his arms and carried me to his car.

It was nice and warm inside the car. Even the leather seats were warm. As Sean climbed back in on the driver's side, he clicked the heater up another notch and then turned to look at me, the look of disapproval and incomprehension plain on his face.

"Do you want to tell me what you were doing?" he asked.

"What are you doing here?" I met his question with one of my own.

"Your dad has been worried sick. When I got to the house, no one had seen you in hours. The two of us looked around. We found your shoes and your stockings, in the garden." He emphasized the last three words again. "I had kind of hoped if I ever tripped over those it would be because I had taken them off the night before."

I blushed as the warmth began to return to my cheeks and at the thought of him slowly undressing me.

"You came to the house?"

"I was at the funeral today too."

I nodded. "I saw you. Thank you."

"I came by the house to check on you. I couldn't very well abandon you to all those old biddies, could I?" He grinned and even in the dim light in the car, I could see the perfect whiteness of his teeth. "Besides, I wanted to bring you something."

"I honestly can't take another ham or casserole."

"Good. Because I would be an ass if I showed up to comfort you with a ham." He leaned in toward me. I pulled back against the door.

"I don't think now is really a good time for that."

"You thought I was going to kiss you? I'd be lying if I said the thought hadn't crossed my mind. But you can relax. I brought you something I thought might help. I put it back here." He reached down behind my seat. I heard a click and soft little noises. "Okay, close your eyes."

I eyed him suspiciously but did as I was told, crossing my arms in front of me to hold the suit coat around me.

"Here you go." Something incredibly soft brushed against my cheek. I opened my eyes. "This is Corianne," Sean said to the small soot-colored kitten that climbed into the crook of my arm and nosed its way into the dark warm cavern of the jacket. "She doesn't have a name yet or I'd introduce the two you properly," he whispered in an aside. "Corianne will take excellent care of you."

"I will?"

The kitten began climbing up the silken lining of the suit coat, her sharp claws scraping and catching in the delicate fabric. I plucked her off, held her up, and looked at her closely, nose to nose. She mewed softly and batted at me before climbing onto my shoulder and settling into my hair.

"I will," I said, managing a small smile.

CHAPTER NINETEEN

THE LAWN IS expansive and leads to the water's edge. I kneel at the water. There is no light to speak of and yet it is shadowy. Morning dusk. The water is impenetrable. Despite the breeze, the surface remains smooth save the occasional water bug skating across the surface or a bubble which rises from the ooze beneath. Gnarled willows bend low over the water, dip and scratch their bony hands, but cannot ladle a drink. Their roots sigh and propagate. On the lawn, peacocks' cries to the morning are like the screams of women. Screams. There in the shadows of the trees. They echo across the water and out onto the lawn. Even the peacocks mill in aimless alarm. The sound is everywhere. It even seems to rise from the water. I lean to peer into the dark surface. What is reflected is not my face but hers. Rebecca's. Something moves in the trees and birds rise en masse.

I sat bolt upright wrapped in sweat-soaked sheets. The back of my hair was wet. Shallow breaths. The screams reverberating. Fully awake, I could still hear them. Unnerved, Maud gave one loud meow as she jumped off the bed, casting a cautious look over her shoulder and heading out the door at a trot. Whatever had been going on in my other world, she wanted none of it.

As my head cleared, I remembered where I was—in Sean's bed, alone. A wave of longing washed over me as I wished for the familiar warmth of him there next to me. As my heart stopped pounding and my breath slowed, I heard screams again. This time they were no dream. They came from outside the apartment building. Quickly, I got to my feet, pulling my robe from the end of the bed, wrapping it around my naked and cooling body. I stopped and listened. Again, I heard screams.

Hurrying to the window, I looked down to the street below. From this vantage I could see no one, but the sounds seemed to be coming from the courtyard. I rushed down the hall to the living room balcony and pushed back the white sheer curtain on the French doors just in time to see a boy running from around the corner and then two more darting from somewhere underneath the balconies out into the courtyard. I pulled open the door and stepped out to take a closer look. Through the metalwork I could see figures rushing around. More shrieks rose and hung in the rain-soaked air. The piercing shrieks of little girls. None of them had noticed me. Moving to the railing, I finally spotted them darting out, laughing, and screaming as the boys chased them.

"Now look. We're the monsters," the oldest looking boy said. "Kenny is a monster with horns and his skin is poison. If he touches you, you *die*." The boy clearly relished drawing out the last word. For effect, the boy named Kenny reached out and grabbed the sleeve of the girl nearest to him. She screamed loudly and jumped away into her friends sheltering circle. A pleased Kenny smirked at the one called Jack.

"I want to be a monster too," said a bigger, heavier boy.

"No, Eric. You're the troll."

"I don't wanna be a troll. Trolls are stupid," the one called Eric objected loudly, disappointed with his assignment.

"Nah, trolls are cool, Eric. You live underneath the grates and when girls step on them they fall into your lair, and you grab them."

"Okay. Yeah, cool." Eric brightened.

"Hey, Jack, what kind of monster are you? Kenny asked.

"I'm a dragon," Jack answered and then narrowing his eyes added, "I have scales and yellow eyes. And when someone looks into my eyes, they're frozen."

"Do you breathe fire?" This question came from somewhere inside the circle of girls.

"Yes, of course I breathe fire. Don't be stupid. Haah!"

More screams and laughter as the girls ran again, flocking, trying to escape Kenny's corrosive touch and Jack's fire, all while keeping track of Eric the Troll's Grate of Doom.

A small smile started across my face. Funny how little had changed since I was that age. The same playground games. I had forgotten the way we used to play like this on the blacktop at recess, especially in the spring when the ground was still covered with snow or spring rains had made the grass too muddy to play football or baseball. At that age, it was a rare and uneasy alliance for the sake of passing the time. Just as now, the boys made their games around chasing us. I thought back to the large, iron-covered concrete wells that sat on either side of the old red door of the school. No one ever seemed to know what the wells were for though there was never a lack of stories in circulation. There were high windows above them, the music room if memory served. The boys would push us into the space between the steps leading to the playground and those wells. The space between the end line of the basketball court to the brick building was the dungeon. We ran around screaming and tried to get away. The boys would herd us like antelope, trying to catch us between the stairs, the "vat" and the building. Those girls who were not caught would try to free us. To prevent escape, the boys would hold us tightly by our wrists or push their bodies up against us, pinning us to the rough brick until we could barely breathe. We were supposed to try. The entire game was built on capture, restraint, and escape. My smile fell away as I remembered the burning pain that followed as I tried to wrench my wrist away. My wrists would be red and throbbing by the time the bell rang to call us back in, my jacket or sweater dirty or snagged from scraping against the brown brick. Just kids having fun, right? But there was always something about it that felt darker, more sinister, even then when Monster was just a game we played.

The damp morning air seeped through my thin robe. I tugged the silk back into place where it threatened to slip away. The children ran through the courtyard and back to the border of the sidewalk as tenants of both buildings began heading out to begin their days. There was the man who lived in the building across the courtyard, below my friend with the Bob Dylan music, who biked on Saturday mornings rain or shine. As usual, he was one of the first up and out. Thin and fit, nothing extra on his frame, his spandex base layers were all designed for aerodynamics and left nothing to the imagination. As he lifted his bike up over the step at the courtyard entrance, I could tell his arms and legs were nothing but hard muscle.

In college, I had spent time with a cyclist. Rob insisted on being called a cyclist. He did not bike. That was for wimps. He trained, his regimen involving cycling at least five days a week for a prescribed minimum number of miles. He hit the gym to build his legs with squats and leg presses. Food was not fun. It was healthy and carefully orchestrated for the perfect balance of energy and nutrition. He put wheat germ in vile looking protein shakes and had an enviable four percent body fat. I remembered the unforgiving feeling of Rob's hard muscled body grinding against me when we had sex. There was no place for my curves to rest. No way to feel that delicious merger along the length of our bodies. His borders were simply too defined. Unrelenting. Aggressive. In the end, so was his personality.

I watched as anonymous cyclist neighbor strapped on his helmet and clipped into the bike pedals, recognizing the pre-ride checklist. He was training as Rob had. Wheels engaged, sprockets clicking softly, he sent out a fine spray off the damp pavement as he headed out. Then there was another click. This one from up above. I looked up just as the balcony door across from where I stood creaked and swung open. The man stepped out, took a deep breath, and seemed to sigh. He was smiling, as I had, but the children were currently nowhere in sight. Was his smile meant for me? I couldn't tell. His eyes were unreadable at this distance. Other than the vague direction of his looking, I could tell nothing. Only that his eyes were open. In the morning shadows, there was no face to study. No expression. Standing there in just my robe, I might as well be standing there naked, and I suddenly felt like I was. I gave a weak smile and hurried back into the apartment.

It never got easier. Being looked at. Being watched. Being fixed to the spot with a look. Limbs ready to move, to run, twitching with stored energy. Stay frozen or run? How far across the clearing? How far to the safety of the brush and trees? And I had smiled politely. Of all things, I had smiled. The absurdity of it made me laugh and shake my head. Terrified and still trying to be polite. The mouse patting the cat on the head as it switches its long feline tail back and forth. The rabbit thanking the fox for eating it. This was just the sort of insight Dr. Lawrence loved. I made a mental note to tell him.

It stayed with me. That hunted feeling. Even as I began the machinations of my day, heating the water for tea, putting food out for Maud, it felt like someone was in the apartment with me. I wondered if I would ever be normal—if that feeling would ever go away. I'd felt it in the cafe the day before as well. As soon as I walked in, I felt it. The pricking in that oldest, most primitive part of my brain. Danger.

I was there to meet Kate, a long-time photography friend of Sean's. From the first time I'd met her and watched the way they interacted I was pretty sure they had slept together at some point. I didn't ask and he didn't tell. If they had, it was long before he met me. That's what I told myself. I was certainly no nun when I met Sean and I didn't feel compelled to give him details about Rob or my others. The truth was I liked Kate and I didn't have many friends.

Kate and I arranged to meet at Café Montegna down the street. She knew when I did venture out alone this was one of the few places I went. Good coffee, a decent bistro fare and given the neighborhood, less pretentious than the name would lead one to believe. Plus, if they weren't crowded, the staff would let me sit for hours. I tipped well. It was a good place to work or read and I liked that it was just a five-minute walk.

Kate arrived first and remembering I hated sitting in the middle of the room, she had gotten us a spot along the wall on a row away from the windows. She was on her phone, as ever, but waved as soon as she saw me come in. It was hardly necessary. Kate was a hard woman to miss. Model tall and thin, she typically put her thick red hair in some magnificent braid or topknot and always wore green somewhere. A very particular shade of forest green, near her face. It might be a turtleneck, a scarf, even a pair of earrings, but it was always there. Her signature. Someone must have told her once that the green brought out her eyes. They were right.

As soon as I stepped inside and started making my way back to the table, I wished I had worn something different. Seeing Kate radiating springtime chic right out of *Vogue* in a green dress and bright floral scarf, I felt instantly dumpy in my jeans, boots, and deep blue tunic sweater. That is when I noticed him. A man, approximately thirty years old, wearing a navy knit watch cap and a slate-colored field coat. I noticed him not only because he did not fit (*the field coat is wrong*) but because he seemed to have noticed me. More than that, he took an unusual amount of interest in me. It was not just that fact that he had looked at me when I came in or looked up when I walked past his table. He watched me. He watched me walk all the way to the table and he kept watching. Even when I had gone past and my back was to him, I could feel it. The warning prickles. I slid into the seat opposite Kate. The entire time Kate and I talked, he watched.

"Hey Kate, did you notice the guy sitting near the register?" Kate looked slowly over her right shoulder.

"The guy in the hat? What about him?"

"He's staring at us."

"Maybe he wants you," she arched on eyebrow suggestively over her coffee cup. "Sean shouldn't leave you alone so long, the ass."

"I'm getting checked out by some creepy stalker dude. Great news, Kate. Thanks."

She laughed that laugh of hers that was always a little too loud, a little bawdy. He looked over. Realistically, what guy wouldn't? Inwardly, I scolded myself for thinking he was looking at me and not Kate. Sean was right. I was getting paranoid again.

"Cori, I'm sure it's fine," Kate added, trying to reassure me. She didn't know exactly what had happened to me in the past. All Sean had told her was that I was a victim of a crime a long time ago and it made me neurotically cautious. I left the details up to her imagination. Yet here she was trying to reassure me. I appreciated the gesture. "Look, he has a notebook or something. He's probably just a writer looking for material."

"You're right. He's watching you anyway."

We went on with our lunch and gradually I became involved in Kate's stories about her work, her posh clients who pronounced their ordinary names with extraordinary affectedness, and her longtime boyfriend Adam, who had just made partner in his law firm. I almost forgot my unease. Kate had been right, I decided. I was overreacting again. Not everything was about me. I needed to get out more. I had become too reclusive, even by my own standards. Gradually, I felt myself relaxing. That was when the man got up, gathering his coffee and notebook, and walked to the tables along the windows nearer to us.

He was just waiting for a different table to open, I told myself. I had my favorite spots. I had done it. Gotten up and moved. That was all it was. I turned my attention back to Kate's story about how one of Adam's coworkers was caught having sex with the copier repair guy in the ladies' restroom. *He is a writer, probably people watching.* But he never took out a notebook and the way he turned his chair, sitting slightly away from the table, it was like he was listening to our conversation.

"Cori?"

"What? I'm sorry, what were you saying?"

"I asked if you and Sean want to meet us for dinner when he gets back."

"Oh, yeah. Sure. That would be great," I answered distractedly.

"When does he get back? Tomorrow?"

"No," I dropped my voice lower. "He called yesterday and told me he was invited to stay in France and do some additional photos for the story. He changed his flight. He won't be back for another week."

"Like I said, I love him, but he is an ass to leave you alone so much. Why couldn't you go along?"

"It's complicated."

"Right. Well, if you get tired of being with a photographer who is too busy looking through his viewfinder to see what's right in front of him, I can hook you up with a nice attorney." Kate winked. "Maybe I will anyway. You know, just to help pass the time." I opened my mouth to answer, but she was already on to the next topic. "Adam and I are going to the opening at the new gallery on Mill Street tomorrow night. I'm hoping to get a show there of my own. You should come. Talk my work up to the gallery owner while sipping expensive wine you didn't have to pay for—my favorite kind."

"No thanks, I have plans." I was trying to be vague, not wanting to go out and not wanting to talk about the fact that I would be home just a few blocks away, especially as the man appeared to still be eavesdropping.

"Ooh, a clandestine meeting. Sean, eat your heart out."

CHAPTER TWENTY

I AM WALKING in a village. An old village. Nothing is paved. The pathways are all dirt and turf. I follow one path, walking past buildings built of stone and wood. People know me here. I walk alongside a fence then head in the back door of one of the buildings, entering a vestibule. Straight ahead is a narrow wooden stairway leading up to another level. Turning to my left, I enter a long room with a wide-plank floor. I recognize it as a pub. There is a worn bar and rustic plank tables and wooden chairs set about. This is my building, my pub, and upstairs is my home. I know this though I have never been here before. A fireplace is glowing softly. A sudden draft sweeps through from an unseen source, stirring the fire and sending soot sifting across the floor like snow. Hot embers tumble out of the fireplace and are swirling. The room begins to burn.

"Christ, Cori," Sean threw his hands out, "You probably scared the hell out of those kids."

"I was trying to help. I thought they needed help."

"Not everyone is in danger. Cori, you need to let it go. He's not in every truck."

I had been out walking, walking along the creek as I did most mornings at my parent's house. My house. There in the morning, trembling with the fresh energy of the day, it reflected everything. Every nuance of every season. During the spring thaw, the water ran clear and cold as if it were coming down from mountaintops instead of small drumlins. On that morning, the creek bed was almost dry. The drought of the summer stretched onward. The trees and wildflowers, the fox, everyone had used up the last rainwater that had rolled down the hills and filtered through the rock. A board placed by neighborhood kids as a crossing plank now sat marooned on top of the rocks and spanned the muddy bed. In between gnawing open the thick green skin hiding prized black walnuts, squirrels took time to issue a warning about my presence.

Unheeding, two children in helmets bicycled, each with a backpack strapped on. They were biking to school. The girl was obviously a new bike rider. Her pink and white bicycle wobbled back and forth unsteadily on the sidewalk as she tried to peddle up the hill. She would try to correct for one zig and end up zagging back the other way. The boy was older. He kept calling out to the little girl over his shoulder, encouraging her in a scolding sort of way.

"Don't move your handlebars so much."

"I'm … trying," she pushed out the words as if they exerted her as much as the hill. "It's hard."

I remembered how challenging it was to learn on these hills, but back then there was no network of sidewalks. When the concrete ran out, I had to turn into the road and crunch through white gravel. A spill meant a badly torn up knee or hand and my mom picking out debris with a pair of tweezers, rinsing the abrasion with rubbing alcohol or hydrogen peroxide while I winced. I watched as they continued their climb along the switchback of the hill parallel to the woods, silently willing the little girl to make it without falling.

A white pickup truck pulled up slowly, approaching the kids but stopping just short of them. It was the same truck I had passed further back; the same one those kids had passed two blocks ago. I had noticed it parked in front of a house. The last house before the woods started. As I always did, I noted every person and vehicle on this stretch, aware that for about a mile, anyone on foot was pinned between the creek on one side and the woods on the other. There were no houses that faced out on to this stretch. The closest ones sat up on the ridge above the woods or through the thicket and on the other side of the creek.

"*C'mon* Megan. We're going to be late."

"I'm sorry. My legs are getting tired."

"Then just get off and walk it."

"That will be even *slower*."

I kept moving, monitoring both the kids and the truck. There were no markings on the vehicle. It could just be a worker checking an address, but it seemed too freshly scrubbed and well looked after. I was too far away to see the make of the truck or even the logo. I took note of what details I could. Four doors. Two in the front and two that hinged at the rear. Suicide doors. They would allow ample clearance to pull a child into the cab. A bike could easily be ditched in the woods or thrown into the truck bed, I calculated. This was the kind of thinking that drove Sean crazy. Morbid. Forensic. Paranoid. I conceded morbid and could even see how he could say forensic, but I never conceded paranoid. Paranoid implied irrationality. My fears were completely rational, based as they were in fact.

The truck pulled ahead past the two children and disappeared around the next curve. I let out an audible sigh of relief. It was just someone checking a map or making a phone call. Relaxing a little, my pace brisk, I tried to go back to listening to the birds and letting my thoughts unspool, but they were still wound up tight.

The slope leveled a bit and the kids were making better progress. I could only imagine how hot and sweaty they would be when they did finally make it to school after having climbed this long hill with their windbreakers zipped up and backpacks strapped on. Of course, their nylon jackets were a damn sight better than the horrible rubber or vinyl slickers I had to wear as a little girl. I still hated even the sight of them, knowing all too well the clammy feeling of being trapped in them, the thin cotton lining soft but ineffective at wicking away the moisture and heat that would build up inside the coat. Then there was the awful creak of them as you moved, and the rubber fabric sticking to itself. Though the fisherman's styling came in handy on the playground when boys threw rain-soaked worms at you. Barring a headshot, the worms would stick to the raincoat and then slide slowly off. Not fish guts but the same principle.

When I rounded the curve, I saw that the truck hadn't left after all. It was still there. The driver had just pulled around the curve and waited again for the kids. As they approached, the driver let them pass and then pulled slowly forward, passing them again before stopping and waiting. This was not my imagination. The driver of that truck was waiting for those kids, shadowing them. Yet they seemed not to notice. My pace became a jog as I tried to keep my eyes fixed on the kids while stealing glances at the truck. As I watched the kids approach it my heart pounded in my throat.

"Hey." I tried to yell but it came out as a hoarse whisper. "Hey!" I tried again. "Hey kids, stay away from that truck!" They didn't hear me. They just kept talking and peddling. Frantically waving my arms, I tried again. "Stay away from that truck. Kids, look out!"

They finally turned to look at me. As they did, I saw the truck door open. Breaking into a full run, I called to the kids to do the same. But they were confused and just stared at me and then at the man rounding the truck. He wore jeans and a plaid shirt, white tennis shoes, with brown hair down to his collar and a beard. As I ran up, he put his arms around the boy and girl who in turn moved closer to him.

"Lady, what the hell is your problem?"

"My problem? You're the one following these kids. You think it's fun to stalk innocent kids, you sick bastard." My hand clutched onto my house key where it sat in the bottom of my jacket pocket. I pulled it out, holding it between my fingers, ready to jab with it if I needed a weapon.

"Megan and Ben, go on ahead. You're going to be late. I'll be right there," he said to the kids. Then turning back to me, "Lady, you've got this all wrong. These are my kids."

"*Your* kids?" I was confused. "Then why are you creeping along following them?"

"It's Megan's first time riding her bike to school. I was following them in case she got too tired. I could throw her bike in the back and give her a ride the rest of the way, but she is too stubborn. She wants to be like Ben."

The kids had ridden ahead, but slowly. They turned and looked back nervously.

"It's okay. Go on. I'll catch up," the father called after them. "Look, lady I think you're probably trying to do something good here, but really, I swear these are my kids." He looked at the key still clutched in my fist.

My face burned with embarrassment. Unable to meet his eye, I looked at his shoes and then at the key sticking out of from my clenched fist between the index and middle finger. I put my hand back in my pocket.

"I'm...I'm sorry. It's just that it looked like you were following them. Well, you were. There was some trouble here a while back and I guess...I'm really sorry if I scared you. Or them." There had been trouble here once. I just hoped he didn't know that it was nearly twenty years ago.

"I didn't know that. Thank you, I guess. For looking out for my kids. These days you never know, do you? He held out his hand. "Jay. Jay Prinzler. My wife and I just moved in up around the other side of the park." He gestured with his head, his hand still suspended and un-met.

"Cori," I dropped the key in my pocket and produced my empty hand. "Cori Dempsey." I didn't offer where I lived. If he ever told anyone my last name, he'd find out soon enough. His handshake was firm and his hand calloused. I laughed to myself. Maybe he was a tradesman after all.

"Well, Cori. Good to know we have a neighborhood watch. Now, I've got to make sure those two make it into school before the bell rings."

My voice trailed off as I finished telling the story.

"Cori. Cori." Sean was standing in front of me, holding me by the shoulders. "Cor," his voice softened as he saw me come back from my memories, "he's not in every truck."

"He could be in any truck. Don't you understand? They never caught him. Not here anyway. If he's not in prison or dead, he'll come back. They come back, Sean. They can't help themselves. I heard the cops say it. He'll be back. And I don't remember his face."

"Well, he's not this Jay Prinzler guy. Logically, he's too young." A deep silence fell between us. "You need to call Dr. Lawrence."

"If he's still practicing."

"You know he is. I saw his number on the notepad you keep on your desk."

"It felt real, you know, with the truck crawling up on them. The way they just stood there. It was like it was happening again."

"I know." Sean put his arms around me. "All the more reason to talk to Lawrence. He will know what to do. I don't. I don't know how to help."

"This helps." I let myself relax into Sean's arms. Let myself enjoy the feeling of being safe down a burrow. "This does too," I said running my hands up inside his shirt.

"This isn't a bad time?" he asked, though he had already run his hands to hollow of my back.

"It's the perfect time." I answered unzipping his pants.

The truth of it was I wanted Sean badly. I wanted him to remind me I was still alive and loved. I wanted him to reclaim me from the hell that filled my dreams every night, to fill every part of me until there was no room for anything else except the heat of his body and the relentless restless ache of mine. I wanted his mouth on mine. I wanted to feel him against me, pushing aside any more thoughts. I wanted to feel anything else. And I did right there up against the wall. I came until my head ached and until I felt him release inside me. Then turning my head away, I began to cry silently.

CHAPTER TWENTY-ONE

SEAN WAS RIGHT. I needed to talk to Dr. Lawrence. It had been at least three years since I had. Things had been good in that time. Well, good might be a stretch, but at least stable. I had not been seeing him with any regularity since just after my mother died. I was on a discretionary basis. Mine. I had called him after my father died, had a couple of appointments, but Dr. Lawrence felt I was as far as I was ready to go.

Doc had told me there were things I was not willing to explore further. Conscious or unconscious, I had hit a point of resistance in my therapy. Sometimes the mind protects itself. My mind could not deny what had happened. The fact of my hypervigilance was proof enough of that. Nor could it, or I, face the totality of what that had meant for me. That's how he explained it. As a result, I became less "participatory" in my therapy. There were things I was withholding and screening. It became a waste of both our time to keep the appointment, Doc told me, if I was not willing or ready to take the next step.

I didn't understand what he meant by at the time. I buried myself in the relationship with Sean. Here was proof that I could have a normal life. After the incident with the Prinzler kids, I could no longer pretend. My life was not normal. I was not normal. Not by a long shot.

I found myself back in the lobby of the high-rise building that housed Dr. Lawrence's office. Tiled in cool black and gray, the lobby appeared carefully staged with potted plants sitting around a Zen-like water wall. Though I already verified by phone that Dr. Lawrence was in the same office on the fifteenth floor, I looked for his name on the wall directory. Emile Lawrence, Suite 1501. No mention of what he did. How perfectly ambiguous. I reached under a silver rectangular ashtray that hung on the wall between the two banks of elevators and pressed the call button. Though a relic now that smoking was banned in public buildings, at ten o'clock in the morning it already held an impressive array of other discarded items that included a wad of chewed pink gum, a crumpled parking receipt, and a small white mint.

Not knowing what to expect from this appointment after my time away, I found my nervousness was growing by the time a man in a gray business suit joined me to wait. Twitchy, I felt awkward as the man and I nodded politely and then returned to staring at the floor while "The Girl from Ipanema," stripped of anything even remotely provocative or Brazilian, joined the occasional and distant chiming and whirring as the elevator cars moved somewhere above us.

It was silly to be nervous, I told myself as the elevator arrived and I stepped through metal doors. I had known Dr. Lawrence for almost twenty years. My hands continued shaking anyway. I hoped the man in the suit would not notice as I pushed the button for my floor. Was he a regular in the building? Did he know what went on in Suite 1501? Could he know that I was one of Emile Lawrence's broken toys?

"What floor?" I asked.

"Sixteen," he answered.

I pressed the button for the sixteenth floor and folded my hands in front of me, hoping to quell the shaking. Breaking with standard elevator protocol, he didn't move further back into the car. He stayed close as if there were ten other people in the elevator with us.

"Thank you." His voice was deep, smooth, and warm. As he looked down at his wristwatch, I could hear a day's growth of whiskers scrape against the collar of his starched white shirt. His cologne was a dizzying blend of amber, patchouli and vanilla mixed with the pungent aroma of freshly brewed coffee, yet I noted he wasn't carrying any coffee. Perhaps he had a meeting in the café downstairs before this I reasoned as I indulged my habit of drafting a backstory for this stranger. He seemed too hip to be a banker or insurance salesman. He could be a stockbroker. Trying to create more space between us, I backed up and leaned against the wall facing him.

When he took out his cell phone, I chanced a glance at his face. Olive skin, square jaw, with dark hair and deep-set brown eyes. The missed shave appeared deliberate. He caught me looking and his eyes flicked over me. I immediately looked away but when he returned to his phone, scrolling though messages, I studied his hands. They had to have been the most beautiful hands I had ever seen. Strong and sinewy, his skin was smooth and looked buttery soft, as if the only work he ever did was at the gym or in the bedroom. His nails were short, both perfectly shaped and perfectly manicured. As the elevator rose, rocking gently, I imagined his hands on my skin. My face flushed in deep embarrassment while another part of me responded very differently. Alone with just him and my steamy thoughts, the elevator car became uncomfortably close and warm.

The elevator stopped on the fifteenth floor after what seemed an eternity. I practically burst out into the hallway leading to Dr. Lawrence's office, muttering "you too" in response to his wishing me a good day. Hurrying on, I went past the faux maple doorways lining the hall and ducked into the ladies' room just across from Dr. Lawrence's office. Turning on the sink, I let the water run across my palms, cooling and soothing me. I lifted my wet hands and gently patted my burning cheeks. In the mirror, they did not appear as red as I had imagined them to be.

"Get a grip, Cori," I scolded myself as I shut off the water and pulled a handful of crinkly brown paper towels from the dispenser and dried my hands. Looking in the mirror one more time, I drew a deep breath and dabbed my face dry. "This is no big deal," I told my reflection and then headed out the door and into the office across the hall.

Dr. Lawrence never had an assistant or at least not one that I ever saw. No one greeted me when I entered, there was just the vague canned air smell composed of the chemical finishes in carpeting, paint, and furniture that caused all office buildings and furniture stores to smell roughly the same. The waiting room had been updated since I had last been here, though the arrangement was the same. To the left of the door was a bookcase, sparsely populated by volumes with faded old red and blue cloth covers and gold lettering on their spines. Sprinkled in were a few curiosities. A large seashell, a small wooden box, and something that looked like an old metronome. To the right of the door was a nondescript gray loveseat and several small armchairs covered in the same gray fabric. A large square-shaped glass table sat in the center adorned with a scattering of magazines and a low heartleaf philodendron, its glossy green leaves and vines climbing over the sides of a red clay pot. I picked up an issue of *Coastal Living* and settled onto the loveseat.

The door to Dr. Lawrence's inner sanctum was in line with where I was sitting. Despite the soft music coming from the small speaker on the corner table between two of the chairs, I could hear the familiar low murmur of Dr. Lawrence's voice and then a higher voice rising and falling. Happily, I could not overhear what was being said. I flipped the pages of the magazine, scanning the photos, but I was too restless and distracted to read. Instead, I forced myself to concentrate on the picture of a white stucco house with a sweeping veranda flanked by palm trees. It was overlooking impossibly blue waters and a deep blue and cloudless sky. Trying to project myself into the photo and onto one of the chaises on the veranda, I imagined the feel of the warm sun baking my body, penetrating deep into my skin until my skin radiated the heat back out. I let myself remember how it felt, vacations at the lake, accompanying Sean as he rowed us out in the boat to a sandbar where he could take photos of wading birds and stretching out on the floor on a beach towel with my bikini top untied, my body an offering to my sun lover who powered me with his delicious heat.

No sooner had I lost myself in my pleasant sun-soaked fantasy than the door opened to Dr. Lawrence's office. Every golden thought evaporated just like that. Out walked a man with thinning hair, a mustache, and wire-rimmed glasses. Not Dr. Lawrence but the patient. I suppressed my surprise and my amusement. I had assumed the higher voice was that of a woman.

"Very good, Roger, I'll see you next time." Dr. Lawrence said as he followed the man through the door.

"Yes, next time," the man named Roger replied, careful to keep his face turned to the side as he scuttled past me and headed out to the hallway. Avoidance behavior, either symptomatic of some deep neurosis or of his being a new patient, I surmised, dropping the magazine on the table as I came to my feet.

"Corianne," Dr. Lawrence said warmly, as if I were a long-lost niece. "Come on in."

Like the waiting room, the inner sanctum had changed little in the intervening years. Without even thinking I assumed my usual position on the sofa. Doc sat down in an updated version of the old brown chair and threw his left leg over his right. His socks looked more expensive than I remembered. Business must be good.

"So, Corianne, what's going on? You haven't come to see me since your father died."

"That's a pretty broad question. Where do you want me to start?"

"Where would you like to start?" he answered cagily.

"Ah, there's the Dr. Lawrence I know and don't always love." My comment elicited a small smile. "I'm still with Sean. So that's good. And I still work as an editor."

"Still working from home?"

"Yes. Still that."

"Well, that's okay, Cori. As we've talked about, it's fine as long as it is not an avoidance. Tell me, are you still having issues with the agoraphobia?"

"I never liked that term."

"Ah, yes. Do you still have…misgivings…about the world?" he re-framed like a skilled cross-examiner. "Is it still difficult for you to trust what you see? Who you meet?"

"I think that's better."

"Okay, then what's not better?"

"I'm still…the dreams. I'm still having them. They were better for a while, but they're worse again. And there was the thing with Mr. Prinzler and his kids."

"Who is Mr. Prinzler?"

I told Dr. Lawrence about how I had practically accosted Jay Prinzler, convinced he was a pedophile, when in reality he was a good father protecting his kids. I told him how the dreams had been worse again since then. How sometimes it felt like I had them even when I was awake.

"That doesn't sound very much like trusting the world, does it? Doc asked rhetorically. Then he added, "Why do you think you're having the dreams again?"

"I don't know. That's why I'm here."

"I think you do know, Corianne. I think you do. What's the one thing that has troubled you more than anything else about the day Rebecca died?"

"Besides the fact that I saw my best friend snatched and she turned up dead? I think that's a pretty troubling thing."

"What else? What about that day made you convinced that Jay Prinzler was dangerous?"

"He was following the kids in his damn truck. It was creepy."

"What else?"

"It was like he was the guy. Like it was happening all over again."

"But he wasn't the guy."

"He could have been." My tone was hard. A defensive reaction, I recognized. "He could have been," I said again more quietly.

"But this man was young. The man who approached you and Re-becca would be much older by now, yes?"

"That's what Sean said," I admitted begrudgingly.

"Then why, Corianne? Why did you react so strongly to this man and this truck? You know. It's why you're having the dreams again." Dr. Lawrence took off his glasses. I remembered this tell of his. He was expecting me to say something important. Something significant.

"Because—" I stopped myself.

"Go on."

"Because I don't know who the hell he was. No one does. He could be anyone. He is everyone." My fingers picked at the hem of my gray cashmere cardigan. "I never saw his face. My monster is still out there."

Dr. Lawrence's forehead moved almost imperceptibly. He uncrossed his legs and put both feet on the floor. There was a long pause where no one spoke. The water cooler let out a low glub as a large air bubble rose to the surface.

"I know, I know. There are no monsters. Just people who do terrible things for reasons we don't always understand."

Doc almost smiled but caught himself and let the any expression fade completely away before going on. "I think we need to give your monsters faces," he said, steepling his fingers. "I think when we do, you'll remember the face of the man who took Rebecca. I believe it's here," he tapped his temple with his index finger.

"You once said, more than once really, that my mind might be protecting me. Then wouldn't it be bad to remember?"

"That is a possibility—just as it is a possibility you didn't see his face. But I think you did. I think that memory is trying to unearth itself. That's why you are having these difficulties. It's like a sliver of wood that embeds itself deep in the skin. I believe it is working its way up from the place you buried it. It's time now to work with it. But I also think it is important to proceed carefully. As I see it, we can do this one of two ways. Here in the office, with hypnosis to try to retrieve the memory, or by working with your dreams themselves."

"How do we do that? Working with the dreams?"

"With something called lucid dreaming. Have you ever felt semi-awake in a dream and part of your consciousness realized you didn't like where the dream was going? Then, the dream changed somehow. Maybe in your dream you are giving a speech but doing so naked. Some part of you realizes this is embarrassing and takes charge from inside your dream, finds a bathrobe, say."

"I can't say I've ever had that happen. I usually just wake up terrified."

"The mind can be trained. It can learn to recognize signals that awareness is functioning in the dream space." Dr. Lawrence was getting increasingly interested in his own idea. Both feet on the floor, he set his glasses down on his notepad, leaned forward, and began to gesture with his hands. I blew on the ember of his excitement.

"Signals? What kind of signals?"

"People who work extensively in this field have identified some common symbols, things that are indicators to the mind that it is operating in this other world. They are things that appear nonsensical. Not unusual in a dream. We often encounter things that don't make sense to us when we are awake thinking back on the dream—if we remember it at all. What is different about this technique is that now a part of the mind, apart from the dream, is aware of these things as they happen."

"Like dreams where you know you're in another time?"

His eyebrows lifted with interest and inquiry. "You've had a dream where you knew you were in another time?

I described to him the dream I had had where I was wandering through an old village and found the house that was really a pub. I described the wind and the fire. How I knew, while I was dreaming, it I was not in my life as it is but my life as it was—my life as it was over a century ago, somewhere else.

"Or at least how my mind constructed a past life," I added. No reason to sound crazy. Crazier. I wasn't sure I really believed in past lives, but I wasn't ready to discount it either. "I guess what I'm saying is that I knew it. I knew it wasn't now."

"That exactly the kind of thing we're talking about. As it happens, disruptions in time are one of the most reported signals." He waxed on. "Usually, they involve timepieces. A watch that shows the wrong time or a clock that is incomprehensible. But what you're telling me is much more elaborate." He sat back, put on his glasses, and began making notes. "Cori, do you still keep a dream journal?"

"Not formally anymore. Sometimes I write things down. Sometimes I write to Sean about them. When he's away."

"I'd like you to journal while we're working on this. When this happens again, when you notice something amiss in your dream, when you are aware that you are aware, I want you to say to yourself, *I am dreaming*. Okay?" He pressed his lips together into a thin line. "Well, that's our time for today."

"That's it? Tell myself I am dreaming and scribble some notes?"

"It's enough for now," Dr. Lawrence said darkly.

CHAPTER TWENTY-TWO

AT THE TIME of Rebecca's abduction, after I ran home and told my mother what happened and the police came, Detective Hanley asked me question after question about what the man looked like. I gave a description of his car, but I could not tell them what the man looked like. Not his face anyway. Not really. I could only answer the simplest, most basic questions. Was he young or old? Did he have dark hair or light? But the car—I never forgot that or the image of Rebecca's face as he pulled her inside it.

There were two theories for why I could not give a description of her killer. One was that from where I stood, which was probably two or three feet from the car, I simply did not get a good look at his face. His face might have been in shadow, or my sight line broken by the roof of the car. There was another theory. A more disturbing one. As the other theory went, I in fact knew the man in the car and had been so traumatized by the event, my mind would not permit me to remember. Indeed, this was so disturbing a theory to the town of Oliver that it was summarily rejected as impossible. There was simply no way someone they knew could be responsible; no way it was a coworker or the neighbor they had beers with at the backyard barbeque. No, our own neighbors decided, if there was a wolf in the fold, it had come slinking into Oliver from somewhere else.

I had come to understand through my sessions with Dr. Lawrence (and reading I had done on my own without his knowledge) that this not knowing who he was, where he was, the threat of someone completely unknown had so haunted me he became everyone to me. I could barely remember the girl I was, the one who loved to go exploring, who swam openly in the faces of strangers, interested in everything and everyone. Yet the agoraphobia did not take over all at once. My fear grew like a mushroom in a dark closet.

You see, more than anything, everyone just wanted to forget. It is what people do when the truth is too terrible, or they would never get out of bed in the morning. The adults around me wanted to forget. The town wanted to forget. They had their memorial service once a year on the anniversary because it was the decent thing to do and in the months between, the events of the past were put away. Those events became more distant, as I suppose they should. If it was talked about at all it was usually in whispers as I went by or as a story used to frighten children into not straying too far. A cautionary tale. Remember what happened to Rebecca Ashworth. In between, people lived their lives. That's what's supposed to happen. No one is supposed to live that kind of sadness every day, but there I was—a walking, talking, breathing reminder of what had happened. They could not forget me no matter how hard they tried. I made people uncomfortable, as if I too were lying along that creek. As if forever, I would have the stink of death on me.

The worst was what happened with Rebecca's parents. From that very first day, the Ashworth's reaction puzzled my parents and unnerved me. At the beginning, Mr. and Mrs. Ashworth were truly angry with my mother and father for calling the police. I never really knew why except that they were extremely religious in an oddly closed-door sort of way and suspicious of the police in general. Much of their family life and their social life revolved around their church, which was not the church, or even the same type of church, as the one where my family or many of my classmates went. In the years Rebecca and I were friends, we rarely went to her house to play. It was always my house, my yard, my mom putting out a snack or inviting Rebecca to stay for dinner. When I did go to her house, there was no music and almost no books, except for the Bible. It was weirdly quiet and uncomfortable. It must have been for Rebecca too because she seemed to prefer to be anywhere else.

Her mother looked a great deal like her, or the other way around. They had hair the same color, the same slender face, and pale blue eyes, but her mother's face had none of Rebecca's joy. Mrs. Ashworth was quiet and mousey. Rebecca's father was tall and lanky. I remember him coming home from work in slightly threadbare navy suit pants and a blue shirt, the same beaten down black briefcase in his hand whenever I saw him.

They barely spoke to my mother and father at the funeral and consciously looked away from me. When we went through the line to offer our condolences, Mrs. Ashworth, her hair wound up tight and wearing a dark dress with tiny flowers and a lace collar, seemed somewhere else entirely. Somewhere frightening.

"Elizabeth, Alan and I are so deeply sorry for your loss," my mother said reaching out for Mrs. Ashworth's hands, her own eyes brimming with tears.

Mrs. Ashworth shook my mother's hand limply and looking at her with vacant eyes recited almost mechanically, "And this is the condemnation, that light is come into the world, and men loved darkness rather than light, because their deeds were evil."

"Mrs. Ashworth," I croaked, partly because I had gotten very thirsty and partly because I didn't know what to say looking at Rebecca's flower draped casket looming just behind them.

Rebecca's mother turned to look at me. Her gaze hovered on me for a moment, something darker moving across her face, and then looking over my head, she muttered icily, "And when ye spread forth your hands, I will hide mine eyes from you. Yea, when ye make many prayers, I will not hear. Your hands are full of blood."

Behind us Mrs. Arnesen gasped audibly.

"Nola," the older woman said grasping my mother's arm, "I don't know why she would say such a thing. It must be the grief. Grief makes people say outrageous things. Things they do not mean. Things Corianne must not hear." Mrs. Arnesen angled her head knowingly.

"Yes, of course, it's the grief," my mother said tersely as she hustled me from the room. My father, who had been talking with one of the neighbors in the back of the room, took one look at my mother's face and wheeled out of the room behind us.

I knew people were whispering, but until that moment it had never occurred to me that they blamed me. Okay, not everyone blamed me, but certainly Mrs. Ashworth did. When we got home my mother drew me a bath, the way they did in old books or movies, and when she thought I couldn't hear her, she talked to my father about getting out of town for a while. That was the first time we headed to the farm. The first time we went to Sheerfolly Chapel. Now I was going back.

As I pulled my small black suitcase from Sean's bedroom closet, I thought about what to tell him. He was due home in a few days from his latest trip and I honestly did not know whether I'd be here. In my head, I spun out the conversation, rehearsing how I would tell him I needed to go back to the farm. I would talk about how it had been important to my mom and now that she was gone, it would help me feel close to her. It was true. Since my father died, I missed her more than ever. I practiced the words softly under my breath as I pulled a pair of jeans off the small pile of my clothes sitting on the bed, folded them in thirds, and put them in the suitcase. Even saying it to myself it sounded too rehearsed. Like I was running lines for a play.

Continuing to pack, I briefly considered telling Sean the truth. I was going to see Bill. I was going to see Bill and the farm was home to me. More than the house in Oliver. More than being here with him. It meant he would ask questions, probing questions I did not want to answer. Questions I wasn't sure how to answer. No, I decided, I would stick with the bit about my mother. It wasn't untrue, it just wasn't the whole truth. Sean and I had planned to talk this morning, but he was late for our call. He was meant to let me know his flight details, so I would know when to expect him. I began to bargain with myself. If he wasn't due for another couple of days, I might not have to tell him anything. I might get to the farm and have nothing to say. Or Bill could refuse to see me. Then I would be back before Sean even knew I was gone. I would wait, wait and see what his plans were and then if I needed to, I would tell him just that much. I was missing my mother.

I went out into the kitchen to make some toast and coffee. Now that I had decided I was leaving my stomach was churning uneasily. Perhaps toast would settle it down. Plus, it would buy me a little more time. As I waited for the toaster, my mind revisited my choice to go. Just thinking about seeing Bill, I felt nervous. With shaking hands, I pulled a small white plate from the cabinet over my head. By the time the toast popped up I had changed my mind about eating and wandered back to the bedroom.

By eleven o'clock, my suitcase was packed, the toast was in the garbage and the dishes were done. When it became clear Sean had missed our call completely, I knew I had run out things with which to procrastinate. I needed to go.

"C'mon Maud," I said swinging open the metal door of the cat carrier in invitation before placing it on the floor. "We're taking a road trip." Maud looked over from the chair where she had been sitting all morning watching me drift from one room to another. She eyed the box skeptically before giving me a bored look. As if to emphasize that she was only getting up because she wished it, she stood, stretched slowly and after she smoothed down an errant bit of fur, jumped down from the chair. Standing in front of the carrier, she gingerly reached out a paw to bat at the soft bed inside, but then withdrew it.

"It's going to be fine. You'll see. It's a farm. Mice, crawling things, a cat's paradise. You'll love it. Now get in."

She acquiesced to my request with a loud meow.

By noon Maud and I had left the city well behind. My body relaxed as the buildings and strip malls of the suburbs gave way to woods and fields, enough that I noticed just how tensely I had been gripping the steering wheel. Pins and needles started in my fingers and gradually spread out to my hands. My shoulders dropped from my ears as the muscles along my shoulder blades groaned. I pushed against the steering wheel and pressed my back into the bucket seat of my black Lexus, part of my inheritance from my father. There were still another three hours to go, but I loved the drive. Maud was less pleased.

With an hour left, I stopped for a cup of coffee at a small restaurant aptly named The Triangle Café for where it sat at the slanting junction of two county highways. I still wasn't feeling hungry but Bette, the only waitress on duty, didn't take no for an answer. In fact, I was doubtful she gave it as an answer much either after I watched her work the room of men, some young and some old, who filed in for an early dinner. I was a fine one to talk. Maybe Bette was just friendly. I let her ply me with coffee and a viscous cup of potato soup that was more bacon and green onion than potato. But it was warm and filled the hollow spot that began growing in my stomach once I started smelling the pot roast, burgers, and fries cooking.

With the smell of heavy diner food hanging on my clothes and having been left alone in the car while I ate, albeit on a pleasant day with the window open wide, Maud was even less enthralled with her arrangement than she had been when we started off. She scolded loudly as I opened the car door, pulled a half full bottle of water out of the cup holder, and flipped the front seat forward to get access to her in the back seat.

"I hear you, little one. I'm a crappy mother." I opened her carrier and clipped a pink leash onto her pink faux rhinestone collar. The collar was ridiculous. It had been a gift from Kate when I first started bringing Maud to stay at the apartment. That was Kate. Always fun and a little over the top. I did have to admit it looked lovely against the silk of Maud's smoky fur. She meowed her assent as I picked her up and took her into the grassy area alongside the parking lot. I cupped one hand, poured some water into it, and then offered it to Maud. She lapped it up daintily, her rough tongue tickling my palm. I got a small plastic tray out of the back of the car, set it down, and poured some kitty litter in the bottom. She sat with her tail swishing from side to side but didn't move.

"Hey city girl, have you forgotten the garden already? And this is your bathroom stop, so make the most of it." I turned my back. Shortly after I heard the crunch of her paws in the litter. Victory. When she was done, I carefully bagged the tray and threw it in the dumpster around back of the café.

Eventually she began to hop after toads and insects she found in the grass. Putting my hand through the loop in the leash, I pulled my phone out of my back pocket and checked for a message from Sean. Nothing. I hoped he was okay. And I hoped he wasn't on his way home. How many nights had I cursed his delays and extra stopovers? Now here I was hoping for them.

"Okay. Time to go," I scooped the cat up and leaned into the backseat to put her in the carrier. She spilled out of my arms like a Slinky, walked back and forth across the seat, and then again entered as if it were her idea. Raising an eyebrow, I scolded. "Look Missy, we don't want to roll in at bedtime and it's going to be a long drive to the hotel in the dark." I was talking to Maud as if she gave a damn. A picture flashed into my mind of me, an old woman in a rundown apartment, surrounded by phone books, a half dozen cats, and old stockings bagging at my ankles while my mind slowly became untethered. Definitely time to go. Remembering all the coffee Bette had poured for me, I ran back into the café for my own break, and we headed out.

There still wasn't much in the area, but I remembered a town called Mason was along the river about twenty miles north of Sheerfolly Chapel. My research showed they still had a small hotel. I had called and booked the night before. If all went well at the farm, I would stay for a few days. If it didn't, I would be out of there by breakfast.

CHAPTER TWENTY-THREE

THE FARM LAY on the other side of town. I drove past the post office, the grocery store, over the river, all the things I remembered from coming here with my mother or Evelyn. There were new things too. Next to the small hardware store was a sandwich shop, part of a national chain, and a Mexican restaurant that opened in what had been the old variety store. Mostly, it looked the same. Cars and huge pickup trucks were angle-parked, their beds full of metal or supplies and big dogs panting in the heat. People stood out in front of the storefronts talking, exchanging their news. As I rolled past, they turned to look at my car knowing immediately I was out of place. I looked at them, nodded subtly in greeting, and then looked away quickly, feeling embarrassed and as if I had already done something wrong by coming here.

Past the Schulz taxidermy studio, the scene gave way to cornfields, long driveways, and houses with faded paint set far back from the road. It had been growing stale in the car and even with the air conditioning on, I was getting drowsy in the heat of the late day sun which baked me through the tinted glass. Even if I hadn't been warm and sleepy, I was compelled to lower the car window, to be closer. Closer to the land. Closer to the wind I saw moving the cornstalks. Closer to the green. The glass kept me part of a different world. I wanted to be part of this one again.

Maud protested the pressure change as the window pulled away from the rubber seal with a loud squeak and the scent of manure swirled in from the neighboring dairy farm and into the backseat, buffeting her carrier. Looking over my shoulder, I saw her attempt to continue her protest only to have it cut short by the wind ruffling her fur and blowing in her face. She closed her eyes and turned her head away.

When I thought of going back to Sheerfolly Chapel, when I imagined it lying in bed next to Sean as he slept, I had always imagined I would park the car somewhere out on the main road and walk up to the farm on my own two feet and on my own terms. Now that I was nearly there, I realized the scene played better without the cat or luggage. Fantasies do not require a toothbrush. My clammy grip on the steering wheel tightened as I slowed down to look for the turn onto Solomon Drive. Bill and Evelyn's place was down past the old Solomon Farm at the end of a long dirt and gravel road they called the driveway. The Soloman name was big here. They had once owned a lot of land, having gotten in early and cheap as farmers pushed west and found vast tracts of prairie that required little in the way of clearing. It was only later they found out about all the rocks that made it a slow, back breaking process to ready the land for planting. Within the first ten years, so the story goes, they sold off the land for the Parson farm to Evelyn's great grandparents, Clive and Edna.

The turn appeared suddenly in the gap between two fields of corn. I hit the brakes and turned hard, dust swirling and gravel crunching under the tires. My purse slid across the seat next to me and then tipped over, its contents clattering to the floor and spilling between the seat and the door.

"Shit." Guiding the car to a stop along the side of the road, I hesitated a second before turning off the engine. I could not let go of the idea of walking to the farm. I had been driving all day and it would feel good to stretch my legs. It would also give me time to think of what to say. The last thirty miles had yielded no inspiration at all. If I thought it would be hard to tell Sean about my coming here, it paled in comparison to trying to find the words to explain to Bill and Evelyn why I was suddenly turning up on their doorstep. I wasn't sure I knew exactly.

Climbing out of the car, I looked down the empty stretch of road ahead of me. If memory served it couldn't be more than a mile to the house. I could walk it. Rounding to the passenger side, I opened the door carefully. A lipstick I never used, a pen, and a half of a roll of mints fell into the dirt. With two fingers, I plucked the items from the dust and gravel. I tossed the lipstick and the pen back into the bottom of my purse, along with my wallet and an assortment of loose change I scraped up from the floor of the car. Peeling the mint wrapper down, I picked the top one out and flipped it into the ditch, thinking to save the rest, then reconsidered and tossed the whole thing into a long-empty paper coffee cup.

Standing up, hands on my hips and staring at the cat, I realized my options were limited. I couldn't leave her with the car as I had before. It was too hot. Hopefully, I wasn't just ducking inside for a few minutes and if I left the window open enough to matter, she would probably pick the lock on her carrier and make a break for it. Crafty, that one. I could not imagine Maud would find her way back here if she got loose. She didn't yet know where here was. I had to take her with me. Fit though I was, there was no way I was going to make it a mile carrying the cat and her damn Winnebago. I scowled as I lifted the long strap of my purse over my head, settling the bag across my body to free my hands. These were precisely the kinds of inconveniences Sean never considered before he surprised me with a cat. But I couldn't imagine not having Maud anymore. She was my alter ego. Or maybe my conscience, albeit with a kind of Bohemian code.

"Looks like it's your day for adventure Madame." I pulled out the pink leash one more time. "This works much better when you hold down the fort and I go out to scout."

Indeed, it was slow going. After keeping her in the car for hours, I had no choice but to let Maud down to walk in the weeds and grass and in her exuberance at having been sprung, she made a beeline right for the fields, first tugging on her leash and then having met my resistance, sitting down stubbornly. I patiently brought her back, but she was enthralled with every smell, every cricket, the caw of every crow, and so the pattern just kept repeating itself. She would head off on her own direction, I would try to correct her and in protest she would sit down and refuse to move. Time and again I had to collect her. At least it gave me time to think, but in the end, I did have to pick her up and carry her the rest of the way or we would never have gotten to the farmhouse before dark. Maud was embracing the country life with gusto.

At last, I could see the circle drive in front of the house and the familiar white clapboard and slate colored roof. It looked older. Worn. Not run down exactly, but tired, like many of the faces I saw here. There were two small pots of flowers on the porch steps filled with bedraggled pansies on pale stems, their faces nearly in the dirt. I remembered Evelyn always keeping huge pots spilling over with bright flowers. I cut across the stubbly grass in the circle of lawn ringed by the driveway, past the small wooden swing Bill had made for me which still hung from the old oak tree, and up the steps. Raising my hand, I pulled up short of a knock.

"Okay, this is it," I said picking a bit of dried cornstalk off Maud's delicate charcoal head. "How do I look?" She blinked and looked bored. "Yeah, that's what I was afraid of."

With a deep breath, I knocked on the screen door. Four solid knocks. More solid than I felt. I waited and listened. Nothing. I knocked again and leaned in close to the door, listening for movement inside the house. Again, nothing. I walked over to one of the large low nine-paned windows and peered inside.

"Can I help you?" came a familiar drawl behind me.

My face burned with a crimson blush that began at my chest and washed up into my face. I knew without turning around it was him and here I was prowling around like some nosey neighbor peeping in. Flooded with nerves, my legs began to tremble. Maud felt my sudden fear and distrusted it. With one quick wrench of her body, she turned out of my arms and landed with a soft thump on the porch floor. Turncoat. I glared at her and then slowly turned around, my fingers pulling at the fabric of my skirt where it stuck to me.

"Hi, Bill."

The question on his face turned to recognition. He stood. I stood. Neither of us moved. "Corianne? My god it *is* you."

"It's me," I said flapping my arms nervously at my side.

"You look … beautiful. Older. And beautiful as I remember you." He started up the steps. "She's not one of ours," he motioned to Maud who had made herself comfortable on the porch swing.

"No, she's with me. Sorry. I couldn't leave her in the car."

"Well now, no need to apologize. We're friendly here at the farm. Some folks even decide to stay." He sat down next to Maud and looking up, winked at me. She sniffed at his outstretch hand and then rubbed against it until he stroked her throat, working his strong fingers into her fur. I could hear her purr from where I was standing. What a shameless hussy.

"Where is your car, if you don't mind me asking?"

"Up on the road. I felt like stretching my legs." Gingerly, I walked over and sat down next to Bill on the swing. He pushed the swing back and we started to rock. One of my sandals dropped off my foot. I let the other one slide off too.

"We'll go get it later," he said matter-of-factly as he unhooked the leash from Maud's collar. "You know you never struck me as the cat type."

"Yeah, I know. She was a gift. When my mom died."

"I'm sorry, Cori. We miss her very much." He put his hand on mine.

It warmed me to hear him say my name again and when his hand touched mine, the lump of sadness and regret I'd swallowed on hard when I left the farm, when my mother died, when my father died, when I moved into Sean's, rose until it took up my whole throat. I was that little girl who had first come to the farm. I had a terrible secret. I pulled my hand away. My eyes fixed on the porch rail, but I saw Bill turn to look at me.

"You haven't said what brings you," he asked after a long silence.

"I'm not quite sure myself. I've felt…I've wanted to come since Mom died. Since before that really."

"Whatever wind brought you, Corianne, I'm glad you're here."

"Thanks for that."

"It's the god's honest truth."

"I think I could use a little truth just now." I hadn't meant to say it and quickly turned the conversation a different direction. "Where's Evelyn? I knocked. No one came to the door. Right, you know that."

"She's upstairs. Didn't want to come down today."

"Didn't want to come down? Why? What's wrong?"

"Cori, she can't walk."

"What? Why? What's happened?"

"She had another back surgery." He ruffled his hair. "It was supposed to be simple. Something went wrong. A fragment of bone. A piece of medical hardware. They're not sure what happened."

"Oh my god, that's terrible. Bill, I am so sorry. I didn't know. Was it malpractice? Did you talk to a lawyer?"

"I suppose we could have. There were lawyers that came around and wanted us to, but Evie didn't want any of it. She didn't want anyone around. Not even me some days."

"How long? How long has she been … how long?"

"Four years. It's why we didn't come to your father's funeral."

"Why didn't you tell me, Bill?"

"Evie made me swear I wouldn't. Said you had been through enough."

I felt like the rug had been pulled out from under me. All the way here, I was thinking about me. About seeing Bill and what I would say. It never occurred to me that they had their own problems.

"Do you want to talk about it?"

"Not here. Not now." Bill stood up, still holding Maud. "Evie knows someone is here. She might have even figured out it is you by now. Nothing wrong with her hearing." A wry smile muscled its way through the tension on his face. He handed Maud to me. "And she'll want to meet that little one for sure."

"Well then, let's go," I said and followed him through the screen door.

CHAPTER TWENTY-FOUR

I WAS AT the house again. The house in the village. This time there was no fire. It was nightfall and there were several people in the pub. A trio of men sat playing a game and trading stories about what they had seen. They were woodsmen. Two of them were older. One of the older men was burly. He had thick curly hair and a long thick beard streaked with silver. His friend also had a beard, but it was fully gray and close-cropped. The second man was of slighter build. The older men were telling stories to the young man, whose eyes were wild with fright as he listened. One held his hands apart wide to indicate the size of something. Some creature. Or his manhood maybe. It was always hard to know when the men got to drinking and telling stories. The young man had thin pale hands, hands that had not seen much work. The other two men had thick hands. The skin on their knuckles was reddened and dry. But there was something about the older man, the one with the curly hair. The color of his eyes, like the ice-cold blue of the sea. I had lived near the sea. It still ran in my veins. As I dropped a pint of beer off in front of him, I felt his eyes on me, and though his hands were rough from the work of living off the land, I knew they would be as skilled on me if I were to welcome him in my bed. My indecent thought was interrupted as a singular sound rose from outside. The long howl of a wolf.

All conversation stopped. It was she. She came each full moon, alone—
and she waited in the woods just beyond the wall which separated this
pub from the woods beyond. She waited for me.

My father did not really take time after my mother's death to grieve. That's what they say, right? That you are supposed to take time for grieving. That there are stages. That it is a process. That's what Dr. Lawrence told me one Thursday afternoon when I stormed into his office and slammed the door. That I was going through the stages of grieving.

"It's quite normal to be angry, Corianne," he said in that frustratingly immovable way. "To feel betrayed. To feel your mother left you."

"With all due respect, fuck you Dr. Lawrence. You don't know what I feel." I thought I saw his face move, a flinch maybe. Looking down at my lap, I stifled a smug little smirk, but I could feel his eyes on me. He was not amused. I folded my arms across my chest and then unfolded them again, finally reaching down to fish a cigarette and some matches out of my handbag. I didn't light the cigarette. I pulled it lightly through my thumb and forefinger, over and over, the delicate paper sliding along my fingers.

"Then why don't you tell me?"

"It's hot in here. Why the hell is it so hot in here?" I got to my feet and walked over to the office window. In the parking lot, gulls circled the light poles, calling to each other in brittle voices. They looked pure white against the gathering storm clouds. And soft. So soft.

"Why are there seagulls this far inland? I've never understood it. They just showed up one day. It must be ten miles or more to the closest lake.

"They're scavengers. Survivors. Highly adaptive."

"Yeah, but what are the adapting *to*? I mean, they need water, right? There's no water in the damn parking lot."

"They need food. Perhaps those waters they come from are fished out. Or too polluted. Or maybe there are just too many of them to all live in the same place, so a few went off to find new water."

Tapping the cigarette against the glass, I laughed.

"You don't know either. You're just making it up. Aren't you?"

"It's a theory," Dr. Lawrence replied.

I laughed again. Really laughed. "I respect that Dr. Lawrence. I respect a good bullshitter. I really do." The last part was less clear as by then I had shoved the cigarette in my mouth. With a snap, the match caught followed by the familiar crackle as the paper caught flame. Taking a quick puff and then exhaling, it became more of a sigh.

"You know I don't like you to smoke in here, Corianne."

"Yes, and I also know you won't forbid it either."

I had been coming long enough that I opened the drawer next to the good doctor's desk and pulled out an old square green glass ashtray. Now it was his turn to sigh.

He stood up and turned on the small cylindrical air purifier that sat tucked behind a slightly sickly-looking Ficus.

"Something tells me I'm not the only one who smokes in here." I motioned with my head and waved the cigarette in the direction of the Ficus.

For a long time, I had suspected that Dr. Lawrence had the odd illicit smoke when no one was here, but I'd never been able to crack him. He would never smoke with me as Bill had. It would be a break with decorum. A breaking down of the boundary between the shrink and the shrunken. Bill. I had tried not to think of him, but since he had phoned, I couldn't get him out of my mind.

"Don't be silly, Cori. Plants don't smoke."

I looked carefully at him, but there was no smile. Not on his face or in his voice. Still, it was a rare attempt at humor. And it hadn't escaped my notice that he called me Cori. Not exactly cutting down the wire fence between us, but he had taken a step up to it. I found I was suddenly grateful for that small kindness.

"I need her. She was always the one who—I could tell her things, you know? I don't blame her. It's not like she chose to get cancer and die, right?" I thought of that talk in the garden. The one where she told me about Martin. "People can't choose to die, can they?"

"Do you think your mother chose to die? Cori? Is there something you haven't told me about your mother's death?"

I thought back to that day in the sunroom. The way we all had to step out. The look that passed between my father and the nurse. Dierdre. Dierdre of the Pink Scrubs. There was something about that day. Something in my father's hand. I had spent many nights going over it until I couldn't bear to think about it anymore.

"I think my mom's heart was broken. Not medically, although I suppose with the chemo…I just think that there was too much. Too much sadness. I think she decided to die is all." I snubbed out my cigarette. I wasn't willing to go any further. There was no point in sharing my suspicions with Dr. Lawrence. They were only suspicions. And I was so tired then. We were all so tired. "Do you think that's possible?"

"The mind is a powerful thing. It can't always win over the body's natural processes, but yes, I think it's possible that one can give up on the will to live and hasten one's death."

"Well, I think that's what happened. I think my mother hastened her own death."

"Does that anger you?"

"Cancer sucks. I guess I can't blame her."

"A minute ago you said you thought your mother died of a broken heart."

"I didn't say that."

"Okay. You tell me."

"I said I thought there was too much sadness, and she chose to die."

"What do you think made your mother so sad that she would give up on her life."

"Me."

"Your mother loved you very much, Corianne. You were no doubt a source of great joy to your mother."

"Maybe once. But what happened with Rebecca. It tainted me. It tainted what she had left of—" I stopped myself.

"What she had left of?" Dr. Lawrence repeated.

"Never mind. It was stupid."

"Let's talk about this idea of you being tainted."

"Let's not."

CHAPTER TWENTY-FIVE

AS I FOLLOWED Bill up the stairs, instinctively sidestepping the squeaky treads even after all this time, I remembered how many sweaty nights I laid in my bed thinking of him. Listening as his footsteps paused at the top of the stairs. Wondering if he was looking at my door. My breath would catch. I could not exhale until I heard him walking toward his bedroom. Their bedroom. Breathing again. Sighing sadly.

I could hear the bed creak as Bill climbed in. Next to her. Sometimes I would hear the brief murmur of voices, rustling, or other muffled noises. Soft moans. I would roll over and face the window, holding the pillow tight against my head so I wouldn't hear. To be fair, I think Bill and Evelyn tried not to have sex very often with me just down the hall. But the summer got long, I imagine. Too long to worry about the teenage girl down the hall. It was god-awful. Both the imagining it and the sick feeling that rose when I did. A vague nausea like when you've had nitrous at the dentist. The disconnected feeling. The hiss of the tank. Vision wavering slightly. The mask over your face and the feeling that you are about to throw up inside it.

There on my side, facing the window, I would try to focus on the moon. If no moon, I would play games with myself. Reciting the lyrics to songs. Saying the Rosary. I didn't have one. A rosary that is. My mother did. She had one with beads that looked like pearls that she kept in a little leather pouch that snapped shut. I had asked to see it on one of those evenings when I sat on her bed talking at her while she got ready to go out for the evening with my father. I loved watching her get ready for the dinners my father's architectural firm hosted. It fascinated me. The way she transformed from the beautiful earth mother I knew into this other woman with diamond jewelry and a tube of red lipstick in a tiny, beaded handbag. While we talked, she let me hold the rosary. I wrapped its beads around my hand and felt the silk of the tassel, studied the tiny image of Mary stamped into the metal badge that sat in the center.

On those nights, back to the door, I would pray to Mary. Spotless Blessed Mary. Blessed Mary without fault. How could she ever understand? Still, I prayed, no rosary in hand, but knotting and unknotting the sheet. *Hail Mary, Mother of God. Blessed are you among women and blessed is the fruit of thy womb, Jesus.* My lips moving, I ran silently through the words over and over again, as if I could be absolved by sheer panicked devotion. *Hail Mary, Mother of God, pray for us sinners now and at the hour of our death, Amen.* It ran together as I recited it faster and faster. *Blessed Mary, make pure my unclean heart.* I would intersperse my own ad libs. I would beg Mary from the sweaty hell-licked depths of my wretched soul. Mary had sacrificed. The pure were always asked to sacrifice. It was why Rebecca had been taken and I had not. I felt the weight of my mother's rosary in my palm. Bill. Bill who I wanted so badly. Bill would be my sacrifice. The price of my redemption.

"Just give me a minute to make sure she's ready for company." Bill held up his hand and motioned for me to stay outside the door.

I buried my face in Maud's soft fur and kissed her, looking sidelong at the open door at the end of the hall. Through the door I could see the white bedspread. The window was open, and the curtains flapped and danced in the late afternoon breeze. I took a step closer.

"Cori? Come in here this minute," came the somewhat cheerful command. I snapped to attention and Maud pushed her paw into my hand, letting me feel the prick of her claws. The door opened and Bill waved me inside.

"Well, how stupid of me to think she wouldn't want company." Bill flashed me a smile. "As soon as she found out it was you, she was already out of bed."

"That would be a miracle, wouldn't it?" I heard Evelyn's voice from somewhere behind Bill. As he turned to let me through, I saw her sitting in a large wicker chair. The arms of it were rolled and the back was rounded, sweeping into a bell shape. I remembered seeing it in on the porch when I used to visit. The wide seat made Evelyn, who had always been slight, look as small as a child. She seemed thinner to me too. Despite the warm day, she wore long pale blue pants which clung to the bones of her knees before dropping into a wide flare. They were old women's pants. The kind grandmothers wore to Mass on Sundays. I imagined her legs, withered as an old woman's legs beneath.

"Corianne Dempsey. What the hell took you so long?"

I froze and then began to stammer. "I, I meant to come earlier."

"Oh, you are a sight for sore eyes. Get over here so I can give you a hug."

I walked over to the weathered wicker chair and leaned down, hugging her with my one free arm. I felt a kiss land in my hair, and I breathed in the familiar warm fresh cotton smell of her.

"Hi Evelyn. God, I've missed you. Say hello Maud." I expected Maud, caught in a moment of affection to which she had not consented, to protest as Evelyn reached out to pet her. Instead, she just peered intently at the woman in the chair. I let her down and she commenced exploring, sniffing tentatively at the blue pants.

"Bill, would you please bring us something to drink. It's hot today and I'm terribly thirsty. I expect Cori is too after her drive."

"Yeah of course. Be right back." The old treads of the stairs creaked as he made his way to the kitchen.

Standing over Evelyn felt awkward but sitting on the bed felt too familiar after all these years. I remembered another chair being in the corner by the dresser, but when I looked around, there was none. I knelt in front of her. Opening my mouth to speak, I found only a silent sadness. Her best friend was gone. She couldn't walk. She couldn't work the garden or walk the land that she loved and lived on her whole life, and here I was for my own selfish reasons. Here with the woman who in some ways had been more of a mother to me than my own, helping me find a way to begin again. Giving me safety.

"I know. I know," she said softly.

A cold crept through me. Hiding my face, I put my head down on her knees. She couldn't know, ever.

Evelyn and I talked for over two hours. I told her about my mother's illness and my father's sudden death—how his heart was too broken to go on. She told me matter-of-factly about her surgery and about the piece of bone that had broken away and lodged against her vertebra. They had showed it to her and Bill on the x-ray afterward. She told me Bill had not been convinced it was as simple as that. That he said the surgeon looked stricken in the post-op consultation, as if he suspected something else had gone wrong. Bill tried to get him to give more detail, but the surgeon had just said, slightly apologetically, that though statistically rare, these things do happen and that there was nothing he could do. Evelyn would likely never walk again. Another surgery would be too risky.

She was very brave as she told the story. Far braver than I ever would have been. There was not an ounce of self-pity in her voice. No blame. That had been earlier, Evelyn said. In the first few months.

"I didn't blame the doctors so much as myself," Evelyn told me. "For even agreeing to the damn surgery in the first place. I hurt before, but I managed. I let them convince me it could be better. I got greedy. And now, well now this is how it is." She waved at the wheelchair folded up and sitting near the door. I was so flustered when I had first come in, I hadn't even seen the wheelchair. Now settled in and perched cross-legged on the bed, I noticed there was also a walker standing on the other side of the bed.

"How do you manage? I mean, this house isn't exactly handicap accessible."

"Oh, you noticed?" Evelyn laughed wryly. "This room is taken up with all my equipment now. Poor Bill ended up moving down the hall."

My eyebrows went up.

"Yes, your old room."

My first thought was relief that I had thought to book a hotel room. The second one was darker. Every night I slept next to Sean, wishing it were Bill beside me, Bill had been sleeping in the bed that held all my sins. I had left long ago. No doubt other people had stayed in the little guest room at the end of the hall. Yet part of me wanted to run down the hall and strip the bed. Wash the sheets. Another part liked the idea that Bill's body might lie in the same hollow mine had— that we shared something sharing that bed, though years apart.

"I didn't think to ask earlier, but you are going to stay awhile, aren't you Corianne?"

"I wasn't sure, showing up unannounced. I thought I'd at least stay a day. I've got a hotel room in Mason for tonight." I had reserved two nights, but I didn't mention that. One step at a time.

"Nonsense. You'll stay here."

"Oh, I don't think that's a good idea. Bill." I motioned down the hall. "I'll just be in the way. The hotel will be fine."

"Nope. I won't hear of it. You staying in that cardboard box when you could be here with us at the farm? I know you miss being here. And what about this one? What is she going to do in a hotel?" Evelyn patted Maud, who had curled up in her lap and fallen soundly asleep.

"I do want to be here. Of course, I do. But I couldn't."

"No buts. It's settled. Bill can sleep on the couch. I know he'll want you to stay too."

"I can take the couch."

Recognizing I had just given in, Evelyn gave a satisfied smile.

"I'll let you and Bill fight that one out. Now, if you don't mind, could I ask you to go give him a hand with dinner? He really is wonderful about it, but I know he'd love the help."

"No problem. I'm on it."

The sun was getting lower. Downstairs the kitchen was awash in orange light as the late day sun, hanging in the western sky, blasted in the kitchen window and door. Bill hunched over the sink washing potatoes as a pot of water boiled and splashed on the stove.

"Need some help?" In an old muscle memory, I grabbed the large white cotton towel off the peg by the refrigerator and tied it around my waist.

"Christ, yeah."

He easily surrendered his post at the sink and moved to the stove, lifting the rumbling cover on a skillet. Steam poured out. Bill pulled his face away quickly, like a turtle pulling back into its shell. I made my way to the sink and the half-washed potatoes, pausing for a moment behind him. I could feel him. Feel the electric current of his body. As he turned to talk to me, I slid past and over to the safety of the sink.

"You're staying for dinner, I hope." With a bang, he settled the cover back on the skillet.

"Yeah, Evelyn invited me. But only if there's enough," I added. "I don't want to be any trouble. After all, I showed up here unannounced."

"You're plenty of trouble, Cori, but you're welcome for dinner. More than enough. Evie eats like a bird."

My face fell as I stood, potato in hand and the faucet still running cold water.

"Cori, I'm kidding. You know that." Yet I knew what he said was true. I was trouble. Always had been. Being here was trouble. The refrigerator door opened and closed. *Hail Mary, full of grace.* "I trust you still drink these." He uncapped two beers and handed one to me.

"Yep." I dried a hand on my makeshift apron and took the bottle he handed me.

Truthfully, I had not had a beer in a long time. Apparently, it was passé to drink beer in the city. Sean now drank wine and top shelf liquor. Beer was too blue collar. Too common. I felt them all gawk at me when I drank a beer. Just to shock them I used to like to wave off the glass and drink it straight out of the brown longneck. Bartenders appreciated the lack of pretense. Sean grimaced and then made a joke about it. With bemused expressions, his friends would resume conversation in their strangely affected accents. Poor Corianne, the hopeless country mouse. My parents were educated professionals. My father an architect, for god's sake. I was educated. Bright, even promising, if you believed my professors. Yet most of the time we were out with his friends, they ignored me. Sean gently urged me to try harder, but I think we all just felt awkward and uncomfortable. It became the same drill. A few members of the group would make the initial overture, asking politely how I was, and then not wait for the answer. I didn't like to talk anyway. Hours I sat listening to their inane conversations about the newest restaurants, who made partner, whose apartment was getting a complete remodel. I was very interested in the remodeling and knew a lot given all the time I spent curled up reading in my father's office or standing next to his drafting table, losing myself in the miniatures while he explained the principles of the cantilever, but I said next to nothing. Not unless Sean, trying to make me feel a part of things, drew me back into the conversation.

I retreated into another space as I had grown used to doing. They prattled on, their voices coming from the top of their throats as if they had some constriction. Especially the women, everything expressed in bored voices, vowels yawned through jaws that could have been wired shut and a hissing sibilance issuing from their bleached white teeth. I could feel myself die a little more as I sat there, wishing I had a cigarette. Sean thought I quit, but I still smoked out on the balcony when he was gone. Or at the coffee shop. To hell with it, I thought one night out at the bar. Excusing myself to go to the ladies' room, I instead slipped out the service entrance I had seen one of the wait staff use. The bar's owner, the one who had brought me the second beer, no glass, stood leaning with his head back against the brick building, smoke rising from his cupped hand. I waved the cigarette I had pulled out of my purse.

"You don't mind, do you?"

"Nah. It's a free country."

"Thanks."

"If I were with those gas bags, I'd be out here too."

I laughed. "Oh, so you noticed."

"You gotta nice laugh," he said. "Never heard you laugh in there."

Being outside, even in the alley, I had relaxed a little and was enjoying my smoke. Now, I straightened back up. On alert.

"Hey, don't worry. I'm not some freak. I just know who my regulars are. Your group comes in enough I remember. And you're kinda hard not to notice."

I blushed in the dark.

"Charlie," he leaned away from the brick and stuck out his free hand. There was a thick Cuban link silver bracelet on his wrist.

"Cori," I answered, cautiously extending my hand.

"I tell you what, Cori," he drew a thin reedy breath, "you let me know when you're coming in and I'll set up a private table out here in the smoking section, alright."

"Does it come with the perks?"

His face broke into a wide smile as he held up the joint pinched in his other hand.

"Yeah, doll. Sure. That too."

The first bitter wash of cold beer hit the back of my throat. I had taken Charlie up on that more than a few nights. It was the one place I went at night when Sean was gone. It was only two blocks from the apartment. I managed to walk it the first time, figuring if I got there by ten o'clock there would still be enough people moving around on the street. I had clutched my keys in my balled fist. By the time I got to the door of the bar, I was almost in a run. After that, I took a cab. At least to go home.

"Really lady?" the cabbie had questioned me when I gave him the address. "You know that's only like two blocks, right?" He craned around and looked at me. It must have been obvious how uncomfortable I was being out at that hour because his face softened. "Hey, whatever. It's a quiet night," he shrugged, shifting the taxi into drive. When I got out of the cab, he handed me his card along with my change. "You call me, okay honey? Most guys, they won't do this mickey mouse kind of fare. But Isaac will take care of you."

On the nights I showed, Charlie would close a bit early, open the old dormer window out back, and we'd sit in the alley talking, listening to Cannonball Adderley and getting high. At one or two o'clock in the morning, Isaac would come back for me. Sometimes he would just wait at the curb out front of the alley and honk for me. One long, one short. Sometimes he would come around back.

"Nah," he'd hold up his hand when Charlie offered him a joint. "I don't need no reefer madness. That stuff scares the hell out of me. But I'll take one of those," he added, motioning to the beer.

I was grateful for Isaac. If it hadn't been for him that last night at Charlie's would have ended very differently. I had considered Charlie a friend. Charlie considered himself something more. The night had gone like so many others before had. We drank beers, got high, and talked music. But that night when I got up to go, Charlie grabbed me by the wrist and pulled me in for a kiss. I pushed him away, but he took hold of me by both shoulders and forced me up against the brick wall. I had liked it when Chuck had me up against the wall in the laundry room at my parent's house. But this wasn't like that time with Chuck. I wanted Chuck. I invited him. This was not like that time.

Charlie tried again to kiss me. This time I turned my head. He responded by putting his forearm under my chin, against my neck, and forcing the issue. Struggling to get away as he tore my blouse open, I felt the pressure against my windpipe increase. I tried to knee him. That's when he hit me hard across the face. My head snapped to one side and bounced hard against the brick. Pain radiated out from the point of impact. I tasted blood. As I tried to focus my eyes, I thought I saw Rebecca standing in that alley, watching. The next thing I knew, Charlie was ripped away from me. Isaac had come for me early. He came running when he saw what was happening.

"Jesus!" he said, shocked when he saw my quickly swelling face and the blood running down from my temple. Then he turned his attention to Charlie, punching him in the gut and then kicking him where he lay. "You little motherfucking prick. Think you're such a man? We'll see how much man you are after I'm through with you."

I reached out and grabbed Isaac's fist right before it connected again with Charlie. "Just get me out of here," I mumbled over my cut and swollen lip.

"Yeah, yeah, of course," Isaac responded. Then he kicked Charlie one more time and we left. I turned to look out of the taxi window for Rebecca, but she was gone.

"Hey, where'd you go?" It was Bill.

I started at the sound of his voice. Yes, that's right. I touched my lip. I was in the kitchen again with Bill.

"Just thinking about the last time I had a beer with a friend," I shivered involuntarily. "What am I doing with these?" I held up a washed potato.

"Just cut them up. I'll throw them in with the meat."

"What are we having?"

"Pan steak. Some onions. Nothing fancy."

"These aren't ever going to get done in time, you know. We should parboil them." Not waiting for an answer, I began opening and closing cabinet doors until I found the covered pot and took it over to the sink to fill.

"I'm glad you're here, Cori."

The pot wobbled even though I held its short black handles firmly in both hands.

"Here, let me get that." Bill stepped close to me and put his hands over mine, taking the pot from me.

"Thanks." It came out more softly than I intended.

Pulling away, I turned back to the cutting board and began slicing the potatoes as if it took all my concentration. I heard the pot bang against the metal burner followed by the click and soft whoosh of the gas burner turning on. I focused on the crunch of the white potato flesh coming away from itself and the clack of the knife against the cutting board. Finally, I found my voice again.

"It must be very hard. Keeping all this going by yourself. Taking care of Evelyn."

"It was awful at first. There was the back and forth to the hospital. Then all the therapy appointments. Finally found someone who will come out here to give her physical therapy. That helped a lot. But it's not cheap." He paused. "She was really depressed. Nothing I did helped. Everything I did was wrong. I didn't know what to do anymore. It was too hard to be together. I ended up moving down the hall. To your old room."

I stopped chopping and looked up. Bill was smiling, leaning against the kitchen counter with one leg bent, work boot up on the cabinet. It was a gentle smile. The smile I knew. The one that had warmed so many dark days. He looked bigger than I remembered. Taller and thicker. Not heavy, although he had put on a little weight since the last saw him. I could see it in his face. The years had softened the lines of his jaw. I liked it very much and wanted to reach out and touch the stubble of whiskers. So different from Sean's clean-shaven face and wiry frame. I wanted to memorize how Bill looked now, lay down a new track, filling in the details I had not been able to recall as clearly anymore. He was broad in the shoulders. Strong from the work of the farm. He had a strong physical presence—gentle and yet powerful. When he stood next to me at the sink, hands on mine, I felt small. Delicate.

"Evelyn mentioned that when she asked me to spend the night."

"She asked you to stay? That's good. Wow. That's huge actually. She hasn't wanted anyone here." Bill took a long drink. "Just one night?"

"Well, I booked two nights at the hotel in Mason. Oh shit, I need to cancel my room for tonight." I looked around, wiping my hands on my towel apron, trying to remember where the phone was.

"I got it," Bill lifted himself from where he was leaning against the kitchen counter, pulled a cell phone out of his back pocket and after a few seconds of searching the phone's memory, hit the send button. I mimed hands on a steering wheel, reminding Bill we still needed to get my car. He nodded as the call went through.

"Yeah, Joe. Bill out on Soloman's. You've got a reservation tonight for Corianne Dempsey? Yeah. Dempsey. Right. Yep, Nola's daughter. I'm calling to cancel it. Yeah, both nights. She's going to stay at the farm with Evie and me instead. What? Well, Joe, I don't think she's big on church, but I'll mention it to her. Yeah, city folks, right. Thanks." Shaking his head, he ended the call and shoved the phone back in his pocket. "Joe says there's a chicken dinner up at the church tomorrow night and you're welcome to come."

"Uh, weird. But okay," I answered, lifting the cover of the skillet and adding the potatoes. "How do you stand it? Everyone knowing everything about everyone here." With the lid still in my hand I asked, "Anything else I need to do?"

"Nah, just let it go." He shook his empty beer bottle. "You ready for another one?"

"Sure."

"Will you be here tomorrow night?" Bill asked.

"Why, you want to go to the chicken dinner?"

"Maybe, smart ass. No, I was just wondering how long I'm going to be on the couch."

CHAPTER TWENTY-SIX

DINNER BEGAN AWKWARDLY with those uncomfortable pauses that grow in the cracks between people who have not been together in a long while. Although Bill had alluded to the fact that she almost never came downstairs anymore, Evelyn had insisted on coming down to eat. I wondered how Bill would get her down the stairs at all. I hadn't noticed a lift or anything of that sort when I had gone up earlier. That was because there wasn't one. Bill had to carry her down. Not a big deal as Evelyn weighed next to nothing, but I couldn't imagine Bill having to do this every day. Not now, not for the rest of his life. After all, Evelyn was nearly twenty years older than I was. Even if he was younger than she was, we were all getting older.

I tried to be busy when Bill came down with Evelyn. When my mother was ill, there came a point when she wasn't particularly proud around family anymore, but when we had a guest, she was extremely conscious about being as gracious and put together as before—basically pretending she was not ill at all. Those performances took a toll on her. I remembered watching what little color she had drain out of her face until it looked gray. I learned firsthand what people meant by ashen. That was usually when my father or I got up and began clearing dishes, commenting pointedly on how late it was. My mother was too polite to throw anyone out.

After so much time away, I was now a stranger here. Yes, I knew the house. I knew Bill and Evelyn. But I didn't know. Not really. I felt torn between letting Evelyn know she didn't need to hide her condition and respecting her privacy. Things were not the same, but it was easier to pretend a kind of normal with her seated across from me at the dinner table, albeit with the walker parked next to her chair where Bill had put it. I tried not to gawk and yet I wondered—if she couldn't walk, what use was the walker? All that aside, it could have been any night the three of us had shared a meal. Except Bill was serving dinner, depositing on each plate a portion of the pan steak and potatoes, ladling the gravy and onions over everything. If it hadn't been for the neat pile of bright green beans, it would have been a grim plate. As it was, it looked vaguely institutional. It must have looked that way to Evelyn as well, but she was nothing but gracious as Bill brought our plates over.

"Ah, thank you my dear. This looks delicious."

"Mmm, yes," I chimed in. It smelled good enough to make my stomach rumble and remind me I hadn't eaten since the diner. Maud must have felt the same. She strode into the kitchen on her tiny white boots looking very much as if the house were hers, stopped at my feet, and gave a plaintive meow.

"Corianne helped with the potatoes, or we'd still be waiting." Bill set his plate down, grabbed another beer from the refrigerator and joined us, sitting at the head of the table.

"So, Corianne, you've gotten fully caught up on our little story here, but we haven't heard much about you. How is your job? Are you still an editor for…what's the name of that travel publisher? Drogheda?" Evelyn unfolded her napkin and placed it in her lap.

My first forkful hovered halfway between the plate in front of me and my mouth, rich gravy dripping. Maud licked her chops and sat at attention, head bobbing as her eyes followed each drop, drop, drop of gravy in case anything might make it to the floor. I shot her a scolding glance before answering. She meowed again as we continued our aside.

"Daufuskie. Yes, I'm still editing travel books. It's good. I mean, I still like it," I set down my fork. Disappointed with me, Maud got up, walked under the table and over my feet, and took up a post next to Bill. "There's not been as much work lately. Not the big book projects. It will pick up again. I've heard about some things coming down the pipe. Of course, that doesn't mean I'll get them."

"You should think about writing your own book. See the world. Your dad left you the house, right?" Bill tore a little piece of steak with his fingers and lowered it to Maud. "Is it all paid for?" Maud reached up with her paw as if to take it.

"It is." I caught Bill's eye and shook my head. He brought his hand back up and rested his forearm on the table, the bit of meat hovering. Nonplussed, Maud lowered her paw, raised it again and then meowed more loudly before sitting down. "But I haven't been staying there much the last few months."

Reaching for my water glass, I could feel the soft brush of the strawberry blond hair on Bill's arm against mine. It was delicious. I lingered a moment too long with my hand on my glass.

"Oh?" Bill stood up, walked over to the cabinet, pulled out a small pottery plate, and put the piece of meat on it before setting it down on the floor next to the sink. Maud had not missed a second of Bill's movements and ran over, nearly tripping him as he made his way back to the table. "Where have you been staying?"

"With Sean, of course." Evelyn chimed in cheerfully.

My face flushed. I had been consciously avoiding the topic.

"Who is this, Sean? We don't really know anything about him." Bill sat back away from the table, brought one leg up across his knee, and grabbed his beer.

"Bill, I told you about Cori's young man." Evelyn said it with all the properness of my father's elderly aunts. I might have laughed out loud if it came from anyone else, but the farm often felt like a place out of time. "You've been seeing him quite a long time now. I remember your mother telling me how he came around to visit when she was ill."

"Yep, a long time. I'm staying at his place in the city. He's not always there much. As a photographer, he travels a lot for work. In fact, he's how I got connected with the travel editing gig. He's on a trip right now, traveling with a magazine writer." Bill grimaced, the muscles along his jaw visibly tightening. I continued, "He worried about me being alone at the house."

"Yeah, being alone in the city is a *much* better solution," he muttered.

"Bill," Evelyn chimed in, "Cori is a grown woman. That's her own business."

"It was hard, after Dad died. It was so unexpected. I had some tough days, it was—" I stuck the fork tines into my potatoes, piercing them over and over until they began to fall apart. *You don't need to make excuses for your feelings. That is what keeps you separated from them.* It was Dr. Lawrence in my head. Damn him and his logic. "I was–*had* a lot of anxiety," I blurted out and then sighed heavily.

"Perfectly natural," Evelyn said gently.

"And Sean, he was there for me. Just as he was when my mother died."

"Convenient." The legs of the chair scraped against the linoleum floor as Bill pushed away from the table. Without looking at me, he picked up his plate, went over to where Maud was still licking her chops and scraped the rest of the pan steak onto her little floral plate, onions, and all.

"Bill," Evelyn brought him up sharply. "Cori, you don't pay any attention to that. It's just that you are family and well, we look out for family around here."

I was angry at Bill's questioning of my relationship with Sean and with his feeding Maud after I had clearly indicated I didn't want him to give her table food. Maud, however, was quite happy to benefit from whatever human drama was playing out and began snapping up the meat, periodically looking over her shoulder like a lioness after a kill in case one of us might move to take it away from her. She could have had all our plates. My food stuck in my throat and Evelyn had folded her napkin.

In truth, Bill had said nothing I hadn't already thought.

"It works for us." It came out sounding defensive and not aloof, as I had hoped.

"I see that."

Looking from Bill to me and back again, Evelyn sighed. "Bill, I think it's time for me to go back upstairs. I'm exhausted." Bill didn't move from where he stood at the sink, hands balled into fists. "Bill?"

"Yeah, yes, of course. Let's get you back upstairs." Bill helped Evelyn rise to her feet by transferring her weight to the walker.

"It was lovely to be altogether again for dinner, wasn't it?" Evelyn said.

"It was," I answered. "And I'll take care of these dishes." I was unsure what else I could offer. Clearly my presence here was not helping anything. After a moment of awkward silence, I went and put my arms around Evelyn's tiny frame. "I'm sorry. I'll go after I clean up."

"Don't be ridiculous. You have nothing to apologize for. You'll stay as agreed."

"I'll get some fresh sheets on the bed as soon as I get you settled." Bill spoke in deference to Evelyn.

"I'm taking the couch," I said sternly and then added, "or I'm not staying."

"Suit yourself," Bill said just before he swept Evelyn up into his arms.

It was odd seeing Bill and Evelyn that way. More than odd. Painful. As I scraped and rinsed plates, I tried to get the image of Evelyn, draped in Bill's arms, out of my mind; her sinewy arms raised around his neck, long fingers of one hand holding the tiny wrist above the other and thin withered legs underneath the blue pant legs, feet covered in the small silk slippers she wore. I had once dreamed of Bill sweeping me into his arms. Dreams can change. Not that I didn't still want Bill. Despite everything, it was agony being near him earlier.

Feeling his leg near mine under the table. The way I wanted Bill had changed in my time away. Or maybe it was that it felt again as it had been. Having been gone for so many years, the intensity of what I felt had faded the way color drains away from a pressed flower. Longing, yes, but colorless, skeletal, and fragile. Being here had reignited something I had forgotten. It was real again. Physical. Present.

There was an edge to his anger with me that revealed a passion I responded to immediately. Evelyn had seen it. I shook when he questioned me about Sean, but not entirely from anger. There was something dark in the way I wanted him—the way I had wanted him that last night on the windbreak. There was something in him that understood the darkness in me.

Adding a squirt of detergent, I watched the sink fill with white foam and plunged the stack of plates into the hot water. I tried to shake off Bill's anger, yet I realized I was savoring it. Bill sounded jealous. It meant he cared for me more than I had let myself believe. His reaction had surprised me and yet it meant everything. This was something I should talk to Emile about. I never met this topic in our sessions head on. I always danced around the subject of Bill. To his credit, Dr. Lawrence never pushed it. Instead, we continued to work with my dreams. They were more frequent again. The fire. The woods. The wolf. I rinsed a plate and set it in the drain board. Reaching back into the soapy water, I grabbed another plate. Something pricked at the back of my mind. I brought my attention back to how I would bring up the subject of Bill with Dr. Lawrence. For the second time that night, the thought of Dr. Lawrence and his untroubled forehead comforted me. My breath deepened and again, I forced myself back to the dishes, back to the present.

As I bent to pick up the plate Bill had set out for Maud, I heard the faint chiming of my cell phone, muffled in my purse. Dr. Lawrence couldn't be that good. He couldn't sense my troubled thoughts from this distance, could he? Choosing to ignore the phone, I turned on the hot water tap again and pushed the small pottery plate with the sweep of blue flowers under the water. Transfixed by the softness of the water on my skin, I watched it rush from the tap and pour into the sink below. As I pulled the plate from the hot water there was a flash, an image. From a dream. A field. Water. Rocks. My hands shook. My breath was coming fast, but I could not get any air. My lungs would not fill. I stepped back, clutching the edge of the sink with one hand, plate in the other, growing so dizzy I thought I would black out.

"Cori, I think your phone is ringing."

I hadn't heard Bill come back downstairs. I jumped at the sound of his voice and the plate slipped from my hand, smashing into several large pieces on the floor. I just stood there looking at it, unable to register what had happened. My chest was heaving, and my hands were trembling. The trembling spread from my hands like a ripple until my whole body shook.

"I'm sorry, I didn't mean to scare you," Bill started apologetically. "Cori? Cori? What is it? What happened?"

When I did not respond, he called my name again.

"Cori!" He rushed over to where I stood unseeing in front of the broken pieces of pottery. I could hear him, but his voice seemed far away.

"Hey." He put his hands on mine to steady them. "Where are you? Where did you go?"

Finally, I managed to lift my eyes and look up at him, or someone looked at him, from deep inside a hollowness.

"It's okay," he whispered. "It's okay, love. Come here. Come on back." As I stood frozen, he wrapped his arms around me and pulled me to him. "You're safe," he said. "You're safe."

He said it over and over as I clung to him. Finally, I began to cry.

CHAPTER TWENTY-SEVEN

"I NEED TO go out and check on the horses before dark. Keep me company?" Bill asked when I finally stopped sobbing.

"Okay. Yeah. That sounds good," I said wiping my eyes with the heels of my hands.

"I'll just go let Evie know we're stepping out for a bit. Be right back. You okay?" He touched me lightly on the arm. The concern in his eyes almost started me crying again.

"Yep, I'm okay now." I followed him to the entryway and picked up my purse up from the small table that sat against the wall next to the stairway. "I'm just going to check my messages."

As Bill headed up, I pulled my phone out and looked at the missed number. It was Sean's. And he was home. Shit. I dialed into my voicemail with a feeling of dread. The tone of his voice was unmistakably angry. A wave of regret washed over me. I should have at least left a note. Regret turned to embarrassment by the time I reached the end of the message.

Corianne? Where are you? I got home and there's no trace of you. Or the cat. Not even a note for Christ's sake. Now you're not picking up. What's going on? Where are you? Are you okay? Call me as soon as you get this. Please. I love you.

The please sounded desperate. What had I done? I glanced up the stairs. I could hear the murmur of Bill and Evelyn's voices, some bumping around, and the creak of sticky dresser drawers. Walking back through the kitchen, I slipped out the back door with my phone. The strength of the signal was wavering from strong to barely there, but it was enough that I should be able to get a call out. I took a deep breath and hit the call-back button.

As I listened to the computerized ringing, I hoped Sean didn't answer. It would be easier to just leave him a message tonight and talk tomorrow. *Please don't pick up. Please don't pick up.* No such luck. He answered on the fourth ring. I tried to remember what I had rehearsed while I was packing. That seemed like days ago now.

"Hi." It was a lame beginning.

"Corianne, what the hell is going on? Where are you? Is everything all right?"

"I'm at the farm."

"At the farm? What on earth are you doing there?"

"I told you I wanted to come out here. That I needed to do this."

"Someday, sure. But on the night I'm coming home?"

"How the hell did I know you were coming home tonight? You didn't tell me. You didn't make our last call."

"I tried calling you from the airport. You didn't pick up. I thought I'd surprise you."

"Well congratulations. I'm surprised." The screen door opened. Bill stepped out, holding a dark colored cardigan. Turning away to shield this conversation from him, I lowered my voice and hissed, "Look, you haven't checked in for days. How was I supposed to know you'd come home early?" I had felt guilty and now I let that guilt turn into anger. It was easier.

Bill lingered nearby, waiting, and clearly uncomfortable. He motioned toward the barn, indicating that he would go on ahead. I raised my index finger and mouthed, "One minute." In my ear, Sean was elaborating on my inconsiderateness. It seemed it was my day to have people lecture me on my poor choices.

"Something could have happened to you. You should tell some-body where you're going."

"There was no one to tell."

"I was worried."

"I'm sorry." I could feel myself beginning to cave as I so often did, trying to sidestep a full-blown argument. "But aren't you the one al-ways telling me I need to get out and do more?"

"And aren't you the one who is always telling me that there is evil around every corner?"

"Touché."

"Jesus, you're starting to rub off on me. I thought one of your boo-gie men had finally come and grabbed you. Or that you had—" After a long pause he added, "I'm sorry. I just want you safe."

"I know."

"You can be impulsive."

"Now you sound like Dr. Lawrence."

"Maybe he's got a point."

"I needed to do this. I need to be here. With people who knew my mother. Lately I've started thinking…look," I changed tacks, "it's just where I need to be right now. Please try to understand. Honestly, I thought I'd be back before you got home." It wasn't exactly an apol-ogy, but it was the best I could do.

"When are you coming home?"

For the first time, he referred to the apartment, his apartment, as my home. It had always been his. My home was the house, as much as he hated my being there. He was good at this. Making me angry and then making me sorry. Saying something thoughtful or something he knew I had been waiting to hear just when I was making some deci-sions on my own again.

"Another day or two. I'll call tomorrow and let you know, okay?"

"Okay. Okay. You're sure you're good? You sound like you've been crying."

"I'm fine," I assured him, knowing full well that my voice was na-sally and thick from all the crying.

"Oh, and I assume you have the cat with you? Or is she at Kate's?"

"Maud is here with me."

"Ah, good. All right then. Look, I'm sorry. It's been a long day of airports and planes. I'm beat. I should get some sleep." The familiar warmth returned to his voice.

"I get that."

"Goodnight then, okay?"

"Goodnight"

"I love you, Cori. You know that."

"I know. Goodnight."

As the call ended, I realized how long my day had been and how tired I was from the drive, the anticipation, and now, the crying. I closed my eyes and drew a long shuddery breath of night air.

"You ready?" Bill called to me.

"Ready." I shoved my cell phone in my pocket and hurried over to where Bill stood waiting for me.

"Here." Bill held out the sweater. "It's still getting cool out here at night."

"Thanks."

I had assumed it was one of Evelyn's sweaters, but as I slid the cardigan over my arms, I realized it belonged to Bill. It smelled faintly of spice, fresh air, and sweat. Long on me, the banded bottom came down to the top of my thighs. The wool prickled against my bare arms. I didn't care. I was wearing Bill's sweater. I tugged up the sleeves.

"It'll do," Bill said casually, heading toward the barn, but there was a flicker of a smile on his lips as he shot me a sidelong look.

We walked along in silence for a while. Every sight, every smell, every crunch of gravel brought me back to my love for this place. It was like waking up, bit by bit. The sound of birds singing a last song as they nested for the night and the air, thick with the earthy smell of things green and growing, reminded me what I had missed while I was away. There was a tangible hum of energy at the farm and my body responded, each cell surging to life, echoing the hum, tuning to it.

"We lost one, you know." Bill's voice broke into my meditation.

"Lost one what?"

"Horse. We lost one of the horses."

A wave of sadness washed over me.

"Lucy," Bill answered my unspoken question. "We lost Lucy."

The quiet fell on us again, heavier now, and we finished the walk to the barn in silence. With a loud clack, Bill slid back the bolt on the door and swung the wood sash up and over. I heard the shuffle of hooves and a few snorts. Bill waved me ahead. Walking in, I saw Knight's massive black head shining like glossy crow feathers. A warm amber light slanting through the window in the hayloft revealed dust motes and bits of hay. I approached slowly and as I did, Knight, lifted his dark eyes.

"Knight?" I was unsure he would remember me after all this time. He looked me directly in the eye but remained motionless. Finally, he made a soft noise, something between a whinny and a snort, and nosed my shoulder. I lifted my hand slowly and he bowed his head to let me pat him on his broad nose. He blustered a little and I pulled my hand back, but he bumped me again and then lifted his nose to my face. I remembered reading somewhere that horses smell each other's breath as a way recognizing each other. In any case, he seemed to remember that we were friends. I heard another voice from what where Lucy's stall had been.

"This is Mac." As Bill said her name, she came over and butted Bill affectionately. He obliged, picking up a brush and pulling it over her with an expert hand. Mac's deep reddish-brown coat gleamed under the brush. Being a Clydesdale, Mac had a short dark mane, which Bill brushed to a point between her eyes which hung over a little more to one side. That coupled with her broad white nose and white legs with their longer hair, made her look decidedly playful. "I brought her in a little while after Lucy died. It wasn't right for Knight to be alone. It took me a bit to train her up. She'd been on the MacAllister farm, and that old son of a bitch couldn't take care of her anymore but wouldn't let her go. Something about it having been his daughter's horse."

"Wasn't she the one killed in a car accident several years ago?"

"Yeah. Wrapped herself around a tree. He won't talk about it, but everyone assumes she'd been drinking. I made three offers on her before that bastard gave her up."

"I get that, I guess. A last connection to his daughter. That would be hard." I thought of the things I still had around that belonged to my parents, including an old wooden box full of letters and a pair of mismatched cufflinks.

"Grief doesn't do that animal any good."

"She's here now, that's what counts, isn't it?"

"Yeah, that's what counts. You should see these two out in the paddock. She's a pest, but Knight is just old enough to be patient with her. She feels safe."

Walking over to the saddlery, I ran my hand over one of the worn leather seats. "I can't get over how much I missed all this. How much I had forgotten. Now I'm realizing it was all still there somewhere. I know that now that I can reach out and touch it."

"That's what the city does to people. It gives them amnesia. They forget things. Important things." Bill lifted the brush up and looked at me over his shoulder. "How do you do it, Cori? How do you live there, knowing what you do?"

"What do you mean, knowing what I do?"

"Does he always talk to you that way?"

"What way?" I assumed now we were talking about Sean.

"Like he owns you."

"How do you know how he talks to me? Were you listening to my phone call?"

"Kind of hard not to. You were practically shouting when I came out. It wasn't hard to figure out what the other side of the conversation was."

"I told you, he's good to me. He worries is all. I should have told him I was coming. I made a mistake."

"He wants to control you is more like it. Own you."

"Like you own Mac."

"No." Bill tossed the brush and wheeled to look at me. "Not like that. I take care of Mac. I know what she needs."

"And I suppose you know what I need and Sean...Sean is just some psycho and I... I fell into his clutches like some stupid little girl."

Bill crossed the barn in three long strides and grabbed me by the shoulders. Mac shifted nervously. Knight whinnied in alarm.

"I do know you, Cori. You know I do." His eyes sparked with something I had never seen before and before I could say anything else, he kissed me roughly.

"Bill, stop it." I tried to wrench free. "You're scaring me." I had imagined Bill kissing me again many times, but I had never imagined it happening like this.

Knight whinnied again.

An old terror rose, closing off my throat and making my voice break. Part of me wanted to run, but even if he hadn't been holding my shoulders, I felt frozen. My breath came fast, but I couldn't seem to draw any air.

"Bill," I pleaded.

His grip relaxed. He peered into my face, his eyes searching mine.

"I know you," he said softly.

"I know. I know you do." Tears were streaming down my face. Bill kissed my wet cheek tenderly.

"I'm sorry, Cori. Please. Dammit. I didn't mean to frighten you. I never want to be the one who frightens you. Please don't cry Coriander."

He hadn't called me that since my mom was dying. Bill had given me that name the day we buried the dead rabbit, there on the grassy windbreak.

"You haven't called me that in a long time." I turned my face away. The fear drained from my body, replaced by wave after wave of regret. My father was gone three years and all I had done was hide from my grief, from fragments of memory and my suspicions about how my mother died. "I'm not even sure she's in there anymore."

"She's there." Bill took my hand in his. "I can feel her. I've always felt her." He let my hand drop and turned his back, running both hands through his gray hair, now winged with blonde.

"Do you remember what you said? Why you called me that?" Among the stalls and hay of the barn, my voice sounded like it came from somewhere outside me at the same time it was close.

"Yeah. Because you grow wild. Because you were already old somehow."

"I'm tired Bill."

"That's because you're always fighting. Like that rabbit. Trying to outrun the coyote. Watching for the hawk."

"I'm tired of fighting. So was my mother."

"You don't have to. Not here. Not with me." He sank down on an old cot that sat along the wall under the hayloft.

"That's new." I pointed at the cot.

"Yeah. Lots of things are new." Leaning forward, resting his elbow on his knees, Bill brought the palms of his hands together, almost as if he was going to pray. "I'm sorry I scared you. I guess I'm tired too."

"It's okay."

"I never want you to be afraid of me. *Me* for god's sake. The only thing I ever wanted was to make sure you're safe."

"That seems to be going around."

"I guess you have someone else for that now."

"Why do you hate him so much? You don't even know him."

"I don't need to meet Sean. I know a guy like that a mile away. He's not good enough for you Cori. You deserve more than being kept in that cage of an apartment and fed a few affectionate scraps."

"That's not fair. He has been there for me. So many times. It was bad when my mom was sick, and when she died. I was alone in that house when my father shut down."

"I wanted to. I wanted to go to you."

"Why didn't you?" The memory of the sight of my mother, wasting away in her bed, arms so thin her veins looked like bits of rope,

pricked at me. The weird sickening smell of her hospice room bal-
looned up from stomach and into my throat.

"I had obligations."

"Obligations?" I was getting angry until I remembered Evelyn in
her room upstairs. At least I had had my father for a few more years,
until the heart attack. "Look, I don't want to fight. You had your hands
full. As much as I wished you to come, you had Evelyn. Have Evelyn,"
I corrected myself. It was an awkward moment and neither of us
spoke. There was only the breathing of the horses.

"I have something to show you," Bill said getting up off the cot and
picking up a lantern-style flashlight off the makeshift shelf nailed up
next to the cot. "Come with me?" He held out his hand. I slipped my
hand in his and felt it enveloped by strength and warmth.

"Where are we going?"

"You'll see."

Silence fell between us again as we headed out of the barn, but now
it was our old comfortable quiet. With a gentle squeeze, Bill steered
me away from the house. We walked to the gap in the split-rail fence
that led past the paddock, out to the fields, and out to the windbreak.

It was still early enough in the summer that the grass was fresh
and green, soft underfoot and against my bare ankles. Its sweet smell
mingled with the musky damp scent of earth still rising from the
fields, which had been watered that morning and were now wet again
with the dew that was beginning to form as the day cooled. I walked
through a fine mist that seemed to rise from the earth rather than fall
from the sky. I smiled, remembering how the mist seemed to form as
the plants exhaled. I had been away from this place, from the earth too
long. Now my body remembered every sensation. The way it felt to
kneel in the dirt, digging, weeding, and tending. My body woke to the
memory of the water contained in its own cells. A boundary disappeared between the ground beneath me, the air, my body, and Bill's.
For a moment, we were all marvelously connected. I took another
deep breath, wanting to draw in that feeling all the way down into my
core and hold it, but the there was something else in that earthy smell.

Something unsettling. I stopped. The open feeling collapsed, severing me from the air. From Bill. I fell heavily, solidly, into the earth.

I jerked my hand away from Bill's. The flashlight dropped to the ground with a thud. For the second time that night, my hands began to shake as a tremor moved through me.

"What…? Cori? Cori what's wrong? Is it happening again? Is it like at the house? Tell me what's happening. I want to help."

I could hear the fear in his voice. It echoed my own. In front of me, a girl's broken body lie in a low creek, smudged with dirt, bits of leaves and dried grass in her blonde hair. Nothing had any color except her blond hair, which seemed impossibly shiny given the rest. Soft and clean. If I leaned close, I knew I would still be able to smell her apple shampoo. Bill's voice was urgent and close. He was repeating my name. I wanted to look at him, but I couldn't pull my eyes away from the girl.

"Cori." Bill had me by the shoulders again. "Cori, look at me. Come on." He took my face in his hands and shook me lightly. "Corianne, for god's sake. Come on now."

I shut my eyes tightly. When I opened them, it was Bill in front of me.

"Oh, thank god."

Pulling away, I turned to look for the girl in the grass. My thoughts were confused. It was like waking from a nightmare, but I hadn't been asleep. My mind struggled to lie down new tracks. The body wasn't here. Bill was here. Why is Bill in my dream? Bill is real. I am with Bill. Where is the body?

"Did you see her? I saw her. She was here."

"No one is here. No one is here, Cori. It's just us. Just you and me."

I looked frantically between Bill and the grass.

"But I saw her. I *saw* her."

"Saw who?"

My hand clenched and unclenched, fingers working the fabric of my skirt. Bill looked down at my hand. Even in my confused state, I saw recognition dawning on his face.

"Who did you see?"

"I'm cold."

"Who did you see, Corianne?" Bill repeated the question more in-sistently.

"Rebecca."

"Rebecca? You saw her standing here?"

"No. I saw her there," I pointed to the long grass at the edge of the field. "Dead."

"Okay, we need to get you back to the house. Now."

"I don't want to go back to the house."

"Cori, you just saw a dead girl. I don't think I need to tell you that's not normal. And look at you. You're shaking."

"I'm cold," I repeated.

"All the more reason to get you back to the house. We can call that shrink of yours. What's his name?"

"Dr. Lawrence."

"We can call Dr. Lawrence."

"I want to go to the windbreak."

"Are you...?" He stopped himself from saying what we were both thinking. "Not now. We can do that tomorrow when it's light out."

"I want to go now." My muscles were rigid. I shivered so much that my voice shook.

"That's a bad idea." Bill set his jaw and studied me for a long mo-ment. "You're going anyway, aren't you?"

"Yes."

"Dammit, you're stubborn girl." He interlaced his fingers and put both hands behind his neck. "I don't like this. Not for a minute. But I'm not about to let you go out there alone. And we both know you're going, one way or the other." His hands dropped back down to his sides as if he threw them. "Are you sure I can't talk you out of this?"

"I'm sure."

"Okay then," he reached down and caught the edges of the cardi-gan I wore, which still hung open, and began to tenderly button each button. "But if you see her again, I'm taking you right back to the house. If I have to throw you over my shoulder and carry you there. Got it?"

"Got it." I answered looking down at his hands working the buttons. Reaching out, I cupped his face in my hands. I felt the warmth of his skin beneath my hand and the bristle of his whiskers. "Thank you."

He took one my hands and kissed the palm softly.

"You're sure about this?"

"I'm sure."

"Okay. Let's do this."

Bill let go of me just long enough to pick up the flashlight from where it had fallen in the grass and then took hold of my arm. We walked wordlessly the rest of the way to the windbreak. It was almost dark when we finally got there. The trees were silhouetted against a sky that trembled somewhere between purple and deep blue.

"Do you remember your way?" Bill's question broke the silence.

"I remember."

I picked my way along the uneven ground and familiar ruts, some of them deeper and wider now, carved out by rain and the endless shifting and heaving of the land. I knew where I wanted to go and pulled free. It was too dark to be sure, but I felt I was in the right spot. Bill clicked on the lantern. It was there in front of us, clearly visible in the yellow light. The place where we had buried the rabbit. One side had sunken, there being nothing left of the rabbit's body to hold it up anymore, while the other side swelled like a great wave of earth. Rambling across it was a spreading clump of purple prairie clover with its phallus of tufted blooms. It seemed right. While the bones of the animal rested beneath, surely its spirit would live above, sleeping in the soft grass and nibbling on flowers born of its body.

I knelt and looked for the white stone I had placed as a marker so many summers ago, running my hands back and forth through the grass. Finally, I felt something. Something cold and smooth. I dug deeper into the tangle of grass and worked the edges with my fingers, prying the object up. There were small tearing sounds as the grass gave way. It was the stone, the underside dark and muddy and the top still bleached by the sun. I wished I could wash it, but there was no water at this part of the farm. None of the irrigators reached here and the reservoir was further out past the windbreak and this field, closer to the land still owned by the Solomons. I crumbled off what dirt I could. It fell back into the grass in cold, damp clumps. Resetting the tiny headstone by twisting it this way and that into the dirt, I felt it grind against something else. My fingers dug in the grass again and worked at prying it loose. Another stone probably. These fields were always giving up rock from their sleeping beds. Again, the tearing where my dirt smudged fingers could not separate grass from what I was attempting to plunder. What came loose was not a stone. It was long and thin. A small bone.

"What is that?" Bill had been standing quietly, holding the light, watching, and now saw me unearth something else.

"It's a bone." I held it up for him to see. He walked over and took it from my hand, turned it over and around.

"That's an animal bone." He cast a glance at the grave. "Likely one from that rabbit. Maybe from the front leg."

I took the bone from his hand and held it up to my forearm. Finally, I lowered it, meaning to replace it where I had found it. I hesitated. There was something in me that didn't want to give up the relic I had found. I felt I was meant to find it. The rabbit had given it to me. I moved to put it in the pocket of my skirt. If Bill disapproved, he wasn't saying. Perhaps after everything I had been through that night he decided it wasn't worth arguing with me.

"Be careful. There are sharp edges on it. And it wouldn't hurt to wash it." He reached into his own pocket and produced a handkerchief. "Here. Wrap it up in that."

Carefully, I opened the handkerchief on the ground, placed the small bone in the center and wrapped it carefully before placing the bundle of cloth and bone in my pocket. As I got to my feet, a surge of something moved through me. I didn't brighten exactly, but I felt I was stronger for having the rabbit spirit with me.

"You wanted to show me something," I remembered.

"Maybe now isn't the best time."

"No," I touched his sleeve gently. "I want to see. What is it?"

He pointed and I felt his other hand settle at the nip of my waist as I turned to look. I gasped. There to the edge of the windbreak, beneath the tree where I had carefully placed my gathered stones, there now rose from a foundation of larger rock, not a wall, but a structure about three feet high and two feet wide. A stone altar, more beautiful and complex than anything I did or could do. There were dried bits of dandelion and wildflowers lining the top edge along with a few smaller stones, a stick, and an old bottle cap.

"When? When did you do this?"

"I didn't set out to do it. It started after you left. I found a stone I thought you'd like, and I couldn't just leave it. So, I kept it. Brought it over here so you would find it when you came back. Then I found another one. And another one. It's your fault, dammit. Because of you I can't help but look at the goddamned rocks. Then you didn't come. And the pile kept getting bigger. I thought I should do something with them all. I thought you'd like this."

"Oh, I do like it. I think it's beautiful. It might be the most beautiful built thing I've ever seen." I squeezed his arm. "When I die, I want to be buried here, with the rabbit, under this old tree. And you will come and leave flowers for us." I kissed his cheek.

"Oh god. You're not dying, Cori. Don't even say that."

"Everything dies. You know that."

"Yeah, okay. Everything dies. But you're not dying anytime soon so stop it right now."

"It'll be alright. When it's time. I think it will be alright. I won't be afraid. As long as—it will be okay." I stopped without finishing the thought.

"As long as what?"

"Do you believe in hell, Bill?"

"No. I think we have plenty of hell right here on earth."

I frowned and lowered my head.

"I guess you're right," I said. But I thought of the dreams of fire, of the visions of Rebecca's body, and I wasn't sure I believed him. Easing my hand into my pocket, I touched the handkerchief to make sure the bone was still there.

"Is that what you're worried about? Going to hell?"

"No, I suppose not. There are just some things I don't want to leave undone. My mother left things undone. Unsaid." I bent down and picked a bit of clover bloom from the grave and set it on the altar with the other offerings.

Bill clicked off the lantern and set it on the rocks. We stood there quietly for a long while before he felt for my hand.

"I love you, Coriander."

"I know."

CHAPTER TWENTY-EIGHT

WE WALKED BACK to the house without speaking. I didn't know how long we had been gone. The house was completely dark, save for the light over the kitchen sink and a small soft glow upstairs. Evelyn's light was still on. She was reading or waiting for Bill.

Bill swung open the back screen door and held it for me as I stepped through.

"We ought to discuss the sleeping arrangements," he said as I ducked under his arm. "You should take the room upstairs. I'll take the couch." He kicked off his shoes without untying them and left them on the braided rug at the door. I enjoyed seeing him in his jeans and socks. I had always felt there was something very intimate about a man taking off his shoes in my company, something erotic in his being completely dressed except for his shoes. I couldn't explain it. I suppose it revealed vulnerability—or freedom. When I was a kid, I was always kicking off my shoes. Now as I thought about it, looking at Bill's feet in heather gray socks to which bit of grass still clung, I'd stopped running barefoot long ago.

"No," I answered. "I think it would be best if you were upstairs—in case Evelyn needs something overnight. I wouldn't know what to do for her." Bill grimaced but could not deny my logic.

"Okay, I'll go get some sheets and some blankets from the linen closet."

"It's pretty warm," I called out softly after him, walking into the living room. "One blanket should do." He turned and looked over his shoulder as he headed up the stairs.

"Not the way you've been shivering tonight."

I shook my head. He was right. Looking around the room for my overnight bag, I remembered that while Bill and I had gone to get my car and move it into driveway before dinner, I had left the bag in back. The curtains were drawn, and I headed to the front door picking my way among the shadowy shapes in the living room guided by the light that fell from the stairway fixture and my memory of where the furniture had been. Mostly, it was still what I remembered, the overstuffed armchair with the ruffled skirt, a brown davenport, and a round end table. A familiar pair of amber eyes glowed out of the corner from under an old footstool.

I turned the doorknob and pulled on the old oak door. Swollen in the warm humid air, the wood groaned against its frame, refusing to budge. Bracing with my left hand against the frame in layers of varnish and dirt that were sticky with age, I yanked hard on the doorknob with my right hand. At last, the door gave with a reluctant squeak. Startled, Maud darted out from the footstool and disappeared deeper into the house. "Sorry," I whispered and slipped out onto the porch.

The car sat as I had left it, parked in the turnaround, nose pointed out for an easy getaway just in case the remainder of the evening did not go well. The large leaves of an old sugar maple stirred slowly in the breeze, its thick limbs taking time to find their momentum. I shivered. Something else felt near to me. Something dark. A sliver of moon slid in and out of thick clouds. I stood stock-still and listened. There was only the sound of the trees, the rustling corn, and the occasional hoot of an owl perched somewhere on the rooftop. That was it, I reassured myself. That was why I felt watched. Though interested in the field mice and other small animals waking up for their nighttime foraging, the owl could surely see me. I made mental note to keep Maud inside at night. The owl might decide she was worth a try.

The dome light went on as I opened the passenger-side car door. My black overnight bag sat on the floor behind the driver's seat, right where I had left it. I grabbed the handles and yanked it up and over the center console. A few cat hairs flew into the air. I was still leaning half in the car when I heard gravel crunch on the driveway. I pulled up with a start, smacking the back of my head hard on the doorframe for the second time that day. As they connected, there was a solid whack.

"God dammit!" I winced and jerked the bag free, prepared to use it to defend myself if necessary. The back of my head stung, and I saw stars. Instinctively, I pulled myself clear and closed the door quickly, knowing the light illuminating me put me at a disadvantage.

"Do you need a hand?" It was Bill's voice coming around the car.

"Dammit, Bill. You scared the hell out of me." The sharp pain and stinging sensation on the back of my head was quickly replaced by a more widely broadcast throbbing. I put my hand up to the back of my head and felt for blood, but my hair was dry. In this case, it seemed I was as hardheaded as Sean always accused me of being.

"Sorry. Are you okay?"

"I hit my head is all."

Bill put his hand over mine. "Let me have a look."

"I'm fine," I said.

"Humor me."

"Whatever." I pulled my hand away and bowed my head down. Bill's fingers probed gently underneath my hair. "Ouch." I winced.

"You've got a fine lump starting. Might want to get some ice on that." His hand lingered for a moment and then taking my head in his hands, he kissed my head softly. "There now."

"Thanks." I lifted my head. My eyes were adjusting to the dark again and I could see Bill's hair ruffle in the breeze. The light coming from the upper window of the house outlined his jaw. One side of his face shone like a sliver of moon.

He leaned in and kissed me softly on the mouth. I didn't pull away this time. My eyes closed. His lips were warm and soft as they caught mine. It was a quiet and tender kiss. And then it was over.

"There now," he said again.

With eyes still closed, I savored it. The gentleness of it. No one had ever kissed me like that. Not Sean, not anyone. I thought this feeling must be what Dr. Lawrence meant by peace. I did not want to run. I wanted to surrender to it, the feeling of being small and safe, and open. The feeling didn't last. I remembered Evelyn in her bed, waiting for Bill. Waiting for morning. Waiting to wake up to a different reality. Or wishing she wouldn't wake up at all. Like my mother. Rebecca never had a choice, that morning and every morning after had been taken from her. Rebecca in her purple dress with the yellow flowers. My eyes snapped open.

"I think I need to go to bed. I'm tired from the drive." I stepped back and held my bag in front of me. Bill took the bag from me.

"Then we should make up your bed."

Inside, Bill had turned on the small brass lamp that sat on the table in the corner of the living room nearest the couch. On the couch sat a neat stack of sheets in different colors, two thin plaid cotton blankets, and a pillow in a white case. I picked up the pillow, which was somehow thin and yet leaden at the same time. The pillowcase was soft and worn, with tidily embroidered pink rosebuds along the hemstitch. I ran my fingers along the flowers, Evelyn's mother's needlework, no doubt. I could feel its age.

"Still the same pillows, I see."

"Like I said, we haven't had many visitors."

"It's fine. Like old times." Setting the pillow on a chair, I set about making up my bed, unfolding an old seafoam green sheet first and tucking it underneath the bottom cushions. Bill opened the white sheet and laid it on top, then spread out one of the blankets. I tried in vain to fluff the pillow before I placed it against the arm of the couch.

"There," I said. "Just like the Ritz, but without the mint on my pillow." Bill opened his mouth to say something. I held up my hand. "I'm kidding." We both laughed.

"There's an extra blanket here," Bill gestured to the end of the couch.

"I think I'll be fine."

"I still wish you'd put ice on that bump." He reached a hand up to check it, but I stepped to the side and started rummaging in my bag, pulling out my toothbrush.

"It'll be fine."

"Right. If you need anything." Bill didn't finish the thought.

"I know where things are," I said, trying to sound nonchalant.

"Go ahead. I'll check in on Evelyn."

"Okay, thanks."

Slipping off my sandals, I headed up the steep stairs, toothpaste and toothbrush in hand. My bare feet hit the cold bathroom tile and I reached back for the old black light switch in the hallway. It clicked on with a loud snap. I closed the white painted door as I heard the door to Evelyn's room open and close softly. Setting about my nightly rituals, I imagined Bill sitting on the edge of the bed holding Evelyn's hand, explaining why he had been away so long, kissing her cheek. Would she know? Did his shirt collar smell like me or were the odors of the farm so pungent, so present, that all she would discern was the scent of his sweat and the land mixed with the sweet and heavy approach of rain. I would know, I thought. If it was Sean. I did know.

I turned on the faucet and bent to the sink to wash my face. The water was cool and had the faint odor of the river. The smell used to bother me, but I had grown to like its soft mossy scent. I had neglected to take a towel from the linen closet on my way in but looking to the towel bar I saw Bill had already thought of that. On the silver bar hung a pale pink bath towel and a matching washcloth. Evelyn had always set out the same special set of pink towels for me when I came to stay.

It felt good to rinse the road from my skin. As I hung the washcloth carefully on the towel bar to dry, I looked in the mirror and studied my face. I brought a hand to my lips. I could still feel Bill's kiss. I clicked off the light and pulling the door open partway, peeked out into the hall. The door to Evelyn's room was closed. The room at the end of the hall was still dark and open. I crept downstairs as quietly and slipped out of my skirt and top, and quickly pulled on an old Georgetown t-shirt I had pulled out of Sean's drawer at the last minute. I rarely wore anything to bed anymore, but I would not scandalize Sheerfolly Chapel by sleeping nude on Evelyn Butchart's couch with her husband upstairs. Not that Evelyn would know the difference, I supposed. Exhausted, I crawled between the sheets, temporarily displacing Maud, who had taken advantage of the fact that I had been busy upstairs to move in. The sore spot on the back of my head burned when it contacted the limp pillow. I winced.

Upstairs, a door opened and closed. There was the sound of running water then floorboards creaking overhead. I waited for the sound of the guest room door clicking shut, but it never came. Straining my ears, I listened in the dark. I thought I could hear a small sigh as he settled into bed. It was sinking in. Here I was. Not dreaming about being here, here— on the couch in the well-worn t-shirt of a man who didn't seem to know how to love me no matter how hard he tried, the man I had always loved sleeping upstairs, and a moody cat sleeping on my feet.

Bill was right about calling Dr. Lawrence. Still, I was still glad he had forgotten. Closing my eyes, I tried not to think of what an impossible situation it was. The feel of Bill's mouth on mine had reignited my hunger for him. *Hail Mary, Full of grace, the Lord is with Thee.* But Mary knew where I had been tonight. She knew what I had done. She knew right now, in this moment, I wasn't really sorry. I wanted the ache. I wanted Bill. And as I fell asleep, I saw in her peaceful face a look of disapproval, maybe even revulsion, and beneath her outstretched arms was a little girl in a purple dress, blood in her shiny blond hair.

The fire came again as it always did, beginning with the sudden draft and the ember which left the hearth and caught fire on the wooden floorboards. Licking the planking, the flames reached out and fed greedily on everything. Table, chairs, and eventually the walls themselves. The pub was empty. Only I knew it burned. I tried to go for water. Finding the way blocked, I called out for help. There was no reply, only the growing roar of the fire and the smoke, which stole my voice. The heat was unbearable. Catching up the fabric of my long full skirts in two fists, I ran for the door and lifted the lock. As it swung open, the fire rushed up the stairs, forcing me out in the rupture of heat and smoke. I fell into the dirt and scrub of the yard and crawled as far away as I could. Coughs wracked my body and my lungs strained to suck in fresh air. The roar grew louder as the window exploded. Looking over my shoulder, I saw Mary standing in the doorway with her placid smile and her arms outstretched. The girl in the flowered dress stood with her, the dark cord of a bruise around her neck, blood staining her silky blond hair, and waved for me to come. I passed out face down in the dirt.

When I woke, Bill was shaking me as I gasped for breath.

"Cori, wake up," he was saying softly. "Cori, wake up. You're having a bad dream."

I sat straight up on the couch, panicked, still seeing the fire. I sputtered, trying to catch my breath. *What was Bill doing here?* Soaked with sweat and trembling, I threw my arms around him.

"Jesus, your heart is pounding. Shh, shh, shh. It's okay now. You're okay." He held me tight and rocked me in his arms. "You're okay. I've got you."

Gradually, I trusted my lungs were filling with good, clean air. The gulping breaths subsided. The pounding of my heart slowed. My head against his shoulder, I shivered and then surrendered to his soft words and the warmth and strength of his arms.

"Do you want to tell me about it?" Bill finally whispered. I lifted my head and looked at him. Tears filled my eyes again and though my mouth opened, no words came out. He stroked my cheek gently with the back of his hand and then held me tightly again. "That's fine. You don't have to talk right now. But you're soaking wet. I think we should get you some dry clothes, okay?"

I nodded again. Bill looked up at the stairs and then toward the kitchen.

"C'mon. Let's get you freshened up and into something dry." Standing up, he held out his hand. I took it, but my legs were too wobbly to stand. I shook my head. Bending down, he scooped me up in one fluid motion. Maud watched with concern. I wrapped my arms around him and let my head fall against his shoulder once more.

Bill carried me through the dark kitchen and out the back door to the barn. Behind the barn was an outdoor shower that he used when the work on the tractor left him so dirty Evelyn wouldn't let him in the house until he at least got the first layer off. I had always wanted to use it when I had come here as a kid, an impulse which my mother squelched. It was like the shower at the pool, I told her. She told me it was not appropriate for a young woman. Now, Bill set me down and stood me under the giant showerhead.

"I'll be right back. I'm just going to get a towel and some dry clothes." He stepped away slowly, holding out his hand as if I would fall when he took it away. "Will you be okay?"

I nodded again. As I waited for Bill to come back, my eyes adjusted to the night. I looked up at the hundreds of stars visible here so far from any city lights. I made out the boxy outline of the constellation Lupus, near Scorpius. A light went on in the barn. The halo of light stopped just before the shower, but the stars were lost to me all the same. Bill came back with one of his shirts and a towel, both of which he set down on a homemade wooden bench sitting to the side of the makeshift shower.

"It's not the Ritz," he echoed my earlier tease. "But there's water and soap. You can rinse off. I'll wait for you in there." He pointed to the barn. I just looked at him. My arms felt like lead. I shook my head.

"C'mon girl," he said it so softly it was almost a whisper. He took my hand and led me back two steps. When I was clear, he turned the faucet. Water made its way up along the old pipe and after a few seconds, burst from the showerhead. Putting his hands on the hem of the t-shirt, he paused. "You okay if I do this?" I nodded once more, and he lifted the damp shirt from my body and over my head. The cool night air washed over my already damp skin. My skin tightened against the cold and goosebumps rose on my arms. Bill's hands were at my hips, fingers working the slim band of my panties away from my body. Bending, he slid them down my bare legs. I stood naked in the night. Naked to this man.

"I'm sorry. This is going to be cold." Again, taking my hand, Bill guided me under the shower. I closed my eyes and let the water pour down over my head, my face, my skin, which had been so hot in the fire. He had pulled on an old pair of jeans and a cotton shirt. Only his feet were bare, yet he didn't worry about the water which splashed and soaked into his clothes, the hem of his jeans acting like a sponge. Reaching around me, Bill took the bar of soap from the shelf. I closed my eyes and listened as he wet the soap, turning it through his hands until it lathered. Then setting it aside, he slid his soaped hands along my arms. I opened my eyes and watched him. His eyes met mine as he washed away the heat, soot, and sweat. I let my eyes close again. His hands moved along my back, my neck and over my breasts, cupping them softly underneath, holding their fullness in his hands for just a moment before moving down over my ribs and stomach. Then bending he washed my legs, not avoiding the place between my legs, but not deliberate in his touch either. He stood again and I leaned back letting the cold water run through my hair and over my face. I took a drink of the fresh water as it ran into my mouth. The water I could not find.

Bill turned off the faucet and the water slowed to a trickle, then drip-dropped onto the raised wooden slats that served as the shower floor. Taking the towel from the bench, he threw it over one shoulder, first wringing out my hair and then patting me down, blotting my hair and drying my skin. When I was dry, he held up the old shirt he had brought from the barn. Obediently, I slipped in one arm and then the other. Pulling it up on my shoulders, he began buttoning it for me just as he had the sweater. Fingers leaving the last button, he leaned in and kissed me, softly again, drinking the drop or two of water which still clung to my lips.

"There now, that's better."

I wrapped my arms around him. His arms answered and came around me, holding me tightly.

"Coriander." He said it as gently as he had done everything else. "My sweet wild girl."

"I don't want to go back to the house. Not right now." They were the first words I had spoken since Bill had shaken me from my dream. My voice was rough. I could feel relief flood Bill's body as I spoke.

"Do you want to tell me about it?" he asked.

"I can't," I said stepping away. The immediacy of it all had begun to recede, but the images were still clear, and I knew I did not want to feel that way again. I wanted to stay here, clean under the stars. Clean as Bill's hands had made me.

"You can stay out here, Cori, but you shouldn't be alone. You've not been feeling well tonight."

"You can't leave Evelyn alone." The reality of where I was seeped into the edges of my consciousness. "She shouldn't wake up in that house by herself. I'll be fine now. I'm used to the dreams. I'll stay right here, I promise."

"I'd feel a lot better if you'd let me call Dr. Lawrence like I wanted. What happened, I don't even know what happened, but it's not normal. Even I know enough to know that."

"I'm much better now." I tried to sound cheerful. Bill regarded my announcement with healthy skepticism. I revised my statement. "I'm okay now."

After some more back and forth, Bill finally agreed to my sleeping in the barn on the cot. He went up to the house to grab fresh blankets and brought me Maud for company. She looked puzzled and wary. Her amber eyes could see fine in the dark. Bill dropped her on the cot where I sat hugging my legs. She let out a loud a guttural sound like a tiny bobcat. From his stall, Knight snorted. Maud lifted her head and stretching herself out, sniffed delicately at the air, trying to learn more about our new roommates.

"See," I reached out and scratched Maud behind the ears. She shrugged me off. "We'll be just fine."

"I'm leaving the lantern here for you. And I'm going to be out here twice before dawn to check on you two." Bill gave me a stern look. "Stay put."

I saluted.

"Cute. You're sure?"

"What's going to happen to me in the barn except for a few spider bites?" My voice had more conviction than I felt. Still, I couldn't stand to be in the house. I needed to be here. Without reason, I knew it.

"Get in under those blankets before you catch your death." He realized his poor choice of words. "You're shivering again."

I swung my legs up and Bill covered me, tucking the blankets tight around me. He looked around trying to locate Maud, who had begun to explore a little further from the cot.

"I'll close the door on my way out and we'll hope for the best. Plenty of ways she could get out of here, but I think she'll stick close to you tonight. I know I would. Try to get some sleep."

And with that, Bill clicked off the light and I was alone again.

CHAPTER TWENTY-NINE

EXHAUSTED THOUGH I was, sleep only came in small bursts. I was afraid to close my eyes again. Afraid to dream. It had not been like this in a long time—since I had felt this hunted, even with walls around me. It was safe here, I knew that. But when I closed my eyes, I saw the grasses. I saw Rebecca, her mouth opened in surprise. Now, I also saw the fire.

My eyes snapped open again. Moonlight sifted through the gaps in between the old barn boards making a triptych of the wall opposite on which hung an old rectangular mirror badly in need of resilvering, a stained and sweaty baseball hat, and a rusted horseshoe. If I squinted my eyes, looked through the boards, and moved my head just so, I could see the first hint of dawn's blue twilight beginning. Bill would be back soon. I had made it through the night. I sat up and leaned my back against the hard boards so that I would not fall asleep again. If I fell asleep, I would dream—and I wanted no more of these dreams. A little longer, I thought. Dawn is almost here. Hang on a little longer. Once the sun came up, it would be okay to walk up to the house.

It had been a long night and despite my best efforts, I grew drowsy again. Twice, my bobbing head woke me. Maybe it would be okay to lie down. I played a little game with myself. If I uncovered my legs, I would get cold and that would keep me awake. It didn't. I fell asleep again. At least this time there were no dreams, just heavy sleep.

The door swung open and thumped against the old iron lass that served as a doorstop. Bleary-eyed and disoriented, I smiled sleepily when I realized that what I saw was Bill coming toward me, a mug of steaming coffee in each fist.

"Rise and shine, girl. We've got work to do today."

"Hmph," I replied, my face still half buried in the pillow.

"Good to see you slept."

As I peeled open one eye again, Bill looked at me and then quickly looked away. He seemed overly preoccupied with finding a place to set down the extra mug of coffee. Looking down, I realized my make-shift nightshirt had shifted and I was in danger of spilling out. More than that, I remembered, I had no panties on. Hurriedly reaching down for the sheet to pull over my bare legs, I felt for the hem of the shirt. It was covering the important parts save the curve of one cheek. I thought I saw a small smile lift the corners of Bill mouth.

Covering up was instinctive. The modest thing, if a little late. Bill was not my lover, at least not by a strict definition. Yet last night he had touched me as gently as a lover would as he tended to my shaking feverish body. He had seen all of me. He had kissed me. At least I had a hazy memory of him kissing me.

"You had quite a night," Bill said, turning back to hand me both cups of coffee now that I had covered myself again. He dragged over an empty white plastic five-gallon bucket and turned it upside down, pulled something out of his back pocket, and sat down across from me. It was my cell phone. "Time to call that doc of yours."

Bill took his coffee and handed me the phone. I went to power it on then tossed it on the bed instead. "But I feel much better now," I insisted.

"Cori, I'm no expert, but what happened to you last night, that looked a lot like some kind of post traumatic shock or something."

"It was just a bad dream," I shrugged, taking a sip of coffee. "A very bad dream."

"Don't bullshit me, Corianne Dempsey. We both know it was a lot more than that." Bill's voice took a hard edge. It was a tone he had never taken with me. Parental. I didn't like it. Bill took the mug from my hands and set it down on the ground. Then he took both my hands in his. "Look, I don't know how much you remember about last night, but you were not all there. Something scared the life out of you, and it was like…it was like you were stuck someplace else. Stuck in that dream."

"I remember." My voice was quiet. "I'm sorry."

"Look," he sighed, kissing both my hands, "Don't be sorry. Just get well."

I didn't want to admit that he was right but the tears that started welling up in my eyes gave me away.

"Okay," I pulled my hands from his, picked the phone up off the blanket and powered it on. "I'll call."

"Good girl."

I powered up the phone and held it aloft, searching for a signal. Finally finding a connection, the phone began to buzz and chime. I had at least three messages. Not bothering to listen to them, I dialed Dr. Lawrence's number by heart, knowing full well at this early hour I would get his answering service. At least I could leave a message and Bill would relax.

You've reached Dr. Emile Lawrence. I'm not currently in the office. If this is an emergency, please dial 9-1-1. Otherwise, stay on the line to leave a message and I will get back to you as quickly as possible.

As I waited to leave a message, the quiet of the morning was interrupted by the sound of a car door slamming somewhere back near the house. Bill popped up, almost kicking over my coffee. He motioned to me that he was going to go investigate and, I knew, try to intercept whomever it was before they rang the bell and woke up Evelyn. I nodded and then heard the line click.

"You've reached the answering service of Dr. Lawrence. This is Darla speaking." The woman's voice was cool and professional.

"Yeah, hi. I'm a patient of Dr. Lawrence's. I need to get a message to him."

"Is this an emergency?" she asked.

Lady, if it had been a fucking psychiatric emergency, I'd probably be dead now, wouldn't I? Aloud I said, "Not exactly."

"And your name?"

"Corianne Dempsey."

"Can you please spell that?" she asked perfunctorily.

"C-o-r- i-a-n-n-e Dempsey, d-e-m p as in Peter s-e-y."

"And what seems to be the problem, Ms. Dempsey?"

Well Darla, my mind has finally become completely unhinged. Aloud, I replied, "I had an acute...episode last night. Nothing psychotic," I laughed, managing to make myself sound psychotic. "Anxiety. I'm a little fuzzy on it all, but my friend thought maybe it was some kind of PTSD thing." That was a lie, of course. I remembered the dream clearly. Remembered seeing Rebecca. What seemed like a dream was Bill scooping me up and taking me out to the barn. Yet here I was.

"And what is the best number to reach you?"

I gave my cell phone number and hung up just as Bill came back into the barn, visibly stressed.

"Sean is here," he announced through gritted teeth.

"Sean? Is here? Now? Why?"

"Yep. Seems he decided to worry about you not being home after all."

"But I told him I'd be home in just a couple of days," I said in disbelief.

"He said he tried calling." Bill was clearly annoyed.

I looked at the blinking blue light on my phone and groaned. "He must have called back yesterday after we talked. I turned my phone off. I didn't have a chance to listen. Shit, I better talk to him." I threw back the blanket.

"Not dressed like that, you won't."

"Sean's seen me in less than this." I swung my legs out of bed and slammed back the last of the coffee.

"Not *quite* like this. Not coming from the general direction of the barn, in the morning, dressed in another man's shirt—and nothing else."

"I don't suppose you brought me a pair of panties."

"I have to say that wasn't the first thing on my mind, no."

"I'm hurt," I teased.

"Let me rephrase that. Your state of undress has been very much on my mind. A plan for sneaking your underthings past Sean was not."

"Fair enough. Any other ideas?"

"I did hang up your wet things last night. With the morning sun, they might be dry by now." He walked out around the side of the barn and came back with my t-shirt and panties. Without thinking, I hurriedly stepped into the panties and started to unbutton the shirt. Bill cleared his throat and turned his head.

"I think that ship has sailed, don't you?" Still, I turned my back, slipped off the shirt and pulled my own t-shirt over my head. I tossed the shirt I had been wearing at Bill, pulled the blanket off the cot and wrapped it around me. "I better go talk to him. He is nothing if not persistent."

"That still doesn't explain you coming from the barn half-dressed and wrapped in a blanket."

"We ladies go where we please, remember?" I answered, scooping up Maud from where she dozed in her silly sparkly collar and with a final flounce of the blanket, made my way to the house.

As I rounded the bend in the path, past the paddock where Knight and Mac were already out grazing, I saw Sean pacing in front of his silver BMW. For as long as I had known him, Sean had always had nice cars. Expensive. Foreign. The day of my mother's funeral, when he found me wandering, he picked me up in a black Porsche. That was the same day he gave me Maud. It seemed incongruous. Sean, photographer wandering the globe and sleeping under the stars, driving a luxury automobile. The fancy car and the kitten. I didn't know about the family money then. It seemed quirky and sensitive, him showing up with a kitten for me. Turns out it was just Sean. He liked to give gifts, liked the grand gestures. It was easy for him to do, and I had loved him for it. Just not the way I loved Bill. I had never loved anyone the way I loved Bill. But we worked in a way. We both liked to be on our own for chunks of time. Yes, when I looked at Sean, I knew we were more alike than I cared to admit.

When he saw me, Sean made a beeline for me, flapping his arms and saying things I couldn't quite hear. I caught the words *Jesus ... weeks ... think ... dead.* It seemed over the top, especially coming from him. I still didn't understand why he was here. We had talked last night, hadn't we? He knew I was here. A day or two, I'd said.

When I got close enough to hear all that he was saying, I realized he was referring to the three messages he had left me and to which I had yet to listen. He stopped abruptly and looked me up and down.

"What on earth?"

"Hi yourself."

"Don't get me wrong, you're a sight for sore eyes, but where were you? Sleeping under a haystack?"

"Something like that."

He kissed me and pulled me in for a hug. "Umm, love, what's that new perfume you're wearing?"

"Oh," I pulled away, "I slept out in the barn last night. The house was too hot."

"The barn? With the cows?"

"No, no cows. Two horses though."

"I come back after months abroad, and you would rather sleep with the horses? My ego!" he mocked, clutching at his heart.

"Sean, we covered this last night. I had no idea you were coming home, or I would have left word. Or been there," I added as an after-thought. "You've not exactly been in touch much the last few weeks."

"I know, I know." He kissed me on the nose. "That's why I am here. The shoot ran over, and I wasn't always where I could get a phone signal. Anyway, I wanted to make it up to you. Thought I'd come out and surprise you. See this place you're always talking about. It sounded important."

"I'm definitely surprised." Maud leaned out of my arms, switching allegiance back to Sean as she often did when he came home from a trip. He purred to her in return as she settled smugly into his arms.

"I've already met Bill." He tried to sound casual, but I heard a hint of jealousy in his tone. "Where is Evelyn?"

"It's early. I suspect she'll still be sleeping if the car doors and voices didn't wake her. I'll take you up to meet her later. First, I need to get dressed."

He did not seem to hear the part about my taking him up to meet Evelyn. "If you want to get cleaned up, I'll take you out for breakfast. I passed a decent looking café in town. Old school Americana. I'd like to take some photos."

Naturally, there was a work angle. "Can't." I shook my head. "Bill said there was work to do today."

"And you have to help? Don't they have farm hands or something for that?"

"I said I would help. This isn't a big operation and they are short-handed right now." I was looking forward to spending the day working and not thinking. I offered no further explanation. "I'll get dressed and go see what that's about. Then I can make us some breakfast here."

I hated how Sean did that. How he came back after so many weeks away and started making decisions. My decisions. Pretending they were ours. I wished he would stop talking. I wanted to walk the farm together, show him this place I loved. He only saw taking me away. I wished we could just be quiet together—the way Bill and I were. Saying and not saying.

Sean was clearly not volunteering to spend the day helping on the farm. Fine. He had his own car. Let him leave if he liked. It was probably better that way. He didn't understand how long it had taken me to work my way back here or how much the place meant to me. How could he? I had never told him. Not really. No. I was not about to leave. I was already anticipating the fight. I realized my chin was lifting and my mouth had already set in the way it did when I was digging in. Beneath the blanket, my cell phone buzzed in my hand. I pulled it out and looked at the screen. Damn. It was Dr. Lawrence.

"I have to take this."

"Right now?" Sean lifted his eyebrows.

"It's important," I said readjusting my blanket before turning my back to him and answering. "Hi Doc. Thanks for getting back to me so fast."

"You made quite an impression on Darla."

"It was quite a night."

"Tell me about it," Dr. Lawrence asked in his shrink way.

I glanced over my shoulder and moved further away from Sean, positioning myself facing outwards toward the fields, hoping that if my voice carried at all it would float out among the drifts of alfalfa or be masked by the rustling of corn. Not that Sean didn't have experience with my nightmares over the years. But this felt different. Carefully, I recounted the dream, including the details that I knew would interest Dr. Lawrence. The fire again, but this time me caught in it. Trying to put it out. Even on the phone, Doc listened in that way he had. As I talked, I pictured him sitting on a golf cart crossing and uncrossing his legs, his forehead still and unmoving beneath a hat or the canopy while his buddies debated woods or irons and yucked it up about their wives shopping habits. When I got to the part about Mary, Blessed Mary Ever Virgin in the burning doorway, he made a little noise that sounded like a "hmm." I paused.

"That's new," he said underwhelmingly.

"There's more. I saw Rebecca."

"You've had dreams about Rebecca before."

"Yes. No. Not in the dream. Well, yes, in the dream. She was there beneath Mary's outstretched arms. Beckoning me, I guess you would say."

"How so?"

"Goddamn it. Don't you start that crap. The way you, I, or anyone would say. Beckoning for fuck's sake. Waving me to come into the fire." I was getting snappish, not wanting to bog down in the bullshit hair splitting. I didn't know how much time I had on this phone consult, but I wanted to get to through the whole the thing and find out if I was losing my mind. "But that wasn't the first time I saw her last night. I saw her twice, earlier. When I was awake. I saw her dead."

There was nothing and then a small noise like shifting in a vinyl seat coming from the other end of the line. Now I pictured him pointing his friends to the phone and then twirling his index finger at his temple in the universal gesture for crazy in the head.

"That's bad, isn't it?" I knew the answer.

"It's significant," Dr. Lawrence answered.

"That's what Bill thought."

"Bill?"

"I'm at the farm. It's a long story. I scared the hell out him last night. I froze at one point. Just froze. I dropped a plate. That was before the dream. After dinner. I woke up from the dream sweating and with my heart pounding. I thought it would explode. I couldn't talk. Couldn't move. He said I maybe was in shock."

"Obviously I didn't see it, but from what you describe, I think he is right."

"What's happening to me?" I wanted Doc to give it to me straight.

"I want to talk more about this. I want you to come in to see me. But I want to ask you a question." I noticed he was not answering mine. "Corianne, is it possible you actually saw Rebecca's body?"

"Last night? I already said I did."

"Not last night," Dr. Lawrence said calmly.

"No," I said as it dawned on me what he was asking. "No, not possible. I wasn't with her again after she was taken. I was with my mother and the police. I never saw her again. Not until the funeral."

"Okay. I needed to ask."

"Why?"

"Because from what you're telling me, it sounds very much like a repressed memory resurfacing."

"A memory? That doesn't make any sense," I frowned. My head was beginning to throb.

"Sometimes we bury things deep in our subconscious that are too painful for us. As children, we might not have a framework from which to make sense of them or assign meaning. We shut them out. Bury the memories. Tell ourselves they are dreams. They are still there though. Not eradicated, they remain. When they surface again, if they surface again, there are often fragments fused to other things out of which we've made a narrative."

"So, you're saying I actually saw Rebecca's body and my mind has jumbled that memory with all kinds of crap. Mental clutter?"

"Not clutter." Of course, he would never use the word crap. "But I'm saying that's one possibility."

Standing on the outer edge of the driveway, I sank down into a crouch, trying to absorb what Dr. Lawrence was telling me. It didn't seem possible that I could have forgotten something like that. It would mean there was a gap somewhere. Time I could not account for that had been backfilled with something else or just papered over. The hole opened and the world I knew seemed to drop through it.

"Corianne?"

"Yes, I'm here."

"Are you still keeping your dream journal?"

"Yes." I had pulled it from its hiding spot before I left Sean's, not so much because I thought I would need it in Sheerfolly Chapel, but because I didn't want him to find it—or worse and even more likely, his housekeeper.

"I want you to write these things down. Everything you can re-member when you wake up from the dreams."

"Should I get back? You said you want to see me, right?"

"I do, but now I don't think you should leave the farm just yet. There is something important happening. Something that seems trig-gered by that place. By the safety you feel there perhaps. If it's possible to stay there, I'd like you to do that. We can talk by phone for now."

"Sean is here you know. He showed up this morning worried because I went away without telling him." I looked over my shoulder for him and saw he was already wandering around with his camera.

"That's unfortunate." It was the closest Dr. Lawrence ever came to a judgment.

"I'm not going back. I already told him that. But should he stay?"

"That's up to you, but I have concerns that any tension between the two of you could hamper your progress. You need to focus on taking care of yourself right now. I want you to be very firm about your boundaries. This needs to come first."

"He won't like it, but he'll accept your recommendation. I don't know if he'll want to stay. He's interested in the place as a photographer. I might be able to recommend some other places he could explore for some shots. He's already said he wants to do some scouting around town."

"Let's talk again at the end of the week, but I want you to call me sooner if anything changes. If the episodes get any worse or you remember something concrete."

"Okay."

"Just try to relax, Corianne. This memory, if it is a true memory, has been buried a long time. It may take time to work its way up."

"Okay," I said again before the call ended.

I pulled the blanket down around my legs and sat in the grass, rocking back and forth, pressing the phone against my head as if that would help me make sense of everything. Bill saw me first and started toward me in a jog. Sean, noticing the movement, keyed in on me sitting there in the grass and started toward me as well, waving Bill off. Bill pulled up short and stood watching as Sean closed the distance between us. It was Bill I wanted to come. It was Bill I wanted to help me make sense of this but here was Sean kneeling in the grass beside me. Avoid tension, Dr. Lawrence had said. I took a deep breath.

"I heard you say Doc. Was that Dr. Lawrence?" The concern was evident in his voice.

"Yes, I called him this morning. I had one of those dreams last night." I tried to downplay my anxiety.

"One of your nightmares, you mean. You've had those before."

"This was different. I guess you could say I had a kind of episode." I tripped on the last word as it came across the threshold of my lips.

"What kind of episode?"

"Shock. At least, well that's what Bill said it looked like. Like I was in some kind of shock. Clammy, shivering, and heart racing."

"That sounds like one of your anxiety attacks."

"No, it was more than that. I couldn't speak. For a little while, I didn't speak."

"Then we've got to get you home, Cori." Sean put out his hand to pull me to my feet.

"No, that's the thing. Dr. Lawrence doesn't think I need to go back." I took his hand and stood up, still clutching the blanket around me.

"Did you tell him about the not being able to talk?"

"Yes, I told him. He thinks it's good for me to be here. That I might be remembering something. He doesn't think I should go back just yet."

"Oh, I don't know," Sean sounded skeptical. "You've been through so much. Doesn't he know that? You don't need to be remembering more or having someone convince you that something you dreamed really happened."

"What he said made a kind of sense."

"So you're going to stay here out in the middle of nowhere—with Bill?"

"And Evelyn," I added. "It feels good here. Like I can breathe. Maud and I will stay. You can head back if you like. Or you can stay. I'm sure it wouldn't be a problem."

"I can't stay, Cor. I've got tons of images to sort through for the story. I need to get back. That's why I came out. Because I wanted to surprise you. I thought we might have breakfast and drive back. To-night, we could go out for a nice dinner and then spend the rest of the night catching up over a good bottle of wine. I'll tell you all about France. I thought you'd want that. You wrote in your letters that you missed me. Missed our time. Here I am."

"And here *I* am." It came out sharper than I intended. I was so tired and confused. He just wanted to spend time together, but I couldn't imagine leaving the farm. Not right now. I couldn't make the choice he wanted me to make. It felt like I couldn't breathe. Why couldn't he just stop talking? I started again, "Look, I love you for driving all the way out here. It's just that this is really important. For a lot of reasons."

"Can I ask you something, Cori?"

"Sure. Of course."

"How did Bill know you were in shock? I mean, how did he know you woke up from a dream in shock?"

"I don't know. I guess maybe he's seen that kind of thing before. Or maybe he knew from the movies. I don't know."

"That's not what I mean, and you know it. Please, Cori." His eyes were locked on mine.

"He wasn't in bed with me if that's what you're asking. I must have been screaming or calling out. You know better than anyone how I sometimes wake up from those dreams." His eyes softened and his soft full lips parted slightly in a sigh.

"Cori, Cori, Cori. I'm sorry." He held out his arms and I moved into their circle. He held me as he had so many times before when I'd been frightened. My body resisted at first, but I was so tired. I turned my head into his shoulder. "I'm sorry," he said again kissing my hair. "You're right. I'm sorry I wasn't here. I didn't realize they'd gotten that bad again. Why didn't you say something?"

"They have. The last few weeks." He was always so confident, so sure of life. It was easy to lean into the habit of him. Easy to give him all the tension and confusion of the last twenty-four hours. When his voice grew tender and reassuring, it made me remember how we used to sit and talk in the garden and the way he had been there for me as my mother slowly faded away.

"Then do you really think it's such a good idea to be all the way out here?" Sean ventured more cautiously. "You should have friends around you. Someone who knows what you've been through."

"Bill and Evelyn know what I've been through."

"I only meant since your parents died. The way you cut yourself off and holed up in that house. Even I—I know you love it here, but Bill and Evelyn, they haven't seen you for years. They don't understand how it gets for you. You were making good progress in the city. Getting out and seeing people. I don't want to see you go backwards. I don't want you to use the isolation of this farm as an excuse not to deal with things."

Tears came to my eyes. I had started feeling clearer here. At the farm I could hear my own voice. Now after weeks away, Sean was here, well-meaning but telling me something different was best for me. I felt confusion return. He was the one bringing the past up and then chastising me for not leaving it behind. His voice began to drown out mine or at least make it sound small. We talked about this. I had talked about it with Dr. Lawrence who had said that this was Sean's conflict. His need to rescue colliding with his desire to wander. It was White Knight Syndrome. He needed the security of my dependency, so he was always reminding me of my weakness and fear. Dr. Lawrence was right. I couldn't do this with Sean around and yet sending him away and staying here with Bill, even if I could lie and pretend it was only the safety of the farm and the connection to my mother that I wanted, felt like a betrayal after all he had done for me. Stuffing down the guilt, I focused on how often he left. It wouldn't be any different this time. We would head back to the city and have a wonderful week together, maybe two, before he got the call about the next assignment. Sean would have to leave again, would want to leave again, and I would be alone in a far more dangerous place—my own dark and turbulent mind. I needed to be strong. I needed to make him hear me. Boundaries, Dr. Lawrence had said. Strong boundaries.

"Dr. Lawrence thinks I need to stay," I began slowly. "To be here to work with this. Just a week. Maybe less. If it's not happening, if I'm not making any progress, I'll drive back early. But I need to give this time. I need to find out."

"Alright. A week," Sean said kissing me again on the top of the head. "I guess we've made it this long. What's a few more days apart?" He reached for me again and smiled mischievously. "But I'd be lying if I said seeing you in my old t-shirt didn't give me ideas." His hands reached up under the hem of the t-shirt and as he cupped my backside, he pulled me up against him. There was no mistaking his intention. "There must be plenty of places to go to be alone out here," he said seductively.

I had always been physically attracted to Sean. Sex was never one of our difficulties. Now though, here, I just couldn't. Not with everything that was storming in my head and in my heart. I took his hands in mind. "I'd love that. Really, I would. But to be honest, I've had one hell of a night. Rain check?"

"You're right. I'm an ass. Forgive me, baby?" Sean smiled but there was a sadness in his eyes, like he knew this time something was different.

"There's nothing to forgive," I said and kissed him long and tenderly.

CHAPTER THIRTY

TEMPORARILY FORGOTTEN AND her leash neglectfully hooked around the side-view mirror, Maud had made camp in the shade of the car. She looked every bit the lioness surveying the savannah, starlings and voles being her antelope.

As we stood at the car, Sean attempted to smooth my russet hair which was curling in the humidity. "Cori, I also came out here because I wanted to talk to you about something."

He looked uncharacteristically nervous. I cringed inwardly. No good conversation ever began with those words. I clenched my jaw and braced myself. Since the time he arrived in my life, I had been preparing for this moment. When Sean told me he found someone else. That I was too broken to love. Or worse, that he didn't love me at all.

"What's that?" I tried to sound nonchalant.

"We haven't talked about it for a while, but I want you to think again about selling the house." Mistaking my relief for disgust, he hurried on. "I know, I know, but you could move in with me, permanently."

"Are you actually going to be there?" It was a bitchy reply and I felt bad as soon as it left my mouth.

"Or we could buy something else for you. Something with a little distance. Distance from the past," he continued as if he had not heard me.

In all honesty, as I moved among my parent's things it had sometimes felt precisely like that—living among things. They were things I had never chosen. It was a museum, a house filled with artifacts of someone else's life. They were my parents, and I honored the connection to them, to the past. Yet what filled those rooms was their past, not mine, not the past as I had lived it, and I didn't know how much of my future I wanted to give to Sean. The future was never a place I indulged much. It was uncertain. Short. The future could be taken away.

"Think about it?" he urged.

"I'll think about it," I said noncommittally.

"Hey, I almost forgot."

He reached through the open car window and pulled a small old book from the dashboard. The leather cover was faded and cracked, held shut with a coated elastic band. The pages were thick with cellulose and lignin. I held it to my nose and smelled the roughly cut fore edge. The scent was warm. The smell of cherry or almonds mixed with a little must and the smell of the leather. I read the spine. Lady Montagu's *The Turkish Embassy Letters*.

"Kate said someone dropped this off for you. Some old cabbie named Isaac. You must have left it. But taking a cab, Cori." Sean looked at me with great seriousness. I thought he was going to scold me for not walking the city more, but he broke into a broad smile. "See, I told you it would be good for you to be there."

It did not escape my notice that he had already been in contact with Kate even though he had just arrived home last night, but I allowed myself to be distracted by the book. It was sweet of him to bring it to me. I ran my hands over its cover. It was not mine and it certainly wasn't anything I thought Isaac would have been reading. His taste veered more to Dashiell Hammett. Perhaps it had gone unclaimed in the lost and found. Isaac remembered how I liked old books. It was such an unusual volume I couldn't imagine anybody would forget it on the seat of a cab. Books like this had lived lives of their own. I looked forward to learning about this one, hoping for a clue about the previous owner. I opened the front cover and saw one word written on the end paper. Sorry. It was from Charlie. His way of apologizing after all this time.

"Thank you for bringing this to me. I thought I had lost it," I lied as I kissed Sean goodbye. It was a small lie. An unnecessary one. They came easier than they should have. They came more often.

Book in one hand, Maud's leash in the other, I headed for the house as the BMW's tires bit into the gravel and Sean pulled away. They say that when you love someone, your natural inclination is to look back when they go. It is human nature to want to make sure they are still there and to fix them in your mind. Climbing the steps of the front porch, I did look back, watching until he was to the road. I waved. A sadness settled heavily on me. Things were about to change again but I did not know how.

I walked in the house as the front rooms of the house were just beginning to glow with the warm light of the rising sun. Happy to be off her leash, Maud promptly disappeared noiselessly up the stairs. I dropped the book onto my overnight bag and pulled out clean clothes, changing right there in the living room. I was just pulling a pale pink tank top over a pair of jean shorts when I heard voices floating down from Evelyn's room. The low murmur of Bill's voice was followed by Evelyn's high and clear one. I inched closer to the stairs. The door to Evelyn's room was ajar. They were talking about me.

"I understand. This is an especially important time for her. Yes, of course, her mother would want us to look after her," she was saying. "And she'll be such a help to you." Something about that last part, the sadness of it that sounded familiar to me. Not the words but the tone of it. It sounded like my mother. In Evelyn's voice was the echo of the way my mother talked to me at the end. One foot in the grave, as they say. She spoke as if she were already gone.

"To both of us, Evie. She will be a help to both of us." Bill had heard it as well. The feet of the bedside chair scraped the wooden floor and Bill's footfalls came closer to the open door. "It'll be nice for you to have another woman here. I do my best, but I'm not...well, I'm me." Evelyn murmured something in reply I could not hear. Before I could scoot away, Bill's boots were on the stairs.

"Hey, there you are." It was a poor attempt to cover my eavesdropping. "I'm ready to work. What are we doing today?"

"Is he gone?" Bill shot a glance toward the driveway.

"Yeah, he's gone."

"I need to bring some more hay bales down to the barn, take care of the horses. I've got a bum wheel on an irrigation boom in the south field. If we don't get more rain soon, that's going to be a real problem. I've got the part, but it would help to have another pair of hands. I remember you used to like to help me work on the tractor."

"I think I did all the talking and you did all the work."

"There are all different kinds of help. Besides, it's a good day to go out there and work on it. Evie has physical therapy today. That's an hour and then she's pretty wiped out and sleeps for good chunk of the afternoon. Her therapist is good. Fixes her lunch and everything before she goes. Not her job, but she doesn't seem to mind. I've told her she doesn't have to, but she says she likes being out here," Bill elaborated. "Frankly, I'm grateful for the extra time."

At the mention of the therapist woman, a wave of protectiveness washed over me along with a small bolt of jealousy. I felt protective of Bill, and of Evie, but I was suddenly feeling protective of the farm itself and that surprised me.

"Bill, is Evie okay? I mean, obviously she's not, but she's not in immediate danger, right?" If Bill noticed my clumsy questions, he seemed to chalk it up to my tendency to be direct to the point of bluntness. He cast an eye at the stairs and waved to me to follow him out onto the porch. We sat down on the steps.

"She's not going to die from her injury if that's what you mean. There are complications though. Things she's more susceptible to now that she's not very mobile."

"That's what I'm asking, I guess. Is she bedridden? Or has she given up?" It was a question I didn't have the right to ask. I clenched my jaw. Stupid.

"Evie is so brave. She didn't give up until well after the first three consults. Every time we went to an appointment, she would have that smile, that light, as if she knew something none of us did. Each time we left it was dimmer. She didn't give up all at once, Cori. Don't be that hard on her."

There was recrimination in Bill's words. A warning. I had said too much. Pushed too far. In fact, it was the first time I had ever called Evelyn "Evie," the pet name that Bill used with her. It showed my arrogance and my insensitivity. He loved Evelyn and I was still a silly little girl to think that my being here after all these years changed any of that. I laid my palms against the tops of my thighs and pressed hard until I could feel the handprints left underneath.

"I guess I was just thinking of my mother. When it changed with her. It was something Evelyn said. But my mother was sick a long time. That's a different thing altogether."

It was true. I had been thinking of my mother. Increasingly I had been back to thinking of the morning she died, and the looks exchanged between my father and the nurse. I remembered the way his hand curled in a small fist, the sound of my mother's breathing as it became ragged and shallow as the space between each breath opened into longer and longer pauses, and the furrow of her brow and creases around her mouth relaxing. The lines were still there, like phantoms, but so too was the young woman I saw in photographs smiling out from under a large-brimmed sunhat, arms full of flowers. In her joy, I could not possibly know Evelyn any more than I could know the young woman in the hat. In their sadness, I knew them both too well. Evelyn wanted to die. I knew she did. I wondered if Bill knew it too.

I wanted to go upstairs and put my hand on Evelyn's, tell her it would be all right. Like the rabbit, in time she would be some place quiet and peaceful. It wasn't that way for Rebecca, but then it had all been different for Rebecca. Her breath had been wrung from her body. That's why she was a ghost. I had once read a book in the dark stacks of the public library about ghosts. People who died violently or with a great deal of fear were more likely to become ghosts. I didn't know if animals could become ghosts, but I suspected their energy stayed around in other ways. In the end, I was sure the rabbit saw his death coming the way anyone would. His round brown eyes said he had seen it. Yes, the ghosting of animals was different. I felt the rabbit's trembling near to me.

"Corianne, I'm sorry. I wasn't thinking. It must be hard for you, being here. A lot of reminders. I didn't mean to snap at you."

"I had it coming."

"No one has it coming." Bill looked straight ahead, but he reached over and put his hand lightly over mine for just a second. "Look, we've got the whole day and lots to do. Why don't you see if there is anything in that refrigerator we can pack for lunch? I'll gather up the tools we need for that pump. We should stay close until the PT shows up, but we might as well make the most of the time when Evie has someone with her. I've needed time to get out there to do this."

"I'm on it."

"See you at the barn?"

"Dibs on driving the tractor."

"We'll see." Bill laughed as he rose to his feet. "I remember how you drive."

"Hey, it was my first time!" I called after him.

Bill strode off in the direction of the barn wearing his soft faded jeans, boots, and an old blue t-shirt. The blue shirt showed off his toned and tanned arms. As I watched him go, I tried to remember if I had ever seen Bill in anything other than jeans. To my memory, he always wore jeans, even in the worst heat of summer. Now I couldn't imagine him in anything else. Except when I remembered him in nothing at all. It was another memory I had tried to push away. Bill's naked body through the partially open bedroom door. It had both excited and embarrassed me. I closed my mind to the memory as I had a thousand times before and headed back into the house to rummage through the kitchen to see what might make a picnic lunch. Passing the stairs, again I paused to listen. Foot on the step and hand on the rail, I wondered if I should go up and say good morning or something comforting. Just then, Evelyn started to hum softly. It sounded bright. Sweet. I smiled and left her to whatever happy thoughts she was managing to have.

In the kitchen, I cobbled together enough for a decent lunch—a loaf of wheat bread tucked away on the counter and something that looked like ham salad in a round white casserole dish. A tentative spoonful confirmed it. I spread ample amounts of the ham salad on bread, enough for three sandwiches, topping each with sweet pickle rounds the way I remembered my mother and Evelyn doing, and then carefully wrapped each sandwich in waxed paper. There was a small blue cooler in the laundry room just where Bill had told me it would be. I was loading it up with the sandwiches and two big slices of watermelon when I heard the therapist's car pull up. There was the muffled slam of the car door and then Bill's voice as he greeted her. No doubt they were exchanging information on how Evelyn had fared since her last visit. I heard footsteps on the porch just before the front door opened and closed. The murmur of voices moved toward the stairs. I busied myself filling a large thermos with lemonade from the pitcher in the refrigerator. Putting the pitcher back, I spotted the beer. As an afterthought, I threw two in the cooler and scooted out the back door.

I waited for Bill out at the tractor. He had already hooked up the trailer to it and in the trailer's bed was a toolbox, a large wheel, and various washers, bolts and other hardware I could not identify. I lifted the cooler and thermos up, wedged them between the machine parts, and covered them with an old quilt I spotted on the shelf in the laundry room. I tucked in the book Sean had brought me as well. When

Bill walked up, I was leaning against the giant back tire of the tractor which stood as tall as I did, watching a cloud of tiny yellow butterflies that rose from the grass.

"You ready?"

"Yep." I pushed myself off the tire.

"You didn't get so busy daydreaming and watching those butter-flies that you forgot about our lunch?"

"I did not." I feigned indignation. "Right there. Under that old blanket."

Bill cocked his head to the side and squinting one eye against the sun said, "Girl, I've always loved your freckles, but I sure to hell hope you've got a hat. Sun's a little stronger here than sitting perched in your big city window."

"I've thought of that. I did spend quite a few summers here." From the back pocket of my jean shorts I produced a white baseball cap which I unfolded and popped on my head before pulling my thick auburn ponytail though the keyhole in the back. Bill laughed and snugged down the brim playfully.

"Like I've said, Corianne. You just tell like it is. C'mon then. You're riding shotgun."

I nudged the hat back up and after one look at the cab of the big John Deere 6E tractor, grabbed what handholds I could find, pulling myself up until I could get a foot on the running board. Bill boosted me the rest of the way as if I weighed nothing, scooping me up with one hand placed unceremoniously on my backside. I scrambled into the smaller second seat. Before I could say anything, Bill had climbed up into the tractor and fired it up. As it rumbled to life, the engine noise made further conversation difficult. I settled in as Bill guided the tractor between the fields of corn down to a smaller square of field bordered on one end by a green copse. He had mown this smaller field down to a golden stubble sometime earlier and the cut hay dried in neat windrows. The lack of rain was good right now for the drying hay, but it made things especially dusty. The cab was enclosed, pro-tecting us from the dirt and bits of dried hay that flew around us. In front of us, the land stretched out in one long, lovely flat ribbon. From under the brim of my hat, I stole a glance at Bill. His face was calm and peaceful, as serene as the land appeared to be.

We went to the irrigation pump first. Aside from handing him things, I was not much help except when I helped him position the massive tire, but he claimed having another pair of hands made the difference. I chatted away while he worked, kneeling in the dirt, sweat glistening on his face and forearms, his tongue sticking out to one side of his mouth. "Uh huh," he would say from time to time. At one point I stopped talking, thinking I was either boring or annoying him. "Well keep talking," he said matter-of-factly. I rambled on, keeping up a steady monologue about whatever popped into my head.

"Sean thinks I should sell the house." It was a subject not really connected to any other. I blurted it out with no introduction. "Too many ghosts."

"What do you think?" Bill glanced up at me.

"I don't know."

"Sure you do."

"You sound like my shrink again."

"Sounds like a smart guy." Bill got up and wiped his greasy hands on a raggedy old bit of flannel that hung out of his jeans pocket. "Now then, if that doesn't do it, I'll have to call someone."

"What's next?" I asked.

"I need to pick up some of that hay. We'll take the bales to the barn to store." Bill picked up the thermos, unscrewed the top, and took a long drink of the iced lemonade.

"What should I do?" I asked looking at him and using my forearm to block the sun from where it slanted between my hat and the top of my sunglasses. I had seen Bill and Gary, the part-time farmhands, manage that hay after it had been through the baler. I knew I didn't have the upper body strength to toss hay bales around the way those two did.

"I'm guessing you've got that book that Sean brought you tucked somewhere."

I crossed my arms. "And what makes you think that?"

"Look, as long as I've known you, Corianne, you've always had a book and your thoughts squirreled away somewhere else," Bill said tapping my temple with his index finger. Standing close like that, his face bent into mine, I could see the glint of sweat in the stubble that shadowed his jaw. Without thinking, I reached up and with the back of my fingers, brushed away a bead of sweat that ran down his cheek. He climbed up into the cab. "You remember your way to the river from here?"

"I think so. I go to the far western end, through the gate, and then take the road past the old blue house."

"You got it. I'll pick up the hay and then drive those bales up to the barn for Gary. He's supposed to come out later today after he picks up some things in town for me. Meet you at the river."

"You're going all the way back?"

"Yep. It won't take that long. I'll leave the tractor for Gary and check on Evie. I'll come back and get you in the truck." Bill retrieved the cooler, thermos, and book from the trailer and set them on the ground.

My mood sunk a little.

"Don't worry, I'll be there. The day is heating up and I'm looking forward to a swim. Now you better get going. You've got quite a walk ahead of you. I just might beat you there." He gave me a wink as he climbed back up into the tractor.

I hadn't thought about carrying the cooler and thermos until after he had fired the tractor back up and took off in a loud, dusty cloud. I'd be carrying them on foot. I shoved the book deep into my back pocket. Following the mown swath between the edges of the fields, I headed off toward the road and the river.

The summer was already changing. I could see it in the color of the fields. Things were turning ripe and golden. The corn was setting its tassels and each plant was now taller than I was. Overhead, a high white contrail scratched the blue of the sky, gradually merging with one long shelf of cloud that skimmed along. Insects buzzed in the building heat of the day. For a stretch, the green of the corn stalks became deeper and the small spaces in between them became darker and more mysterious. Corn rose on either side of me in walls that seemed to stretch on endlessly, whispering as its broad leaves stirred in the breeze. My thoughts felt as thick and deep as those spaces.

Sean being here this morning had upended me more than I cared to admit. It had been easy to surrender to the farm and to visions of the past. In the comfort of Bill's company, I had begun to feel brave enough to remember. It had been easy, too easy, to let life with Sean become a distant dream and easy to outrun the doubt that crept into my mind whenever he was away. I had never meant to stay with him and yet years later, there I was, living in his apartment and sleeping in his bed. How had that happened? Was fear keeping me there or the freedom? I liked to think being in a long-term relationship proved I was better, but being in one you didn't ever have to work at was like sitting by the exit. I had grown to trust Sean, mostly. And I did love him. But it was different than with Bill. I had always loved Bill and always trusted him. From the moment I got out of the car with my mother all those years ago, he and Evelyn had been there for some of my darkest days. Now, I had trusted him with one my darkest nights. The answers I needed were here. On the farm. I knew it.

When I arrived at the big metal gate, my hand was sweaty and sore where the plastic handles of the thermos and cooler dug in. I unwrapped the rope from the latch, lifted it and swung the huge gate open. On the other side, I set my burdens down on the sandy soil and wiped my hands on my shorts before swinging the gate closed and resecuring the rope in a figure-eight knot. Beneath my feet, the ground changed from grass to road, all faded pink and dusty. It sparkled in the sun like broken glass. Looking up and down the road, there was nothing to see except farmland. No cars. No trucks. Just the fields I had emerged from and more fields across the road. Turning the other way, I looked down the road, toward the river.

The sun was high overhead now and the air was so humid it seemed thick enough to swim in. A languid breeze rose from somewhere deep among the roadside corn, smelling earthy, cool, and sweet. It pushed the haze that hung in the air, stirring it slowly, but offering no cooling. Beneath my ponytail, sweat gathered along my hairline, finally coming together in one giant drop that let go and ran down the back of my neck. I pulled the baseball cap off my head. The bits of curl that had slipped from the elastic band were stuck to my face. I was busy trying to swipe away the hair that had plastered itself down when I heard something behind me. I froze, listening. I whirled around. There was no one there even though just a second ago I had sworn I heard footfalls behind me. Remaining motionless, I strained to listen to the sounds underneath the breeze and the rustling of corn stalks.

Peering nervously into the corn, I called out sharply, "Who's there?" No one answered. It must have just been a trick of country sound—the fine gravel and sand on the shoulder crunching under my tennis shoes and reflected by the wall of corn, but I couldn't shake the old feeling I was being watched. I scolded myself for being paranoid, but I stayed wary, picking up both my things and my pace. I never even noticed that I dropped my hat. Bill would be at the river waiting, I told myself as I hurried on. I needed to stay on the road until the blue house. I would be a sitting duck until then. Then I could turn off onto the path that led down along the bank.

"There's no one there, Cor. No one is there," I muttered to myself under my breath, hustling as best I could, the cooler thumping against my thigh and forcing me into an uneven gait. I was going to have some dandy bruises.

At last, I reached the little house. Its paint had once been a rich blue, though I had never seen it so, even when I first came to Sheerfolly Chapel with my mother. It had faded even more in the intervening years and from its uneven stripes I discerned that the paint was now peeling away from the clapboards altogether. As a girl, I had thought it looked like a blue gingerbread house springing mysteriously from the corn; an enchanted house that watched me with its long dark eyes. It bore the letters RGS in script up on the peak on the front of the house, or at least the outline of the letters, the actual letters having either fallen off or been taken down many years ago.

RGS. Raymond Garrett Solomon. The middle of the three Solomon brothers, and from all the stories, the most interesting one. He had refused to farm and run off to New York, or some said Paris. He was a dangerous, they said. "An eccentric," the old women in town had tittered. Deep down, they were excited to believe they knew a real live maverick. I wasn't sure being bored with rural life counted him as an iconoclast, but I had no doubts now, as I thought back to their clucking, that in his day Raymond Solomon had been on the minds of more than a few farm girls as they rolled on their stockings for the church social on Friday nights—and then again as they arrived at Confession on Saturday morning with those same stockings run and balled up at the bottom of a handbag.

He never stayed in town long, but each time he came back, hope swelled in his father's heart. That is how they told it anyway. His father kept the old blue house by the river for Raymond so that he could come and go without his mother's watchful eye upon him and to save her from an early grave, scandalized as she was by the drink, the noisy parties, and the women.

A rusted out old Ford pickup the color of a green bottle fly sat at the top of the gravel driveway, chrome fenders hanging slightly. I had never known that truck to move and doubted it had ever run at all. Still, I watched as I always did for movement, some sign of life at the old place. There was nothing. Not even Raymond Solomon's ghost creaking a few old porch floorboards for fun. I set my things down under the big black metal mailbox that leaned crazily on its post and took three tentative steps into the driveway. Again, nothing happened. There was no barking dog. No one opened the front door to greet me or even to chase me off. Emboldened, I walked a few more steps down the driveway, keeping my eyes fixed on the house.

The driveway was flanked by two very neglected rose bushes, each one grown to the size of a decent hedge. They were heavy with huge, fully opened soft pink blooms. A drift of fallen petals covered the ground and as I walked past them, the scent of roses was thick and heady, reminding me of the scented guest soaps pressed into the shapes of rose blossoms my mother used to keep in the guest bathroom. Up close, I realized the porch was longer and deeper than it appeared from the road, like a veranda. I turned and looked back up the driveway. I had wandered too far from the road. Stupid girl. Casting one look back at the house, I ran all the way back to the mailbox. Hands on my knees, I bent to catch my breath. After a quick swig of lemonade from the thermos, I hurried on and swung down past the house onto the beaten grassy path that led down to the riverbank.

Crushed beer cans and cigarette butts attested to the fact that it was still popular with a certain crowd looking for a place to party away from prying eyes. Ducking my head, I wound my way beneath the branches of pine trees, trying to avoid the needles that snatched at my hair, pulling more bits from my ponytail and streaking them with sap. As I neared the riverbank, the trail of grass and dirt finally gave way to a thick layer of dried pine needles and sand.

"There you are slow poke." Bill was already on the bank, kneeling at the water's edge. He cupped water in his strong, broad hands and drew it up to his face, wiping away the dirt and sweat of the morning. Drops fell from his jaw and darkened his t-shirt. "I found your hat in the road. I was starting to get worried."

"I didn't realize I'd dropped it. How did you get past me?" I still held both the cooler and thermos, or I would have my hands on my hips in annoyed disbelief.

"Sorry, let me help you. You do alright?" Bill rose and wiped his face with the front of his t-shirt, revealing the taut muscle and a trail of hair spreading out across is stomach the same strawberry blond color as the thick waves of hair on his head. I sighed softly and then quickly cleared my throat to cover the sound.

"I have a few new bruises is all."

Bill smiled and hurried over to take my burdens from me. "Sorry, I should have done that." He walked over to the old quilt I had put on the back of the truck this morning, which he had already spread out on the bank, and set everything down on one corner. My empty arms felt heavy and quivered as I tried to lift them to brush back the sticky piney bits of hair from my face. Inside, I felt as unsteady. When Bill called out, I had been thinking of the conversation with Sean, the dreams, and the abandoned house; I felt as empty inside, except I had ghosts, who refused to leave.

"You alright?" Bill asked it again, but this time we both knew he was not talking about my arms.

"I don't know. Bill, what if I'm going crazy?"

"Come here." I walked toward Bill's outstretch hand. Tentatively, I reached out with my own. As our fingers touched, his hand enveloped mine. It was strong and warm. "You are not crazy, Coriander. Not at all. You've seen things. Things you shouldn't have had to see. You feel things. Things no one else feels. That doesn't make you crazy. It makes you beautiful."

I kept my eyes on our joined hands, too self-conscious to look Bill in the eye. Of all the things I had ever thought about myself, beautiful was never among them. Yet a part of me let myself believe it now when Bill said it. I smiled shyly, but my smile faltered as the shadow of self-recrimination and guilt crept back in. It was wrong to feel this way. I was not supposed to like the way his compliment made me feel.

With other men it always was about what they could take from me; how I could fill their void, their needs, with my body. It was about expediency. Even with Sean, it was about what he needed. His need to be needed. Even when he gave, he took. Bill wanted me. I knew that. And I wanted him. But it felt different with us. The way we touched was like another layer of our long conversation. Bill knew me, who I was, and he understood who I had been before all the darkness. Sometimes when I was with him, I thought it was possible I could find her again too.

We set out lunch and ate, talking among the birch and pine trees. I looked out at the river. Its dark surface floated in one direction while the clouds slipped by in the other. Watching the water made me feel relaxed and drowsy. Birds and tiny ground squirrels were alert to the food that spread out on the blanket. They hung near the edges of the trees, waiting of us to finish so they could claim any scraps. Every so often, one of them would hop through the grass, coming a little closer to investigate. I tossed a crust of bread toward a squirrel and waited.

"When's the last time you fished?" Bill asked as we put away the last of the food.

"God, I don't know. The last time I was here probably."

"Well then, I won't give you too hard a time when my stringer is full and you're still baiting your hook."

"That sounds like a challenge."

"It is."

"Okay, you're on. When?" I asked.

"Right now," Bill answered. "Before you can chicken out. Tonight, you eat what you catch."

"I don't just carry a rod and reel with me."

"I got you covered," Bill said walking back along the tree line, opposite the direction I had come from, to where he had backed his truck.

"No wonder I didn't see you when I got here."

From the truck bed, Bill lifted two rods and reels, a bucket of minnows, a small box, and a large net.

"You're optimistic."

"As I recall, you're a hell of a fisherman."

"I was like twelve when I caught that bass. And the only reason I got the damn thing up was because you helped me set the hook." Bill handed me the box, an old wooden Corona cigar box with a brass latch that I had used as my tackle box.

"Ah no. That's not how I remember it. You were whispering to that fish. Bewitching him, like a mermaid."

"Mermaids bewitch men, not fish."

"Now that too, girl. That too."

If I am honest, I had thought Bill and I might sleep together that afternoon. I had entertained the thought that he may have brought me to the riverbank and away from the house so we could lie together away from the farm, away from responsibilities. Away from Evelyn. I wanted it to happen. I wanted to know what it felt like to have his weight on top of me. It was probably better, the way it ended up; the two of us standing silent in the weedy shallows, casting lines and sidelong glances, sharing a cold beer, and beginning to know each other in a way we hadn't before.

We managed to catch enough fish for dinner, although Bill caught far more than I did. Still, I hauled in enough to say I helped.

"You know I'm not cleaning these, right?" I laid the wet rods in the back of the truck.

"Not how it works, sister. You catch, you clean. Just like always."

I wrinkled my nose.

"You're not suddenly getting squeamish on me?" Bill laughed. I shrugged in response. "Fine. I'll put them out of their misery, but you're on scaling. That's the messiest part anyway. Damn things fly everywhere. With this weather, we need to at least gut them soon. Here, hold this." Bill handed me the stringer. It jangled as the deep green rock bass thrashed trying to free themselves from the metal band that ran through their open mouths and gills. "We got any ice or water left in that cooler?"

I reached up and lifted the lid. "Yep. It's still about half full, some ice, mostly water."

"Well, it'll have to do for a bit." He lifted the stringer up and laid the fish in the cooler. The shocked fish renewed their struggle briefly. "Not ideal, but it'll work. Good thing it's a short drive back. I'll clean them just as soon as we check on Evie. C'mon, get in."

I swung up into the truck. As I closed the door, the sounds of the river and the wind in the trees stopped as abruptly as if I had just stepped into a soundproof booth. After the day of having the farm and the river all around me, a deep sadness settled in—an anticipatory loneliness. It wasn't that I minded being alone. I was used to that. I had grown wild again in Sheerfolly Chapel. In the city, there was no whisper of wind in the giant stands of trees. No burble of the river as it eddied and finally spilled over slick, shiny rocks. It would be back to people upon people, buildings that blocked the sun, and the sound of traffic. The chorus of birds would be replaced by the hostility of car horns, the back-up alarms of garbage trucks, and the hollow metal clang of dumpster lids. Maybe a few pigeons cooing. On a warm day, I could look forward to the music of the watcher across the way. My sadness grew larger until it consumed even the present moment. It took with it the sky and the sun. There would be no Bill. I dreaded going back and as my sense of dread increased, so did the close, closed in feeling of the truck.

The driver's side door opened, jolting me back into the summer afternoon. As Bill got in and sat next to me, I drew a deep breath. Clinging to Bill was the scent of the river, fresh and mossy, smelling of both air and earth simultaneously. I wanted to always remember the smell of that afternoon and be able to take it with me. As soon as Bill turned the key in the ignition, I hit the button that powered the window. As the glass slid down, I drew another breath of the river air.

"Thank you." I wanted to reach out and touch him.

"For what?"

"The fishing. The picnic. For saving my tackle box all these years. It was nice."

"It was, wasn't it? A good break for both of us." And with that, Evelyn was back in the truck with us. I turned my head and looked out the car window.

As we bumped along the narrow path, tree branches scraped against the side of the truck. I fidgeted uncomfortably in my seat, the sound registering uncomfortably in my body. My fingers whitened as they closed into balled up fists. I put my bare feet up on the dashboard, bracing myself against the sound. Bill reached over and put a hand on my knee.

"How are you doing?" he asked for at least the tenth time in twenty-four hours.

"I'm okay."

"So, what are you going to do with the house?" Bill asked, returning to my rambling that morning in an effort to distract me. He had been listening after all.

"I want to sell," I began, laying out the discussion I had been having in my head on the drive to farm, "but I don't want to stay at the apartment. It just not where I am supposed to be. I want to belong somewhere. I do, belong somewhere, I mean. I can feel it. I just don't know where that is yet. You know?"

Bill drove in silence for a while. "You belong to the land, Cori. Always have. Don't you know that? The way it speaks to you." He looked over at me and added, "If not here, somewhere."

"I know I'm tired of running. The ghosts keep coming for me no matter where I am."

"Then stop running. Make a stand." I knew he was talking about more than the house now. He was talking about Sean.

"Where? How?" I leaned my head against the door column. "Everywhere I go, I'm the thing they fear. They see it in me, Bill. You see it. I know you do."

"I see you, Coriander. I always have."

We had turned out onto the main road, parallel to the train tracks that ran along the river. A long train was making its way at a high speed, indicating it was no longer carrying any cargo. The train's big engine had already passed. I heard the long whistle signal a warning at a crossing well ahead. This close to the tracks, the ground shook. My head ached from the heat and the beer I had consumed with lunch. I let it drop back against the headrest. I could feel the rumbling of the train where my feet rested on the dashboard. Lifting my head again, I looked out at the train cars clattering past; tankers, flat beds and old rusting Canadian Pacific boxcars tagged with spray paint, some open, flashed at the road like a gap-toothed smile. When we were kids, there were stories about hobos riding the rails in open boxcars. I wondered if anyone did that anymore. Then I saw something else. Not the train itself. There was something in front of the tracks, in the tall grass and Queen Anne's Lace.

"Bill, stop! Stop!" I had to shout to be heard over the passing train. Bill hit the brakes and the truck skidded to a stop on the shoulder, dirt and gravel flying.

"What? What is it?"

"Something. There." I pointed. "On the side of the tracks." I was already getting out the truck, the last part of what I said lost in the heavy thud and screech of the end of the train moving down the rails. Rushing forward to get a closer look, I saw something long, something about the size of a child. No, longer than that. Standing next to the shape was a little girl, shiny blond hair and a dirt smudged flowered dress that came to just above her scuffed knees. I stopped short.

Turning to Bill as he rounded the side of the truck, I looked pleadingly into his eyes. "Tell me that isn't … tell me that isn't a …person." I was asking as much about the little girl as the figure in the grass, but I knew the little girl could not be there.

"I don't know," Bill said grimly. "I need to go look. Wait here."

I should have kept it to myself, but I grabbed his arm. "Bill, she's here. Rebecca is here."

He took me firmly by the shoulders. "You have to let me go look."

My arms fell to my side with fists like two weights. The soft fabric of Bill's well-worn shirt brushed against my arm as he pulled away. Gravel crunched under his boots as he made his way across the culvert and climbed up the other side, trampling a path through the tall grass and wildflowers. I turned my back, afraid to find out what was there. It seemed like an eternity before he spoke. Finally, I heard him yell something, but between the sound of the retreating train and the pounding in my ears I could not make out the words. I turned back toward the tracks.

"What?" I called out in a thin and reedy voice.

"A deer. It's a deer."

"Is she—?"

"Not quite. Corianne, get the keys out the ignition. You'll need the keys. My hunting rifle. It's in the truck box. Bring it."

I ran to the truck, turned the ignition off, and yanked the keys out before sprinting to the back of the truck. Stretching up on my tiptoes, I pulled up on the lift gate as hard as I could. It dropped with a bang, and I scrambled up into the bed, hands shaking and keys rattling. I tried one key and then another and another. Finally, the padlock clicked open obediently. I didn't like guns. They scared me and reminded me of the policemen who had occupied our house in the chaos that followed Rebecca's disappearance, firearms in their stiff black holsters. Bill tried to teach me to shoot once by putting old tin cans up on a fence post. He thought it might be good for me. Get me over my fear of guns. I hated it. There was no time to think about that now. I lifted the rifle, thankfully still in its case, from where it lay in the box and then hurriedly slid down off the truck. The edge of the bed scraped along my thigh on the way down, but I barely felt it. I started to run, then remembered the gun and dropped to a brisk walk, moving toward Bill as fast as I dared.

"She's in bad shape." Bill said, unzipping the case. "She's got a broken hip, at least. Punctured lung."

I made myself look down at the deer. Blood was bubbling from her black nose as she took sharp, shallow breaths. White bone stuck through hide on one of her legs. I swallowed the bile that rose to burn the back of my throat. There was a loud click as Bill chambered a bullet.

"Wait. Wait." I knelt beside the deer, holding my hand over her as I looked for a place to touch her shattered body that I thought would not cause her more pain. I looked at Bill, tears streaming down my face.

"We have to Cori."

I nodded mutely. Finally, my hand came to rest on the top of her head, near the still alert oval of her ear with its soft pink interior. I could feel her body trembling as I leaned in and whispered to her, "Time to go, sweetheart. It'll be okay. It'll be fast." Her ear flicked and her soft brown eyes looked into mine. I knew they would soon be distant and cold, like the rabbit's eyes. I looked up at Bill again, who nodded. She did not seem to mind my touch, or maybe she couldn't feel it. I stroked her head gently. "I'm so sorry, brave one. I'm so sorry. It's not fair."

Bill put his free hand on my shoulder. "It's time. Go wait by the truck." Sensing my hesitation, he spoke to me firmly. "Go on, now."

Taking my hand away, I rose to my feet. The deer startled with my movement and began trying hopelessly to get to her feet. "Shh," I whispered, patting the air as I backed away. "It's okay." I kept saying it, even once I was well clear. Repeating over and over, "It's okay." She knew.

Arms crossed around me, shivering, I had just reached the truck when the shot rang out. I turned to look for Rebecca, but she was gone.

CHAPTER THIRTY-ONE

BRIGHT AND HOT as the day was, I shook with cold. I could only watch mutely as Bill climbed up in the back of the truck, replaced his rifle in the box and locked it.

"I called the Sheriff. They'll send someone out to pick her up." He said it quietly but matter-of-factly. "It was the humane thing to do, Cori."

I nodded. It was. I knew it was and yet I couldn't help flinching a little as Bill wrapped the quilt around my shoulders. The same quilt we sat on enjoying our lunch just a few hours ago. At the touch of his hands, I started to cry.

"Come here," he turned me to face him and wrapped his arms around me.

"Bill, I saw her. Rebecca. By the deer. That's how I knew."

"You've been going through a lot. Sorting through all that past stuff. The dream. Then Sean showing up here." There was undisguised disapproval when he got to the part about Sean. "Rebecca has been on your mind is all. That's why you saw her."

"Maybe." I had stiffened in his arms, spotting drops of deer blood on his shirt and then the blood on my own hands. Sensing the change in me, Bill looked down.

"I'm going to walk back to the water. Rinse my face," he said. "Walk with me."

I walked silently by Bill's side, holding the quilt around me. As we reached the water, he pried it away from me and taking my hands pulled me down to my knees. He plunged my hands into the cool river water and washed them just as he had washed me the night before, then patted my face with his own hands, clean and cool from the water. I sat down on the balled-up quilt and stared at my wet hands. I could still see the blood.

Bill peeled off his shirt, dropping it near me, and went back to the river. I looked up, watching him as pulled off his boots and waded into the edge of the water to wash his face, droplets of water wetting the fluff of reddish blond hair that rose from his chest. Perhaps he felt her blood seeping in as I had because he stood and without hesitation, totally undressed. His back and legs rippled with muscles built by a lifetime of work. He was as beautiful as I had always imagined.

He waded into the water and then dove under, gliding unseen out into the dark of the river. I watched him disappear under the water and then got up from where I sat—and took his shirt. Rolling it up, I stuffed it under my arm. I hadn't thought about doing it. I just did it. I saw Bill cutting back toward the shore with quick, clean strokes. Back on the bank, he picked up his jeans and looked around, puzzled by the shirt's disappearance. I held it tightly against my body.

"I took it," I confessed, and got up, handing him the quilt with one hand.

"My shirt? Why?" Bill asked, as he began toweling off.

"It has blood on it."

"Right. Of course. I probably have an extra t-shirt in the truck."

I wanted to reach out and touch him. Feel the river water running off his body, but the image of the doe with her oval ear and knowing eyes intruded. I turned away, my face beginning to burn with the old shame. Clutching the shirt, I began walking.

"We should get back. I'll meet you back at the truck," I called over my shoulder.

This time, we set out for the farm in silence. We pulled into the driveway just after four o'clock by the dashboard clock. Bill swore softly under his breath.

"What's wrong?"

"I hadn't realized how long we were gone."

"I'm sure Evelyn is fine. She would have called your cell phone, right?" I was trying to reassure Bill. "She's probably sleeping. You said she's always tired after her therapy."

"You're right. She's probably sleeping." Bill looked at me and gave me a gentle smile. "Some fun day, huh?"

I forced a small laugh. The images in my mind seemed like those of two entirely different days. In one, I woke to Bill bringing me coffee in the barn. In the other, we washed away the blood of the dead doe.

Bill reached over and gave my hand a squeeze. "I'm going to run up and check on Evie. I'll be back to help unload the truck." I watched Bill stride to the house and head for the kitchen door. He was obviously deeply concerned about Evelyn having been alone that long.

I opened the door of the truck and pulled Bill's blood-spattered shirt from where I had tucked it under the front seat of the truck. I wanted to get rid of it immediately, but as I rounded the back of the truck, I remembered the fish we caught were likely running out of ice. Hesitating, I let the shirt drop to the ground then, ignoring Bill's instructions to wait, I climbed into the truck bed. Now full of fish, the cooler was heavier than I thought and harder to balance as most of the ice had turned to water. I slid the container to the end of the lift gate and climbed back down, hoping I could lift it down and at least get it as far as the shade of the big maple. It was awkward, but I thought I could manage. I couldn't. The remaining ice and fish shifted, bringing the full weight into my body at once. I had no choice but to let the cooler crash to the ground. The ice and fish slid out onto the dusty earth.

The fish, suddenly thrown from their icy stasis, instinctively slapped against each other and the hard ground, their topaz eyes fixed in awful lidless stares, mouths gaping, gills struggling uselessly to pull oxygen from the steamy air. Water from the melting ice pooled briefly and then disappeared into the thirsty ground, leaving only a dark shadow.

I knelt to pick up the fish but froze with my hand outstretched. The image of the dying doe, her leg shattered, rushed back to me. Death followed me. It had followed me here. Rebecca had followed me here. A new panic rose in my body. I had brought it here, to the farm—to Bill and Evelyn. Struggling back to my feet I snatched up Bill's shirt and took off for the barn in a full run. I flew in the open door and dashed to the wall where I knew Bill hung tools. There it was. The small shovel hanging exactly where I had remembered it. The old rusty s-hook squeaked and then snapped down as I eased the shovel handle from its curve.

After having let them graze in the pasture for the morning, Bill must have put the horses back in their stalls before he drove to the river. Knight gave a snort, reminding me he was there. Reminding me that Lucy was gone and he, too, had been alone. I set the shovel down and walked to him. He nosed my shoulder firmly, then with another snort, pulled his head up abruptly, his ears pricked forward. He must have smelled the deer's blood on the shirt, which I still held in my hand. I dropped it on the floor next to shovel.

"It's my fault, Knight." I ran my hand along his broad forehead. He shifted, still wary, but I could feel him gradually relax. I kept stroking him, leaning my head close and whispering, "It's my fault. I brought it here." This time a low knicker rose from deep in Knight's throat. He may have been trying to reassure me, but we both knew my guilt. After giving him a good pat, I walked over, picked up the shovel and shirt, and headed for the windbreak.

There on that familiar rise of earth, partitioned as it was from the rest of the world by the trees and the tall rows of corn beyond, I began to dig. The place I chose was near the small grave of the rabbit and its tiny cairn. Using the edge of the shovel, I chopped through the tangle of grass and tree roots as I hollowed out a new space. I dug furiously, dripping sweat stinging my eyes. Unwilling to stop, I simply licked away the salt drops that ran into my mouth. When the shovel no longer suited, when the dirt I had piled up spilled in on the earthen walls, I threw the shovel down and dug with my bare hands, carefully prying rocks from where they had slept for decades or more and setting them to the side.

Finally satisfied with the new grave I had dug, I picked up the shirt. Holding it close against me, I took a strange comfort in the soft feel of the worn threads, inhaling the pungent odor of sweat mixed with death. Rhythmically and systematically, I folded the shirt in tight crease after tight crease, transforming it into a tidy parcel of fabric. Gingerly, my fingers brushed a spatter of blood as I folded. I expected it to feel wet. Instead, the fabric felt rough and stiff where the blood had soaked in and dried. Placing the shirt in the hole, I grabbed a handful of dirt and closed my fingers around it. The earth was cool and moist, but like the blood, it had already begun to dry in the heat of the summer afternoon. Bits of it sifted out through my clenched fist. I tossed what remained in on top of the shirt and reached for another handful. Then another and another. When that was not fast enough, I scraped the dirt in by the armful. Finally, there was no longer enough loose dirt to scrape from the tangle of grass and where the blood-spattered shirt had been moments ago, there was just a mound of freshly turned earth. I set about smoothing it, patting it with my hands. When it was close enough to level, I picked up the three largest rocks that I had pulled out of the hole and laid them on top.

I sat back and swiped at the sweat dripping off my face with my forearm. It didn't feel better, just finished. I hadn't had a cigarette of any kind since I had arrived at the farm. Now I craved one. I remembered the old stash I had kept in the tin here on the windbreak. Even if the tin was still there, I guessed it had leaked. Nothing inside could be any good anymore, but there was always the chance.

Though Bill had built the stone altar nearby, the familiar piece of fieldstone was still at the base of the tree. He'd left that piece. Pulling it aside, I saw the tin, still neatly wedged in the space where I had first hidden it. It was rusting considerably but the seal was still tight. It took a bit of doing to pry open the lid. Finally, it came loose. I smiled and pulled out the slightly crumpled Marlborough Lights pack and a shook it. There was a small rattle as two cigarettes and one joint dropped into the thumb-sized opening in the foil. I pulled out the joint, put it to my lips, and reached for the small green Bic lighter that I had tucked away in the tin along with some other small souvenirs. The wheel of the lighter had also corroded and did not move easily. Determined, I worked the wheel with my thumb. Eventually, it began to move more easily. I brought the lighter up to the joint and tried again. The flint gave up a small spark, but no flame. I flicked the lighter repeatedly, feeling the small metal wheel bite into the side of my thumb. At last, the mechanism gave a satisfying snap and a small yellow flame rose with a low hiss.

The ancient joint caught quickly. The smoke burned my throat as I drew the first breath down deep, held it for a moment, and then let it go with a sigh. Taking the tin with me, I went and sat between the rabbit's grave and the fresh one I had made for the deer. I took another drag of the joint as I looked through the other small items I had left behind. A stub of a yellow pencil, its point long gone. Underneath that was the Mass card from my mother's funeral. On the front of the card was a portrait of Mary, standing on clouds, her arms outstretched, palms turned up, in that familiar way of Holy portraits. One bare foot peeked out from her belted white tunic. Her blue mantle fell in gentle folds across her arms, and her head, covered in white, was ringed by twelve stars on a field of blue sky where the gloaming clouds opened at her head.

My father must have chosen the design, appropriate given his wife's Marian devotion. I imagined the two women talking, mother to mother. I turned it over and read the Memorare, the first letter rising importantly above all others in an antique script:

Remember, O most gracious Virgin Mary, that never was it known that anyone who fled your protection, implored your help, or sought your intercession, was left unaided.

Inspired by this confidence,
I fly unto you, O Virgin of virgins, my Mother.
To you do I come, before you I stand, sinful and sorrowful.
O Mother of the Word incarnate, despise not my petitions, but in your mercy, hear me and answer me.
Amen.

Sinful and sorrowful. Indeed, I was that. I laid back on the old grave, placed the prayer card on my chest, and drew again on the joint. Old and dry, it burned hotter and more quickly, stinging my fingers where I held it. I watched the smoke rise and began to move my lips in the Memorare. *Remember, O most gracious Virgin Mary. I fly unto you. Despise not my petitions.* How long had I cowered in my bed, praying to gracious Mary, asking her to despise me less than I despised myself? What could she do for me that she had not already taken it upon herself to do? After all, I was still here. It could have been me in the casket with my hair spread across the soft white satin pillow while my parents wept. I looked up at the clouds building in the afternoon sky, bottoms flattening out and darkening, tops growing taller. My parents had wept. My mother had certainly wept. I heard her through closed doors and in muffled conversations. Her little girl no more. She knew and she cried. I wondered if anyone else would have cried peering into the casket at my eerily placid face. Rebecca's face had looked posed and painted. The undertakers had made her cheeks too rosy and tinted her lips. Her body, in a high-necked white dress, was otherwise obscured by the large number of white and pink flowers strewn across it and draped around and over the casket. She would have like that part, I thought. Buried among the flowers.

Remembering that I had not yet looked at all the mementos, I sat up and reached for the tin. Two items remained. The first was a tan and white rabbit's foot keychain complete with tiny nails. Ghoulish and sad. No wonder I had buried it. The other was a button—thin, white, and pearly like the inside of a seashell. It was about the size of a quarter, with four holes for threading. Something about it had disturbed me enough to shut it up with the keychain. I rubbed the disk between my thumb and forefinger. It was not mine. I knew that much. I stared down at it in my dirt-smudged fingers. Slowly, a memory took shape. I closed my eyes to let it come into focus. I saw Rebecca, in her purple flowered dress, laughing and talking as we played on our way to school that day. I tried to focus on the image, not the emotion, as Dr. Lawrence had taught me. I walked next to Rebecca, admiring her new dress. Like the girl who wore it, every detail was perfect. The lace set in at the neck and epaulets along the waist, decorated with beautiful pearl buttons. The button dropped from my fingers as my eyes flew open. Digging into the ground with my heels, I wheeled, pushing myself away from it and kicking over the tin in the process.

"There you are," Bill called out as he strode up. "I've been looking all over for you. Why was dinner laying in the driveway?" His voice trailed off when he saw my terror-stricken face. I kept my eyes down worried about what he might see in them.

"What is it, Corianne? What's happened?"

I pointed to where I had dropped the button in the grass. Bill walked over, looked down and seeing the button, bent to pick it up. "This? I don't understand."

"It's hers."

Whose? Your mother's?"

"No," I shook my head. "No. It's Rebecca's."

"Rebecca's? I'm afraid I still don't understand, Cori. What's it doing here?"

"I had it in the box."

Bill bent down again and picked up the tin. "She must have given it to you, Cori." He was about to put the button back in the tin.

"No. She wouldn't. She couldn't. It's from her dress. It's from *that* dress. The one she was wearing. Bill, how did I get a button from the dress she was wearing that day?"

"I'm sure there's a logical explanation," he offered reassuringly. "Maybe someone thought it was yours."

I shook with cold. As an adult, I knew if the police had found a button, any button, it would have ended up in an evidence bag. Not with me. Not buried in a tin with a few stale cigarettes, a joint, and a ratty good luck charm. Bill sat down and put his arms around me. For the first time, he noticed the patch of freshly dug dirt.

"You mind telling me what's going on here?"

"I buried something."

"Something?"

"It's stupid."

"Try me."

"The shirt. I buried the shirt," I confessed.

"My shirt?" Bill said with surprise.

"Yeah."

"You buried my shirt. Why would you do that?" He was trying to be patient with me.

I just fixed him with a long look.

"Right, stupid question." Bill's eyes fixed on mine. I looked away. "Corianne, are you stoned?"

"Not really."

"Not really? Is that a category? Look, I wouldn't mind except you didn't wait for me." He laughed despite himself then sobered again. "Yeah, bad joke."

"Bill, I'm scared. Why do I have it? That can't be good."

"I know. I know." He pulled me close and kissed the top of my head. "Do you remember anything else?"

"I loved her dress. I was jealous."

"Well, maybe she knew that and gave you the button."

"No, there's something else. I feel it." I looked down at my hands and my shorts, both covered with dirt. My head started to pulse again. I brought the heels of my hands to my temples, trying to either to force the memory from my head or keep it locked up. I could not be sure which I wanted.

"Maybe we should leave it for now," Bill suggested.

It was too late. I saw Rebecca again and not as part of some exercise. She was laying in the grass as I dreamed her or imagined her. There was dried grass in her silky blonde hair and dirt smudged her pale arms. I knelt beside her. Knowing I could not wake her, I took her hand in mine. Her skin was cool and soft. Gently, I plucked a leaf from her hair. I looked a long time at her laying there. She could have been sleeping like in one of our games, except that no one slept like that. One of the pearl buttons had lifted, the threads that had stitched it down at her waist broken and torn. I pulled on it and it came away.

"That's a good girl."

It was man's voice. I was not supposed to have the button. At the sound of his voice, my hand closed around it in a fist.

CHAPTER THIRTY-TWO

WHEN I OPENED my eyes, I felt sick and disoriented. My head felt as if it would split in two. I grabbed Bill's hand. I knew now what I had seen was a memory, and yet I did not understand it. I could not make it fit with the rest of what I knew. I had never been there. I had run.

"You're white as a sheet. What is it? Corianne, what did you remember?"

"I was there. Bill, I was there. I saw her."

"Where? Saw who?"

"Rebecca. I saw Rebecca lying in the grass. Dead."

"You've imagined seeing her before."

"No, this was different. This time I wasn't imagining it. I was remembering. It was a memory. I know it was. I was there, Bill. Kneeling beside her. I touched her. I took it. I took the button from her dress. How is that possible? What was I doing there? Why did I do that? Who does that?"

The questions tumbled out one after another as I frantically searched both my memory and Bill's face for answers. He had none to offer me. He tried to pull me into him. I pushed him away. It hurt to have him touch me precisely because I wanted it so much. If he touched me, I knew there would be no keeping the darkness from touching him. He must have sensed what I was thinking.

"Corianne, we've talked about this. It wasn't your fault."

"And this is the condemnation, that light is come into the world, and men loved darkness rather than light, because their deeds were evil." Those had been Mrs. Ashworth's words to me as my parents and I paid our respects. The accusation in her eyes came flooding back to me. I repeated her words, feeling a cold darkness crowding me. "And when ye spread forth your hands, I will hide mine eyes from you: yea, when ye make many prayers, I will not hear: your hands are full of blood."

"What?" The shock was plain on Bill's face. He reached for me again. Again, I backed away.

"It's my fault." I choked out between sobs.

"Look, I don't know whose been filling your head with all that damnation and hellfire Bible shit, but it wasn't your fault." Bill grabbed me firmly by the arms before I could pull away again. "Do you hear me? It wasn't your fault. You were a little girl, Coriander. A little girl, for Christ's sake. Now, we're going to go call Dr. Lawrence right now. And we'll figure this out." Keeping one eye on me, Bill let go long enough to pick up the button, toss it into the tin and snap it shut. Then grabbing me by the hand, he yanked me to my feet and pulled me down the path back to the house.

"It's going to be okay. It's going to be okay," Bill repeated under his breath as we made our way toward the house.

"I can't go in. Bill, promise me you won't make me go into the house. I couldn't face anyone right now, especially Evelyn."

He stopped walking and turned to look at me for a few long seconds, trying to read my expression. "You'll stay put on the porch? While I go get your phone? Promise me."

"I'll stay. I will. I swear."

Bill ran his hands through his hair and sighed deeply. "Alright, let's go."

We started again, rounding the corner by the kitchen door, and heading around to the front. I almost ran into him as he stopped again abruptly. I heard him mutter under his breath, "Oh Jesus, not now," but I could not see what he was reacting to—not at first. Then I saw. It was Sean. He was back and sitting on the porch swing.

I looked at Bill, my eyes wide.

"I'll get rid of him," he said through clenched teeth.

"No." I grabbed Bill's arm. "No, I'll talk to him. I owe him that."

Bill immediately protested. "You're in no shape."

"Go get my phone. Call Dr. Lawrence. His number is in the phone. Explain to him what has happened."

With that, I walked up the front steps and took a seat on the swing next to Sean. Maud was on his lap, clearly happy to see him, and he seemed happy to see me. If he noticed my edginess, he chalked it up to our earlier conversation.

"What are you doing back?" I asked, reaching over to rub Maud's throat with a dirt smudged hand. She purred, not minding that my hand was trembling, but did not leave her privileged place on Sean's lap.

"Wow, you really did work all day didn't you," he laughed, noting my dirty and disheveled appearance. Then he grew serious. "I didn't like how we left things Cori. You're clearly going through some-thing—and I want to be there for you. Just as I've always been."

"Going through something. Yeah, you might say that."

"I love you, Cor. You know that."

"I do. It's just not a good time." I paused. Unsure of how much to tell him, I decided on the truth. "I remembered something today. Something about the day Rebecca died."

"That's good, right? That's what you wanted."

"It wasn't what I expected. Not that I even know what I expected. I was with her somehow. I remembered seeing her, dead."

"You're just remembering her funeral."

"No, not like that."

"Oh. Oh god. You mean—" Sean said as he realized fully what I had been saying. "But how is that possible? You weren't there. You had run for help."

"That's what I thought. What I remembered. But now this, this changes everything. So, do you see? I'm no good for anyone right now. I need to figure this out. I need to know who I am. I need to know if I am who they say I am, Sean."

"Who says? Don't worry about me. I'm not going to leave you on your own with this. I know who you are."

"I'm seeing things when I dream and now when I'm awake. Bad things. They followed me here. You know it's true. I'm barely hanging on."

"Let me help."

"I don't know how."

"What about Lawrence? Does he know what's going on? Should I call him?"

"Bill went to phone him. To tell him."

"Okay, then I'll drive you back to the city. Take you to see the doc." Sean was desperate to help.

"I don't know. I don't know what to do."

"Corianne," Bill said as he came up to the porch.

"Did you talk to him?" I asked, hopeful.

Bill nodded but did not immediately say more when he saw Sean sitting next to me.

"It's okay. You can talk in front of him. I told him."

"Does she have an appointment? I can take her." Sean's eagerness annoyed me.

"No. Not exactly," Bill said, turning to me. "Dr. Lawrence is coming to you."

"He's coming here to the farm?" A small measure of relief flooded my body. I wouldn't have to leave the farm. I would not have to leave Bill.

"The doc said he had something he had to take care of today, a call or something he needed to do first. He'll leave just as soon as he can.

I gave him directions. But he might not get here until late tomorrow morning."

Another night. I would need to get through another night. I rubbed my forehead.

"One of your headaches? Sean put his hand on my back.

"Yes."

"Does she have her Valium with her?" This time Sean spoke to Bill as if I were not there.

"I don't know, do you?" Bill asked me, looking concerned as I had never mentioned being on medication.

"I haven't taken Valium in a year." I chose not to mention my other anti-anxiety meds and Sean chose not to pursue it.

"How about a glass of water or something?"

"Yeah, that would be nice." I agreed mainly to give him something to do.

"Straight through to the back," Bill gestured.

As Sean disappeared into the house, Bill knelt in front of me. Reaching up, he pushed the curtain of my hair aside. "I told Dr. Lawrence that Sean is here. He said it is up to you if he stays. That the most important thing is that you feel safe. I agree."

Hearing Sean returning, Bill stood up and took a step back but stayed near me.

"Here we are," Sean handed me the glass of water and stood looking anxious. My hand shook and water splashed on to the porch and Maud.

"Thanks." I took a sip, steadying the glass with both hands and used the time to figure out how I was going to say what was coming next. "I appreciate that you came back, Sean. I know you want to help. I really do. I just need to rest, try to get some sleep tonight, and wait for Dr. Lawrence."

Anger clouded his face as he looked between Bill and me. I gave Bill a look that requested a moment. He read my cue.

"I better clean those fish off the driveway before this young lady smells them. Frankly, I'm surprised she hasn't already made a beeline." Maud looked up casually at the mention of her name before returning to licking the water from her fur.

"Look, Sean," I quickly added. "Why don't you stay at the hotel in Mason. Come back in the morning. I won't really know anything more until I talk to Dr. Lawrence anyway and I need a quiet night. I'm going to be resting. Go. Wander with your camera. There are some great spots to get photos, like that old bridge I told you about. Come back in the morning. I'll be fine here. Doc is on his way."

I could tell he did not like the idea, but he had no counteroffer. He looked at Bill walking away and then turned back to me, a look of tenderness and vulnerability on his face I had never seen before. I took his hand and tried to reassure him.

"I promise I'll call if I need anything."

Sean nodded and bent to kiss my hand, patted Maud on the head, and headed for the driveway. Just before he got in his car, I saw him turn and say something to Bill. I couldn't hear what was said, but they shook hands.

I watched Sean drive away for the second time that day. This time I felt regret, but there was already too much crowding my mind and the pulsing in my head only grew worse as I tried to think about our future. I had no energy to spend there. I stretched out on the swing, pulled the cat into my lap, and closed my eyes.

When I woke, the sun was setting. Even this late in the day, the last rays were hot on my skin. Cooler air was there waiting beneath the trees for the sun's absence. Hidden in fields and branches all day, robins and grackles moved across the lawn looking for dinner. I sat up a little and adjusted the small pillow that had appeared under my head. Bill must have done that. As the breeze slackened, clouds of punkies gathered and drifted through the air en masse. Butterflies hovered over the pots of flowers for one more drink of nectar before heading for bed and the voices of nearby crickets grew steadier as the sun slipped lower. The faded flag, which had hung off the porch for as long as I could remember, rippled briefly and then dropped limply again.

The screen door squeaked as Bill stuck his head out to peek at me.

"Hey, you're awake," he whispered. I smiled right before I remembered I didn't have a right to be happy.

"Thanks for the pillow."

"I was afraid I'd wake you."

"I never felt a thing. I guess I was really out." It suddenly occurred to me that I had fallen asleep with the cat and woke up alone. "Where's Maud? I hope she didn't run off."

"She's fine. She's in the house. Up on Evie's bed."

"What an opportunist."

"Evie loves it."

"Good, I'm glad." I sat up and drew my arms around me, fighting off a chill.

"You hungry? I made some pork chops for Evie and me. Nothing fancy, but I could fix you a plate."

"Sorry about the fish fry."

"They were small anyway." I could hear the old tease in his voice.

"Maybe a little something would be good."

"C'mon in. Get a sweater. I'll warm a plate up for you."

"Thanks." I got up slowly, feeling heavy-headed from my long nap and the headache, which had finally started to move back into the background.

Bill banged away in the kitchen as I searched for the sweater I had worn the night before. Realizing I probably left it out in the barn, I looked up the stairs. Evelyn probably had one I could borrow, but I was hesitant to go up there. What would I say? I had turned her quiet house upside down. Sean had come and gone twice. Her husband was off who knows where for hours, not to mention I had practically had a nervous breakdown the night before. I had put one foot on the stairs, weighing the walk to the barn over going upstairs, when Evelyn called out to me.

"Cori? Is that you?"

"Yes, coming." I hurried up the stairs. "Hi, I didn't want to bother you," I said standing in the half-open doorway, "but could I borrow a sweater? I think I left mine out in the barn."

"Of course. Help yourself." Evelyn waved me to the closet to my left. There were dark circles under her glassy eyes. I tried to be casual as I flipped through the hanging clothes, my hand finally coming to rest on a gray oversized cardigan. She laughed. "That one's Bill's. I don't know how it ended up in there." Her speech slurred as if she were a little drunk.

"Oh, I didn't realize." I blushed and started to put it back.

"Don't be silly. Wear it if you like it."

Keeping my back to her, I pulled the sweater from its wooden hanger and slipped it on. Like the other borrowed clothes, it smelled of Bill. I closed my eyes and breathed in the scent of him.

"I understand you've had quite a day."

"I know. I'm sorry, Evelyn."

"Sorry for what?"

"I brought my problems here. You don't need that."

"It seems to me that you spend an awful lot of time apologizing for something that never was your fault, Corianne."

"Maybe."

"Come here," Evelyn motioned to me. I walked over and sat in the wicker chair next to the bed. "Do you want to talk about it?"

"Not just now. It's all a little confused right now." I fixed my eyes on the top of my white Keds. Neither one of us said anything for a good long moment.

"You know, Cori, your mother loved you with all her heart. You were everything to her. You and those flowers of hers."

"I know," I said softly. I wondered if Evelyn knew about Martin—about how much my mother had loved him to the very end.

"You know she might not have always gotten it right, but she did what she thought was best for you. Mothers protect their daughters. With their lives if necessary."

"What do you mean?" It was an ominous thing to say. "Did she tell you something?"

"I'm just saying if she was here…well, I think she would have wanted to be here, to help you with all this."

What my mother wanted I could not know, but I was clear on one thing—if she were here with me in this, I would be looking for answers rather than comfort. The truth was shuttered up somewhere in my head and it was coming open one slat at a time. She took the terrible truth, whatever it was, to her grave. She and my father both. There was no one left who could tell me what really happened that day. If that was parental love, I didn't think too much of it just now. I rose and kissed Evelyn on the cheek.

"I better go have something to eat. Can I bring you anything? Do you want me to shoo her out of here," I inclined my head in Maud's direction.

"No, I'm fine. Bill and I had some dinner while you were resting. Plus, I love this little one." As I stepped out into the hallway she called after me, "Cori, you'll have more answers tomorrow. Try to rest tonight."

"You too, Evelyn." I headed downstairs, my body wrapped in Bill's sweater and my head tangled in dark visions. I was missing the time when they only intruded on my sleep.

While Evelyn and I talked, Bill had set a place for me at the kitchen table. I sat down in front of a plate filled by a large pork chop, a biscuit, and some overcooked looking green beans. Pulling a faded cloth napkin onto my lap, I picked up the biscuit and tore off a bite.

"You'll be needing this," Bill said, handing me a cold bottle of beer. "Remember, I'm not much of a cook."

"No, I'm sure it's fine. It looks very good. I'm just not feeling especially hungry."

"Eat."

"Keep me company?" I asked poking at the beans with my fork.

Bill lifted his own beer in affirmation. "I'm yours for the night." He smiled and then his expression grew serious again. "Can I ask? How was Evie when you were up there?"

"She looks tired." I took a bite of pork chop. Admittedly, it was delicious. The meat melted in my mouth, tasting of apples and cinnamon.

"Yeah, that's what I thought too. I think she's in a lot more pain after her therapy today than she'll admit." He seemed to have a further conversation about this silently with himself.

"You worry about her? Getting hooked on the pills. Taking too many." In my dark mood no subject seemed off limits.

"Sometimes."

I pulled off another hunk of biscuit. "I think you're right to worry." Evelyn's glassy eyes were familiar to me. They looked like my mother's did when she was on morphine.

"Why? What? Did she say something to you?"

"No, no, nothing like that. Just a feeling. Forget it. Forget I said anything. I don't know what the hell I'm talking about."

"What's it like, Corianne? Being that close to death all the time?"

I tried to choke down the biscuit as tears filled my eyes. It stuck halfway. I swallowed hard on it and washed it down with a long drink of beer.

"I didn't ask for this, you know."

"I didn't mean that. It's just, sometimes it feels like it's here, you know? Like death is in the house. It isn't you. Oh god, Corianne. No, it is *not* you. I first felt it after her accident. More since the surgery— since they did that to her."

"It feels pretty much like this." I put my head in my hands and closed my eyes. "It's like seeing a shadow, a ghost moving out of the corner of your eye and turning just a second too late. You know it's still there. It just moved. It's waiting someplace else."

"I hate it."

"Yeah, me too."

Bill pushed back his chair and got up, leaving the kitchen. I heard him heading upstairs, I assumed to check on Evelyn. I got up and scraped the rest of my dinner into the garbage, put my plate in the sink, and grabbed the cardboard six-pack of beer, now just four bottles, from the refrigerator. Careful not to let the screen door slam, I walked out and headed toward the barn guided by the house lights, the rising moon, and instinct. I sat down on the old rough-hewn wooden bench near the outdoor shower, setting the pack of beer next to me. I wanted a cigarette badly. Most of my nights were sleepless but I knew this would be longer than any that had come before. Using the edge of the bench, I popped the cap off a longneck the way Bill had taught me that last summer and took several long swigs, making mental calculations for when Dr. Lawrence might arrive. Bill was right. Best case, he would not be here until after breakfast. He had said he had something to do first. Even traveling light, you go home, throw some things in a bag, and grab a toothbrush. Then figure in stops for gas. Sleep.

I tried to remember something good, a time before all this on which I could focus. A time when the tall grasses were an invitation to an endless day of happy exploration and the nights meant heavy-limbed empty rest. It smelled like rain though there were only a few clouds in the sky. Summer was like that here. You could smell the change rolling over the prairie when it was still hundreds of miles away.

My head was getting pleasantly thick from the beer which I drank entirely too fast. The crickets' voices stopped and started, trading off, one group picking up where another left off. I lost myself in the sound and wished I could pull it up over me like a blanket. If only I had a cigarette. The random thought had become a fixation. I thought of the one left in the pack in the tin, but I didn't know where Bill put the tin. I had some in my purse, but that was back at the house. I stood and started to pace. Maybe he kept some somewhere. I knew he never smoked around Evelyn, but he always had the odd smoke with me. Now I was betting he didn't only smoke with me. No, he had his own stash somewhere. I went into the barn and looked around, checked the small shelf by the cot and even patted down the pockets of the old coat that hung on one of the hooks. Nothing.

"What are you looking for?" Bill leaned against the doorway, a beer in hand. He had entered on feet as quiet as the damn cat.

"You're on to me." I tried to shrug off the fact that he just caught me rifling through his things. "I need a cigarette."

"And you thought I'd have some?"

"I thought you might." He stared at me for a moment, like he was trying to decide if I was telling the truth, and then walked lazily to the shelf. "I already checked there," I volunteered, further incriminating myself.

Bill paused, raised the bottle of beer, and pushed it against a board above the head of the cot. The board flipped outward and with his free hand, Bill reached up and pulled out a pack of cigarettes.

"You have to know where to look."

"Look at you with your secrets." I took him in with equal parts of amusement and admiration. I never thought of Bill having secrets. It made him sexy in a way I had never considered. From his pocket, he produced a small brass lighter and handed it to me. There was an inscription, but the brass was too heavily tarnished to make out what it said. After lighting my cigarette, I held the lighter out to Bill. He leaned in. The end of his cigarette glowed as he dragged hard on it to make sure it caught. I closed the lighter with a satisfyingly solid snap.

"Hey, is that my sweater?"

"Yeah."

"It looks better on you." He turned and walked out. He was in a mood. This was a side I had never seen. I followed him back to the bench. I sat, but Bill was now the restless one. He put his foot up on the bench and took another long drag. I waited. "Look, I'm sorry about earlier."

"No apology needed." We finished our smokes in silence and dropped the butts in one of the empty beer bottles.

"It feels like it won't ever be light again. Doesn't it?" I said finally. "Like everything that's gone before is someone else's life you're watching on a screen." I sighed hard. "The way it aches. That's what tells you it's your pain. That's how you know."

Bill reached over and cupped my face in the palm of his hand. He just held it there. Just like that. Dropping his hand, he stood up and turned to look out into the darkness. I reached out and let my fingers stroke his gently. His hand closed around mine, then all at once, he turned and pulled me to my feet. His mouth collided into mine. He kissed me roughly and urgently. He pushed the sweater from my shoulders and buried his face in my hair, in my neck, murmuring "Coriander. My beautiful sad Coriander."

But as his unshaved face scraped against my skin, as he undressed me, as my hands hurried his own clothes to the ground, it was not my sadness that ravaged me. When he lifted me and I wrapped my legs around him, it was not sadness that entered me. As we fell down on the old cot, the fire that had burned across my dreams lapped all around me, consuming me. Welcoming me. Welcoming us. We were both broken now.

CHAPTER THIRTY-THREE

HE WOULD NOT stay. I knew he could not, and so I savored each minute we laid together, hot skin touching. There were no words, just restless hands and mouths. Finally, he rose to go. I sat up and watched him dress in the dim light.

"Corianne." He reached back for me though he faced the door. I took his hand.

"I know."

I listened to him walk away and when I could no longer hear the crunch of his boots, I climbed back into the old gray sweater, pulled up the blanket, and stared into the darkness, all my senses still highly tuned. Memorizing exactly how he had felt, still feeling where he had been, until I fell asleep.

My sleep was heavy at first. Then the dreams came. Confused and fragmented. Walking with my mother in the garden. The Virgin Mary appearing along the stone wall, smiling at us while blue fire ringed her feet. Rebecca's casket floating in the river. Old grain silos rising along the banks like ancient round towers. I woke with a start just as the casket began to open and a small white hand floated up in the water.

Heart hammering, I sat up, eyes straining into the dark. I was unsure where I was until the cool night air sifted through gaps in the boards and settled on me reassuringly. I was in the barn. I was safe. At least for now. Perhaps, I thought, the things I had left to fear were not in this world.

"Another bad dream?" The sound of Bill's voice from somewhere in the dark startled me and I jumped.

"God dammit." My voice was raspy from the late night, the beer, and the cigarettes. I peered in the direction his voice had come from but could not see him. "How long have you been here?"

"Not long. An hour, maybe less." He shifted and I realized he was sitting down against the wall on the other side of the space, under the hooks where his coat hung.

I got up and walked in a slow shuffle, stepping gingerly with bare feet toward his voice, my arms held out in front of me because I could not remember if the path between us was clear. When I was right in front of him, Bill reached out and put his hand lightly on the side of my knee so I would feel where he was. I turned around and slid down to sit next to him.

"I thought you might be cold. I brought you the big blanket from your bed. The couch. Whatever." He flipped the blanket open and I felt the gush of air in my face, the brush of fabric against my cheek as he wrapped it around me. "I've been watching you sleep."

I knew the blanket was an excuse. I had blankets out here.

"Thanks." I wasn't sure what to say next. We fell into silence. Finally, I spoke again. "Bill?"

"I don't know," he answered.

"Yeah, neither do I." I put my head down on his shoulder. Bill lifted his arm and pulled me in against him, wrapped his other arm around me and held me tight. I fell asleep again sitting there, listening to the rise and fall of his breath.

I woke for the second time in the intimacy of that soft time before dawn and Bill's embrace. My neck ached as I lifted myself upright and leaned back against the timbers of the barn wall. Bill was awake, looking straight ahead. He had never closed his eyes. We had slept like soldiers, him letting me doze while he kept watch. Feeling me stir, he turned and gave me a small smile.

"Good morning."

"Morning." Tentatively, I reached out and put my hand on his arm. He smiled again, reached over to brush the hair from my face, and kissed me tenderly. "I'm glad you slept."

"I'm sorry you didn't."

"Do you know what I love most about the farm?"

"No, tell me."

"The order of it. The rhythm. The work. The way everything lives and everything rests. Really rests. There is a freedom in the certainty of it. And there is an hour, this hour, when everything is quiet, and still, and new. Even the wind hasn't woken up yet. It is completely pure. You can get really empty in an hour like that."

I said nothing and put my head back on his shoulder in silent apology. I had brought everything but stillness with me. Chaos had surely followed me to Sheerfolly Chapel. Now, the chaos in my mind was unraveling outside of it. I would always leave a trail of destruction. That is what Mrs. Ashworth meant when she looked me in the eye and quoted John 3 to me. I had looked it up in my mother's family Bible with shaking hands. There was something in me that chose the darkness. *Because their deeds were evil.*

When I found out about Martin Hayden, about how much my mother loved him, loved him even all the years she was with my father, how she wished I had been his child, I thought that was it. That thought or longing—my mother's sin— somehow lived in me. I told myself that was why I had never felt right anywhere but running through those fields chasing grasshoppers. Eventually, the shadow fell there as well. Now I knew a portion of my mother's torment, and in my recklessness, I had made it Bill's.

"I'm sorry, Bill." The words finally came. "I've never really been good at being still."

He kissed the top of my head. "I'm not. Sorry, that is. You, Coriander, you are like the air right before a storm. I knew it the moment we met. I've always loved that about you. The thing about chasing storms—you can't mind getting caught in it."

My cellphone chirped. Bill pulled it out of his pocket and looked at the number. "You ready?"

Dr. Lawrence drove to the house, pulled around the circle and stopped his 1963 black Mercedes convertible with its round headlights pointing toward the road. Bill let out a low whistle of appreciation.

I didn't know whether to hug Dr. Lawrence or try to appear totally nonchalant meeting him in completely abnormal conditions. I went with the latter.

"Glad to see my sessions have gone to good use, Doc." Dr. Lawrence was neither uncomfortable with my suggestion nor apologetic. Bill stepped forward and offered his hand.

"Dr. Lawrence, I'm Bill. Thank you so much for coming."

"Bill, I'm glad you called." Then Dr. Lawrence turned to me. "Corianne, how are you feeling? We're you able to get some sleep last night?"

"Yes," I answered too quickly. Then added, "A few hours. Dreams again."

"We'll talk about those and what happened yesterday," he said looking from me to Bill and back again. I thought I detected a small flicker of recognition cross his Mount Rushmore face. "We have a lot to talk about, but perhaps we could start with some coffee. It has been a long night. Would that be all right with you?"

"Yes, of course," Bill jumped in. "I'll go get a pot started. Corianne, why don't you show the doc around? Let him stretch his legs."

We walked around the outside of the house, then down past the barn and the paddock while I narrated with what I knew about the farm, how it came to be in the Parson family, and how Evelyn had inherited it. Most of the rest he knew from our sessions. The Suttons and the Parsons, Evelyn's family, had become good friends back when the Parsons bought the land from old man Soloman. My mother and Evelyn had known each other as girls just as Rebecca and I had.

We stopped along the pathway to the windbreak. I did not want to take him there. It felt like too sacred a space. I pulled the pack of cigarettes from my back pocket that I had lifted from the barn before going to meet Dr. Lawrence in the driveway. Now I offered one to Dr. Lawrence. He just looked at me stonily.

"No thank you."

"Well, I know you don't mind." I tossed my hair to one side and leaned in to light a smoke.

He met my sass and raised me one.

"So how long have you been sleeping with Bill?"

He said it just like that. No preamble. No warning that the session had begun. He just lobbed that question at me like a Molotov cocktail he watched explode at my feet.

"What? No coffee and small talk? Wow, it's a good thing I'm not the fragile type, Doc. You know, some head case who has nightmares and sees dead girls."

"Come on, Corianne. You've never been one for coddling. You made that plain by the time you were twelve. I won't start now."

"I like you better with the chair and fake ficus."

"The ficus is real." He paused before going on. "You want me to give it to you straight, so now do the same for me. It's a simple question, Corianne. Why are you avoiding it?"

"I'm not avoiding it."

"Then answer it."

"Last night," I exhaled a long stream of smoke. "It just happened last night." When Dr. Lawrence looked at me, I saw that almost imperceptible flicker of his left eyebrow. "I swear to God, it was the first time. Look, you encouraged me to stay here. You know how I feel about him."

"I encouraged you to work with the memories that were surfacing in a place where you felt safe. This was, of course, always a possibility."

"It just…happened."

"Do you know why?"

"I felt...lost. Scared. We both were. The dreams are back." I tried to change the subject.

"How are you feeling this morning about it?"

"How do you think?" I snapped back. I took another drag on the cigarette. The length of gray ash grew, hanging on the end until I finally flicked the butt end with my thumb. "Everything I touch, everything that touches me, dies. I don't want that for him. I love Bill. I always have."

"Let's start there."

"What about your coffee?"

"Oh, I haven't forgotten. Let's walk." As we walked slowly back to the house, he let me be quiet for a minute and then asked, "Where are you most comfortable here?"

The windbreak flashed into my mind immediately, but I didn't say it. I thought of the house. The kitchen? No, I didn't want to talk there in the house with Evelyn upstairs. The barn, but—Dr. Lawrence saw me hesitating.

"Corianne, we will have the best result if we do this where you feel safe, but it also needs to be a place that is meaningful to you."

"There's a place. It's just a strip of land between two of the fields. A windbreak with some trees and grass. Bill and I buried a rabbit there once—when I was young. It's where I go when I'm here. When things get—"

"I remember. Good. Do you feel you can take me there?"

I paused, chewing on my lower lip. I looked down and then looked up at Dr. Lawrence with a sidelong glance. If I wanted my answers, I needed to do this. "Yeah. Yeah okay." I gave a small nod. "We can go there."

"I need to get something from the car." Doc said. "I'll do that and perhaps there is some way we can take the coffee to go. I'd like to get started."

"Sure. There is a big thermos. I'll get it." I turned toward the house and then turned back to Dr. Lawrence. "Are you going like that?" I pointed to his crisp trousers and oh-so subtly striped dress shirt and loafers.

"I'll be alright," he said.

"You might want to change your shoes," I tossed over my shoulder as I walked away.

"What about Sean?" Bill asked as I was screwing the top on the thermos.

"What do you mean? What about him?" My mind wasn't tracking. I was distracted with Dr. Lawrence here and anxious about starting our session on the windbreak.

"Sean, he's planning on coming back here this morning, right?"

"Oh Jesus. I can't." I could feel several emotions rising in me, not the least of which was guilt.

"He's not here yet," Bill said looking out the front window. "I might be able to head him off with a phone call. You go, Corianne. Go out the back and get Doc. If he shows up, I'll handle it."

"How? Invite him in for coffee?"

"Maybe. Look, just go. You don't need him in the middle of this right now. Doc said you need to feel safe, right?"

I hesitated. It didn't feel unsafe around Sean. He had been there for me when my mother died after all. But it was true it would be more than I could take on right now.

"Corianne, it's not going to be a short conversation. You know that. You need to go. I swear I will explain to him that Dr. Lawrence needed to talk with you alone."

"You're sure?" I asked, my hand resting for a moment on Bill's arm.

"I'm sure. Now go."

"Okay." I started toward the door. "Wait. Maud, I want to take her with me." I dashed to the mudroom where I had seen her stalking a cricket. She was there with the now deceased cricket under her paw.

"Oh Maud. Honestly, what did that cricket ever do to you except have the misfortune to get stuck in here." I had the awful pink leash in my hand and hooked it on Maud's collar.

"Are you sure that's a good idea?"

"She'll be on her leash."

"The rabbit?" Bill reminded me. "Oh, forget it. Just go."

"She's a cat not a dog," I said as Bill swung open the screen door. I ducked under his arm. I wanted to kiss him but seeing Dr. Lawrence waiting for me I said simply and honestly, "Thank you for this."

Dr. Lawrence stepped forward and said something to Bill in a low voice he thought I would not hear.

"Keep the phone close."

As it turned out, Dr. Lawrence had agreed with Bill's instinct to intercept Sean. A "later conversation," he had called it. Doc had a leather messenger bag with him. I hadn't bothered to ask what was in it. His notepad and pen no doubt. Instead of his usual reading glasses, he wore sunglasses. They were not like Sean's gunmetal aviators, more Gregory Peck. There were even fewer clues now to his thoughts, but I felt like I had a new insight into Dr. Lawrence seeing him outside the office.

The heat of the day was already beginning to build, and the wind had picked up so that as we walked down the grassy way between the fields out to the windbreak, the corn told its stories. Dr. Lawrence paused and looked around as we came up on the windbreak. The big oak tree, the stone altar, and the patch of curated green grass looked weirdly out of place next to the fields of corn rising and falling as they did in tidy rows along the swells of earth toward other smaller breaks before running to the rye fields, golden tassels waving.

We sat under the sheltering arms of the oak, its shade already welcome. Dr. Lawrence unscrewed the top of the thermos and poured coffee into the lid cup. He offered me the first cup, but I waved him off.

"I think the last thing I need right now is coffee." I busied myself securing Maud's leash around an old stump so she could explore then settled down across from Dr. Lawrence and leaned back on my hands, watching her. She soon became enthralled with all the movement and new smells. She crouched down and watched the crows cawing from the gnarly oak tree, the tiny voles who crept through the grass, and everything else moved on that island.

"Tell me about the dreams." Dr. Lawrence asked.

"The same to start. Fire. The Virgin Mary. But last night, last night was different. I was walking with my mother in the garden. Mary came to us. The fire was around her. Blue fire. And the casket." I stopped.

"What casket? Your mother's?"

"No. No, it was Rebecca's. It was floating in the river. She reached for me." I pulled my legs up and hugged them tightly.

"Okay. Good. Let's go back and talk about what happened yesterday at the river." Dr. Lawrence sipped his coffee.

"Aren't you going to take notes?" I asked motioning to his bag lying in the grass.

"Would you like to me to?" he asked.

"I don't give a fuck. I just know how you like your notes."

"Tell me about the river. What happened at the river?"

"Nothing. We fished." I laughed at the memory. "Bill took me fishing. We were trying to catch enough rock bass for dinner."

"Did you?"

"Yeah. Well, not enough for a feast, but yeah, we did."

"So that was pleasant."

"Yeah," I laughed. "It was pleasant."

"How do you think that connects to your dream?"

"I don't think it does.'

"Talk to me about what happened after you left the river, after the—"

"Throw me that can," I interrupted. Dr. Lawrence tossed the empty soda can in my direction. I picked it up, pulled out Bill's cigarettes, and promptly lit up. Maud lifted her head and taking one whiff of the smoke, practically wrinkled her pink nose in disgust before turning back to her latest quarry—a hapless little toad.

"We were driving back to the farm," I finally continued. "The railroad tracks run right along the road there. I heard the train." I closed my eyes and listened to the memory of the train rocking and clicking down the tracks. "I saw something. By the tracks."

"What did you see?"

"Rebecca." I opened my eyes and looked at Dr. Lawrence. "It was Rebecca. I was sure of it. She was standing there in that dress. Except it wasn't her. When Bill went to look, it wasn't her. She was showing me something."

"She was showing you something? What was it?"

"A deer. A doe." My eyes were welling with tears as I remembered the sight of her. I thought about the feel of her body trembling beneath my hand. "She had been hit by the train while trying to cross the tracks. She was so beautiful. So broken. Bill said she wouldn't make it long. He thought it was for the best."

"What was best?"

"She had to be put down. Her leg was shattered, she was…she was—" I was breathing harder, and my hands were shaking. "There was blood and bone. Bill sent me to the truck to get the rifle—I stayed with her as long as I could. I didn't want her to be alone, you know? I put my hand on her head. She looked at me. I think she knew." I finished what was left of the cigarette and crushed it out on the can. "Look, you know all this." I ran my hands through my hair. "Bill told you all this on the phone yesterday."

Dr. Lawrence did not directly acknowledge the phone call or what I had said, but his questions shifted.

"What happened after that? What happened when you came here to the windbreak?"

I sighed. "I had Bill's shirt." Seeing no reaction from behind the dark glasses, I continued. "It had blood on it. I buried it." I mumbled the last part, turning my head.

"You buried it?"

"Yeah, over there. Near the rabbit." I waved my hand at the small circle of freshly turned dirt. Defensively, I added, "Well, I couldn't very well bury the deer, could I?"

"Okay, you buried the shirt. Then what?"

"I wanted a smoke. To settle my nerves, I guess. I remembered I had a tin stashed out here from when I used to visit. There were a few old cigarettes, a joint—the tin seemed airtight, so I lit up. That's when I found the button. That's when I remembered."

"Tell me about the button."

"It was a flat pearly button. I had seen it before. It was Rebecca's. It was on that dress, the one she wore that day. There were two buttons. Here and here." I pointed to my waist indicating where they had been sewn to the dress she wore. Then I saw…I remembered. Rebecca was lying there." My stomach turned as I thought of her body twisted unnaturally.

"Take your time. Remember, you are safe here at the farm."

"She had…a dried leaf in her hair and there was dirt, on her arm." I touched my arm as I spoke. "I pulled the leaf out of her hair, touched her. She looked like she was sleeping. But when I…her skin was cool."

"You're doing very well, Corianne. Stay with that memory. What else do you see?"

"One of the buttons is hanging from broken threads. I took it. I knew I shouldn't, but I couldn't stop myself. It was so pretty I wanted it. But I wasn't there by myself. There was a man. I heard his voice. I hid the button in my hand."

"What did he say?" Dr. Lawrence asked gently.

"That's a good girl." I shivered. "Who was he? Was that him, her killer? Why do I remember being there? I wasn't there. I ran. I ran." My breath was coming so fast now I was almost hyperventilating.

"You're doing very well, Corianne. This is much farther than we have ever gotten."

"But who is he? I want to know. Is this even a real memory? It *feels* real." My mind was buzzy and unfocused. I was feeling lightheaded, like when you stand up too fast. Everything was starting to swim in front of me.

"Take some deep breaths. Try to relax and when you feel ready, I want you to close your eyes."

I did as Dr. Lawrence instructed. I breathed in and out, slowly, aware of my pulse thumping away in my throat. I looked over at Maud sitting at attention, watching everything, her tail swishing slowly back and forth. I imagined the feel of her dark silky fur under my hand when I rubbed the top of her head. Gradually my breathing slowed.

"I'm ready." I closed my eyes. "Now what?"

"Go back to the man's voice. Where was he when you took the button?"

Reluctantly, I went back into the memory. My kneeling view of Rebecca. My hand reaching out to take the button, closing around it. I frowned. "I'm not sure. I can't see him."

"Listen to his voice," Dr. Lawrence guided me. "Where is it coming from?"

My hand closed around the button. I could feel its hard outline pressing into the palm of my hand. *That's a good girl.*

"He's behind me. I can't see him. Just his shoes. They are black. He wants me to go with him. He has me by the hand. I still have the button in the other. I don't want him to see. I'm not supposed to have it."

"That's very good, Corianne. Now look up. Can you see his face?"

His big hand enveloped mine. I tried to look up. "No, I can't." My eyes snapped open. "I'm sorry, I couldn't see his face. I was kneeling and it was bright behind him." I uncurled my hand and looked at my palm. "I had to hide the button. I held on to it tight, so tight it left a red ring in my hand. Why do I remember that and not his face?"

"Our memories are not always sequential. Especially when it's a traumatic memory as yours is."

"I don't understand any of this." I was tired and frustrated.

Dr. Lawrence pulled his sunglasses off and hooked them on his shirt pocket. His face looked strangely empty without glasses. He had his notepad on his lap. I hadn't noticed when he took it out. He looked at me a long time without saying anything. We just sat in silence. Finally, he spoke.

"Corianne, I believe these are real memories you're accessing. They have been coming in flashes, bits and pieces before, but you couldn't remember the main parts. You weren't ready. Remember, your mind protected you. You were very young and these things you experienced, the things you saw, were very frightening. And as we've discussed previously, a part of you felt very guilty because you lived."

"But how can we know they are real?"

Dr. Lawrence steepled his index fingers and brought them against his full lips. I had always thought he had a very sensual mouth. It was in such contrast with the rest of his very controlled demeanor. His eyes moved from me down to his messenger bag.

"Corianne, I did a little research before I drove here."

"What kind of research?" I asked. I thought he had looked up some study on traumatic memory loss and he was going to unroll a bunch of psychological jargon on me.

"I talked to a friend in the DA's office. She put me in touch with the detective who worked your case. He is still on the job."

"Detective Hanley? Why?"

"I asked him to pull the police report on Rebecca's death." He looked again at his bag.

"Is that it? It's in there?"

"Yes. I read it through before I headed here. I thought it might shed some light on this. On these new visions or memories."

"And did it?" I was sitting with every muscle locked in anticipation.

"It did." Dr. Lawrence paused and then continued. "The man that you remember, the man with the black shoes—Corianne, that was Detective Hanley."

"What? How could that be? I didn't meet Detective Hanley until he came to the house. He talked to me in the kitchen."

"He did come to the house, but he found you there first. With Rebecca's body."

Of course, I had known somehow when I had the vision about Rebecca, about touching her and taking the button, that it was more than a hallucination or a waking dream. I had told Bill as much. It was real. Yet now, faced with the reality, I felt more confused than ever. More afraid.

"How is that possible?"

"As I said, when we witness something too traumatic, the mind protects itself. In your case, deleting a portion of the events and then splicing two memories on either side together, like splicing together two pieces of celluloid. Quite simply, the film or memory you have been reliving has been edited—by you."

The ramifications were terrifying. The truth, the real memory, could be so much worse than what I had lived with all these years. My headache was intensifying again. I grabbed the right side of my head where a dull ache alternated with a sharp pain.

"Corianne, tell me what you're feeling right now."

"My head, it's pounding. I feel lightheaded. My chest feels tight."

"Okay," Dr. Lawrence said calmly, but I could tell he was concerned. "We've done a lot. That's enough for now. You need to rest." He pulled his phone from his pocket and hit a button. He stood and turned away from me, talking into the phone in a low voice, but I could hear everything he said. "Hello, Bill, it's Dr. Lawrence. We are done for right now. Is everything in hand there? Yes, yes, I see. Could you walk out and meet us? I think it would be good for her. Reassuring. Fine. Good."

"Dr. Lawrence," I continued as soon as he had ended the call, "I want to know. I need to know."

"I understand, Corianne. But right now you also need to rest. You're trying to process this new information. It is important we don't go too fast. You need time to catch up with yourself. Why don't you collect Maud and we will walk back, maybe have a little something to eat?"

"I'm not hungry," I answered, but I got to my feet, gathered the leash, and picked up the drowsy Maud. Dr. Lawrence waved me in front of him. I was to lead the way. I walked along the path not really seeing anything until Bill appeared in front of me like one of my hallucinations. He took Maud from me, holding her like a football. The warmth of his body as he wrapped his free arm around me was real enough.

"It must be 90 degrees out here and you're shaking like a leaf. Come on. It's all right, girl. It will be all right."

Bill walked me straight to the barn. I looked at him quizzically, then at Dr. Lawrence. "I thought we were going back to the house?"

"Would you prefer to go to the house?" In his typically frustrating way, Dr. Lawrence answered my question with a question.

"No. I mean, I'm so tired."

"You should lie down but eat a little something first. You haven't had anything to eat all morning." Bill suggested. I shook my head no. "At least have something to drink. Some water. It's so hot."

I took the bottle of water he offered and took several good-sized gulps. Almost immediately, I wanted to throw up. I shook my head and handed the bottle back to Bill.

"Come on." Bill handed me the cat and led me into the little room below the hayloft, to the bed we had shared the night before. Without another thought, I slipped off my shoes and laid back. Bill wet a cloth and laid it on my forehead. The compress felt good. I wished it could cool the inside of my head too.

"Don't go," my voice rose in a plea.

"I'm not going anywhere. And she is going back to the house with Doc."

Dr. Lawrence poked his ahead around the corner, looking more out of place than ever in his posh work clothes. Bill deposited Maud in his arms. I smiled smugly at the sight of Maud with my shrink. Birds of a feather.

"Bill, can I have a word?" Dr. Lawrence asked.

"Yeah, sure." Bill cast a worried look my way. I nodded. The two men stepped outside.

As their voices rose and fell, a word or two would filter through my fatigue: *psychogenic amnesia, trauma, reorganize.* I was much too tired to stitch those words together into anything more and it was soothing just to hear their voices. The only two men other than my father I had ever really let myself deeply trust. And Sean. Where was Sean? Was he here? My eyes felt heavy and began to close. I opened them again, trying to focus on the knot in one of the oak beams running overhead. Before long, they closed again. Every time I might have drifted into sleep, I snapped awake again, afraid of what new images I might see against the darkness. Eventually, I could hold them open no longer.

I stand at the edge of a subterranean tidal river, holding my hands together like a book, palms turned upward. Resting in my hands is a dark-colored salamander. As I look at it, lying there in my hands, a tenderness for this being washes over me. Overcome, I begin to cry softly. Instantly, I know it is especially important to put the creature in the water. I wade into the water and holding it gently, I move it slowly through the water as I would to revive a stunned fish before releasing it. I do not mean to let go of the salamander and yet it leaves my hand. I panic until I realize it is swimming on its own. I watch it for as long as I can, but the water is dark and the salamander disappears within a few seconds, into water nearly the same color as its back.

"It just doesn't make any sense." I hoped my irritated tone would mask the way this new dream still unsettled me. There was something about the underground cavern and the murky water.

"I think it is quite interesting. In fact, it makes rather a lot of sense." Dr. Lawrence was making notes on the pad. "The salamander is an amphibian. It is inherently of two worlds, living part of its life in the water and another part on land. If I am not mistaken an amphibian such as your salamander begins its life in water. In swimming away, it would be returning to its origin. It seems reasonable that in one possible interpretation, and of course there are many, the subterranean river would be your unconscious, the part of your mind you are trying to recover. That would account for the hidden quality. The murkiness of the water. You said you felt moved by the salamander. Why do you think that might be?"

"I don't know. It was strange. The thing was really ugly. Creepy, you know, in a primordial way. Like those fish with no eyes that live in caves." I was poking at the ground with one of the sticks that had come down off the oak tree in the last storm.

"Follow that," Dr. Lawrence suggested.

"What? The fish with no eyes?"

"No. Well, yes. If that's where it takes you."

"Doc how is this going to help me remember?" I threw the stick as hard as I could out into the field. It made a whistling noise as it sliced the air near my ear. "Go get it Maud." She opened her eyes a slit, bemused, and then closed them again.

We had been sitting underneath the tree for close to an hour and had not progressed past my crazy dream. I stood up, feeling restless, and brushed the grass and dirt from the back of my shorts. With a defiant look in Dr. Lawrence's direction, I pulled out another cigarette and struck a match. Rather than lecturing me, he simply rolled the empty can my direction.

"What about Sean? If he gets here and I'm not at the house. I've seen the way he looks at Bill. Complete contempt."

"And undoubtedly, he sees how Bill looks at you. Sean is a smart guy. He understands the importance of what is happening here and from all you've told me, he is very supportive of the work you are doing. I don't think he'll jeopardize that for jealousy. He loves you."

I clenched my fist. I didn't want to need Sean's support. I certainly didn't deserve it. I opened my mouth to say as much and then closed it again.

"Corianne, when you're ready, let's try again. When we're done here, we can work on quitting smoking again."

Did I see a flicker of amusement on Dr. Lawrence's face? I took one long last drag off the cigarette, the end glowing hotly. "I just feel like I'm going to crawl out of my skin." I snubbed out my smoke and sat back down.

"Try not to think of anything specific right now or what will happen next." Dr. Lawrence began in that soothing tone of his. "I want you to just close your eyes and take a deep breath. That's it. And again. One more." He allowed a long pause. "Now, we'll begin very simply. Tell me where you are."

"I'm on the farm, in Sheerfolly Chapel. With you."

"How do you know? What tells you that?"

"I don't know. Umm...I feel the sun. I can smell the earth. And water. I can smell water, from the big irrigation sprinklers in the fields. Some of the spray gets picked up and carried on the wind like rain. I hear your pen scratching on the paper. Crows cawing."

"How does it feel to be here?"

"It feels good. Peaceful."

"Can you remember another time when you felt this way, Corianne? Do you remember another time when you could smell the earth? A time when you heard the birds and felt calm and happy?"

"I used to feel like this when I was running though the fields when I was a little girl. I would swish through the grass with a great big stick playing explorer. It felt like I was the only one, you know? Like I was the first person ever to walk there. There were some twisty old oaks by the creek, and I would go and try to catch frogs—"

"What is it, Cori? What did you remember?"

"Rebecca. She was by the water. In the tall grass by the creek. With the dried-up leaf in her hair. I wasn't supposed to go there. I was supposed to wait."

"Who told you to wait?"

I closed my eyes tighter trying to make sense of the fractured images that were flashing through my mind.

"It was a man's voice."

"Detective Hanley?" Dr. Lawerence asked.

"No, no someone else. He's telling me to wait." My mouth formed the word wait and I touched my finger to it. "We're crouched in the grass. He puts his finger up to his lips and he mouths the word *wait*."

"What else?"

"He has a gun."

"A gun?" Dr. Lawrence did his best to mask his surprise, but his voice rose a bit too much at the end of the question.

"Not like a handgun. Big." The image came into better focus. "It's a rifle. A hunting rifle, like the one Bill used to put down the deer."

"Can you see whose holding it?"

"His hands. They are dirty. Greasy. But I can't see his face." Frustrated with my lack of recall, I frowned. As frightening as the memory was, I needed to remember. I took a deep breath and tried again. "It's…no. That can't be right." I stopped myself. "It's Mr. Emory."

"Mr. Emory? The farmer?"

"Yes. The one whose fields we cut through. He is holding my arm. I can see Rebecca, but he won't let me go to her. I don't understand."

"Then what happens. Just visualize the memory. Try not to think ahead of it."

I drew in a sharp breath.

"Corianne?"

"No, I don't want to."

"We've come this far, Corianne. But we can stop now if you don't feel ready for this."

My mouth had gone completely dry. I licked my lips and swallowed hard. My throat felt thick like cotton. "No," I managed. "Let's keep going."

"Okay, you're there crouching in the field with Mr. Emory. Then what?"

"A man, the man, the one from the car. He's kneeling over Rebecca. He hears us. Hears me in the grass. He looks up. He sees us." My hands were turning over and over each other, fingers knotting and unknotting. The memories were coming so fast now I didn't need Dr. Lawrence to prompt me. They tumbled out.

"He saw us and stood up. I had already started running. Running to Rebecca. To help her. The man, he came toward us. Toward me. That's when Mr. Emory fired. I heard the crack of the gun. It was so loud. He took it in the shoulder. It kind of exploded. His shoulder. His shoulder was torn apart. I looked up at him, his face, his eyes. He was so surprised. But then his face got all angry and he reached for me. He had a belt or something in his hands. That's when Mr. Emory fired again. The man dropped the belt and clutched at his stomach. There was blood all over his hands. He fell near me. Mr. Emory told me to go. To run. I tried calling to Rebecca. She wasn't moving. I didn't want to leave her and started toward her again. Mr. Emory shouted at me to go. I looked back at him...at Mr. Emory. I didn't know what to do. I had to step around the man on the ground. He was making scary gasping noises. I was afraid he was going to reach out and grab my ankles as I went passed. I froze. Then I heard Mr. Emory's yelling at me again to run. I ran. I ran as fast as I could."

I was sobbing. There it was. All of it. The violence and the gore. The horror I felt. It was all there. I promptly threw up.

CHAPTER THIRTY-FOUR

THERE WERE THINGS that still weren't clear even with what I remembered that afternoon. Detective Hanley had found me with Rebecca. I couldn't remember why or how. It took more time with Doc to unearth the rest. He stayed at the farm for several more days. Bill tended to me as he had Evelyn for these past years, cooking things he knew I liked to tempt me to eat. Sean stayed close. He came to the farm most afternoons but went back to the hotel in Mason for the evenings. I was glad he was near.

"I found her, not the police. How could I forget that?" I asked Doc in the last session at the farm.

"How could you remember?" Dr. Lawrence said quietly.

"I ran to the creek. She was already dead."

Dr. Lawrence put his hands in his lap and said grimly, "In these cases, the victim usually is killed within the first few hours."

"But I remember talking to Detective Hanley at the house? How?"

From underneath his notepad, Dr. Lawrence produced the brown file folder I had seen earlier.

"As I told you, when I knew I was coming here, I called to speak with Detective Hanley to see what light he might be able to shed on this. He was good enough to let me see the case file. I was not able to take the actual file with me, but he did let me make some notes and made me a copy of the transcript of his interview with you. Corianne, according to the police report, you led Detective Hanley and the other officers to Rebecca's body.

"I did?"

"Not directly. You led them to the field. After you'd been home. Hanley tried talking with you, but you took off running. There were reports of a little girl with auburn hair running into the field. Neither of you had arrived at school. That was the first alarm. Then Rebecca's abduction, everyone was on high alert. Neighbors told the police they had seen you. Detective Hanley followed your path and discovered you kneeling by Rebecca's body. No one knew how to account for the missing hours. Until now."

I closed my eyes again and felt Detective Hanley take my small hand in his large and strong one. *Cori, it's okay. These officers will take good care of your friend. Come on, let's get you home. That's it. That's a good girl.* It was Detective Hanley's voice I had remembered hearing and it was his face that I saw silhouetted when I looked up.

"He wanted me to get in the back of the police car, but when he opened the door, I wouldn't get in. Not until later, when I went with my mother. I just froze. It looked too much like his...the seats. Like the man's car."

"Do you remember what came next?"

I fought my way through the fog that had settled over my memory and the fear that had risen in my body when I remembered the car again. My jaw was tight, and both my hands had closed into fists.

"We walked. We walked all the way back to the house. He never let go of my hand." Tears were streaming down my face. "I had the button in my other hand. I thought I would get in trouble, so I hid it in the pocket of my father's coat and then in my room." Wiping away tears only to have them replaced by new ones, I turned again to Dr. Lawrence. "But at some point, I brought the button out here and put it in the tin. I have no memory of doing it. That's still blank."

"All this time, all these years, I was certain he was still out there. Certain that he followed me. Certain he knew where I lived. That he was going to come back for me."

He took a moment to clear his throat before he answered. "You may remember that in time. Your brain is extremely busy right now putting everything back in the proper order. It is why your hallucinations and visions seemed so real and immediate. You were reliving fragments of memories. As bits of information rose to the surface, you were experiencing them as events happening now, in the present. Or woven into dreams. Not as past events. Now they have context again within the larger framework of the event."

"The hallucinations and dreams will go away now?" I asked hopefully.

"In theory," Dr. Lawrence answered cautiously. "It might take some time, but yes, in many cases like this, they do recede and eventually cease."

"In theory. Okay. Well, those are better odds than before."

"You still have a lot of work to do, Corianne. You do understand that? But you have your feet on solid ground now."

"Yes, I understand."

"Doc?" I asked as we stood and began walking back to the house. "What happened to the body? What about Mr. Emory?"

"Detective Hanley's report makes no mention of Mr. Emory or finding a body other than Rebecca's."

I stopped walking and turned sharply to look at Dr. Lawrence. He kept walking slowly in his expensive loafers and his now rumpled trousers.

CHAPTER THIRTY-FIVE

I LAID DOWN on the riverbank, closed my eyes and waited. After several minutes, I opened them again. I was still alone. Alone with new memories. I had left home to run through the fields that had always held me like a daughter. Rebecca had been my sister. We had made it so.

One day when we told our mothers we were riding bikes, we snuck down to the creek. Once there we gathered dried grasses, leaves, seedpods–whatever we found that looked curious and medicinal, and we piled them up on a flat rock. We lit a fire with matches I had stolen from my father's study. Rebecca had brought a length of silken green cord from her mother's sewing basket. While the fire burned, we clasped wrists, my palm to the inside of her wrist, and her palm to the inside of mine. Carefully, Rebecca wound the cord around our two wrists. She had written a special poem for the occasion. I had forgotten the words long ago. Something about asking the nature spirits to recognize our sisterhood. Then we dipped our personal sacred objects into the water. Mine was a crow feather, hers, her lucky rabbit's foot. We traded as a sign of our trust. Rebecca said it was important that the moon be in a certain phase for the ritual. Neither of us could be out at night so far from home but we could see the moon rising that day. Rebecca was certain the time was right. To seal our sisterhood, we smoked a cigarette that Rebecca had stolen from her older cousin Brian. I was quite a bit older before I realized we had shared a joint. We were now sisters forever. Two weeks later, she was dead.

I missed her. She understood me in a way no one else could. Had she lived, well, I knew the odds were against us staying close as we grew up. She was perfect Rebecca Ashworth with her silky blond hair and her family's plans for her, and I was Corianne Dempsey, hopelessly wild down to my unruly hair. Perhaps, I thought about it now, we had remained friends because she had died.

My headaches were better again, but the fatigue was still bad. I had been resting and sleeping a lot the last few days, and I preferred to be alone. Everything reminded me of something. The grief reborn each day. My memories were reshaping themselves daily. Now, the cool water lapping against the bank, burbling over rocks, took me back to the hours I used to spend alongside that creek. My favorite time there was just after the rain, when instead of stagnant old water, it managed a real current. There was a place not far from where Rebecca was found, where I found her, marked by the long line of a birch tree which had fallen and lodged in the whorl of branches of an aged oak, where a series of large white rocks stuck out like a shelf. In the driest weather, there might not even be a trickle of water on them. It was a different story after the thunderstorms that brought the heavy summer rains. As the water ran off the grassy fields and down the hill from Mr. Emory's farm, a small waterfall would form. With the water tumbling over the rocks and the trees forming a green archway overhead, it felt enchanted.

I got up and waded into the river, trying to keep from slipping on the rocks slimy with algae and the silt deposited by the tireless current. I watched the water splash up and around my ankles. The water looked brown from all the fine sand particles the current was stirring up and my skin was lit to a ghostly white by sunlight piercing through the shallows. Something sparkling on the riverbed caught my eye. I reached in and pried it up with my fingers, rinsing it in the current. It was a bit of granite, pink and flecked with gray and black, two inches in diameter. Pushed up from the deepest parts of the earth, it had once been molten, but cooled long ago there where it had slept. Sand had worn it down, but the hints of its old, jagged edges remained.

The chilly water lapped at the backs of my knees as I walked further out. Somewhere down the river, an outboard motor coughed to life and then hummed down the waterway. My feet had grown numb to the cold. Pushing the bit of quartz into my pocket, I waded in deeper, letting the cold bite higher, until I was nearly chest deep. I wished it could numb all of me.

I had wandered out quite far and the current was stronger, nearly pulling me off my feet. I dug my toes into the silt and imagined planting myself like a water lily. I relaxed my arms and let them rise and float in the warmer water at the surface, inhaling deeply the smell of life that masked the smell of death. Quietly, I began to recite a poem. It was by a Latin American poet. I had read it in a book Charlie had given me to read. The poem haunted me. I learned it by heart. When Charlie found out, he gave the book to me to keep, just as he had sent along the other with Isaac.

I am a river, going down over wide stones, going down over hard rocks, my path drawn by the wind.

The trees around me are shrouded with rain.

The words reached deep inside me and hauled up something powerful. Vaguely hopeful. Unbearably sad. Picking up my feet, I brought my head back and stretched out fully on the water. I could feel my hair spread out, my body rocking gently in the current, the sky in its blue expanse above me, and the water holding me like a fallen leaf. Neither part of nor separate from but letting me participate in the experience of being river.

I am a river, descending with greater fury,

With greater violence,
Whenever a bridge reflects me in its curves.

I was to get no further. The sound of Sean shouting out across the water interrupted my recitation.

"Cori. Cori, what are you doing? Come back!"

I did not turn or give any other sign of having heard him. Not outwardly. Not right away. Instead, I listened to the silver sound of the water lapping at my ears. He continued to shout my name from the shore, growing more agitated. Finally, I waved my hand, turned myself over and started to swim. I had drifted quite far and set about pulling myself against the current, back to the bit of sandy beach where I had entered the water. My wet clothes slowed my progress. Halfway there, my legs began cramping from the cold and I struggled just to hold my position. Finally, I broke the deep pull and made it to the shallows where I could touch the bottom and put my feet down among the weeds and silt.

I rose from the water feeling heavy in my body again. Too tired to lift my legs much, I splashed and lumbered awkwardly. Sean kicked off his shoes, and ran into the water, hauling me the rest of the way into shore.

"Are you okay? Jesus. You scared me to death. What were you thinking? He grabbed me by the shoulders and shook me slightly to emphasize his point. "You can't do shit like that. No one knew where you were. For all we knew, well Christ, Cori." He hugged me tightly for a moment. "I'm just glad you're alright."

I was going to argue that there had been no danger, but I was too tired. Tired of fighting. Tired of trying to make what was in my head make sense for everyone else when it barely made sense to me. Instead, I just stood there shivering, with water dripping from my hair and the tatters of my cutoff shorts, not saying anything at all.

"We better get back. Everyone is worried." He turned and taking me by the hand, began to walk. It was a motion he had repeated endlessly through our years together, but this time something in me resisted. Something old. I wrenched my hand from his. He turned and looked at me, uncomprehending.

"Let go." My voice was quiet but firm. "I'm okay."

"Cori, what's wrong with you?"

"Don't touch me that way. I don't like it when you touch me that way."

It took him a moment and then as it dawned on him, as he realized what I was referring to, his confusion turned to disbelief. "Cori, I would never hurt you. You know that."

I could find no words.

"You think I would hurt you?

"Please understand."

"I don't. I really don't. I love you. And I've been on this roller coaster with you for years now. I've been out at this farm because that's what you needed."

"But you haven't been with me. You've been everywhere else but with me."

"You're the one who wanted me at the motel."

"I don't mean now. I mean before. Before I came here."

"I have to work, Cori. See people. I can't stay shut away like you can."

"Then go, if it's so horrible being with me." My inner Dr. Lawrence looked disapprovingly over his reading glasses. *That is not constructive, Corianne.*

"You're twisting my words." Sean paused and when he spoke again, his voice was calm and silky. The seduction that had made me go to bed with him in the beginning. "Corianne, I love you. I've loved you since the first moment we met over that stupid scone."

It would have been so easy to let that be the end, but I dug deep for the courage to say what had to come next.

"I think you loved the idea of me as something to rescue and fix more." I smiled sadly, remembering how he checked in on me throughout my mother's hospice. How he had found me the day of her funeral. "And you did rescue me. I love you for that." I placed my hand on his cheek.

He put his hand on mine and started to speak, but I stopped him.

"You rescued me a little like you rescued Maud. You wanted to save her, but not be responsible for her—so you gave her to me."

"Oh come on, I gave you a kitten as a gift because I thought it would be something good for you. I thought you'd like her. Don't psychoanalyze me, Corianne. There was no ulterior motive."

"I do like her. She's become quite good company. We understand each other."

"You really can't trust anyone, can you? Not even me. Not even after all this time." The anger and sadness were written plainly on his face.

"It's not about that."

"Yes, it is. How do you do it, Cori? How do you manage to go through life cut open and still not feel anything?"

Tears sprang to my eyes.

"I feel everything," I said.

We were both quiet for a long minute. Finally, Sean spoke again.

"I had hoped with all this, with you having your memories back, you could finally leave this all behind. Start fresh somewhere. We could. Together."

"Somewhere?"

"I thought we could go to France for a while. See what kind of life we might have there."

"It's not a good time."

"It's the perfect time. You'd love it." Nervously, he rushed on. "You would love the history."

"What would I do? I don't know French. How would I make a living?"

"You could take time off. Do your own writing. We could find a real Paris atelier. You know, with the windows you love, and Maud…she could sleep in the sunbeam. Or a farmhouse."

"You like the city."

"Not all the time."

He made it sound so good, part of me wanted to say yes. It would have been easy to just surrender myself again and let him take care of everything, take care of me the way he did. Easy to pack my suitcase and open it in the new life he was painting. Yes or no. Simple enough, but I could not form an answer. It was not just indecision that gripped me.

"Think about it," Sean said, kissing me softly on the cheek. Then he turned and walked back up the path to the road.

I watched him disappear behind the tree. Expecting him to turn around and look for me, I was surprised to find myself disappointed he did not. My heart was beating fast. Alarms were ringing all throughout my body, each with a different message. Go. Don't go. Run. Stay. Beneath them, beneath the anxiety, I was feeling something else beginning to rise. Something underneath the deep, deep sadness. Something even more than the crushing grief. Now, after all the years of being so afraid, I found living in this body with me was something else. Anger.

CHAPTER THIRTY-SIX

WHEN SEAN GRABBED my hand, it was like a fissure opening up, releasing a molten core. Never in all the years since Rebecca's abduction, since her death, had I ever allowed myself to be consciously angry about it. Any of it. Now anger threatened to eclipse everything else.

First came the rage that shook in my body, then the hot tears that seemed to come without end. Finally, there was the sick shock of it returning down through the layers into my core. I had found Rebecca's body. My parents had lied to me. Betrayed me by their silence. All those years my mother had watched me struggle with nightmares, even stumbling across my dream journals, and she had never said a word. Never asked. I expected that from my father. I could tell, even when I was so young, all of it made him deeply uncomfortable. So uncomfortable he locked himself away in his study. I knew I was broken. Loved, but broken. And they just kept shelling out for my sessions, hoping Dr. Lawrence would fix me.

They were well intentioned, Dr. Lawrence would tell me later, defending them, surmising from what he knew of them that they feared talking about it would retraumatize me. Ironically, it was the silence more than anything else that did that. A child left alone in the dark, not understanding what had happened. Left alone in the darkness with partial memories, remembering a different past, all the while the truth seeped up through the floorboards and came down the chimney.

The man, that fucking man in the car, had taken me just as sure as he took Rebecca. He had stolen me from my life. I had not died, not that day. It was much, much slower, the half-life of the violence that took me. There were not bruises around my neck to see or torn clothing. No one could see the darkness he planted inside my body, the one that ate me from the inside out. Yet whoever I was then, whoever it was I was becoming, had not come home. No, he took me, her, the moment he called two young girls over to that car. The darkness. I had felt it immediately in my body and housed it in the terror I took in. I felt the cold touch of it again as if for the first time and doubled over and wretched again.

My mind managed to forget some things, bury them even, but my body never forgot. And each time one of the sick phone calls had come, I felt dirty all over again. I prayed. Not to God, but to Mary, Ever Virgin, with her serene face. I had begged Mary night after night to please, keep me safe. I promised I would stay in the house if only she would protect me. *Please make me clean. Please let me forget. Please let him be dead.*

I screamed. Right there on my knees in the dirt on the riverbank, I screamed, pounding my fists against my legs until they were red and my throat felt shredded. Until I collapsed in sobs. Bill was checking on the repaired irrigation pump in the nearby field and thought he might find me at the river. He came running. Pulling me into his arms, he held me and rocked me until the sobs became shuddering gasps. Finally, he whispered, "Come on girl, let's go find Doc."

Dr. Lawrence said it was a positive development but tranquilized me anyway. Sean had already left. I never told him exactly what happened after he had gone. Part of me felt shame. Another part of me thought telling him would only make him feel bad, like it was somehow his fault. He couldn't have known.

For weeks after that, I worked to get my bearings. Taking long walks by myself, running my fingers over the small rabbit bone I now kept with me. Trying to find the space to breath. I barely talked to Bill and not at all to Evelyn. If she knew, if my mother had dragged her in somehow by confiding, I was not ready to know it. I felt hollowed out inside. Void of anything. It did not take me long in those empty days to realize Sean had been right about one thing. I could not go back to Rossmore Drive and the house that had belonged to my parents. There was nothing there for me now—not even safety. I would sell the house. It had never been mine. I was without a home. The only place that had felt like home to me in years was the farm, the windbreak, scattered with pieces of me.

Evelyn was the one who suggested I stay on in Sheerfolly Chapel. I had finally gotten up the courage to talk with her again though I never mentioned what had happened. One morning when she and I were having breakfast in her room, she brought up the subject. "As good a place as any to find yourself," she said. Then she put her hand over mine and just held it there. The moment she touched me I knew she knew. Bill and I had not been together since that night. I could not say that we never would again. I wanted Bill and, by the way he looked at me, the way I felt his hand on the small of my back, or how he brushed the hair back from my face, it was clear he still wanted me. But if I came to him again, or him to me, I need to be clean again. To feel like I could come to him new. I didn't know how long that would take, or if it was even possible.

Six months was all it took to sell the house given all it had to offer and its location. The couple who bought it had a little girl and boy on the way. At the closing, the husband beamed at his young family and talked about what a lovely old neighborhood it was. When he gushed about the miracle it was to find such a beautiful house so close to the school, I shuddered involuntarily. I sold many of my parents' things, keeping just those pieces that really spoke to me of them, like my father's drafting table. Like me, they would have a new life.

"We're here, Maud," I announced as I pulled into the driveway of our new home. The rusted pickup was still in the driveway. Maud lifted her head and blinked at the tired blue gingerbread house, clearly unimpressed. "I hope Raymond Solomon doesn't mind cats," I said as I swung the car door open.

THE END

ACKNOWLEDGEMENTS

I WOULD LIKE to express my deep appreciation to Reagan Rothe and the team at Black Rose Writing for your supportive and organized approach and for being open to new voices. Thank you as well to the editors at *Modern Poetry in Translation* for permission to reprint portions of "The River" by Javier Heraud. Writing is a solitary act, but that doesn't mean one is alone. Over the years, I've been fortunate to cross paths with some wonderful writers that I can now call friends. A huge debt of gratitude to Reed Farrel Coleman, who peered at my poetry bones, thrown like runes, and suggested I had a novel in me–and then hounded me firmly, but good-naturedly, until I finally finished a draft. This book simply would not exist without your encouragement and no-bullshit feedback. Heartfelt thanks to Scott Zieher for more than 30 years of friendship and swapping correspondence, poems, and critiques. Thanks also to Kathie Giorgio and Sandra Tully for their friendship and fellowship through the years. My deep appreciation to Carmen Kuhling for being one of my first readers and for her enthusiastic support, friendship, and deep understanding. To Meta McKinney, my friend, I thank you for your warm heart and insight. To my sisters, Anne Jozwiak and Elizabeth Jozwiak, you're simply the best. I can't imagine being on this journey called life without you. I still think our early, lost writing collaborations might have started it all. To my wonderful sons, Connor Eull and Thomas Eull, who thought it was cool to have a mom who was a writer, I thank you for your patience, interest, and for always being my biggest fans. I love you both more than I can say. I hope this book makes you proud. To my husband and partner, Tom Moylan, I am grateful for your love, listening, and unfaltering belief in this book. You can now say, "I told you so." Mom and Dad, I wish with all my heart you were here to see this day, and, in my heart, I think you are.

ABOUT THE AUTHOR

Kathleen Eull is a novelist and poet. Her poetry has appeared in *Emergency Almanac, Echoes, KNOCK, pith* and as part of the *Verse and Vision II* project at Gallery Q in Stevens Point, Wisconsin. In addition, her interview with poet and artist Scott Zieher appears in his second book *IMPATIENCE*. Kathleen is the owner of Pyxis Creative Solutions, LLC and has worked as a publicist specializing in the promotion of small press authors for more than a decade. She also works as a certified meditation teacher and certified Reiki therapist at Bell Heather Healing, the complementary holistic practice she founded in Limerick, Ireland. A native of Wisconsin, she currently divides her time between Wisconsin and Limerick. *Intercessions* is her debut novel.

NOTE FROM KATHLEEN EULL

Word-of-mouth is crucial for any author to succeed. If you enjoyed *Intercessions*, please leave a review online—anywhere you are able. Even if it's just a sentence or two. It would make all the difference and would be very much appreciated.

Thanks!
Kathleen Eull

We hope you enjoyed reading this title from:

www.blackrosewriting.com

Subscribe to our mailing list – *The Rosevine* – and receive **FREE** books, daily deals, and stay current with news about upcoming releases and our hottest authors.
Scan the QR code below to sign up.

Already a subscriber? Please accept a sincere thank you for being a fan of Black Rose Writing authors.

View other Black Rose Writing titles at
www.blackrosewriting.com/books and use promo code
PRINT to receive a **20% discount** when purchasing.

Printed in the USA
CPSIA information can be obtained
at www.ICGtesting.com
JSHW081043081023
49625JS00001B/30

9 781685 133221